THE
GIRL
FROM
PARIS

BOOKS BY ELLA CAREY

THE
GIRL
FROM
PARIS

ELLA CAREY

bookouture

Published by Bookouture in 2021

An imprint of Storyfire Ltd.
Carmelite House
50 Victoria Embankment
London EC4Y 0DZ

www.bookouture.com

ISBN: 978-1-80019-219-5
eBook ISBN: 978-1-80019-218-8

In memory of Esta

"A thing of beauty is a joy forever." John Keats

"An artist is someone who has learned to trust in himself." Ludwig van Beethoven

CHAPTER ONE
VIANNE, PARIS, MARCH, 1918

The way to get through difficult times is to create a thing of beauty. Vianne forced herself to focus on the words that Maman had whispered at the outbreak of this calamitous war. Gossip blistered around the table at the once famous Parisian restaurant La Violette, but Vianne focused instead on her fingers guiding a fine silver needle through the hand-stitched pintucks on her mother's evocative summer dress. Vianne concentrated, her head bent over the handmade creation of frail lace, tiny, delicate crocheted flowers, and white cotton lawn, the fabric base carefully trimmed and replaced with insertion lace and crochet in zigzag patterns so the gown was apparently seamless. The disapproving clicks of Madame Roger's tongue scalded the air in the restaurant that had once been the coquettish queen of the Belle Epoque. Now, the famous bar was closed and the tin-pressed ceilings no longer echoed with the languorous chatter of men in pale linen suits and women lounging in lace dresses just like Maman's. Even the never-ending clack of knitting needles didn't conjure up a homely feel. Around the table, a dozen Parisian women sat knitting balaclavas and socks, knowing they were bound for the thousands of young men who were hunkered down in the stinking cesspits that were the trenches of Northern France.

For the last four years, first at school and now here under La Violette's still radiant chandelier, Vianne had knitted her way through the war. She'd completed sewing up today's balaclava and now she stroked the mother-of-pearl buttons and hand-worked loops that fastened the back of her mother's exquisite gown. Balaclavas might be Vianne's reality, but Maman's lace dress was her fairy tale.

When someone unfastened the restaurant's glass door—with its zigzag strips of paper to provide some protection from the terrifying attacks on the city—the women's chatter came to a stop. For one trifling second, the room did not ring with fatalistic talk of the German bombardment of Paris since March 23; how their assaults had shaken the city with such intensity and from such a height, it seemed the shells might have rained down from the stratosphere; how every time a Parisian walked along the streets, they couldn't help but scurry along, head down, as if that would protect them.

This morning, Papa had told Vianne and Maman over breakfast that the French military had worked out it was not bombs being dropped by Zeppelins—as everyone at first thought—but instead vast and powerful bullets shot from cannons. He had regarded Vianne and Maman over the top of his glasses and said that three large gun emplacements had been discovered hidden north of Paris. So far, twenty shells had hit the city each day for several days, until everything had turned quiet.

Mysteriously so.

For the last few days, silence had cloaked the city like a sinister haze.

A flurry of cool air blew into the restaurant from the Champs-Élysées along with the whir of delivery vans and trams. These days they were driven entirely by women, streaming along the rain-soaked boulevard.

Maman closed the door behind her and Vianne anchored her needle in her pincushion, her blue eyes turning toward her beautiful mother breezing in with the wind.

There was a silence around the table as all the women turned their eyes toward Maman.

"Well then!" Maman pulled off her gloves and unpinned her fashionable hat with its wide brim and bow, her tawny eyes seeking out Vianne's. "I have wonderful news!"

Wonderful? Maman's bravery, her optimism, her faith that all would be well was something Vianne clung to, as bereavement after bereavement tore at their friends. Husbands, sons, and brothers were being slaughtered in catastrophic battles day after relentless day, and every second woman in Paris was in mourning. Just today, Vianne had hurried past people queuing up at the train stations to leave Paris, terrified the deadly gun attacks would begin again.

But Maman and Papa would not leave Paris. It was very unlikely that a shell would ever fall on them, very unlikely, Papa and Maman assured Vianne. They were a charmed circle. All their married lives, they had loved each other and there had been hardly an argument. But while they remained safe in their home on Rue de Sévigné, even when the city rumbled and shook with explosions, no one else dared imagine themselves immune to the devastation of this war.

Vianne drew her hand up over her pinned-up blond hair. "Good news?" she whispered. She had forgotten such a thing existed.

"Anaïs and Jacques are coming home, darling. They are both coming to Paris! For their birthday. I will have all my children at home again." Maman slipped across the restaurant with the lightness of a schoolgirl.

Vianne lay the delicate dress down on the worktable, pushing her chair back in anticipation of her mother's embrace, and closing her eyes in relief as she breathed in Maman's favored Chypre de Coty. Sandalwood, bergamot, irises, and jasmine: as far away from the grim realities of the last four years as one could imagine. That was Maman.

"I am so excited I can hardly breathe," Maman whispered into

Vianne's shoulder. She took a step backward and held Vianne's hands. "We will have a birthday celebration. A proper party!"

Vianne nodded, swallowing down her tears of excitement, spiked with the dread that pierced her stomach these days. They had all lived every day for four years with unrelenting uncertainty about the safety of Vianne's older twin siblings, Anaïs and Jacques, while they were both far away in the battle zones of France. The fear for them that bit at Vianne was almost unbearable at times. As the war dragged on, year after year, it seemed all Vianne and her parents were doing here in Paris was enduring a long bleak period of waiting, as news of loved ones was scarce.

"Anaïs will be here at the very same time as Jacques?" she said, clasping her mother's hands.

Maman could hardly speak. "Yes, and so, *chérie,* we will *all* be together. The whole family. I can hardly explain what this means to me." She turned to the room filled with staring women, sending a tear-filled smile toward her oldest friend, Marguerite Clément, who blew Maman a kiss right back. "We shall celebrate."

The disapproving Madame Roger laid her half-completed balaclava down, folded her arms, pinched her mouth, and muttered about unnecessary flirtations and women undermining the seriousness of the war.

Vianne caught the way Maman's friend and kindred spirit Marguerite raised her brow to the ceiling. Marguerite's soft auburn hair shimmered under the glittering chandelier.

"You have finished your work here today, Vianne?" Maman breathed.

"But of course," Vianne said.

She reached for the lace dress, folding it carefully, wrapping it in calico and laying it into the large soft cotton bag that she'd brought in this morning from home.

Vianne sent a sidelong glance toward the censorious Madame Roger. "I have finished knitting," she said. "And Maman?" she added, a little wickedness spurring her on. "How many jars of money did you collect for our French orphans of war?"

"Four jars full," Maman said, placing her arm through Vianne's, oblivious—Vianne was certain—to Madame Roger's stiff stance. "My head is ringing with the clatter of my little metal bowl, and I will fall asleep tonight with my own words sounding through my ears: 'For our wounded, please!'"

"Well then." Vianne placed her soft bag over her shoulder, feeling the thud of her journal moving toward the bottom of the bag beneath the stunning lace confection. "I think we *definitely* deserve a party." She looked pointedly at Madame Roger. "My older sister Anaïs has been nursing in the occupied territories, and Jacques has been in the trenches. There is no disgrace in honoring those who are sacrificing years of their life to keep us safe."

Madame Roger's lips tightened into a rigid line. Vianne felt the softness of Maman's hand resting on her shoulder.

Vianne lowered her eyes. "I hate to think what they have both seen." She had been too young—only fourteen when the war broke out—to contribute properly, and she'd had to wait at home while her brilliant older siblings went away. While Jacques was expected to enlist, Anaïs too had chosen to act.

Sitting here in Paris sewing socks could never compare with Anaïs's bravery. Vianne's older sister would sweep into the house when she was on leave, her starched white nurses' uniform only serving to highlight the flash in her toffee-colored eyes, the beauty of her figure, and the determined, strong temperament that Vianne had always idolized.

Anaïs had left Paris to train at the best nursing school in Belgium at the merest hint of war. When the French government directed in 1914 that women were to remain at home because it was argued that they would weaken, not strengthen, the French cause, Anaïs had written to Maman and insisted that she join the thousands of females bombarding the Ministry of War with offers to drive ambulances, fly planes, set up hospitals and form military auxiliaries like those in Britain. But the women were turned away because it was proclaimed that French masculinity would win this battle.

Anaïs's brilliance, her determination to put herself right in the middle of the action, was something Vianne could never hope to emulate. Her sister's stories of tending to the bloodied, wounded men who came in from the trenches both astounded and horrified Vianne on Anaïs's rare visits home.

Papa tried to protect Vianne from the whispered conversations Anaïs had with her parents about the terrors in the occupied parts of France where she'd worked since the middle of 1915 when she crossed the border back from Belgium. Vianne had listened outside the open door of the dining room at home to stories of German soldiers taking civilian hostages, of their raping women and burning villages, her fingers curling and sweating by her sides as Anaïs talked of women not reporting rapes because no officials took their stories seriously, how these attacks in Northern France were public affairs, witnessed by civilians to cement the reality of conquest.

As the youngest, Vianne had never tried to light a candle to her brilliant older siblings, but she'd seen the way her parents and their friends admired the dazzling twins and had realized that the only way to win the real admiration and love of everyone around her would be to do something that made her stand out in her own way.

When she'd discovered that she could knit and sew five times faster than any of the women who came to work at La Violette, quicker and more beautifully than any of the girls at school, a tiny flame had flickered to life within her, and she'd felt a sense of possibility that she'd never known before.

Sometimes, when she couldn't sleep for worrying about Anaïs in the field hospitals near the dreaded, freezing battlefields, or her brave brother Jacques in the mud-locked trenches, Vianne would sneak out to Papa's study, turn on his lamp and begin sketching her very own fashion designs on his craft paper with her pastels, layering her imaginings with tiny printed notes, carefully taping swatches of fabric to the pages of her growing journal: cashmere, suede, muslin, cotton, organza, and offcuts of the finest Lyon silk that she'd collected from haberdashers in the Marais district where she lived.

Her imagination had got her through the deepest nights of the war, and the dream of a brighter, more carefree time when luxurious gowns could be worn again made her hope they would come out of the war and find a better future for herself and for Anaïs and Jacques.

As the war rolled on, the north of France with its textile mills had been devastated when it was occupied. German soldiers emptied the textile factories, even down to stripping the unfinished cloth from the looms, and requisitioned them. The damage done to the region and the French economy was devastating. The price of wool climbed dramatically because one third of all French textile workers had been employed in the factories in northern France. But the price of silk dropped because Lyon, with its long history of silk production, had come to the rescue and kept the army and the domestic fashion industry of France supplied. Over the course of the war, silk became cheaper than wool. Parisian couturiers willingly incorporated more silk into their collections, and silk was even added to woolen weaves. Vianne would walk through the damaged streets of Paris, with its war-wounded and its refugees, piles of rubble and boarded-up windows where German bombs had fallen, stopping to admire the gorgeous silken creations that still, despite everything, spilled from the hearts and hands of the top couture designers of France: Jeanne Paquin, Jeanne Lanvin, Gabrielle Coco Chanel...

Gradually, a dream had seeded and grown within Vianne as she read in *Vogue* magazine how these enterprising and talented women had ensured their industry continued to survive the war. Many of them had started off modeling clothes, but they were now helping the French economy as they earned millions of francs of revenue. *Vogue* praised Jeanne Paquin for her business acumen and noted that men did not dare challenge her genius for business organization. Vianne had read how these legendary women were in a class of their own: hard-working, astute judges of style and business, they were also excellent money managers. Thanks to their resilience and determination, they had helped to cement France as the world leader of fashion even in the darkest days of the war.

What if one day Vianne's reveries could turn into something real? Something she could be proud of, something she could call her own?

"Marguerite, you will come to Rue de Sévigné on Saturday afternoon?" Maman said to her dear friend, pulling Vianne back to the moment as they prepared to leave La Violette. "We will need to begin the party early if we are to be done by the curfew at 8 p.m."

Vianne glanced through the taped windows of La Violette to the Champs-Élysées outside. When the blackouts began each evening, searchlight beams combed the Parisian sky for invaders, casting a tragic glow on the city and creating a sense of urgency, a desperate need to get home, which was still terrifying and strange.

"Of course I shall come to the party." Marguerite sent Maman one of the smiles that lit up her entire face, her brown eyes dancing. "I will be there for the twins' birthday, my dearest Marie-Laure."

"I cannot wait," Maman said, tucking her arm into Vianne's.

"And what will you wear, Marie-Laure? Something new?" Marguerite asked.

"Oh, I hadn't thought." Maman raised an elegant brow.

"But, you see, *I* am thinking, Maman. So that is very fortunate, no?" Vianne squeezed Maman's hand. She had found in Maman's sewing room an exquisite piece of black Lyon silk, which she itched to embroider with vivid trailing flowers, pansies and leaves all intertwined. But there was not the time to do this by the weekend.

Instead, Vianne had been working on a piece of peach-colored silk. She had cut out the dress pieces to her mother's measurements, having mocked up her pattern in calico first, and it was now draped over the dressmaker's model that Maman had given her for her last birthday. Her journal, filled with sketches of the dress from every angle, was by her side as she applied the finishing touches. She had drawn her model against the backdrop of a wrought-iron balustrade, carefully mimicking the fashion drawings of the day, those that she'd studied in *Mode du Jour* and *Le Journal des Dames et des Modes*. She'd studied the sketches of illustrators and artists such as George Barbier, Eduardo Garcia Benito and Gerda Wegener in fashion magazines whenever she had a moment to herself.

The bright colors and decorative motifs these artists used were inspired by Orientalism and, as a tribute to this, the dress she was designing for Maman would be flowing, the peach silk adorned with embroidered roses and curling motifs picked out in miniature glass beads around the base. The loose-fitting matching jacket that swept over the simple silk slip and fell just to the ankles would be embellished with intricate flowers, and edged with a modern motif in detailed silver thread, reminiscent of the exquisite fabrics used in Japanese kimonos.

Vianne was fascinated by the work of the designer Paul Poiret, who had been one of the first to introduce more straight-shaped silhouettes to women's dresses. But more than that, he'd employed exoticism and theater in his interpretation of haute couture. He was an apostle of Orientalism in design, and his loose, wrapped, kimono-style coats, his diaphanous tunics with Chinese, Persian or Japanese motifs edged with gold fringes or fur and worn over harem pants were as if from another world.

Vianne, having adored her trips to the theater with Maman and Papa before the war, had been dazzled by the Ballet Russes and the sets that had taken Paris by storm, ablaze with color and exotic sensuality. And out in the streets of the city, she used to stare in awe at the modistes wearing turbans topped with aigrette, or ostrich plumes secured with jeweled ornaments and paired with fantastical tunics. This was when fashion had become her fantasy, her way of escaping into a world filled with beautiful things.

And now, in some modest way, she yearned to bring the beauty, the exoticism of other countries into her work, despite the war. And one day, she promised herself, she would travel the world and see it all for herself, seek inspiration as Paul Poiret and others had done. One day, when the war was done.

In the meantime, she'd stay up all night sewing for the rest of the week if Maman could look beautiful in something Vianne had designed herself.

Of course, she'd made up several daytime tailored suits of the sort that were fashionable right now for both herself and Maman out of the patterns in magazines, but to be able to finally bring one of her own dreamy dresses to fruition from beginning to end, to show that she wanted to make Anaïs and Jacques' birthday as special for everyone as possible, to help them relive the glory days of being together as a family and looking forward to a better future when the war was over, would be just the thing!

Above all, the dress would be a thank you to her mother for holding them all together.

Madame Roger thumped her fist on the table and muttered something under her breath. "You are having a party when so many are grieving?"

"Oh, Madame Roger, it is a family birthday. Please," Maman said.

Madame Roger's brow knitted darkly.

"Come, Maman. We have menus to plan." Vianne pulled on her gloves. She did not wish to listen to Madame Roger for one second more.

"Vegetable casserole, using my homegrown bounty," Maman said.

"I saw a recipe for an apricot cake using dried apricots and bread," Marguerite added. She packed up her knitting and tucked her hand through Vianne's other arm.

They farewelled the women around the table and strolled out into the grand Parisian boulevard. The rain had stopped, and the Champs-Élysées was fresh with the smell of wet foliage while the last of the day's sunshine poured yellow streaks onto the sidewalks through gashes in the thick gray clouds.

They walked, arms linked, up the avenue. Come 8 p.m. it would be the darkest boulevard on earth, all the beautiful lamp-posts that used to stand like beacons in the midst of the streaming traffic stranded in darkness.

But there was light on the horizon this weekend. A party. And Anaïs and Jacques. How Vianne adored her mother's philosophy, and how it would come into play this weekend: *you must not waste one minute of your life. Not when you can enjoy it, not when you can live it to your heart's content.*

And right now, the thought of the twins coming home held the promise of making her feel fully alive again.

Minutes later, Vianne pushed down her nostalgia as she passed by Papa's favorite art nouveau Métro station sign on the Champs-Élysées. Before the war, he'd taken Vianne on a magical expedition around Paris to spot the graceful signs that had transformed the Métro into a thing of great beauty. Now, the posters that lined the station walls promoted charity work for the wounded, mutilated, orphaned, and imprisoned, for those sick with tuberculosis in the Haute-Garonne.

Vianne came to a standstill on the platform with Maman and Marguerite, her eyes drawn to a poster of a woman holding a collection bucket, her arms open wide, her pretty face made up to perfection, her shoes polished, as she carried out voluntary work in the name of the war.

Vianne clutched tighter to her dearest Maman's arm. It was worse for Maman's friend Marguerite. Memories must tear so very cruelly at Marguerite's heart every time she walked out her front door into the streets of Paris since she had lost her husband Gerard, a commander at the battle of Verdun. Vianne followed her mother and Marguerite quietly onto the train.

When the train rumbled to a stop at the Hôtel de Ville station, Vianne walked with the two older women through the crowds of exhausted Parisians in the station, past the canteen run by the

Croix Verte, where young girls provided food to the wounded. Vianne admired these girls, who would work overnight as the trains came through stations all over France, while their mothers sat by, knitting and tending to the stoves. A limp group of men lined up in front of the canteen with the sign of the green cross, several on crutches, one with a broken arm, a sight they had now become used to seeing.

Maman chattered with Marguerite as they walked past the magnificent Hôtel de Ville. The rows of chestnut trees bore gaps where some had been cut down for firewood, while limbless men and demobilized soldiers in worn army uniforms begged for change on the street corners, and most of the women walking past were dressed in black. They passed down Rue de Lobau and then left toward the Église Saint-Gervais, the beautiful church where Vianne's family had always worshipped and where Maman was heading, resolute, right now.

"You want to say a prayer of thanks for my brother and sister's homecoming this weekend, I know it, Maman." Vianne squeezed her mother's arm. At least Saint-Gervais had been spared the removal of its great windows, unlike beautiful Notre Dame. Those famous, majestic windows had been stripped of their stained glass so it could be stored for safety, and in their place yellow window-panes now washed the interior only with a tepid light. All that the people of Paris could hope was that, one day, the sun would beam through all the colors of the windows and shine a kaleidoscope of beauty into the cathedral once again.

"I shall light a candle and, in my heart, I shall give a great cheer. I am certain God will hear me, darling."

"Of course he will." Vianne's lips curved to a smile.

Marguerite bade them farewell and moved away across the beautiful square toward the home she used to share with Gerard in Place des Vosges.

Vianne felt a strong sense of stillness wash over her as she stepped into the magnificent church and stood with Maman in the vestibule in the hushed, reverent place of worship.

Maman approached the table of unlit votive candles and selected one, lighting it with a match from the box that sat nearby. She bowed her head in gratitude for the safe return of dear Anaïs and Jacques, before placing a centime in the small collection box on the wall.

Vianne followed suit, closing her eyes a moment while she held the fragile flame atop the slim candle in her hand, the cool, soft wax warming beneath her fingers. The practice of lighting a candle for loved ones was imbued with a poignancy that Vianne had never imagined would come to mean so much.

That evening, Vianne sat in Papa's library on his antique gilt wooden chair, his books lining the walls from floor to ceiling, and a warm fire glowing in the hearth. The small wooden chest filled with embroidery thread that Maman had bought when she'd first taught Vianne to sew sat on a small table by her side. The skeins were wound carefully around small spools so they did not get tangled up. Maman had helped her select the most beautiful soft pastel colors, antique violets, dusty roses, desert sands and misty gray greens.

Vianne slid the silk that she was going to decorate through her embroidery hoop, tightening the screw until it was held firmly. Her brow furrowed in concentration and the sound of the fire crackling was the only soft noise to break up the quiet. She drew a set of leaves using her chalk pencil that could be rubbed away, to accompany the roses that she'd already embroidered along the selvage.

She smiled gently to herself, remembering Maman teaching her to split the embroidery threads for dainty, fine work. Vianne did this before choosing her needle. Starting at the base of the design, she followed the line of the drawing with her needle and thread, her fingers working quickly and surely. Once she was stitching, Vianne fell into that wonderful place where the real world was lost, and she was completely immersed in her own imaginings.

She lifted her head with a jolt at the sound of a small knock on the door.

"Maman?" she asked. How long had she been working? The sound of Papa chuckling filtered through from the living room, but Vianne had asked her parents if she might sew Maman's dress in the quiet space of the library, where the fire was already lit and where Maman would not have an inkling of what Vianne was dreaming up for her to wear at the party this weekend.

"Can I come in, darling?" Maman asked.

Vianne slipped the soft silk, still stretched across the embroidery hoop, into a basket by her side and moved her work behind her chair. "I have hidden your surprise," she said.

Maman came in and stood by the fireplace, her long blond hair falling loose around her shoulders. "We have another lengthy day tomorrow," she said. "Don't overdo it, darling."

Vianne smiled, the intensity of her concentration this evening and the excitement she felt at the chance to sew something truly beautiful for Maman still giving her a sharp focus after the day spent knitting for the war. The last thing she wanted to do was go to bed.

"I know you have a passion for needlework," Maman continued. "But—"

"Oh, it is true," Vianne said, leaping at the chance to tell Maman exactly how she felt. Whether sewing had found her, or she it, she did not know, but the most important thing was to make clear to Maman that it was what she wanted to do. "My love for sewing is so much more than a passion," Vianne explained, her eyes shining. She stood up out of her chair. She clasped her hands. "It is *everything* to me."

Maman tilted her head to one side. She lifted her chin a little. "Sweetheart..."

"We have spent the entire war putting clothes last," Vianne pointed out.

Maman frowned. "Well, yes, I do see that, but—"

"Food, coal, firewood has come first, and rightly so. We've all gotten by mending old garments before buying new ones, walking around with black armbands, or in many cases, wearing uniforms or dowdy workwear on the street."

"Darling, I hardly think we can complain about this. And I've been very fortunate to have you at home to make me some lovely, tailored costumes to wear."

But Vianne held up her hand. "No, Maman. There is something more. Something beautiful and creative and wonderful that we have all forgotten to think about, but in times of distress, I think this is more important than ever. It is the cultivation of beauty."

Maman sat down on the sofa, her gaze lingering on the flickering flames in the grate. She sighed. "I always knew that one day my wise-seeming words would come back to haunt me, but go on, darling girl."

Vianne smiled, her words tumbling out. "French fashion is thriving, Maman. Despite the war—or maybe because of it. The couture industry is the only luxury industry that the government has allowed to function. And why?"

"Something tells me you are going to answer that yourself, chérie." Maman's smile was knowing.

"It is because the industry is far too important to France for the government to impose restrictions or regulations on it, and it is wonderful for morale. It is because France dominates the fashion industry, and no one wants to see that change." Vianne lowered her voice, sending a quick glance toward the door, as if Papa might overhear. She came to sit by Maman. "I have discovered that working in haute couture is very much what I want to do with my life, Maman. I want to get a job as a midinette, a seamstress at one of the ateliers run by the women who are driving our fashion industry from strength to strength."

Maman turned to face her. "I cannot imagine what Papa would think."

Vianne squeezed Maman's hand. "Papa is a businessman, Maman. Surely, he will understand that if I want to devote my life to such an important industry for France, then that is not a bad thing."

"Your *whole* life?" Maman tilted her head to one side again. "Darling, no woman in our family has ever worked for money. I know you love to sew, but couldn't you content yourself with sewing for me, for Anaïs when she is home, and for yourself? I think we could explain away the fact that we don't hire a dressmaker, but to have you working for an *income*?"

Vianne softened her tone. "Despite the destruction and all the devastation of the war, fashions have renewed themselves every single year, new fashion magazines have launched, and Gabrielle Coco Chanel has forged ahead. Jeanne Paquin helped negotiate better conditions for the midinettes." Vianne lowered her voice once more. "What if I could be like these enterprising women one day? All I am suggesting is that I work my way up through the trade—a trade that is keeping France's spirits up and creating employment for thousands of women."

Maman reached across, tucking a loose strand of Vianne's blond hair behind one ear. She smiled, a wistful expression falling across her beautiful features in the firelight. "I admit, I admire your determination. While you were speaking, I was thinking how wonderful it could be for you to become sneakily independent and successful through a craft that women are allowed to master."

Slowly, Vianne lifted her eyes until they locked with Maman's. "Maman, you are a genius," she whispered. "That is entirely how I shall put it to Papa. No man would stop a woman from *sewing*."

Maman leaned forward and drew Vianne into a hug. "Well then," she said. "You know that if it were entirely up to me, I'd tell you to fly from the rooftops and follow your dreams with all your heart. Sewing has been something that brought my mother and I together, just as it united us when I taught you the craft of needlework. It has connected generations of women in our family to one another. If sewing can connect one of us in turn to the wider world, then I am all for it."

Vianne leaned closer into her mother's embrace.

. . .

Early the following morning, Vianne stepped out of her family's apartment onto the Rue de Sévigné with its charming, cream-painted Parisian buildings, their windows gilded with black wrought-iron balconies, elegant lamps decorating the second stories. Her wartime leather lace-up shoes made soft thuds on the old cobblestones. Above, blue sky bloomed between the rooftops, and the sun glittered on the windows that were closed and taped up against the chill March air and the threat of guns.

Vianne turned into the wider Rue Saint-Antoine, her breath curling from her lips. Women pedaled by on bicycles—female letter carriers working for the PTT postal service dressed in peaked caps and tailored uniforms—while female automobile drivers passed in navy button-down coats, sitting behind the wheel, no longer in the passenger seats.

Vianne had become a woman in a city now run by women.

Outside the *boulangerie*, queues of Parisians were already lined up to buy the standard loaves of bread the government had introduced two years ago, the *pain national*: national wartime bread made with a rustic flour to strict measurements. It was a restriction that Parisians were tolerating, but Vianne's papa ate his while pinching his nose and willing the war to be won and soon, so that the nation's proper bread could once be enjoyed again, because what was Paris without baguettes? Every morning at breakfast, he never failed to mention, too, the fact that butter had been replaced with margarine.

Vianne moved down the sidewalk, past the local café, the bookstore, and a scattering of boutiques, until she crossed Rue de Turenne and came to a stop outside her father's beloved antiques store, Celine. She pulled off her leather gloves outside the plate-glass windows. Inside, Papa was lovingly adjusting one of his treasures, a terracotta Processional Virgin, her body stuffed with straw, her original dress made of tattered cotton, her porcelain head tilted slightly and her palms open. He'd be moving her so she could catch the best light.

Vianne stepped into Papa's poetic and refined world, the world of his own imaginings, and he came toward her and kissed her on both cheeks.

"Good morning, Papa," she said, stepping back and smiling into her darling father's blue eyes. Eyes that matched her own. He raked a hand over his graying hair, thinning now. But Maman said he would always be her handsome Gabriel.

"What has brought you here, *ma mignon?*" Papa asked.

Vianne tapped his hand with her gloves. "I have a surprise for Maman, and there is something else I want to talk about with you."

He raised a brow and wove his way to his desk at the back of the store, turning on the lamp and settling himself in his leather chair. Vianne followed him past a living-room table adorned with Italian landscape art; a marble bust of Venus; a pair of golden-colored velvet-covered chairs; and a display of perfume from the Grasse perfumeries, on a late nineteenth-century curved table painted and carved with gold leaf. *The Belle Epoque.* That glorious time before the war which so often filled Maman's and Papa's conversations and sometimes had them weeping for the memories of those wonderful years. Vianne sighed and stopped right at the piece she had come here to discuss with Papa.

She stood under a chandelier, its crystal pendants and beads ready to hold electric candles. "Dearest Papa," she said, her breath catching at the sight of the stunning jewel in a glass cabinet in front of her. "I have never asked you such a favor as I am about to, but you see," she went on, her voice catching, "I am making a gown for Maman to wear at Anaïs and Jacques' party this weekend."

"Oh, *ma petit.*"

She searched his face, wanting to impress him, wanting him to tell her what a wonderful idea this was. Wanting him to tell her that he thought she could create something worthy for Maman to wear at the most important event the family had held for a long time, and that her dreams of working in haute couture were more than fairy dust. But this did not happen, so Vianne took a deep breath.

"Papa," she said, her heart beating fast. "I have been thinking for some time that I want to show you what I can do." She had to make him understand, see her for the young woman she was becoming, not the young girl she used to be. She leaned her elbows against the perfumery. "I'm not just little Vianne anymore. I have dreams and aspirations of my own." She sighed. "Oh, there is no point lingering and waiting to tell you. The fact is, I'd like to try to get a job as a midinette, working for a couturier." She chewed on her lip and held his gaze. "I want to find a job in haute couture."

Papa raised his head, a fountain pen poised in his right hand.

"It is a dream I have been thinking about while the twins have been away," she went on, beating down the quiver that threatened to spill into her voice. "To work as a skilled seamstress for a couturier, creating clothes of beauty and luxury. I would like to contribute, in the smallest way, to the industry that is so important to France."

Papa placed his fountain pen down on his desk. His brow creased and, slowly, he shook his head, but Vianne knew she had to try again.

"The fashion industry is earning millions of francs of revenue for the country, Papa. To work in this area would be to contribute to France. It is true that the leading couturiers, Paul Poiret, Jean Patou and Maison Worth, all closed their doors at the start of the war, allowing their designers to serve their nation, but they had all opened again after a few months."

"Vianne—"

"But it is the women who inspire me, Papa. Women designers who have cemented their importance in the profession, becoming the heads of major fashion houses. Jeanne Paquin, Jeanne Lanvin, Jenny, and Gabrielle Coco Chanel... these women guide the fashion choices of thousands of women in France. They are governing the fashion destinies of many continents that they have not even visited."

He rubbed his hand over his chin. "These women are not like you, *ma chérie*."

"But yes, they are," she whispered. "And I suspect they are a little like you. You know what it is to be surrounded by beautiful things each day, what it is to give people something to inspire them, something that allows them the time to admire the poetry of life that has been taken so cruelly from so many people during this war."

"Vianne," he said. "*Ma mignon.*" He closed his eyes a moment. "You are a protected child, from a loving family. You would not survive in the world of the midinettes. Last year, you know, the midinettes went on strike, marching down the Rue Saint-Honoré from the Place Vendôme, chanting their rights to raises and days off." He waved a hand in the air. "Sweetheart, you wouldn't cope with the long days, the bad working conditions." He leaned forward, his arms resting on his leather-topped table. "Darling, while I know you have these fancies, the fact is that it would be insupportable for you to join the working classes as a midinette." He lowered his voice. "There is nothing glamorous in being poor. And with a working-class job you would put off any upper-class suitors." He reached out to stroke a tendril of her hair, but she pulled back.

Vianne did not waver, her gaze meeting his own. "What if I were successful?"

"Midinettes are laborers. I will never forget seeing thousands of female seamstresses marching through Paris. People were amused by them, Vianne. Yes, the couture industry is rarefied, moneyed, and I know that the fabrications you are seeing in magazines are inspiring you, but the fact is, seamstresses work hard and live somber lives. Let's not entertain these ideas anymore, eh?" He moved across the room and patted her on the head. "*Petite fille,* your sister will be home soon. Your brother. Help your maman prepare for them." He lifted her chin. "Sweetheart, you are beautiful. That is the most precious accomplishment a woman can have in this world. Forget your notions of working slave hours. You deserve to lead a wonderful life. After this dreadful war, when the men who have survived come home, someone special will fall in love with you, and he will give you the life you deserve: children, a family. Happiness. Don't limit yourself, *ma bébé*. There is no need to work, to labor away."

Ma bébé. Vianne drew her arms around her body. Children, a husband? Yes, perhaps. One day. But for now, her fingers yearned to sew, her heart dreamed of beautiful designs. She wanted to create her own beauty, not be a man's beautiful thing, and she feared that if she could not follow her passion, her life would be permanently colored gray.

The death, destruction, decay and waste of the last four years had only served to galvanize her further. Life was something you could not take for granted. Anyone could be burned out with the flick of a trigger, the stab of a bayonet, the choice of a government to send an entire generation to be slaughtered, right here, on their home soil, in France.

She stared at Papa.

He tilted his head, sending her a smile. "You are so like your maman. Always dreaming. I will have to look after you, protect you from getting too lost in your reveries."

But Vianne sighed. It was not Maman who was lost in her dreams. Vianne knew she'd inherited her imagination from her papa.

She was aware he could also be stubborn. Arguing with him right now would not produce the support and understanding she needed from him.

"I have a wonderful idea for the dress I'm making for Maman this weekend. But I need to borrow something from the store."

She turned her huge blue eyes to him, knowing he couldn't resist, giving him the smile that she had inherited from Maman, the smile that had won him over when he fell in love at first sight years before with the beautiful girl from warm and sunny Provence, whose sparkling eyes and shining hair had captivated him, along with her sense of youthful joy that was a complete foil to Papa's quieter nature. Being with Marie-Laure, he could come into his haven, be with his beloved antiques, but then return home to Maman's constant love.

Vianne had grown up with parents who adored each other so very much. She understood what love, in its best form, could be, but why should the hope of such a love cancel out her own dreams? She pushed these thoughts aside for now.

Vianne opened a secret drawer in a little bureau by the window, a bureau that Papa would never sell, and withdrew a key. She turned the key in the lock of a glass cabinet, taking out, with great care, a brooch in silver filigree set with diamonds, with a clasp at the back so that it could be attached to a gown.

"This," she breathed, holding the glittering clasp in her hand. "I want it to fasten the flowing peach silk dress that I'm making for Maman. It has a slip underneath of soft silk, and a flowing robe that I'm embroidering and beading that needs to be fastened at the waist. Please, Papa, can I borrow it?" She turned the exquisite brooch over in her hand, and it glittered under the chandelier. "It is beautiful. Just like Maman. I want to show everyone what I can do, and I want Maman to be the star of the party this weekend. She deserves something special. Don't you agree, Papa?"

Papa's eyes softened, and Vianne knew he must be imagining exactly how Maman would look wearing the gorgeous clasp. He dropped a soft kiss on Vianne's head and she closed her eyes. She was fortunate beyond words not to have lost any of her family in the last four years.

In her hand, the brooch flared under the light.

CHAPTER TWO

VIANNE, PARIS, MARCH, 1918

Fingers of light stretched through the shuttered windows in Vianne's bedroom on Good Friday. A clear sun threw its pale glow onto her cheeks. She opened her eyes, turning over in her bed with its golden damask cover, stretching her arms up until her fingers stroked the bedhead. It was upholstered in black and gold decorated silk, topped with a little canopy that sat like a crown, its point attached to the ceiling. Papa's discovery, of course. He'd told her stories of how the coronet-shaped canopy had once graced the bedroom in some magical chateau.

Vianne sat up, her ears trained for the wail of an air-raid siren in the distance, the crash of a falling cannonball, the screams of people out in the streets. They'd had four whole days with not one attack in Paris now, and while Parisians were outwardly stoic in the shops, on the trolley cars, in the Métro, and talk was that the German offensive on Paris must be over, Vianne feared that it would be impossible for the Germans to have stopped. She'd read worrying reports in the newspapers about panic that there might be plans to attack important sites such as the Eiffel Tower—a vital communications point exchanging messages with Washington. The monument was encircled with a ring of heavy barbed wire, while a system of anti-aircraft guns defended the Paris icon from

German airplanes and Zeppelins, but would they be able to deflect a massive rain of shells?

Vianne shuddered. It was impossible to know whether it was better to live in ignorance and not read the constant, heartbreaking news, or whether to stay informed and worry incessantly for her family and for her fellow Paris citizens, for all she loved about her city. Sometimes she worried that her family would never again live the life they'd once loved, but in many ways, she knew, they were the lucky ones.

She reached for her *robe de chambre*—her dressing gown—and, throwing it over her shoulders, she tugged on the midnight-blue velvet sleeves. And then she heard it. Not the sound she dreaded, but voices, laughter, just as she'd anticipated ever since Maman revealed that Anaïs and Jacques were coming home.

Her heart hammering in her chest, and her mouth too dry to utter cries of delight, Vianne fluttered down the hallway, flying into the dining room, where the family were already gathered for breakfast. Papa was seated at the head of the glass-topped, delicate table, which Maman had set, even for breakfast, with vases of daffodils and white napkins folded just so, antique crystal shining against the pretty pink and white china plates. Maman sat, framed by the painted-silk intertwining floral panels that lined the walls, and either side of her were Vianne's dearest Anaïs and Jacques.

"*Ma coco!*" Anaïs pushed back her chair and opened her arms wide, her tawny eyes shining in that way that Vianne had missed for an age.

Vianne enfolded her sister in her arms, closing her eyes against Anaïs's white nurse's blouse and apron. Anaïs's navy-blue cloak rested over the back of her chair, and her long blond hair was swept into a soft bun, tendrils falling around her cheeks. Even in a nurse's uniform, Anaïs could never be anything but charming and elegant. Her beauty was legendary in Paris, and she had been a jewel in the eyes of many young men—men who were now battling in the trenches or, horrifyingly, buried beneath the clay in northern

France. She had to shake the disturbing thought away as she and her sister separated.

"And dearest Jacques."

Somehow he too was there next to her, her brother in his officer's uniform, the skin around his impossibly blue eyes, with their black lashes, darkened now with shadows and secrets that were new to Vianne. Her older brother's shoulders seemed thinner and stooped, and a cigarette dangled from his fingers.

She rested her head on his shoulder. "Oh, you poor dear," she whispered.

He took a shuddering breath and coughed. Vianne clutched Anaïs's hand tight while she held onto Jacques.

And right then, Vianne promised herself she would not allow her brooding, private fears about the German raids on Paris to ruin this precious weekend.

She listened, instead, while Anaïs sat proudly in her uniform, telling the stories she could never write in her short postcards home, which, like the postcards from Jacques, usually only told the family to remain patient and brave, and that she sent her love to them. Now, Anaïs talked about how she'd served as a confidante for some of the men in her care at the hospital in Ypres, where she'd been stationed since the summer of 1915. She dropped her eyes and spoke of how she'd sat stoically alongside her patients, sometimes during their final moments of agony. And she looked at her family and told them she'd developed a burning hatred of war.

Despite the horrors Anaïs described, it was impossible to help feeling envious that Anaïs was doing something to make things better for France. Vianne had to find a way to convince Papa that she, too, was worthy of using her own skills to contribute.

Jacques was silent, finishing one cigarette only to reach for another. Nobody commented on the way his hands shook as he reached for the packet time and time again. Maman had noticed this, and every so often she reached across the table to pat her son's hand, curling her fingers around his, making him feel safe. Though he smiled back at her bravely, Vianne saw the line of sweat that coated his upper lip.

By the afternoon, Vianne laughed in a way she had not done in months, pure joy bubbling up inside her until she might burst. If there was one thing she'd learned in this war, it was that spending time with the people she loved must be the greatest pleasure on earth. For one afternoon, she swung along the quai on the edge of the Seine, the water rippling in the sunshine, her arm linked through Maman's, Anaïs on Maman's other side, the three of them catching the interest of men home on leave, with their shining blond hair and their laughing smiles. Maman regaled Anaïs with stories of Papa turning his nose up at his war-rationed breakfast every morning and the dour Madame Roger in the knitting circle who would ruin anyone's breakfast, whether in Paris or not.

"You must not, my dearest girls," Maman said, "let this war destroy your faith, your hopes, your dreams. You must still live your lives."

There was a pause for a moment, and Vianne sensed Anaïs's quiet contemplation of their mother's words just as she had when they were small and shared a bedroom. Maman would sit on the edges of their beds at night, telling them stories, some of them invented, some of them the old fairy tales, and they'd listen to her as she suddenly grew serious, her eyes filled with something deeper that was always there inside Maman alongside her ability to enjoy life to the full.

"Vianne," she went on, turning to Anaïs, "has developed a talent for sewing. She has found that she is quick with a needle and can turn out beautiful work in no time at all."

Vianne blushed, her senses tingling as her sister turned her gaze her way, Anaïs's expression one of genuine interest.

"I have a surprise for your birthday on Sunday, Anaïs," Vianne said. "I am eager to show you all that I have done." *What I want to do.*

A passing soldier stared at Anaïs before winking at her and swaggering by. Vianne's older sister must have sent him one of her famous lightbulb smiles.

"You can't give me a hint about this surprise, *ma coco?*" Anaïs said.

Vianne shook her head solemnly, feeling a little thrill at Anaïs's unwitting use of the name of Coco Chanel. She'd made Maman promise not to peek for the last three days while she worked on the gown. "You must all wait. How many people are coming to the party?" she added, eager to change the subject.

"Oh, twenty, I think," Maman said. "It will be wonderful to have our closest friends, or," she lowered her eyes to the pavement, "those of them who remain."

"Well, I cannot wait for Sunday, and I am looking forward to catching up with all my friends at church today," Anaïs said. "I have missed everyone terribly." Her hands reached up to the necklace she always wore, a seventeenth-century pendant from Papa. Inside it was a tiny picture of Maman.

They turned away from the Seine, stopping at the cobbled Place Saint-Gervais, the gracious buildings opposite the lovely old church looking kindly down on the crowd of one hundred or so people gathered outside in the square for the afternoon service.

Vianne shielded her eyes and looked up at the familiar church's dear façade, with its soaring roofline, and tall stained-glass windows, their beauty outside only hinting at their ravishing colors inside, the quiet contemplation, and the tall heavenly arches.

All this, and having Anaïs by her side again, lent a feeling of stability, a reminder of the days before the war. While no one knew whether those days would ever return, or what the world would look like after all the upheaval and tragedy of the war, here, outside the church, with the people milling about, there was a sense of promise that the light might return to France one day.

A cool wind flurried through the square, and Vianne drew the jacket of her tailored costume around herself and stood aside, but Anaïs moved straight into the middle of the crowds, sending her friends into flights of excitement. Maman was right beside her, kissing her own friends and acquaintances on the cheek in turn.

Vianne still waited on the edge. Another cold breeze whipped through the square, and a fresh flurry of pigeons scattered away into the iron-gray sky. She took a step back, her mood of a moment ago blown away with the wind and the sound of the pigeons' wings fluttering inside her stomach as they swooped away over Paris.

Suddenly, the idea of sitting through Mass under the tall gothic windows seemed stifling. Home beckoned, where it was warm, where she could lose herself in her sewing, where she could escape the surly sense of fear that had haunted her these past days, no matter how hard she tried to fight it. After all, she did need to sew Papa's precious antique clasp onto Maman's dress, for she had not had a chance to do this, and she would not get an opportunity to do so again this weekend: Maman and Anaïs had made plans for every waking moment. And there was the party to prepare for, cooking to be done, flowers to be cut and arranged... Vianne had become used to helping in the kitchen and with household tasks since their help at home had been reduced to one maid of all work. With the men sent off to fight, and women taking up traditional male working roles, the war had meant the number of servants had dwindled and there was a shortage. Now was not the time to sit in church, now was the time to add the finishing flourish to her very special surprise for Maman.

Vianne took in a breath, her decision made. Easing her way through the sweet gathering of women, children and older men, the beloved gray-haired fathers and grandfathers of Paris who were determined to remain brave in the face of all the uncertainty surrounding them, Vianne tapped her mother on the shoulder. She whispered that she'd like to go home and work on her surprise, that she'd also help the maid prepare their supper, and sit and talk with Papa, who did not frequent church regularly like the more sociable Maman, but who was content to devote himself to his faith in contemplative moments. She would take the time to sit with Jacques, who was with dear Papa, and about whom she was worried, although they were all putting on a breezy, brave air around him so as not to upset him further. So many men had returned as ghosts of themselves from the battlefields. Poor Jacques was not alone in whatever tormented him.

Maman patted Vianne on the arm and told her she thought it would be all right to miss the service.

Vianne stood a moment and watched her maman disappear up the steps and through the arched doors of the church, surrounded by her friends, and then swallowed hard at the sight of a lone man crossing the square, his cheeks sunken and hollow in that way they'd all come to dread. She turned around and walked all the way back home with her head down and her arms folded across her body against the growing wind.

Ten minutes had not gone by when a foul blast lacerated the air, its echoes booming through the Marais district like some deafening drum, before beating a low rumble toward the Seine. The entire ground shook beneath Vianne's feet, where she had been watching a river barge, catching her breath before she went home. She was still unsettled by the wind that had whipped up and was buffeting her along the Quai, her hands resting gently on the balustrade at the water's edge, but when the roar gutted her insides, it lodged there like a cold stone. Her stomach caved, and her body buckled. She gripped onto the railings, her sense of gravity tumbling and her top half seeming to want to dive headlong into the river as she found herself staring down at the water's surface. The reverberations tore through her insides and then seemed to flow out of her and ripple along the old gray river, until, like dying thunder, the growling dissipated. Reflected in the water, Vianne was certain she could see Maman's face.

And then, a moment of silence. Terrifying, dead silence, where all Vianne could do was prop herself against the handrail, until slowly, she turned, still leaning against the rail for support, and finally, her fingers flew toward the necklace that Maman had given her for her fourteenth birthday, so long ago now it seemed, the year the war broke out. The year she'd promised Vianne they would survive this. As a family. They were untouchable. Maman was going to keep everyone safe from harm.

All at once, everything came to life. Sirens rent the air as ambulances screeched along the Quai de l'Hôtel de Ville. People screamed; a woman rushed by carrying a child, her hand protectively burying the little one's head to her breast; another child, perhaps six or seven, navy-blue coat flying behind, ran along holding her mother's hand, her eyes catching with Vianne's for one horrible second before her maman swept her away.

Vianne, her feet stuck to the ground like a pair of bricks cemented to their foundation, managed to pull herself free and run, her heart racing in her chest, her stomach aching as if smashed in two by a boulder, and her mouth filled with the metallic taste of terror.

She had to get back to Saint-Gervais church. Whatever had struck, it must not have struck her family.

But then why had she seen Maman's face in the river? Why had her lovely reflection appeared there, only to die away, in a split second, when Vianne reached out to clutch it? Or had she turned mad and panicked, seeing a vision of her adored Maman because, like every other Parisian, she'd developed a morbid fear of German bombs, carrying this around with her like some unbearable weight on her back?

She only made it a little way up Rue de Brosse when she was cleared aside by a police officer, swept back onto the sidewalk as an ambulance, then another and another reeled up the road.

And in front of her, the roof of the great old church where her mother and sister had been worshipping was buckled by a gaping hole. Pieces of wood and debris hung out of it, clearly visible from the street, and when there was another, gut-wrenching collapse, the murderous sound of collapsing masonry shook the air, people screamed and Vianne vomited on the sidewalk.

A woman's arm eased her up to standing again.

"*Maman!*" Vianne wailed, her eyes darting, her hands shaking, tearing at her coat as she battled to rip it away, suddenly burning with heat. "My maman and my Anaïs are in there! I have to get them!"

But the woman disappeared, and a police officer stopped everyone from moving, and Vianne turned to ice. She stood there, a silent, solitary figure even after the crowds dispersed, or were directed away, and she did not move for what seemed an age, while all around her she heard, but hardly registered, talk of the front half of the roof collapsing onto the congregation, huge great blocks of masonry killing all the worshippers in that section of the church.

And after she knew not how long, when Maman and Anaïs did not emerge, and the police told everyone there were no more survivors, she bent her head, her face ashen, and knew that all the lights had gone out.

That night, Papa went to bed, shell-shocked after Vianne had told him the tragic, heartbreaking news. Vianne stood alone and stared at the thin sliver of light that shone out from underneath his bedroom into the empty, silent hallway.

At one o'clock in the morning, unable to sleep, sit, function, drink water or manage any food, she slid down against the wall outside Papa and Maman's bedroom, her head buried in her hands, her shoulders shaking while her stomach ached—ached for the loss of her beloved mother whose life had been cut off at the age of just forty-two, and for the sister who would never grow old alongside her, who would never know the joys of having her own children, whose bravery nursing deep in the war zones of northern France had gone unrecognized and unfulfilled before the end of this dreadful war.

Jacques, ashen, was alone in the salon. Vianne, crippled with her own grief and shock, had been unable to get him to speak, and she knew he was still up, sitting on Maman's green silk sofa, staring at the Turkish rug on the floor, his hands hanging between his legs, not resting against the tapestried cushions that Maman had sewed so lovingly when they'd first bought the apartment on Rue de Sévigné. A jar of flowers that she'd arranged just this morning sat on a side table, and she'd put the silver coffee set out for the weekend, the best one because people would be dropping by to visit, the twins being home. Except now there would only be Jacques.

In the soft lamplight, Vianne had been unable to bear seeing her brother turned to stone.

Marguerite Clément had arrived that evening, her copper hair shining under the lights, her brown eyes strained with grief and shock, and she'd tried to coax the family to eat. In all this flurry, telegrams had been sent to Maman's surviving cousins in Provence. But there were not many relatives left. The war had taken its toll on the younger generation and she'd been an only child, her parents both dying over ten years ago.

Vianne knew that Jacques would grieve especially hard for his brilliant sister whom he leaned on because Anaïs was ten minutes older and always stronger than he. Anaïs had been the leader. Along with Maman, she'd brought something irreplaceable into the family.

How could they go on without either of them?

Vianne reached out, and with her tapering, elegant fingers, she stroked Papa's white-painted bedroom door. She could never replicate what Maman or Anaïs had been to their family, but she would do all she could to take care of Papa and Jacques.

CHAPTER THREE
VIANNE, PARIS, NOVEMBER, 1918

Vianne pushed her way through the streets of the Marais, beating a path through the crowds, fighting like a fisherman's wife to find a way through the impenetrable, overwhelming mass of Parisians screaming with joy as they thronged in the squares, the laneways, the boulevards, jamming the riverside quai. Not an inch of space was free. At home, Papa, devastated and broken, had taken a dramatic turn for the worse. He'd never recovered from Marie-Laure and Anaïs's deaths, and his slow decline had hung over the house like a heavy mist since March. His grief was more than mourning, it was total collapse. Vianne had to find the doctor before it was too late.

The air rang with bugles, people belting out the "Marseillaise," soldiers and sailors in uniform grabbing girls and kissing them until they swooned, young boys riding atop wartime cannons as they were wheeled through the streets accompanied by cheering crowds. Banners hung across the laneways and were pinned to the grand Parisian buildings. *"L'Armistice est signé! La Guerre est gagnée! Vive la France!"* The armistice is signed! The war is won! Long live France! People waved American, British and French flags from the balconies and the buildings were awash with red, white, and blue.

Vianne should have been celebrating too, looking forward to the future, but she had not been able to stir Papa this morning. He was unconscious, still breathing and lying in the bed that he'd shared with darling Maman throughout their married life.

Vianne's sweet, gentle father had never returned to his beloved antique store after the loss of his adored wife. Vianne's insides had prickled with worry because he'd shown no interest when one of his most trusted clients sold the contents of her entire chateau, begging Gabriel to come and value her precious things and help her sell them, insisting that no one else would do. Papa could have made a fortune, let alone spent time lovingly taking care of a cache of treasures, the thing he once adored the most. It would have been a distraction, a way for him to rediscover his faith in life. But he had lost that faith in the world since Maman and Anaïs had been killed. Papa had done the very thing that Marie-Laure had warned Vianne and darling Anaïs not to do on the day she died: he had stopped living his life.

Vianne lowered her gaze, stuck in a heaving mass of people outside Saint-Gervais church, the knot in her stomach tightening, and her hands shaking as she reached out of habit for the black armband of mourning that she still wore around her upper arm. It hadn't helped that the gruesome details surrounding Maman and Anaïs's death, along with ninety other worshippers, some of them her family's friends, had come out in all the newspapers.

Saint-Gervais had been the victim of the massive German goliath of a gun that the French had discovered positioned north-east of Paris, a gun that sat on a vast turntable, nothing like it ever created in the world before. It was enough that someone could have envisioned such a murderous instrument, but to have then spawned it and used it was beyond comprehension. Vianne had read in horror how this gun could accommodate huge shells; how it could, for the first time ever in history, fire those shells twenty-five miles into the sky, shooting them into the stratosphere until they came down to land on Paris' unsuspecting citizens who didn't know where they would strike. The gun was a triumph of German engineering. It was the executioner of Parisian lives.

It had let rip on Maman and Anaïs and torn their family apart.

Vianne wrapped her coat around herself and pushed on, battling the sickening feeling in her stomach at the thought that she might be an orphan by the day's end as she negotiated the revelers and merrymakers enjoying this longed-for day.

She was glad for all the celebrations, glad for the bright smiles on people's faces, and for the way they sat again at the little tables that looked out over the streets, sipping coffee. But none of this could bring back Maman, Anaïs, nor her papa from whatever place of private agony he'd gone to the day his beloved was killed.

Vianne's only hope was the elderly doctor who'd tended their family since she was small. She could not get her father to a hospital. An ambulance would take hours to get through these crowds. Papa, not rousable, was in a state of decline but would hardly be classed as an emergency, not when boys were still being wheeled back from the war flat on their backs and filled with shrapnel.

It was almost impossible to imagine them, out in the trenches on the Western Front, downing their guns in silence at eleven o'clock today for the very last time. The fighting was over. After four long years, the men would be coming home—or what was left of them, since she'd read that it was estimated over eight million soldiers had perished.

The newspapers today proclaimed that the Kaiser had abdicated. The Germans—their population starving and their armed forces driven back at last due to the involvement of the Americans—had requested an armistice. President Wilson of the United States of America had forced a piecemeal surrender upon the German high command that could not be reversed and France was no longer at war.

Pushed hard up against a man's back, Vianne sent the bravest smile she could muster at a young boy of perhaps twelve waving a newspaper in her face. He'd been spared, but what about his older brothers, fathers, uncles, or even his mother and sisters? Had they too been caught out on that devastating Good Friday in March? Someone pulled out a bugle and Vianne forced out the unwelcome thoughts that still haunted her. The reason there had been a lull for a few days before the attack on Saint-Gervais was because the gun could only shoot sixty to seventy rounds before the barrel needed to be rebored. That is what the German forces were doing in the quiet days before they butchered Maman and Anaïs. While Vianne had been repairing the tiny rents in Maman's lace dress so she could wear it in the summer of 1918, the German forces had been reboring the barrel of their enormous gun to murder her in cold blood.

Vianne maneuvered herself out of the masses, knocking against the closed door of the doctor's surgery on Rue de Lobau. It would take another half an hour to fight her way home, and she only prayed it would not be too late. Too late to save the man who'd always been the family's rock, but who had fallen like a dry leaf from a dying tree when the love of his life had been taken away for good.

"Mademoiselle Mercier?"

Vianne's breath came in short gasps, her lips soaked with sweat despite the chilly, late-fall afternoon, the back of her hand flailing to her forehead as the doctor opened the door and took in her appearance.

"Your papa? He has taken a turn for the worse?"

She closed her eyes and steadied her breath at the sound of the kind doctor's voice. Tears streamed down her cheeks freely. How could they possibly get home to help Papa when the streets were an impenetrable mess?

The end of the war was wonderful. The destruction of her family was forgotten in the celebration.

But the doctor took her arm in his bony hand, shouting with the authority of a man half his age, shoving his way through the barrage of people. Warning them it was a matter of life and death.

Parisians had lived with the threat of death for the past four years, and so people cleared a way for Vianne and the doctor to pass. Vianne pushed alongside him, exhaustion unfolding in waves through her insides. She'd ended up running Papa's business single-handedly since Papa had given up, going into the store daily, selling the treasures that Papa had once so lovingly put on display, tending to them just as he used to do, reaching out to his list of most valued clientele and carrying out the multitude of administrative tasks in the evenings. It had been hard work and most days Vianne would set up early, and work long into the night, but it had been a distraction from the gnawing, gaping fear that gripped her due to her father's decline and had gotten her through the long, lonely months since the German gun killed Maman and Anaïs.

What was more, she'd learned how to run a business, a business which she'd not only kept afloat, but for which she had increased sales due to the fact she loved chatting to people about beautiful things. And, mindful of the restrictions on people's budgets due to the war, the new pieces she'd purchased for the store, such as a tiny artist's mannequin with a lace collar, a carved linden silver mirror from the time of Louis XVI, and a miniature brooch with a portrait, had been savvy acquisitions that she'd still been able to sell on for a strong profit.

Jacques would be so very proud of all she'd done to keep the business running while he'd been away at war. He'd had to return to the front soon after the loss of Maman and Anaïs, and his colorless, leaden demeanor, his blind acceptance of what was going on in the world, along with the fact he had not talked beyond a few words to Papa about formalities and had seemed unable to communicate with Vianne, had worried her just as much, if not more, than Papa's withdrawal into the sanctuary of his bedroom. Her only relief was that he would be coming home now. She just hoped her father would be there when Jacques arrived.

Finally, not knowing how much time had passed, only aware that she had to stick close to the doctor, and follow his back, they were pounding up the stairs to the apartment in Rue de Sévigné.

Marguerite opened the front door, her usually immaculate copper hair falling in tendrils from her face, her eyes downcast, and her cheeks as white as a laundered sheet. When she raised her eyes to meet Vianne's, the expression on her face told Vianne everything she did not want to know.

She collapsed into the older woman's arms when, with a little shake of her head, her kindly family friend confirmed the dreadful news that had threatened to spill out and take hold all day.

They were too late. Papa was gone. He'd died of his broken heart.

Ten days later, Vianne sat, her hands clasped on her lap in the salon at home. Opposite her was Jacques, returned from the trenches after being hospitalized for the last two months with a shrapnel wound to the arm. He sat there under Papa's delicate tapestry that hung from floor to ceiling behind the green silk sofa and repeated the words that had astounded, shocked, horrified her the first time they came out of his mouth.

Her body rigid, and yet her stomach roiling toward her feet, Vianne sat trying to make sense of her brother's words.

"You will need to find a husband, Vianne, and in the meantime, somewhere to live. I can only provide you with a small allowance until you are married. But I cannot do anything more than that for you. It is time for you to grow up—just as Anaïs and I had to do, while you have stayed here, safely at home."

She glared at him, her breast rising up and down. He could have no idea how his words inflamed the worries that haunted her throughout the war—that she was not as worthy as her older siblings, that she had not done enough. Part of her, treacherously, accepted his admonishment because deep down she had felt this herself, but her other half screamed for understanding. It was not her fault she was the youngest. He had no right to patronize her or blame her for this.

And yet, he held the reins. Jacques had inherited the entirety of Papa's estate. And he could do with it as he liked, although his obligations to his sister appeared to have slipped to the furthest corners of his mind.

"As soon as I am married, my wife, Sandrine, will be moving into the apartment. She will be taking Maman's place. It is important she is not encumbered."

This was so unlike the Jacques she had known before the war. The coldness of his sentiment was breathtaking.

Vianne stood up and paced toward the window, pulling the lace curtains aside and staring down at the street below. Fall was turning to winter. Outside, women were bundled in coats. Still, people had to queue for rations, and the young men in the streets looked vacant, their faces pinched, white, cold. Women who had manned the businesses, the transport systems, the stores, were being turned away from their jobs, many of them left unemployed and unable to find work now the men were home.

And her own brother was turning her out.

Vianne squeezed her eyes shut. In good faith, she'd taken care of everything these last months, so at least the family would have the business intact, and yet, as soon as he had returned, her brother wanted to ship her out.

"My new wife will hardly be able to manage with my little sister about. She needs to take the apartment and make it her own home. Goodness knows it will be difficult enough for her with all the memories here."

Vianne bit back her response. Papa's treasured collections of porcelain in the rosewood cabinets, the Turkish rugs, the onyx table lamps, the tapestry-covered chairs.

"It's all too old-fashioned," he said.

Papa was an antique dealer! Vianne wanted to scream and beat her hands on her brother's chest. *Have you no respect for his life's work, for the family we were, for Maman's beautiful things?*

She turned to face him. "So, you are turning me out," she whispered, "After I single-handedly ran the business every day for the past eight months, ensuring that you had a thriving antique store to inherit when you came home. Ensuring that the bills were paid and the apartment secure. You are joking, I do hope, Jacques."

There was a knock at the door, and the maid, whom Vianne had managed to keep fully employed, appeared at the salon with a young lady next to her.

Sandrine Roche. Vianne simply gazed at the woman, holding out her hand like a wooden doll when Jacques introduced her to the nurse who'd taken care of him in the field hospital where he'd recovered from his shrapnel wound. Sandrine averted her gray eyes away from Vianne and leaned in to receive Jacque's embrace.

Sandrine sat herself down on the sofa, right where Vianne had been a moment earlier, and reached up to pat her neatly styled hair. She was blond just like Anaïs, just like Vianne. Was Jacques looking to replicate his lost sister in his wife?

And was he turning the one person who reminded him of his past, out into the streets?

Vianne was left with her mouth falling open and only the ability to stutter her dismay in front of the quiet young woman sitting in her family's salon.

Jacques had come into the room this morning, early, before breakfast, while Vianne had been working on her journal for a few moments of precious time, sketching an evening dress and pasting a tiny piece of silk georgette next to the design. She'd fashioned her drawings in the barrel shape and imagined black seed beads and tiny metallic beads to decorate the simple silhouette. She knew that detail was going to be everything in the coming season, and was inspired by the simple, modern lines she was spotting in the windows of the couturiers she made a point of passing by.

But she'd laid down her pencil in surprise, her hands clutching her cutting scissors when he'd told her how, after losing the last four years battling amid filth and mud and stench, he'd fallen in love with a young woman and didn't want to waste any time.

Under usual circumstances, Vianne would have been ecstatic for him, but there was a cold urgency to his voice that frightened her. She had never expected either the speed with which Sandrine would be installed in the apartment, or with which she would be removed.

"I understand your desire to move forward, and to live properly after all the devastation of the past few years..." Vianne chose her words carefully now, mindful of Maman's philosophies when someone did you a wrong—to try to show compassion, but not be walked over—in the hope there could be a compromise.

She sent Sandrine a tentative smile, hoping, perhaps, for something warm in return, a flicker of Anaïs's radiance, a hint of Maman's humor, her positivity and warmth.

But Sandrine simply looked down at her own hands that were folded neatly in her lap.

Vianne's palms began to sweat and a wave of heat flushed through her body. She opened and closed her mouth several times. Was the girl going to allow Jacques to ruin Vianne's life? This was not good for either of them.

But Jacques and his bride-to-be simply sat there, and in the face of their implacable serenity, Vianne had to fight the urge to pick up one of Papa's antique plates and crack it in two over Jacques' head.

"I see," she said instead, her own voice strangely calm. "So, I am homeless." And to think, she'd been working so hard to make Jacques proud of her when he came home!

Sandrine adjusted the folds of her blue dress and pressed her lips together, her eyes following Jacques adoringly as he stood up and paraded across the room in a straight line, quite the opposite of the way Vianne had paced in circles. He stopped in front of the fireplace, assuming the stance that told everyone he was the master of the house. And as he did so, Vianne noticed the line of sweat on his upper lip, the way his hands trembled as he curled his hands into fists by his sides. Vianne had no rights, no voice, no agency to fight him on this. She had never felt more like anyone's subordinate than she did on this day.

Jacques had always been uptight, even panicky on occasion, but he'd never been domineering until this point. It was true he'd followed Anaïs's lead, fretting if he was required to make a decision, until his twin sister would step in and make it for him. Once when Anaïs had disappeared for several hours on the neighbor's pony one summer in the Loire Valley, Jacques had been inconsolable, certain she'd fallen off and was in a ditch. Anaïs had been Jacques' protector, but Jacques was not going to care for Vianne.

Vianne's pulse flared into life. "So, on this small allowance, you are proposing I find a latchkey and move into an unfurnished home on my own?" *How could you, Jacques.* And yet, the thought of living with this woman, with this meek and strange Sandrine, why that was impossible in the extreme! Sandrine seemed so unlike the bright, lively spirits of Maman and Anaïs who had so filled their home with love and laughter.

Vianne reached out and leaned against the windowsill, her hands pressing into the painted wood.

"You will go and live with Marguerite Clément," Jacques said.

Vianne's head flipped up, and she stared at him. "Marguerite?"

"I have spoken with her, and she insists. She will take care of you and find you a husband. I don't see anything wrong with the arrangement." His voice was low and blurred.

Vianne insisted on meeting his gaze, but he bit on his lip and turned away.

Everything is wrong. My independence. My life, the dreams I hold dear. Vianne's hands itched to curl around her journal. At present, it was under a cushion on the sofa. *Do my hopes and plans matter nothing to you? Am I simply a vassal to be parted with, an inconvenience to be handed to the nearest family friend and done away with?*

Vianne glared at Jacques. "How can you live with yourself?" she whispered. "How can you treat me as if I am some package that needs to be housed until I can be completely disposed of so that I'm no inconvenience to you? What would Anaïs think?"

His eyes flickered, but he shook his head.

"It will happen for you, dear," Sandrine said, speaking for the first time, her voice tentative. "You will meet someone who will move your heart."

Vianne's eyes blazed.

"*Migno—*" Jacques said.

Vianne clutched her fists to her sides. "I am not your *mignon*, nor your *coquette*, nor your *bébé*. I am a fully grown young woman who has kept things going while our darling papa was falling apart!"

"You are conjuring up problems in your head. You've always done that, had too vivid of an imagination. You live in a fantasy world; you dream things up. You need to go." His tone became more urgent, as if he were beating out the words, justifying something he knew as well as she did was wrong, until he convinced them both it was right.

She backed away. He was scaring her. Was he attempting to imply that she was mad, that her love for designing beautiful garments meant she was somehow half-baked?

"Oh, I am leaving, Jacques," she whispered. "I shall walk to Marguerite's home right now, and tomorrow, I shall collect my clothes, and my personal effects. I will," she went on, hardly knowing what she was saying, "also be taking certain special items from Maman's wardrobe, because I know she would have wanted me to have them." She shot a parting look at the silent woman sitting on Papa's couch. "Maman did not simply wear her clothes, she shone in them."

Jacques's brow clouded. His jaw clenched.

Vianne collected her journal, clasped it to her breast, and eyed her brother straight on. "I will never live my life in the way you've planned for me. In the last four years, I have grown up. And one day, Jacques, I vow I will startle you. I will impress you, just as I was going to impress Maman and Papa. And then I am certain you will respect me, and you will not dismiss my designing as madness."

Jacques lowered his voice. "You need to go. Now. Please. And one thing, Vianne?"

Vianne's hands shook; she balled them into fists by her side once more.

"Don't ever talk of Anaïs as if you knew her better than me. Don't ever ask me what she'd think. Don't ever mention that I'm alive and she is dead, and especially, don't remind me that you are alive and she is gone for good."

Vianne stood, poleaxed. She wiped a tear away that was falling, lone, down her cheek. "I miss her too, Jacques. I miss them all. And they would have given me a roof over my head."

Jacques' jaw was set. He turned his back to her.

Organizing her journal, her shoulders pulled back, Vianne swept out of the salon, and walked in precise, measured steps to her bedroom. She collected her valise from her bureau and, her hands working quickly, she put great care into selecting clothes she would take with her. She packed a bag, folding her favored garments neatly, because despite telling Jacques that she'd be back in the morning, she knew she'd never be coming back to Rue de Sévigné again.

And then she drew out another valise, a larger one which she'd manage if it killed her on the short walk to Marguerite Clément's home in the Places de Vosges. She tiptoed into Maman's bedroom and, in the moonlight that pooled in through the window, she collected Maman's dreamy white lace dress, the one she'd reworked in the restaurant on the Champs-Élysées all those months ago.

Her fingers nimble and sure, she reached for the peach silk gown that she'd designed for Maman to wear at Jacques and Anaïs's birthday party, swiping at the tears that threatened to spill down her face. Finally, picking up a photograph of her parents and Anaïs, she packed up, turned on her heel and made her quiet way out to the front door.

Vianne stepped out into the freezing Paris night air, a lone young woman with only two suitcases and a dream.

But at least she believed in her own dream, even if no one else did.

CHAPTER FOUR

VIANNE, LE HAVRE, FRANCE, FALL, 1924

Vianne stood at the port of Le Havre amongst the crowds on the Quai d'Escale. In one hand, she held her ticket out of France, and in the other, she clutched her passport tight. She was proud of the fact that inside her passport, her occupation was listed as "seamstress."

SS *Paris*, the great transatlantic ocean liner, loomed in front of her like some impervious grande dame. The majestic ship's chimneys were bright and polished, her great black hull was shining and invincible, and yet it still seemed hardly possible that this impressive beauty would take Vianne all the way to New York.

A stiff breeze whipped up the quayside and the great steamship's foghorn let out a boom that hit Vianne in the stomach and stirred up the brewing vat of emotions that had plagued her ever since she'd made the momentous decision to leave France.

Vianne would be forever grateful to Maman's oldest friend, Marguerite Clément, for providing a temporary home in her charming apartment in the Place des Vosges. Once Vianne had finally secured a position as a midinette at a small fashion house on the Left Bank, she'd worked like a demon, long hours, six days a week, saving all that she could while insisting on paying Marguerite for her board and food. She'd sketched deep into the

night after days spent embroidering embellishments and buttons
and sequins on wealthy Parisian women's gowns, having worked
her way up from junior seamstress to pattern maker before finally
honing her skills as an embroiderer, which had proved madly
useful with the current trend for highly decorated garments in
haute couture.

But, despite her determination to work hard and make good on
her promise to herself that she could be someone, just as grand, just
as wonderful, as Anaïs and her maman were, Paris was breaking
Vianne's heart. It was impossible to shake off the memories that
preyed upon her in the city where she'd grown up, and where her
family were now only ghosts from the past. A past that would
haunt her everywhere she went: in the Tuileries Gardens where
she used to walk with Anaïs and Maman, their arms interlinked, or
amongst the quiet sculptures in the Louvre where she and Papa
used to sit and chat, and most of all, walking down the Rue de
Sévigné past the apartment where before the war they had all lived
blessed lives, but where now Jacques and his wife lived instead.

The months following Maman and Anaïs's deaths in 1918 had
been the toughest, most dreadful of her life. Watching Papa fall
apart had been heart-rending, cruel, tragic. Standing alone while
Jacques had sent her away had been humiliating, mortifying,
unspeakable.

Despite this, she'd tried so very hard to take an interest in the
new Paris after the war. She'd gone along to the burgeoning jazz
clubs, the dance halls, and she'd joined her friends in outings to the
countryside. But by winter last year, with its many long dark
evenings, she'd realized she had to free herself from the deep
sadness that accompanied her like a heavy cloak, even as Paris was
coming back to life. She'd gotten herself through her heartbreak
and her grief, no matter how tough and lonely it had been, but
now, it was time to properly pick herself up and live her life.

Vianne knew, deep down, that the only way to move forward
from the bitter losses that the war had flung upon her family would
be to make a completely new start.

And that meant leaving Paris. She needed to get away from all the memories of a time that was gone now, but where to?

She'd found the answer in a bookshop by the Seine.

F. Scott Fitzgerald's *Tales of the Jazz Age* was a book that Vianne devoured. Curled up in the window seat of Marguerite's salon, she'd been entranced by his stories of parties, of endless fun, of a lifestyle in America imbued with a spirit of freedom and most of all with jazz. She'd read of luxurious lifestyles, of soirees where people danced to the latest tunes in their own living rooms wearing up-to-the-minute clothing.

In America, it was said, there was stability and no dark, lingering shadows of war. Vianne read how the United States would rise to lead the world. It was the country that welcomed strangers, a land of immigrants. Vianne had found herself asking, would America allow her to follow her dreams, and could she one day hope to design the wonderful dresses which Fitzgerald wrote about?

Vianne turned back to take one final look at the hundreds of people who had flocked to the docks to see SS *Paris* depart. She sent up a silent message of love to Maman, Papa and Anaïs, and promised them that she would make them all proud—hugely so. She'd live enough of a life for all four of them at once.

But then, Vianne stopped. A cache of porters, pushing trolleys weighed down with fabulous trunks, was clearing the way through the line of waiting passengers and coming up to board the ship. She stood in awed silence while two of the most beautifully dressed women she'd ever laid eyes on sashayed onto the boat as if they crossed the Atlantic at least every month. Vianne stepped aside for them, taking in the magical labels that covered their trunks— Acapulco, Casablanca, Marrakesh, the Orient Express. Vianne could only imagine the garments that were packed away in those trunks.

Vianne knew that tonight, no matter how crowded her second-class cabin was, she'd be trying to capture in her journal the dresses that these fabulous women wore. One of them, a beautiful blond woman who looked to be in her early thirties and was clearly of great wealth, floated along in her dress of cream silk georgette with a water-lily motif, silver thread and glass bead embroidery. When she and her companion walked past, a hush fell over the crowds gathered on the quay, and Vianne would have been deaf not to hear the murmurs of "Emilie Grigsby" as the second woman walked by.

Vianne stood still, entranced, just as everyone else on the docks was, it seemed, by the beautiful middle-aged woman whose red-gold hair escaped from her fashionable hat, and when she paused a moment, almost theatrically, before boarding the ship, there was a collective sigh of admiration passing through the crowds at the woman's striking, violet eyes as she suddenly smiled and lifted her hand in a tiny wave.

"Emilie Grigsby," a woman breathed next to Vianne.

"Who is she?" Vianne murmured, taking care not to be overheard as she could almost reach out and touch the woman's dress, a dress that had simply come from none other than Coco Chanel. It was made in two parts from wool jersey—one of Chanel's trademark fabrics. Vianne studied the unlined skirt with its deep waistband that was topped with a short sweater edged with satin. The sleeves hung softly and were similarly edged with black satin cuffs.

"Why, dear," the woman said, in the American accent that Vianne knew she was going to become familiar with in the coming months. "Emilie Grigsby had a liaison with Charles T. Yerkes, and he built a mansion for her in New York."

Vianne watched as Emilie paused, smiling genuinely at the captain of the ship, who was greeting first-class passengers, before she and her companion disappeared to the top decks for their journey, never to sully themselves by setting foot in second class.

"Emilie is a patron of artists, sculptors, musicians and writers," Vianne's knowledgeable neighbor continued. "She's regarded as one of the most beautiful women in the world, and now spends most of her time in London, but it looks like she's accompanying Katherine Carter to New York for a while."

"And who is Katherine Carter?" Vianne asked. The glamorous women moved into the magical realms of first class that Vianne would never see, and she turned to the woman next to her, who lent her a knowing smile.

"Why, Katherine Carter is married to one of New York's great industrialists. She owns a beautiful mansion on Fifth Avenue and is a major society hostess." The woman tilted her head to one side. "May I ask why you are so interested in them? Would you like to meet a wealthy gentleman who could provide you with the accoutrements that Miss Emilie and Mrs. Carter enjoy?"

Vianne shook her head. "Oh, no," she said. "I want to design their wardrobes, you see."

The woman raised a brow, and the queue moved forward again, the glimpse of extraordinary wealth and privilege disappeared with the breeze. "Well, my dear," the woman said, "that is an extraordinary and modern ambition, but, you know, anything's possible in New York."

Vianne clasped her suitcase and, her heart lifting as it hadn't done in years, she took her last step from French territory and entered the magnificent ocean liner that would take her halfway across the world. She vowed to herself that one day, just like Gabrielle Coco Chanel, she would design beautiful clothes for the likes of the women who had just stepped aboard the magnificent SS *Paris*.

A week later, Vianne stood on the decks of the ocean liner, staring out to sea as night fell over the watery world that unfolded differently each day. But the changing, mercurial sea was the mysterious entrée to her new life. Vianne had spent days nursing nausea since SS *Paris* sailed from Plymouth. While gutted with seasickness in the small cabin she shared with three other women, she'd nevertheless tried to pore over her sketchbook, determined between roiling, rollicking bouts of sickness to sketch dresses that might be worthy of the likes of Emilie

Grigsby and Katherine Carter. Vianne listened, ears pricked, as her cabin mates chattered enviously of the fabled first-class cabins on board the ship, whose luxury, it was said, no other liner could emulate. They were full of tales of how, in first class, a valet could be summoned at the click of a finger and there was a cinema room, dancing halls, long, beautiful promenades, and staterooms fit for an exhibition, each with their own color scheme.

Vianne stared out to sea now, letting her eyes rest on the last seagulls of the dying day, which followed the ship with their vain hope of grabbing scraps of haute cuisine that the first-class passengers enjoyed in their dining saloon. It was three decks high, so it was said, with tables on indoor and outdoor decks, and paneling of Ceylon lemonwood.

The upper echelons of SS *Paris* had been described as a floating France.

Vianne often imagined what life aboard this seaborne hotel might be like for the women whom she'd seen boarding the ship, as she'd finally made her way to the second-class dining room through the Grand Salon de Conversation once she acquired her sea legs, trying not to stop and stare at the beautiful dome adorned with a grand skylight, its luxurious soft carpets and grand wide staircases leading to the upper decks.

Vianne jumped when someone pressed their hand onto her arm, and she turned to come face to face with a young woman, well dressed.

"Miss Mercier?" the girl said. "Excuse me? I'm sorry to bother you."

"*Oui, bonjour.*" Should she have spoken English? Her cabin mates were French, and she'd not spoken much English on the voyage yet, but Papa and Maman had insisted that she, Anaïs and Jacques learn the language, and now she was only thankful that she was fluent because she was going to need to be so in order just to survive in New York.

"You are a seamstress?" the young woman continued in that

strange and fascinating American accent that Vianne's ears were still becoming accustomed to hearing.

Vianne nodded. "Why yes, I am," she said, unsure why this was of interest.

The woman's shoulders seemed to slump with relief. "Oh, well, we need you straight away. There is a wardrobe malfunction in first class. It is a serious emergency that requires immediate attention, Miss Mercier." The young woman flushed, but took a breath, as if determined to get her point across. "We need the services of a seamstress and a cabin boy told me he'd seen you out here. Would you come with me and help us out?" She cleared her throat. "My employer will pay you, Miss Mercier."

"But of course." Vianne sent the girl one of her winning smiles. She didn't add that there was no need to pay her, she'd pay someone herself for the chance to walk through the fabled first-class.

Ten minutes later, Vianne was in the rarefied world she'd never dreamed she would see. She climbed the grand staircase in the Salon de Conversation, resisting the temptation to stop and stand atop the sweeping stairs, staring down at the ordinary passengers who were forbidden entry to the mysterious and magical first-class echelons. Vianne, instead, climbed steadily, her heart beating in her mouth at the thought of finding inspiration from the stunning garments that the liner's wealthy passengers would be wearing at sea.

They skirted the edges of a luxurious music and lounge room, where plush upholstered chairs were dotted around small tables, and Vianne glanced across at the gorgeous slip-on cocktail dresses the women wore, one embroidered all over in gold, its peach-colored lining made of chiffon as far as Vianne could tell, and another catching her eye in bright shades of red, with several rows of deep flounces below the hips.

Vianne couldn't help the thrill of excitement that coursed

through her veins when her companion led her up a grand corridor and opened a polished wooden door into a room carpeted in pale cream, with geometric patterned wallpaper and a pair of soft feather beds. A woman dressed in Chinese-style pajamas decorated with oriental floral motifs sat at a modern, lozenge-shaped mirror with her back to them. When she turned around, Vianne realized that she was face to face with one of the two stunning passengers whose luggage and traveling clothes she'd admired while she was waiting to board the grand ship. Katherine Carter and Emilie Grigsby.

"Oh, Adrienne," Mrs. Carter said, addressing her maid. "There you are at last. Do tell me that the companion you have with you has come to mend my poor evening dress." She arose from her velvet-covered stool and moved across to one of the pair of mirrored wardrobes that graced the charming room.

Through a pair of open doors either side of the dressing table, Vianne spotted not one but two marble bathrooms. She sighed at the thought of her own cabin, with its clutch of four bunk beds complete with thin, hard mattresses and plain gray blankets. The shared restroom was a long way down the corridor.

She bit down a taste of nostalgia at being surrounded by such beautiful things, because Mama and Papa used to take such delight in decorating their apartment with great care and taste.

"Mrs. Carter, this is Miss Mercier, a seamstress who was recommended to me," the maid said.

The exquisite Mrs. Carter inclined her head toward Vianne and stood aside while her maid opened the door of the wardrobe and reached inside, carefully removing a chiffon gown of pale blue decorated with irregular embroidery in a semi-abstract geometric clamshell design, with an asymmetric hem. Vianne trained her eyes on the way the beaded pattern seemed to be expanding, giving a feeling of movement when the maid laid it carefully out on the bed.

"You see, Miss Mercier, one of the clamshells has a loose thread and we have lost some of the beads. It is quite worrisome as we do not have anything to replace them with, and Mrs. Carter is particularly keen not to lose any more embellishments."

"Indeed," Mrs. Carter said. "Do you think you can mend it?"

Vianne took a close look at the gown, taking great delight at the quality of the fabric, the fine beadwork. She sighed. It might be months, even years, before she had the opportunity to work with haute couture in New York.

"Have you experience handling such fine work?" the maid asked, leaning in next to Vianne.

Vianne, her eyes trailing over the problem, nodded. "But of course. I worked for a small designer in Paris who used only the best fabrics. I can mend the loose thread for you, and ensure the clamshell looks complete, and I shall do so invisibly. You won't see a thing. Nor, importantly, will anyone else. Would you prefer me to do so here, or would you like me to work somewhere else?"

"We can't have you taking the gown away from the cabin," the maid said, looking slightly horrified.

"Oh, Adrienne, we are on a boat. How far could Mademoiselle Mercier go?" Mrs. Carter said. She appeared bored with the entire situation now and returned to her toilette at the mirror.

Vianne's lips twitched at the way Mrs. Carter pronounced her name as if she were a native-born French speaker. "When you return to New York, it should be possible to source replacement beads, but in the meantime, you don't want to lose any more of these precious pieces."

"Oh, wonderful," Katherine Carter murmured. "Give this delightful girl the sewing kit, and do draw me a bath, Adrienne."

"Of course, Mrs. Carter," the maid said. She opened a walnut cupboard cunningly inlaid into the wall above one of the beds, and handed Vianne a sewing kit, filled with cotton of every color, and tiny shining scissors along with needles and pins. "You can work on the bed, Miss Mercier."

Vianne set to work, while Adrienne busied herself in the bathroom, and soon, the suite was filled with the gorgeous scent of bubble bath.

Half an hour later, Vianne had painstakingly mended the dress. It had been tricky but also a pleasure to work on the beautiful garment. She checked her work until she was satisfied before glancing longingly at the wardrobe where she'd caught a glimpse of other gorgeous gowns. Imagine what inspiration was hidden behind those firmly closed doors!

"I'm glad you found me," she confessed to the young American maid. "Because it would have been a disappointment for anything to happen to this dress. The trick of the beading—seeming to move due to the irregular embroidery—is something quite extraordinary. I imagine it would look beautiful when it is worn by Mrs. Carter."

"Oh, it does," the maid said.

Just then, the door opened, and Mrs. Carter's companion from boarding appeared, her glorious red-gold hair dressed with a diamond tiara and her extraordinary violet eyes shining with good health and sea air. Vianne's own eyes widened. Emilie Grigsby, who'd been described as the most beautiful woman in the world, was looking at Vianne with an odd expression on her face.

"Oh, so you're entertaining in the room, are you, Adrienne?" the beautiful woman said. "Darling, you know I never stand on ceremony." She looked pointedly at Vianne.

"Oh, no, Miss Mercier is a Parisian seamstress, who has just mended Mrs. Carter's chiffon gown."

Emilie Grigsby sashayed into the room and Vianne found herself quite starstruck. The woman kicked off her shoes, pulled the bejeweled tiara out of her shining hair, and laid it down on the bedside table. The heavily beaded cream Egyptian-style dress she wore, with its geometrical-shaped embroidery, gave her an even more statuesque air. Vianne busied herself putting away the fine needles and thread she'd used to mend the dress.

Just then, Mrs. Carter swanned out in a fresh pearl-gray-colored silk wrap. Her hair, cut fashionably short, framed her wide cheekbones and soft jawline.

Vianne stood up and held up her chin. She had no idea how to relate to these sophisticated, wealthy American women and, her heart hammering in her chest, she held Mrs. Carter's gaze. "Your dress is fixed, Mrs. Carter," she said, holding it out to show the woman.

Not sure whether Mrs. Carter would deign to respond to her, Vianne prepared to leave. But, to her surprise, both women looked carefully at the dress.

"Marvelous," Emilie Grigsby said. "You'd hardly know I'd caught my diamond bracelet in it at all."

"Well, I quite agree, Emilie dear," Mrs. Carter purred in her soft voice. She lifted her head, her beautiful eyes taking in Vianne properly as if for the first time. "I noticed you when we boarded the ship," she said. "You have such an elegant and charming way about you. It's so very French. Tell me, why are you going to New York?"

"I hope you're not only after a husband," Emilie Grigsby said, her extraordinary eyes crinkling into a genuine smile. "Because I think you've got some living to do before you settle down, dear."

Vianne raised a brow. "I want to find work, initially as a seamstress for a designer in Manhattan." She lowered her voice. "I have ambitions, one day, to design the sort of haute couture you are both wearing." There, she'd said it. She knew she was being bold. But something told her these two unusual and beautiful women would not condone anything ordinary at all.

Vianne's companions exchanged a glance, and the room was quiet a moment.

"Well then," Emilie Grigsby finally said. "You must go and work for Eloise Chapelle. Tell her I recommended you. Several of my close friends back in Manhattan have her make their day dresses and even the odd evening gown because she's so good. You'd do well to start there, and you won't be exploited, dear. She'll take care of you."

Vianne flushed, for one moment, quite lost for words. She wasn't expecting a woman of Emilie Grigsby's cachet to show any interest in the likes of a Parisian seamstress on her way to New York. "I am most appreciative," she said. "Thank you."

"Of course," the beautiful woman said.

"Thank you for mending my dress," Katherine Carter added.

Vianne clasped her hands in front of her. And right then, despite all the uncertainty and the heartache of the past years, she felt a sense of what might be possible. After all, she was going to New York, so who knew what was in store?

CHAPTER FIVE

VIANNE, NEW YORK, FALL, 1924

Vianne hugged her portfolio to her chest, her fashionable, wedge-heeled shoes tapping against the sidewalk on Park Avenue and her navy all-wool skirt with double box pleats swinging. She hoped her tailored blouse with its small frills and white French voile was professional and suitable for the most important interview of her life.

The chance to work in the house of Madame Eloise Chappelle, dressmaker to Manhattan's wealthiest clientele, was an opportunity afforded to her by a kind recommendation from none other than Emilie Grigsby herself; it would be Vianne's biggest lucky break.

Her heart beating with anticipation, Vianne dodged by well-dressed gentlemen in fashionable loose-fitting suits and women in cloche hats. She tried to relax and focus on the miniature gardens that ran down the middle of the grand avenue that were laid out with grass and green conifers, lending this uptown scene an air of graceful respite.

But the sounds of Midtown still rang in Vianne's ears, trolley cars so jam-packed with passengers that they hung out of the windows and hovered on the running boards, traffic officers holding great swathes of pedestrians at bay with whistles and white gloves, cars bumping along the streets, their spare tires perched jauntily on their backs like lifebuoy rings.

Broadway, Fifth Avenue, with its gorgeous, carpeted stores, the Plaza Hotel, Riverside Drive, Coney Island. Since arriving in New York, Vianne had seen them all. She'd wandered around Central Park with her heart aching for France, while forthrightly stamping down any feelings of nostalgia for Paris and telling herself, firmly, that New York was the most exciting city in the world.

She turned into East 63rd Street, deep in the Upper East Side, the heart of elite New York.

The fact that she was Parisian, Vianne knew, had also helped secure her a chance of winning the position with Madame Chappelle, but still Vianne could hardly believe she had a chance in a hundred with such a well-regarded dressmaker. In her letter inviting Vianne to this interview, Madame Chappelle had made no bones about the fact she was impressed with the years of work Vianne had undertaken as a midinette in one of Paris's up-and-coming smaller couture houses. She may not have worked for Chanel or Jean Lanvin, but everyone knew that Paris led all the international trends.

Her heart in her mouth, Vianne stopped outside the elegant building that housed the atelier she prayed would accept her and welcome her into its fold.

One thing was certain. She simply *must not* mess this interview up.

Vianne raised her gloved hand and knocked on the black-painted door in front of her. In the picture window, there was a gorgeous display of evening gowns and Vianne allowed herself a split second to take them in.

Fashioned out of chiffon and lace, chenille brocaded crepe with feather trimming, black lace and satin, the garments were in the very latest style—drop-waist dresses—one even with the very new cape effect forming the sleeves. This was tipped to be one of the key styles of fall and winter and it was impressive to see the feature already on display. Two of the dresses had fabric flowers at the side of the drop waist—also the very latest fashion trend.

Vianne clasped her hands tightly. She had scoured the season's forecasts before her interview, her growing cache of fashion magazines stacked neatly on the small wooden desk in the tiny single bedroom in the boarding house where she was lodging out in Brooklyn until she could afford better. But all the while, her heart was here in Manhattan, where the excitement and glamor of New York was taking place. She couldn't wait to be a part of it, and her spine tingled with excitement every time she strolled around the Manhattan streets.

When the door opened, Vianne sent a bright-eyed look toward the young woman who sashayed out of the door. She was dressed in a deep-red fur-trimmed coat: the collar, cuffs, and border enriched with what Vianne knew was beaver fur. The young woman looked Vianne up and down, and Vianne blushed, recognizing her *joie de vivre,* the girl's confidence that Vianne used to show in abundance before she lost Maman, Anaïs and Papa. She sighed and reminded herself firmly that she hoped to replace what she'd lost with something even stronger. It was what Maman would want.

Trembling with a blend of nerves, anticipation and excitement, she entered the dressmaker's atelier.

As soon as Vianne was in the door, the tightness in her shoulders only intensified at the sight of the elegant surrounds. The room was worthy of a Parisian salon. Soft rugs graced the shining parquet floorboards. An understated chandelier hung from the lofty ceiling, while Louis XVI chairs were dotted around the walls, and in the back corner another exquisite gown was on display, one in pale pink chiffon with elaborate crystal and rhinestone embroidery and fringe draping from the shoulder.

Vianne took in a deep breath and waited at the little table in the opposite corner.

Two doors led off from the entrance hall, and from behind one of them, Vianne could hear the familiar sound of women chattering. Listening carefully, Vianne discerned the sounds of at least four voices. The seamstresses working out in the back rooms.

She knew she was ten steps ahead of herself, but she had to wonder, what would it take to rise to the level of Madame Chappelle?

Another door opened. Two women came out and Vianne glimpsed a charming room beyond, with pale carpets, and a full-length oval mirror in front of which was draped the beginnings of a chenille brocaded crepe gown on a cream velvet chair.

Vianne straightened herself up, trying to stay inconspicuous, trying to allow Madame Chappelle the time to say farewell to her client without interruption.

But Madame Chapelle's eyes scanned Vianne just as quickly as the woman who'd just walked out the door. "Good morning," she said.

"*Bonjour*, Madame Chapelle, I am honored to meet you," Vianne said, forgetting herself for one split second and adding the "h" in "honored." "My name is Vianne Mercier."

"I see you haven't cut your hair," Madame Chapelle said, addressing Vianne directly, while placing a light kiss on the cheek of the woman who was departing. "But you have that certain Parisian flair."

Vianne pricked up her ears. Madame spoke with an accent that was not from New York but that was American of some kind.

Madame's departing customer regarded Vianne in an *I am above worrying about what people think of me but you are not* kind of New York way, swished her fox fur around her shoulders and left the building, the door clicking softly shut.

Vianne gulped. This was it.

She followed Madame Chapelle across the salon. Madame stopped at her antique table, eighteenth-century Tuscan, with gold leaf and a Carrera marble top. Vianne allowed herself a sad smile. Papa would have come in and described every piece of furniture in the room, enchanting Madame with his knowledge of all her precious pieces. He would have *charmed* Madame Eloise Chappelle.

Instead, Vianne, mustering as much grace as she could, held out a hand to the tall, impossibly slim, auburn-haired woman with the slight dappling of freckles across the bridge of her nose and the tops of her cheeks and shook her hand.

"I am more than excited about the chance to work here," Vianne said, embellishing her English with just a little too much Parisian clip.

Madame Chapelle narrowed her slightly hooded brown eyes, enhanced with a toning brown liner and pale eyeshadow as a contrast to her deep-red lips. The woman had flair in bucketloads. Her hair was cut just below her ears and swept to one side, waved in the very latest style. But it was her outfit that was extraordinary. It flowed from her, and if the emphasis had been on relaxed dressing ever since the war, then Madame Chapelle exemplified that.

Her striking green dress of georgette crepe, with its paneled drop-waisted girdle to which were attached two charming flowers, flowed toward her black suede high-heeled shoes, fastened with pearl buttons over the softest of stockings. Her figure was exquisite and gave a perfect line to the dress.

Vianne sighed. She knew she'd only be out the back in a working pinafore if Madame Chapelle decided to stop looking down her nose at her and deigned to give her the job. And still, she'd be fortunate. Most dressmaking jobs in New York were in the Garment District, in factories spilling with girls sitting in rows under harsh lights for long days, with latchkeys around their necks and no one to go home to but their cat.

Vianne straightened up. She didn't even have a cat. Not yet.

"Why haven't you cut your hair?" Madame Chapelle repeated.

Vianne, to her horror, turned quite red. Her hair was the last vestige that she had left of Maman and Anaïs. Their long, wavy, blond tresses had been their pride and joy. She cleared her throat. "Why, I simply have not had the chance," she said. "I have been acquainting myself with New York, and my first priority is to find a position, Madame Chapelle."

Madame opened a drawer in her table and drew out a silver cigarette box, taking out a cigarette, only to hold it unlit in her hand. She regarded Vianne, her hand tapering elegantly from her slim body. "Well, you'd better come and sit down," she said, in her extraordinary compelling accent, waving Vianne in the direction of her two velvet chairs. "I'd take you into my office, but we'd have to pass the girls out the back to do that, and I want you to myself for a while." Her voice trailed off as if she were waving the words away with her beautiful hand.

Vianne settled on a soft velvet chair, her hands tracing over the plush armrests, reveling in their touch after the hard wooden chairs at the boarding house.

"Tell me why you left Paris," Madame Chappelle said. "Why come to New York when the fashion industry is so obviously centered in France? Most New York girls dream of going to Paris, so why are you going the other way?"

Vianne held the woman's gaze. She'd anticipated this. She took in a breath and decided to simply tell the truth. "It is because of the war," she said.

"The war? That ordeal was over in 1918."

"*Mais oui,* but I lost my mother and my sister in a bombing attack, and my father died on Armistice Day of a broken heart." There, she'd said it without breaking down.

Madame Chapelle sat back and folded her shapely legs. "I'm sorry," she said. Her expression did not soften, but her voice did, just enough. "So, you wanted a new life, and you chose New York, I take it?"

Vianne nodded. She folded her hands in her lap.

"How long are you planning on staying?"

Until I have my own atelier. "I have no plans to leave, madame. I want to stay in America for good." After all, there was nothing to return to in Paris.

Madame seemed to consider this. "I'm not going to feed you a lot of baloney. I don't have time for that, nor do I have the inclination."

Vianne bit back her smile. Who knew what "baloney" was, but she was drawn to Madame Chapelle. The woman had something. A languid elegance in the way she lounged, the way she was comfortable in her own skin. Vianne was certain Madame Chappelle could have walked into any salon in Paris and become the center of attention, but beneath this, there was an astuteness, which Vianne recognized as her papa had shared the same attribute.

"This position," Madame said, "is not just for a seamstress."

Vianne's hands stilled in her lap.

"I have too many customers to look after on my own." She leaned a little closer, her hands expressive. "I have my seamstresses, all of whom have been with me for a very long time. They are loyal, hard-working, and I can trust them to reach the *very* high standards that I, and my esteemed clientele, expect."

Vianne nodded.

"What I need, though... now, is someone who can manage three roles. Otherwise, I employ three people, and that, Mademoiselle, would not do."

Vianne held Madame's gaze, her fists gathered tight. "Of course not, madame."

"You told me when you wrote to me that you are able to work fast."

"But of course. I was the fastest and most accurate and careful midinette in the couture house where I worked in Paris. Therefore, I was—how do you say?—elevated and given some of the most complex work to do. I am an experienced and accomplished pattern maker and embroiderer. As the current couture and evening fashions are all about embellishments, embroideries, and decorative beading on the tubular dress, I am skilled in all of these areas."

Vianne paused. She'd brushed up her English since she'd arrived in New York, by engaging anyone who'd chat with her in the boarding house in conversation. She'd even been trying to think in English as much as she could.

She smiled at Madame and went on. "Then, I was put in charge of a group of girls and I not only carried out my own work, but supervised theirs as well, always checking for attention to detail, for accuracy and that they did not take any shortcuts with the careful work required."

Madame's brow furrowed. "I can only imagine that it was quite the risky step to leave a position where you were given such responsibilities, Miss Mercier."

Vianne fought the urge to loosen the tight collar of her blouse. This was where she would not disclose the fact that she wanted to do exactly what Madame was doing right now. She wanted a business like this of her own, a place where her imagination could have free rein, where she could turn her clientele into polished versions of themselves. But she must not get ahead of herself. Instead of saying a word, she simply inclined her head in agreement.

"You also told me that you have designed and made your own clothes, along with clothes for your family and friends?"

"*Oui*," Vianne said. She bit on her lip, but her hands reached down almost of their own volition to the garment bag she'd brought along with her, and from this, she brought out the Oriental-style silk dress she'd designed for Maman for the weekend she died. Carefully, forcing her fingers not to shake, Vianne held up the peach-colored gown of silk, tiny glass beads and blowsy embroidered roses. Vianne's heart lurched at the sight of the antique silver clasp that, in the melee that was 1918, had remained attached to the gown since Vianne had borrowed it from Papa at Celine.

Madame peered forward. "May I?" she asked, reaching out.

"Of course." Vianne sat back, every breath she took measured, her feet wanting to fly off the ground.

Madame took an age. "Extraordinary," she finally whispered. She raised her head, her brown eyes warm. "This is almost indistinguishable from a piece of haute couture. Are you certain you sewed it all by yourself?"

"Why yes," Vianne breathed.

Madame clicked her tongue. "Well then, have you anything else to show me?"

Vianne reached into her handbag and pulled out her journal of sketches, fairly bulging with tiny fabric samples and notes.

Madame took the book in her elegant hands, turning the pages, slowly examining each design, until she came to the drawings for a sequined evening dress that was Vianne's own favorite idea.

"Oh, my," Madame breathed, her eyes drinking in the voluptuous sequined tulle dress. "This is so pretty. The sequins look as if they are spilling over the body in a glistening cascade."

Vianne leaned forward, breaking into a small smile at Madame's endearing words. Forgetting her nerves for a minute, she traced her own fingers over the familiar sketch, borne out of a cold winter's morning in Paris. She'd been sitting looking out over the misty Place des Vosges, the lovely old square with its brick and stone buildings and its central park shrouded in mystery, the sun just rising, and reflecting all its colors in the dear windows of the old houses in turn in a glorious arc. She'd wanted to design a dress that made her feel the same sense of awe. Awe at its beauty, its allure, its promise of enchantment and excitement, the magical way it captured the light.

"Well, you see, the silver sequins are backed with gold," she told Madame Chappelle. "They overlap because I wanted to create a fluid, rippling effect."

Madame nodded, her eyes drinking in the sketch.

"I want the dress to reflect the surrounding light, and color," Vianne explained. "I would align the sequins so very carefully, you see, to emphasize the structure of the bodice, which has a draped front formed by two flared ties that curve around to fasten at the back." Vianne reached across and turned the page in her journal, showing Madame her other preliminary sketches for this dress, the way the skirt draped to just below the knees, the beauty in the detailed bodice.

"Ah, yes," Madame whispered, her voice so soft it was barely audible. "Extraordinary. And most original. It is not derivative, which I love."

"The dress is sleeveless," Vianne added, "as you see. And it is made in deep blue tulle onto which the gold-backed silver sequins are tamboured."

"The low, V-shaped front neck is very unique," Madame said. "The plunge back, with those lovely wide straps, the way the dress falls to the knees is perfection."

Vianne lifted her eyes to meet Madame's serious expression.

"There would be plenty of movement for the legs, for dancing, Mademoiselle Mercier."

"*Oui*," Vianne said.

Madame handed the journal back. She tented her hands, and looked Vianne straight in the eye, her own brown eyes clear and honest, Vianne thought to herself.

"What I want," Madame said, "is a junior designer."

Vianne sat up. She could hardly breathe, let alone speak.

"Some of the duties for this role will be more mundane, of course. You would be assisting me, undertaking tasks such as finding fabrics and helping with finishing touches for my collections." She waved her hand, still holding the cigarette in its holder in the air. "This is what I expect of all my staff, whether they are seamstresses, pattern makers, or embroiderers. We collaborate when the need arises, and all pull our sleeves up to contribute."

Vianne nodded. "Yes, I understand, madame."

"But the difference in this new position," Madame went on, "is, as I said, that it is threefold. I want someone who can meet with some of my customers and who can come up with concepts on a day-to-day basis for my clientele."

She wanted Vianne to consult with her clients? Vianne forced herself not to jump out of her chair in delight.

"I also want someone experienced enough to supervise my staff, a woman who can oversee the development of patterns and the production of garments." She leaned forward in her chair.

"What I am saying is that I would give you the agency to follow a client's garment through from beginning to end."

Vianne's eyes shone. The chance to listen to the clientele, to do what she loved, designing her own garments for them, and then to see things through to fruition, it was what she'd been doing in her spare time, and to be paid to design her own creations, with a ready-made client list and to work for a woman as well regarded as Eloise Chappelle was more than a dream come true, it was the embodiment of her fairy tale.

"Why, this would be glorious," Vianne breathed.

Madame's bow-shaped lips formed a little smile. "As well as designing, liaising with some of my long-standing clients and supervising production to the very highest standards, I would want you to analyze trends in fabrics, colors and shapes for me."

"But of course." She squeezed her hands together, pressing so hard that she might burst.

"Above all," Madame said, "I want someone with an exceptional eye for color, the ability to visualize things in three dimensions, and most of all a designer who has a real passion for clothes."

And right then, Vianne sent the woman a smile that would make Maman proud. "Well, then. You have gone and found yourself exactly the right woman for the job, madame."

Madame sat back in her seat. She crossed her legs, tapped one foot up and down in the air. "Very well," she said. "I have a challenge for you. Before I take things any further, I would like you to not just tell me, but *show* me what you can do."

Vianne lifted her chin. "I would be delighted, Madame Chapelle."

Madame let out a little laugh, tilting her head back in the most charming manner. But it was as if she was including Vianne in her little joke, not excluding her, and Vianne felt her shoulders melt a little as she returned Madame's smile.

"I have a plan in mind, Mademoiselle Mercier."

"Call me Vianne," Vianne burst out suddenly. "Please, madame," she added, lowering her gaze.

Madame leaned forward, and right then, she took Vianne's hands. "I have not—no, I have not ever, I can tell you, met a young woman who shares my passion, who has such flair for design, as you," she said.

Slowly, Vianne lifted her eyes.

"But," Madame said, holding up one finger, "we have to observe formalities before we get too far ahead of ourselves. Let's do this final test before I can definitely offer that you come work with me."

Vianne pressed her lips together, her eyes almost filling with tears. She had not felt such joy since Maman died. "*Oui*," she nodded, unable to find the English word.

Madame chuckled. "If you keep speaking French, my dear, you'll have my clients eating out of your talented hands."

Vianne bit on her lip. She could be anywhere in the world, she was so delighted.

"Now," Madame went on, "I want you to come with me. I want you to meet one of my favorite clients." Madame stood up.

Vianne, taking this as an invitation to do the same, stood up too, and fairly hovered next to the elegant woman.

Madame draped herself in a green, fur-lined coat, for the October day was uncommonly chilly.

Vianne stood, uncertain in her blue skirt and white lacy blouse.

Madame held the door open. "You can talk to my client, you can come up with the concept, you can come back to the atelier and sketch the gown, and you can oversee my women and bring the gown to completion. This will be your trial," Madame said, stepping out into the street and clipping along. Madame stopped on the corner of Park Avenue and East 63rd Street. "I can tell you one thing…"

"Yes?" Vianne breathed. At this point, if Madame had told her they were eating those dreadful American "hot dogs" for supper, Vianne would have willingly sat down and somehow managed to get the things off the plate and into her mouth.

"You know, we are going to *have* to cut your hair."

Vianne felt her mouth twitch.

Madame placed her gloved hand on Vianne's shoulder, her head tilted to one side as if she were considering something else. "Do you need a place to live?"

Vianne nodded, her heart hammering in her chest, but her head moving up and down in precise movements that she hoped conveyed confidence.

"Well then, if all goes well with my client, Mrs. Adriana Conti, you can live above the atelier with Lucia, my pattern maker."

"I'd love to," Vianne whispered. And right there, in front of one of New York's glamorous skyscrapers, with cars sailing up Park Avenue and all the chaos and excitement of Manhattan right at her feet, Vianne could have hugged Madame.

But, instead, the older woman walked up to the doorman and spoke to him with all the confidence in the world. "Madame Eloise Chappelle for Mrs. Adriana Conti." There was that strange drawn-out lilt to her voice again. She turned to Vianne. "Madame Conti's son, Giorgio, is opening a very modern new restaurant, Vianne. It's going to take up the entire ground floor of this building." She waved her gloved hand vaguely around the boarded-up windows, from whence workmanlike noises came. "Madame Conti wants something grand to wear to the opening night. I'm going to let you design the dress. Well, I'm going to let you give it a try. How about that for a trial by fire?"

"Thank you," Vianne said. Had she taken on more than she should? "I am determined to do you proud."

Madame sailed into the marble foyer of the gracious building and Vianne trotted behind her like her an ingénue.

If only my brother Jacques could see me now.

"I didn't mention," Madame continued, "that Mrs. Conti's son is one of the most handsome and eligible bachelors in New York."

Vianne's eyes rounded.

Vianne folded her hands and followed Madame to the grand elevators.

"Don't you be distracted by Giorgio Conti, my dear," Madame

said, waiting for the concierge to let them into the elevators. "He's a charming, sophisticated man. And you," she added, tilting her head in a knowing way, "are an extraordinarily beautiful girl."

"Madame Chappelle," Vianne said, "I am never going to risk my reputation, let alone yours. The chance to design for you is enough. It's just the cat's meow!" She could have hugged herself at the way she threw the new phrase she'd picked up since coming to New York into her conversation. She might be feeling a little lost being so far from Paris, but she was overwhelmingly excited about fitting into modern Manhattan and she had no intention of chasing after Giorgio Conti, or anyone else for that matter, above finally making her dream come true.

Madame let out a chuckle, and she swept into the elevator, her eyes lighting up with a smile.

CHAPTER SIX
ELOISE, NEW YORK, FALL, 1924

Everyone said that imitation was the best form of flattery, but all Eloise Chappelle knew was that copying was stealing, and it hurt. She clipped down Madison Avenue, gathering her green coat close against the unexpected chill in the October air. Immersed in her thoughts, she shut out the noisy Manhattan surrounds, allowing relief to wash over her after this morning's interview with Vianne Mercier. The young woman had astounded Adriana Conti during their private appointment, and Vianne and Eloise were returning tomorrow with the initial ideas for Adriana's very special dress. Vianne Mercier was not only a gifted young woman, but the girl was French, beautiful and might just be the ammunition that Eloise needed right now.

Eloise hurried down to Macy's, Herald Square. Her decision to accept a luncheon invitation from Lena Davis was unnerving her, and the best way to deal with that was to keep moving and not stop to dwell. Eloise was keeping up appearances when it came to her clientele, and of course not one soul knew how much Lena Davis was affecting things behind the façade Eloise always wore, but the fact was, the other designer was derailing Eloise's confidence. She'd become used to the certain type of nausea that bit at her as Lena rolled out copy after copy of

Eloise's original designs, showing these stolen ideas off on the runways of New York, in the leading fashion magazines, blaring in Macy's windows, though this was no fault of the department store.

In the meantime, Eloise was struggling to design, to sew, to inspire her staff, to come to terms with the fact that someone would steal the original garments that she'd worked so hard to design and that were worn by Eloise's society clientele, while blatantly claiming them as their own. The fact was, Eloise needed someone to pick up the needle she'd dropped. It was as if she'd been swept aside in a storm and it was all caused by Lena Davis.

Lena Davis, married, wealthy, well connected, was a tour de force. She had first approached Eloise at a fashion parade in Saks, singling Eloise out at the show, many of which were popping up in department stores all over New York. Fashionable people these days rolled their eyes and said that it was not possible to go out for luncheon in a department store restaurant without a flotilla of models gliding at head height along a runway while you sipped your coffee and tried to make polite talk.

Lena Davis, who back then had a small dressmaking business off Madison Avenue, had told Eloise how she admired her work. And Eloise, even though all her instincts had warned her away from the elegantly dressed Mrs. Davis from the moment she'd seen how the woman was trying to ingratiate herself with anyone who was in a position of power, had been flattered.

Now, she was paying the price.

She'd told Lena how she'd worked out that fringes below a dress would allow the wearer to dance the new modern dances freely without restraint. She'd explained how her vivid orange silk velvet flapper dress that she had spent hours designing with great care, with its slim velvet belt around the drop waist and its skirt of orange and peach-colored streamers, each one lightly breaded and staggered where they were oversewn to the dress, would form the most exquisite delicate hanging fringe. She'd openly chatted about how proud she was of the way this fringe reflected the light with two different shades, while only enhancing and emphasizing the linear shape of the dress.

Next, she knew, Lena Davis had copied Eloise's velvet dress in aquamarine and azure. What was worse, Lena's imitation of Eloise's design had launched Lena's couture career before Eloise's dress had seen the light of day.

Eloise had sat with her head in her hands in her private office after reading in countless newspapers how Lena Davis claimed to every fashion magazine that she'd woken from a dream right around the time of the parade at Saks and *seen* that belted, two-toned fringed velvet dress right in front of her eyes. She'd boasted that the idea just came to her. Eloise had been sickened to her core.

Lena Davis designed under one name, *Pearl*. In a sudden explosion, Pearl had become synonymous with the reproduction of Parisian couture in New York. Eloise's mouth had dropped open when Lena had made an exclusive, lucrative agreement with Macy's to sell a selection of her garments each season in the store, designed exclusively for them, and only sold in their "salon of dress," with its special "French" showrooms that admitted only the most elite of clientele.

Eloise, despite lunchtimes spent stalking around Central Park so she could breathe, despite her attention straying and a lump forming in her throat when she was fitting clients, could not abide designing for a department store herself, where seamstresses and milliners worked twelve-hour days, laboring in stifling "sewing rooms," with the summer sun beating down through skylights onto their shining, sweaty faces. Stories abounded of seamstresses, milliners and apprentices, some of whom were not even paid for their labor, becoming so exhausted they would faint at their desks.

Eloise had stuck to her mandate that she'd only run a specialty couture house, where her clientele would be provided with made-to-order clothes, not ready-to-wear as in those department stores, and where her seamstresses would be properly paid. Occasionally, her girls—Lucia, Adeline, Goldie, and Mollie—worked late, but that was of their own choice, if they were preparing a very special garment for a special client. In this way, she'd kept her staff for years, but things were getting harder, and she just couldn't keep up with Lena Davis and her stranglehold on the market. If Eloise played her cards right and gave Vianne Mercier enough free rein to exercise that creative streak, the girl could be Eloise's best chance of rising above the copyist who was stealing her designs.

While she'd made lists of possibilities about what to do, Eloise could not risk her own reputation by claiming that Mrs. Davis—wealthy, vain and surrounded by a coterie of admirers—was in fact copying Eloise's work, even if they both knew it.

A scandal was the last thing she needed, and she knew Lena Davis was playing on that.

But the months rolled on, and Lena Davis had taken that dress and varied it, and like the true copyist she was, with not an ounce of her own creativity at all, she'd begun to imitate Eloise's other gowns, even the way she accessorized her garments, with flowers, belts, embellishments.

The only soul who seemed to notice was Eloise. The rest of New York appeared to be oblivious, and Lena Davis was going from strength to strength.

And yet, today, Lena had invited Eloise to lunch, and she had no idea why, but she had not wanted to turn the invitation down and she had been curious to find out what Lena wanted.

Eloise stood at the corner of Park Avenue and 34th Street, bringing a hand up to shield her eyes from the sudden streaks of yellow sun that poured from the heavy clouds. Occasionally, she still missed the great Texan skies where she'd spent her childhood, and the sense of endlessness that only the flat lands could bring.

She squared her shoulders and reminded herself sternly of what her adored late papa, a rancher on the Texas frontier would have said about Mrs. Davis and her copying ways. *"Don't trust that woman any further than you could throw her, Ellie. You have every right to be madder than a wet hen 'bout this!"* Eloise allowed herself a smile at the memory of her adored papa, after all, he'd been a fine businessman himself.

Until he'd lost it all.

Eloise moved forward, shuddering.

Back in the late 1870s and 1880s, he'd made huge profits moving his herds north on the trails that led from southern Texas to the Kansas railway towns, when coveted Texan longhorn beef was selling for a fortune in the cities on the east and west coasts. Eloise's daddy had been right in the thick of things.

But when change had come, it had come swiftly and brought destruction for the smaller-scale ranchers in its wake. Barbed wire fences had broken up the grazing lands, ending open-range ranching, and as trail drives became obsolete and railroad cars carried cattle to the big city markets, droughts, blizzards, fires, and predators had wiped out herds across the great state. Prices for beef had dropped when Texas Longhorns were quarantined due to tick fever.

Eloise's papa had knocked the dust off his boots, hung up his ropes, packed up and sold the wooden ranch house with its wide verandas overlooking the dusty plains where Eloise had been raised, and he'd ridden off with Eloise and her mother to New York, only to suffer a heart attack and die of exhaustion when they were halfway here.

Eloise, devastated at the loss of her beloved papa, had found herself having to support her mama on her own at the age of twenty-one. She'd picked up the broken pieces, gotten work as a seamstress, saved like mad and finally started her own business from scratch. Her mama, Pepper, kept house in the apartment they bought together down in the Village and had a constant stream of guests. They still lived together now, and twenty years later, Mama Pepper was her greatest supporter and her staunchest ally, not least when it came to the predicament with Lena.

Pepper had knitted her vivid auburn brows and told Eloise that no proud Southern girl would let the likes of Mrs. Lena Davis hold a candle to Eloise's blazing fire.

Eloise only wished she held her mother's certainty. It was true that she had loyal clientele—of course she did, well-heeled Upper

East Side matrons like Adriana Conti who would order entire wardrobes from her. But they weren't the bright young things whom Lena Davis was attracting. They weren't the flappers, the new generation of women who were redefining fashion, and that was where Eloise had every finger crossed that Vianne might come in.

Eloise stepped into Macy's, the store's sparkling glass counters floating atop polished wooden bases, while the chatter of customers and saleswomen served as a distraction for Eloise's nerves. And those nerves bit hard as she passed by the makeup counters and ascended the gorgeous wooden escalators to one of the restaurants.

Eloise's heart dropped to her knees at the sight of her luncheon companion, already seated, her fox fur draped over the back of the banquette, her short raven-colored hair gleaming, and her red lipsticked mouth curled into a smug smile.

And then Eloise stopped. Because Mrs. Davis wasn't alone. From where she stood, Eloise could see the back of a familiar man's head.

Eloise frowned before drawing off her gloves and making her way to meet Lena's unlikely companion. She closed her eyes for a minute when Lena called out to a passerby while Eloise stood there, ignored.

"You made it," Lena said, turning finally to Eloise, and extending a perfectly manicured hand, the nails dripping deep red. "It's good of you to join us. We weren't sure if you were coming, so Eddie took the liberty of ordering Manhattan cocktails."

Eloise's smile was tight as she placed her coat with great care on the back of the banquette. "I would always let you know if I had any plans that would affect you, Lena," Eloise said.

She extended a hand to Eddie Winter, the editor in chief of *Bella* magazine, the New York publication that considered itself to be the very top resource for women who were the first to buy the best. It was the leading magazine in America, for both daywear and couture.

She hated to think what Eddie Winter was doing here, but

suspicions slivered their way through Eloise's veins, and she held Eddie's outstretched hand a moment too long, as if reluctant to let go and allow this luncheon to begin.

He turned his face toward Eloise, his tortoiseshell glasses framing his chestnut eyes, and his light brown, slightly curling hair combed neatly to one side. He was, of course, dressed right up to the minute in a relaxed daytime suit.

Eloise took care to keep her own expression as cool as a clear blue lake, but her neck was stiffening. It felt suddenly overheated and very crowded in this restaurant.

"Well, Eloise," he said, "I'm glad you finally made it, because I'm mighty excited about this story we're doing on the pair of you."

Eloise's eyes narrowed, and she turned to Lena Davis, but Lena busied herself with her cocktail, peering in at it as if it held all the answers she sought.

"Bless your heart, Eddie, but I'm not following," Eloise said, her "*I'm*" coming out like a southern "*Ahhm.*" "Mrs. Davis has not informed me of any story about..." she took in a breath, "the pair of us being featured in *Bella* magazine." Her instincts were never to be rude. It was not the way she was raised, and she'd certainly not come this far by stooping down low. She drew herself up to her full height and reminded herself who she was.

"Dearest Eloise," Eddie said, sipping his cocktail and reaching for the luncheon menu. "We thought it would be a wonderful thing to feature a lead article about the pair of you together, since you've both come up with such awe-inspiring fringed velvet dresses. I know our readers will be fascinated by you both. We want to know where you got your inspiration, and what you have tucked up your sleeves for us all next."

Eloise flushed and drew her hands into tight balls as she sat down. *Just say no, don't give excuses to folks who don't deserve any, you must hold your head high and walk away.* She could hear her papa's voice, even after all these years.

Eddie's eyes narrowed and he regarded her. "It's wonderful exposure. Now then. Where shall we start?"

Eloise shot Lena a *darn you* stare. But the other woman simply held her gaze, her green almond-shaped eyes opaque and infuriatingly hard.

Eloise stared right back, and for one awful moment, she fancied herself lost in the other woman's tough little world. A world that was devoid of decency, and respect, and kindness—values that Eloise was not going to give up for anyone.

And then something shifted. As she sat there, face to face with the demon who'd bit at her night and day for two years, she simply saw the truth. There was nothing there, nothing behind those darned eyes of Lena's, other than falsity and lies.

And she, Eloise was better than that. She was the real McCoy.

"Well then," Eloise said. Her insides were clattering around like a bag of marbles, but she titled her head to one side. "I'm *happy* to help with your article, Eddie. But on one condition. And one condition only."

Eddie pulled out his silver cigarette box and placed it on the white tablecloth.

Not knowing why, perhaps just because it was shiny and it seemed like a bargaining chip, Eloise pushed that cigarette box until it sat right in the center of the table and caught the light from the overhead chandelier.

"I want to be interviewed first." She'd saved herself before, and by goodness, she'd do so again. "Privately, about the real story behind my dress. Because I designed it first. The whole concept of the velvet and the soft sloping fringe was my original idea."

Eddie slid the cigarette case back toward himself, opened it, and lit up. He narrowed his eyes against the smoke. "Well, then," he said, his voice low. "You know, I'm a magazine man. I love a sensational story."

"And I have something fascinating for you," Eloise continued, drawing out the "I," extra, extra-long, just like she'd heard her mama Pepper do back in the old days when she was roasting some poor neighbor who'd gotten under her skin. "I always deal in originality and the truth when it comes to ideas, designs, and the clothes I put on *my* client's backs. Anything else would be a lesser achievement by far. Don't you agree, Mrs. Davis?"

Lena's hand stilled on her cocktail glass. "You can't steal an idea," she said, her voice slimy as a snake's. "Two designers could both have the same idea and interpret it differently, *Miss* Chappelle."

Eddie Winter sat back and folded his arms. Eloise did not miss the tiny quiver of his brow, the upward tilt of his lips, the sound of his satisfied, *This is tantalizing and I'm not saying a darned thing to ruin it*, sigh.

"Is that right?" Eloise said. "You see, I wouldn't know. Because I always come up with my own concepts from the very outset, Mrs. Davis. Otherwise, I'd just be all hat and no cattle, wouldn't I?" Eloise leaned forward, and Mrs. Davis's strange flat eyes still did not waver. "I've more ideas than you can shake a stick at. You've underestimated me, Lena Davis. The only regret I have is that that I overestimated you when we first met."

Eddie sat stock-still.

But Eloise lifted her chin. "Y'all know that a dream isn't a very original excuse, is it now? Wouldn't you say that's been done before, honey? But then, what would you know about originality, Mrs. Davis? Seems it's a thing that eludes you."

And right then, Eloise felt a little kick of something. It was an old feeling she'd not experienced in a while. Not since Lena Davis had stolen her ideas and hung them out for the world to see.

What Eloise had back was confidence. She had her gumption and it felt good. After all, why should she be bullied out of the limelight by a competitor, and one who had no originality at all?

Lena Davis placed her cocktail glass back down, picked up her handbag, apologized to Eddie, not to Eloise, stood up, and walked out of that restaurant. If Eloise was right, the woman's ears were burning red.

"Well," Eddie breathed, his mouth twitching. "Game, set and match." He handed her the cigarette box, Eloise took one, and he lit it for her. "Now, want to tell me what's really going on?"

Eloise took a sip of her cocktail and raised a brow. "A Southern girl won't tell a journalist anything and you know it."

Eddie chuckled. "She'll never have your class."

Eloise handed Eddie the small plate of salted almonds that sat on the table. "Bless your heart, Eddie," she said. "I'm back."

His eyes twinkled behind his glasses, and he rolled up his sleeves and sent her a wink.

I'm going to take my ideas and make them a whole lot better than that thief ever did.

With that, Eloise reached for her menu, and ordered the best filet mignon in the restaurant. Oh, her daddy did not die for nothing. She would make certain of that. And with her new young designer, Vianne Mercier, there was *nothing* she could not do.

Eloise knew that together, they had ten times the potential of any copycat.

"Cheers," Eddie said. "Now, you want an exclusive in *Bella* about your new season collection? Folks are talking about the gorgeous fabric flowers you're pinning to your belts."

"Let's shoot out the lights," Eloise said. "And you can throw your hat over the windmill and hallelujah the county, Eddie." And she toasted the air with her cocktail.

CHAPTER SEVEN

VIANNE, NEW YORK, FALL, 1924

"Open your eyes, Vianne Mercier."

Vianne cracked one eye open and gasped at the reflection that stared at her in the mirror in the back room of the couturier on East 63rd Street. Her long blond hair was all cut short with a snazzy side parting, and it sat softly below her jawline, making her blue eyes seem enormous, while her dark lashes stood out against her skin even more than they used to somehow. The tiny mole on her left cheekbone seemed even more prominent. She brought her hand to that cheek, her mouth falling open. Behind her, Madame Chappelle's pattern maker, Lucia Martini, placed her scissors down and rested her hands on Vianne's shoulders.

"Oh, my," Lucia said, her own brown eyes crinkling with genuine warmth, and her cherub lips forming a grin. "Someone's looking mighty keen!"

Vianne caught Lucia's gaze in the mirror that Lucia had appropriated while Madame Chapelle was out at some luncheon in Midtown with another New York designer. When the other seamstresses had all gone out, Lucia had stayed right here, and insisted that she turn Vianne into a modern girl.

Vianne blinked hard. She reached a hand up to the unfamiliar short, soft waves that framed her face. Without her long tresses, her head felt a great deal lighter, but also very strange.

Lucia reached down and took Vianne's hand in her own. "I know, it's crazy, isn't it? Seeing it all chopped off and gone. But I'm hoping that tomorrow, you'll wake up and enjoy the benefits of not having to dress that long hair. Also," she said, leaning down close to Vianne's hair, "it will be much easier to dance, and that's the next thing we need to get you doing, now you're a New York kind of girl."

Vianne took one quick glance at the floor, littered with her blond tresses. She closed her eyes against the vivid flashbacks of her, Anaïs and Maman.

Lucia's voice filtered into the quiet room. "See, now you can look life straight in the eye and tell it what you want."

Vianne sent the girl a smile. "*Oui*," she said, still feeling a little wobbly at having lost all her hair. "Well, that does not sound like such a bad way to look at things."

Lucia swung across the sewing room. Framed by the window that overlooked a back alleyway, the petite girl suddenly twisted her feet and kicked her legs and swung her arms at the same time. "Come on, then! Fancy practicing your dancing with me?" She kept going at a terrific pace.

Vianne tilted her head to one side. She glanced around the workshop with its high ceilings, the room flooded with natural light. Three long tables ran from one end to the other, while along one wall several beautiful black sewing machines sat ready for work, their built-in bases resplendent with patterned wrought iron. Along another wall, there were rows of little shelves holding buttons, ribbons, beadings, cotton, wools, silks and bows, and the back wall was fitted with hanging rails, along which were a collection of half-finished charming garments, each one hung carefully so as not to touch its neighbor. Vianne only had to glance at the gowns, slips, chemises, coats, dresses, jackets and skirts to see the garments here were constructed of the finest fabrics there were.

When she'd walked into the workroom earlier today after the

consultation with Adriana Conti, and Madame Chapelle had introduced her to the girls, there'd been the busy hum of treadle sewing machines, and two of the other seamstresses, Goldie and Mollie, had been draping a dressmaker's model with a cream satin cape, complete with an ermine collar, the lining decorated with a printed, checked motif.

Lucia threw her head back, her own short black hair emphasizing her wide cheekbones. "Didn't you have the Charleston in Paris, honey?"

Vianne raised a brow and folded her arms. Somehow, telling Lucia she'd been too down in the dumps to give all the new dances a go back in Paris did not seem like a good idea with such a spectacular display happening right in front of her eyes.

Lucia shimmied over to a long bench under the window. She opened the lid on a phonograph and turned to Vianne, her face lighting up. "Come on!"

"You're allowed to listen to tunes out here?" Vianne asked. Such things would never happen in Paris. The seamstresses in the couture house where she'd worked in France had been supervised strictly, and despite the midinettes having famously and successfully gone on strike in 1917 demanding, as Papa had so ruefully told her, an "English" working week with a day and a half of rest and a raise of one franc for the seamstresses, there remained regimented rules as to the girls' conduct in the workrooms. At the end of each day, Vianne's back had ached, and she'd looked forward to the walk from the tumbling buildings in Paris's garment district to the Place des Vosges after hours of laboring over luxurious clothes the midinettes could never afford, many of them with desperate finances and only one income to support themselves, and often their children, because so many men had been lost in the war. Music and dancing had never been an option.

Lucia turned, one hand poised on the wide needle, a record ready to go on the turntable. "Why, Miss Ellie's a wonderful boss underneath that brusque exterior she's been showing you. She doesn't mind if we do something a little hotsy-totsy occasionally.

Otherwise, we'd all go stark raving crazy just working all our days."
Lucia flashed a pretty smile, and slipped the needle down onto the
record, filling the room with the sounds of one of the dances that
was sweeping America this year—the Charleston. "Now," she said,
her voice ringing clear over the fast-paced music. "The Charleston
is the bee's knees! If you're going to go to any party that's worth
going to, you'll have to know how to do it."

Vianne reached up and patted her newly cut hair. And at the
same time, she felt a smile playing around her lips. Something told
her she was going to like this girl. Something told her she was going
to like New York too. And something told her that if she stood up
and tried to do this crazy dance with Lucia, she'd feel more alive,
and more carefree than she had in years.

"Come over here, girl from Paris," Lucia said. She stepped to
one side, her chest heaving and her eyes bright with the exertion of
it all. She left some room for Vianne to stand next to her underneath the long window that ran the length of the room.

Vianne, her mind made up, stood up and slipped over to stand
by Lucia.

"Now," Lucia said. "Follow me. I'll show you the steps." She
started with her toes, one foot at a time stepping forward, then
back, back then forward. "Slowly at first. One two, three four, five
six, seven eight," she said, shimmying along with the music. "Now,
let's speed things up!"

Vianne copied. The music was infectious, joyous, and soon her
feet were tapping forward and backward, and her knees were
wobbling, and she was laughing out loud in a way she'd long
thought she'd never do again.

"Next," Lucia said, running a hand through her dark curls,
"We'll go in with our toes, and then we'll go out. See? It's easy.
One, two, three, four, five, six, seven, eight. Faster now!"

She sped up. "And now, if you're feeling really sassy, you can
get your arms going and put it all together! Dance with me!"

And before she knew it, Vianne was swinging right around the
whole room with Lucia, keeping step with the lithe girl, her face

flushed, and her heart beating full of some kind of wonderful she'd never felt before. They shimmied over Vianne's cut lengths of hair, shuffled along beneath the window, and wobbled their legs and waved their arms between the worktables until the music stopped.

Vianne leaned on a workbench and sent Lucia a shining smile. "Well," she said. "That was just the most fun I've had in an age!"

"I'm mighty glad to hear that," Lucia replied. She still bounced on her toes. "And that's only the start of it. Wait until we get you out to the clubs!"

But just then there was the sound of talking outside the closed door. In one horrible second, Vianne's eyes flew to Lucia and back, but the girl's focus was trained, unmoving, on the door, even though her chest still heaved up and down from the exertion of the dance.

"Lucia!" Eloise Chappelle pushed the door open, holding it wide while a man with curly brown hair and tortoiseshell framed glasses sauntered in by her side. Vianne and Lucia's boss and the owner of this entire salon folded her arms and took in the tendrils of blond hair that were decorating her floor, her eyes flying from this to the phonograph with its open lid. A red flush spread from Madame's décolletage all the way up to her cheeks.

Vianne's hands flew instinctively to her short hair, her eyes swerving from Madame to the gentleman and back.

The man's brown eyes lit up, and he bit back a grin. Vianne frowned at him and, ridiculously, he winked at her.

"I will clean this up right away, Miss Ellie," Lucia said, marching across the room to a cupboard and pulling out a broom. "You see, I took the liberty of cutting Vianne's hair, like you wanted, and I did so well away from any garments."

Madame Chapelle stood in silence, her mouth working, but no words coming out.

Only the swish of Lucia's broom broke the awful, painful silence.

Oh, she would lose her job, her one chance of success before she'd even begun! Vianne's hands flew to her face, and she side-stepped out of Lucia's way.

"Eddie, I'd like you to meet two of my seamstresses, Vianne Mercier, straight from Paris, and, as you see, apparently with fashionable and very freshly cut hair... And my long-standing pattern maker, Lucia Martini, who should know better than to use my workroom as a hairdressing salon." Madame Chappelle arched an auburn brow. "Girls, Eddie Winter here is the editor of *Bella* magazine."

Vianne drew her hand to cover her mouth.

But Lucia leaned on her broom and sent the gentleman a winning smile. "I'm straight from the Village," she said. "But I'd sure like to see Paris one day."

"Well, sadly I'm neither from the Village, nor Paris," the mysterious, handsome Mr. Winter said, his chestnut-colored eyes crinkling into a warm smile.

Vianne didn't know whether she'd imagined his voice softening and his eyes darting her way when he spoke of Paris. She stared, horrified, at her boss and the handsome companion she'd brought in, from underneath her eyelashes.

"Well, I'm charmed, I'm sure." Lucia continued her furious sweeping, piling up all Vianne's hair and then collecting it up with a dustpan and small brush. Finally, Lucia rubbed her hands together, having tipped the remains of Vianne's Parisian locks in the trash. "I'm sorry about all this mess. Girls from Paris sure go in for long hair!"

Madame Chappelle shook her head, but Vianne was certain she heard her chuckle.

"Well now, it's interesting to see what goes on behind the scenes in a couturier," Mr. Winter said. His voice was mellifluous and charming. He sounded like a well-educated sort of man.

"Oh, enough, girls. Y'all need to get back to work," Eloise Chappelle said, waving at Vianne as well.

"I wouldn't dream of interrupting your... clearly arduous

labors." Eddie Winter pressed his lips together again and glanced at the trash bin, his eyes twinkling.

Vianne opened her mouth to say something—anything—because she was feeling like a gaping fish, only to close it because, right then, the door burst open again, and with a flurry of chatter and laughter and pulling off woolen coats, Madame's other seamstresses flew inside.

Adeline unpinned her velvet hat, the color of deep red wine, her glossy light brown curls bouncing against the collar of her pricey-looking coat, and her bright blue eyes taking in the handsome young man and narrowing just enough to show an interest in who he was.

"Eddie," Madame said. "This is Adeline. Adeline specializes in my most detailed work, ribbon work, embroidery and beading."

Adeline, her cheeks becomingly flushed from the fresh air, looked Eddie up and down. "Hello there, Eddie," she said with an inviting smile.

Vianne took in the way the girl moved with confidence across the room, not stopping to give Eddie Winter any more attention than she deemed he deserved.

Eddie leaned against one of the sewing machines, crossing his legs in front of the built-in base.

"Mollie and Goldie, come on, girls, say hello to Mr. Winter," Madame Chappelle said. "Mollie and Goldie focus entirely on garment production, Eddie. These girls are my trusted and valued seamstresses. When required, they step in and help Adeline with some of the beadwork. As you see, we all operate as a team. I design, hand my concepts to Lucia, who works them into patterns, Mollie and Goldie mock everything up out of calico, fit it to our dressmaker's models. Then, only when I have approved the cut, do they start fashioning the real garment out of the fabric that we intend to use."

Mollie pushed a stray piece of brown hair away from her face, her button eyes surveying the handsome man. "Madame Chappelle didn't mention a gentleman seamstress was joining our ranks."

"Well, I think it's grand," Goldie spoke up, her green eyes framed by straight blond hair. "We just got a girl from Paris, why not some good-looking swell as well?"

Eddie burst out into laughter, and Madame threw her hands in the air, striding across her workroom. She stood, framed by the window, the afternoon sun forming a halo around her auburn hair. "Mr. Winter is the editor of *Bella* magazine. He's writing an article," she said. "About me. Not that you need an explanation for his presence, girls."

Vianne stood rigid on the spot. If today had been any indication at all, working for Madame was going to be anything but dull.

"I think you've forgotten someone's job description," Mr. Winter said, turning to Vianne.

Vianne froze in place.

Mr. Winter folded his arms, and she was certain he sent her a wink. "What do you do, girl from Paris?"

"Vianne is a junior designer." Eloise Chappelle walked over to stand next to Vianne, resting a hand lightly on her shoulder. "She will be assisting me with some of my clientele, coming up with concepts, and then, should I require her to do so, she will sew and embellish garments as well." Madame Chappelle lowered her voice. "So much is in the embellishments these days, Eddie. Most fashionable dresses follow the tubular line, so it's vital that we can come up with details to ensure our garments stand out, and that the simple form is enhanced, but not overwhelmed, by decoration."

Vianne, feeling a shot of confidence under the handsome young man's gaze, tossed her newly cut hair.

He sent her the frisson of a smile.

"Right, back to work," Eloise Chappelle said. "Eddie will be interviewing me for one hour, then I have Mrs. Patterson coming in for a fitting at four o'clock. I will need her cape to be pinned up and ready, Mollie."

"Yes, ma'am." Mollie's button eyes darted toward the silken cape that Vianne had admired this morning.

"Then, at five p.m. sharp I want to see you, Vianne, with your sketches for Adriana Conti." She stood with her hands on her hips. "Off you all go!"

There was a general flurry, and Goldie and Mollie settled down at the sewing machines. Soon, they had threaded them up, their feet were on the pedals, and the whir of them working and chatting filtered through the air. Lucia settled down at her table, drawing out her pencil, her attention focused on the pattern that was spread out before her.

Vianne could have hugged herself, she was so at home here, despite the embarrassment of being caught out with her hair cascading all over the floor.

She moved to a worktable, but Adeline stopped right in front of her, laying her hand on Vianne's arm. "I didn't know Miss Ellie had hired a junior designer," she said, her bright blue eyes catching with Vianne's. "And I didn't know you were French until just now. My mother's family are from Lyon. My ancestors spun silk into high-fashion garments for generations. So you see, mademoiselle, embroidery is in my blood. Can you say the same? Hmm?"

"I'm looking forward to working with you." Vianne kept her tone even. She recognized the implication in the other girl's voice, and she'd dealt with envious girls back in Paris, as well as girls who thought they were better than Vianne. The trick was to hold her ground and never explain herself, even if the girl's heritage from the city of Lyon in France, with both its tradition of silk embroidery going back to the 1500s and as the starting place for the Silk Road, sounded illustrious.

Adeline stood still a moment, before finally letting Vianne go and slipping to the back of the room, where she picked up a deep green dress and settled down, reaching for pots of tiny glass beads.

"Off you go, Vianne," Eloise Chappelle said. "You have quite the task ahead of you. Madame Conti is one of my most meticulous clients."

Vianne jumped at Madame's voice. She hadn't realized her boss was still standing in the doorway, Mr. Winter right by her side. "*Oui*... pardon. Yes," Vianne said, stumbling over her English and making her way to the front workstation.

She picked up the initial sketches she'd started before all the commotion with her hair and the phonograph came about. Her hands shaking slightly, and only imagining what stern words Madame Chappelle would have in store for her this afternoon, she bent her head over her drawings, took a deep breath, forced herself to focus, and dived into her work.

This was her first design for Madame Chappelle, and she needed it to shine.

The afternoon drew on, and Vianne had nothing. She'd ripped pages out of her own sketchbook, screwed them up into little balls and piled them up on her table. For the design would have to be stunning for the wealthy, olive-skinned, dark-eyed beautiful woman in her early fifties for whom Vianne had been assigned to create the perfect dress.

Aware she was putting herself under terrible pressure for "Miss Ellie," as the seamstresses called her, Vianne scanned the ideas she'd forced out of herself so far.

They were terrible. Awful. Utterly uninspired.

Vianne stood up and went to stare out the front window at the narrow street.

"Something wrong?" Adeline asked, her voice tinny and high against the whir of the sewing machines.

Vianne didn't turn around. "Not at all," she said, using her French accent.

She sighed at the sight of passersby rushing along the street so purposefully. From in here, she could see hats and glimpses of gloves and suits and dresses as people rushed by. Everyone in Manhattan looked as if they had somewhere to go. It was so purposeful here, so different from those lost years in Paris after the war, when, after the flush of victory had passed, everyone had gone about their daily activities looking bereft, unsure how to process all the losses, all the indescribable pain of their sons, husbands, cousins, brothers, never to come back. Here in New York, it was as if the weight of the war had been entirely shrugged off.

The last thing she wanted was to forget Maman, Anaïs and Papa. And yet, Vianne knew she had to move forward. Had to allow herself to forge a new life without them, somehow.

Being in New York was supposed to be her cure, instead, her losses still hollowed her out like an aching cavern which no one she met here would ever understand.

Could she find her own freewheeling spirit, that love of life that she'd once taken for granted, ever again?

Carrying out beadwork and embroidery, being told what to do to exact specifications was one thing, but creating something beautiful from scratch was quite another. And sitting here, with her job on the line was as far away from drawing pictures and fancies in her bedroom at Marguerite's house as she could get.

Behind her, Lucia was adding the finishing touches to her pattern. The slip, which would be of navy silk, was to go underneath a dress of navy lace, and Lucia had chatted away about how she wanted a little of the slip to show above the deep V-neck of the dress, for modesty, and also because the silk slip was going to be so beautiful in itself.

In contrast, Vianne had fussed and fiddled, but nothing had come about. Her fingers wanted to reach up and feel the familiarity of her long hair. She struggled with the desire to go to the trash bin and peer in it to take one last look. One last look at the tendrils that Maman had stroked when she kissed Vianne goodnight, sitting on the side of her bed in Paris, the antique clock's soft ticking sending her off to a dreamy, untroubled sleep.

She pressed her forehead against the window, her mind whirling with options: lace, velvet, silk, sleeves or sleeveless, beads or stunning embroidery, or both. She needed something fantastic to win Madame over, not to mention Adriana Conti herself.

Vianne frowned at the bustling on in the street. Red hats, blue hats, hats with feathers, cloche hats that were made of green velveteen.

And then, she saw it.

A woman stopped to look in a window on the other side of the street, slower than the other New Yorkers, and on her head was a hat patterned in black and white flowers.

Black and white.

How about that?

Feeling a sudden stirring of something, Vianne slipped back to her desk. Pushing aside the reams of wasted paper, filled with drawings that would never see the light of day, she put her head down and, her hands working quickly and efficiently, she began to sketch.

"I am ready, madame." Vianne was at Madame's door at five o'clock on the dot.

Madame Chappelle was perched on the edge of her desk, her long legs crossed at the ankle, waving her empty cigarette holder and eyeing Vianne. "Come in, Vianne." She held her cigarette holder aloft. "Don't worry. I'm not going to smoke in the atelier, but I do like to wave something about. Occupies my hands, you know."

Vianne smiled at Madame, took a breath and placed her precious sketches in Madame's other outstretched hand.

"I have come up with something that I hope will be worthy of such an important event in Mrs. Conti's life. I have designed a sleeveless, tubular black-and-white dress, made entirely of metallic thread ribbon work, bound by metallic thread, that will come with a black diaphanous evening cape with contrasting chenille trim."

"Black and white, only?" Madame Chappelle said.

Vianne nodded, beating down the shaky sensation that threatened to loom up and overwhelm her. "Yes," she whispered, only just managing to not speak French. "I want Mrs. Conti to look stunning, and I think that a striking palette of black and white will create this effect."

Outside, the light was fading over Manhattan. From Madame's office, right off the main reception hall, the sounds of people clipping by on the pavement lent something of an urgency to the meeting. Evening was on its way.

Madame frowned at Vianne's sketches.

Vianne cleared her throat. "The black and white metallic ribbons, of which the entire dress is fashioned, will be coiled and intertwined into flower and circle motifs." When the idea had blossomed in her mind as she walked away from the window, having seen that singular black-and-white hat, Vianne had visualized how the soft, metallic black and the cream would complement Mrs. Conti's dramatic features without overwhelming her. The diaphanous cape would lend a sense of theater to the outfit, suitable, Vianne knew, for the opening of a brand-new, fashionable Upper East Side restaurant.

She closed her eyes a moment, remembering all those theater performances back in Paris that she went to with her parents before the war, Diaghilev's Ballets Russes, with their enchanting costumes. Despite all the tragedy and sadness of her journey to this day, she tapped into the memories that had inspired this dress that she believed in. It was all she had to prove that she could design clothes that would bring joy and delight into people's worlds here in the fabulous city of New York.

"The handkerchief hem of the dress will be trimmed with cream ribbon rosettes," Vianne continued, her fingers gliding along the sketch. "They will lend a little nuance to the bold design."

But Madame was focused on the cape. "The chenille trim on the black cape would be contrasting. Cream against the diaphanous black?"

Vianne nodded. "*Mais, oui.*"

Madame's brows knitted together, and she ran her fingers over the design for the cape. "I think the addition of a second and third black chenille trim on the cape would add depth, drama. I think there should be a black chenille trim around the top of the cape as well as at the hips, to anchor it, and to give a luxurious feel."

Vianne caught Madame's eyes. She was right. And she was embellishing Vianne's idea. Oh, hopefully that meant she liked it! "Yes, madame," Vianne said. "Because the cape is see-through. When it is held up behind the dress, the cream chenille piping would line up with the knees, your second line of black trim would line up with the hips, and the top black trim you are proposing would form something of a cape over the shoulders, while the remainder of the cape would offer the viewer a clear sight of the dress."

Madame went back to examining the sketch. After an age, she lifted her head.

"The ribbon work will take hours. Days. Have you considered that?" She looked thoughtful. "This sort of couture work is almost beyond any price."

Vianne pressed her lips together. "I will do what it takes." She spread her hands expansively. "I am new to New York. I have plenty of spare time on the weekends, and in the evenings."

"I don't want to exploit you, and I will charge Mrs. Conti well, but the amount of work will be staggering... it's not something I've seen before. Vianne?" she said suddenly, her voice rising. "You came up with this concept *this afternoon*?"

"Yes, madame." Vianne folded her hands in front of her.

Outside, the streetlamps came on, sending a yellow glow into the office. Madame leaned her hands on her desk. "My staff call me Miss Ellie," she said, her mouth curving into a smile. "Vianne, why don't you call me that too?"

Vianne placed a hand on her chest. "Thank you," she whispered. "I'm honored."

"I have not seen anyone come up with something this extraordinary so quickly, in all my time working, in all my years. Except," she said softly, lowering her voice, "when I've done so... When I *used* to do so," she said, sounding wistful now.

Vianne held Miss Ellie's gaze. "Thank you," she said again,

simply.

Miss Ellie handed Vianne her sketches back and spoke in a matter-of-fact voice. "I want you to go back and add in the rows of black trim to the cape, and some additional shoulder details."

"*Oui*, madame—"

"Miss Ellie," Miss Ellie corrected her, sending her a quick smile.

Vianne nodded, her heart beating wildly. She'd done it. She'd conquered all the doubts and the turmoil and the sadness and the darned excitement at being here, and she'd done something to make Miss Ellie proud! Not to mention herself If only her dear Maman and Anaïs were here to see it.

Miss Ellie picked up a glass paperweight. "How about settling you into the apartment above the atelier, immediately, Vianne? I have two rooms up there, and only one is occupied now. Lucia, I know, would love your company as, at the moment, she is quite alone."

"I would love that." Vianne hugged her sketches to her chest, a sense of excitement bubbling up inside her.

"Do you have much luggage?"

"Two suitcases," Vianne said. "All packed in the boarding house." She regarded Miss Ellie. "They are locked. I didn't want to leave my things out, just in case."

Miss Ellie sighed. "You poor girl. But now you are here, and..." her voice softened, "we at the atelier treat each other like family. My girls are everything to me, and that is why they stay with me."

Vianne bit on her lip, ridiculous tears threatening to spill down her cheeks. "Thank you," she said simply.

"Very well. If your bags are packed as you say, please write your room number down, the name of the boarding house mistress, and I'll have a driver swing out to Brooklyn and pick your things up. They'll be ready and waiting for you up in the apartment after you've had dinner. There are plenty of charming little restaurants around here." She waved her unlit cigarette about again. "Now, go put the finishing touches to your work, find some dinner, and have a wonderful beauty sleep." She arched a brow. "We are meeting with Adriana Conti at eight a.m. sharp in the morning. I shall see you here at half past seven to debrief."

Vianne nodded, her eyes shining. "Yes. Of course. I don't think I'll sleep a wink!"

Miss Ellie's eyes crinkled. "You'll need your sleep, Vianne. And one more thing..."

Vianne's hands stilled on her sketchpad.

"Always remember. You are one of my girls and that means you take care of yourself. When it comes to young men, there are plenty of them who will want to flatter a beautiful girl like you. Just don't let that interfere with your work."

Vianne nodded. "I am not after a beau," she said, the Americanism still sounding strange on her lips. "I have no desire to put my career at risk."

Miss Ellie's warning was stark, but real. Vianne had been told by the boarding house mistress that there was huge suspicion of married women in the workplace. They were seen as pin-money workers who were competing for jobs with men, menaces to society, selfish creatures who ought to be ashamed of themselves. In some states, marriage ban work laws were in place, restricting women's employment. And businesses had been banning married women from work for decades.

No. Vianne was all too aware that if she wanted her career, she would have to adhere to the rules. Women might work before marriage, but they were to return to the home sphere once they wed. Women who sought work after marriage were met with hostility.

"It is the reason I have remained independent, and single," Miss Ellie said. "I have sacrificed love for my career, and all my seamstresses are doing the same. You see, Vianne, love and work outside the home don't mix."

"You have my word, Miss Ellie." Vianne gathered her sketches and went out into the empty corridor. After all, she wasn't in love, nor did she plan on falling in love.

CHAPTER EIGHT

VIANNE, NEW YORK, FALL, 1924

The following morning, Vianne stood outside the elevator in Mrs. Adriana Conti's apartment building on the corner of Park Avenue at eight a.m. sharp. From behind a set of double glass doors, mysteriously blocked off with brown paper, the sounds of builders shouting, hammers rapping, and saws slicing reverberated through the building, where, apparently, Mrs. Conti's son was transforming the entire ground floor into a swanky restaurant.

Vianne's stomach churned with nerves as she stood alongside Miss Ellie and waited for the elevator to sweep them up to Mrs. Conti's home. If she could take the client aside right now and convince her just how important it was that she love the metallic ribbon work design, Vianne would do so on the spot. But Mrs. Conti had no idea that Vianne's future, and Miss Ellie's assessment of Vianne's skills, were at stake with this dress, and the fact that Mrs. Conti's opinion was going to be subjective did not make things any easier at all. Vianne had spent one night in the apartment above the atelier, and she hoped to spend many more.

She took a deep breath, reminding herself how just this morning in Eddie Winter's *Bella* magazine, Miss Ellie had read out loud how lamé, jewels and feathers were in the ascendant this fall. So, that meant that the gown with its chenille trim resembling

black and white feathers and the striking metallic ribbon that
Vianne had opted for were not only original but utterly up to the
minute. If she could continue to use her instincts and guess ahead
of trends, she'd strive hard to be more than a strong addition to
Miss Ellie's couture house: she'd try to be Miss Ellie's grandest
asset yet.

When, finally, the elevator took them up to the thirtieth floor of
the tall building, and the private doors slid open to afford entrance
right into Mrs. Conti's fabulous apartment, Vianne almost fell into
a swoon. Yesterday she'd been so bedazzled by Miss Ellie, and
intimidated by the fact that the design of Mrs. Conti's dress was all
going to be down to her, she'd hardly noticed the stunning home
that they'd stood in. But now Vianne's practiced eyes took in the
striking, modern reception room. There was not one antique piece
in sight, but Papa would have been delighted with the apartment
anyway. Soft gray carpet was decorated with geometric patterns in
contrasting rich red and black, while a modern, low-slung art deco-
style sofa covered in deep-red velvet sat opposite a pair of stylish
bucket-style white velvet chairs. A marble and glass table graced
the space between them, and on the walls, there were modern art
prints and round mirrors. A pair of tall black vases filled with
white lilies graced a side table, and Vianne's shoes sank into the
luxurious wool carpet underfoot.

Miss Ellie leaned forward and kissed her client's cheek. "Dear
Adriana, Vianne has something extremely special to show to you
today. Just as we promised. Just as we promised, dear."

Mrs. Adriana Conti inclined her head so that her luxuriant
dark hair, cut to align with her jawline, was tilted slightly to one
side. Her wide cheekbones, dusted with just a little rouge, caught
in the sun streaming in from the huge windows that overlooked
Park Avenue. The woman's almost-black eyes were made up to
perfection, and she extended a long, bare brown arm and laid it on
Vianne's shoulder. "Well, if this exquisite girl can design as beautifully as she is dressed today, then I am certain to be charmed by
what she has in mind for my son's launch party."

Vianne sent the elegant woman a wide smile and thanked goodness for Miss Ellie and Lucia's foresight. Lucia had pointed out how Mrs. Conti had a real eye for fashion and that anyone who stepped into her apartment should be dressed as if she were going to an event. Miss Ellie had sighed and shaken her head and then decided to loan Vianne a dress for the visit. She'd chuckled that Vianne had got away with a professional look on her visit yesterday, but today called for something more.

Now, Vianne folded her hands in front of the rose-colored chiffon dress she wore, the flower on the drop waist designed in contrasting pale pink.

Mrs. Conti sashayed through her apartment with all the confidence in the world, up a long hallway painted white and dotted with softly lit lamps, before opening a door, and waiting for Vianne and Miss Ellie to go straight on into a glamorous dressing room. Its walls were lined with art deco paneled mirrors and a chaise longue covered in red velvet sat next to an adorable little red table with a mirrored top. A dressmaker's model stood in one corner, and against the wall there was a lacquer side table adorned with a handheld mirror, a set of silver-backed brushes, and a silver tissue box.

"Very well," Miss Ellie said, turning to face the room, her own elegant figure shown to perfection in a dove-gray georgette crepe dress. "Vianne, please tell Mrs. Conti what you have planned, my dear."

An hour later, Vianne shook Mrs. Conti's hand. "Your design is stunning," Mrs. Conti said, her soft, olive-skinned hand lingering in Vianne's. "I cannot wait to see the result."

Vianne allowed warmth to flow through her, and she was certain her cheeks were flushed bright with relief. Relief and excitement, for she too could hardly wait to see Mrs. Conti wearing the black-and-white gown.

Miss Ellie leaned forward to kiss Mrs. Conti on the cheek.

When the client pulled back, her beautiful features lit up with excitement when the private elevator doors opened.

"Giorgio!" Mrs. Conti reached out to embrace the tall man who'd appeared out of the elevator like someone in a dream. But right as Mrs. Conti went to kiss him on the cheek, the young man's eyes diverted straight to Vianne and stayed there, not moving one bit.

He was the most gorgeous man she'd laid eyes on in an age. Perhaps forever. She forced herself not to stare at his face, but only found her eyes drawn to his tanned arm against the rolled-up sleeve of his white shirt. He had a pencil stuck behind his ear like a butcher, despite the fact that his dark hair was cut smooth and close. His eyes were velvet and his teeth were pearly white when he smiled.

"Well, hello there. Where did you come from?" the young man breathed, his eyes kindling against Vianne's. He patted his mother on the shoulder and came toward Vianne with his hand held out.

Vianne took his outstretched hand. Despite the sigh she heard coming from Miss Ellie, she held eye contact with him, her fingers jolting to life at the feel of her hand in his palm. Just one second, then she would walk away and never lay eyes on him again.

"So. You're the young fashion designer my mother has been talking about non-stop since yesterday." Mrs. Conti's son spoke with a slight accent, rolling his r's and drawing out his vowels. Vianne recognized it as Northern Italian. Before the war, Papa had worked with clients from Northern Italy who came to Paris expressly to buy from him.

"Giorgio." Mrs. Conti broke the silence. "This is Vianne Mercier."

"Come and see my restaurant," Giorgio said, suddenly, his eyes still stuck on Vianne. "Come down and I'll show you. Both of you," he said, including Miss Ellie in his enchanted circle.

Slowly, Vianne wheeled around to face Miss Ellie. She had no doubt what her boss would say, but still...

"Bless your heart, Giorgio. Unfortunately, right now, Mademoiselle Mercier and I simply must get back to work," Miss Ellie replied. Behind the Southern treacle, Miss Ellie's tone was glittering steel. "Right now," she went on, magnificent, "we must take our leave of you folks and wait until the first fitting, which is scheduled in a week's time. Just for the mock-up, you understand, Adriana. And, perhaps," Miss Ellie said, shepherding Vianne toward the closed elevator doors, "it will only be me, next time. Vianne came up with the concepts, but my seamstresses will be making the dress."

Vianne opened her mouth in protest. She'd promised Miss Ellie she'd work weekends to carry out all the ribbon work. She was keen as anything to throw herself into fashioning the first ever garment she'd been commissioned to create.

But despite standing there like a gaping fish, not one word would come out from her lips. Every nerve in her body tingling, her pulse thumping in her throat, she let Miss Ellie shepherd her into the elevator, while her boss smiled and dipped her head at the man standing there in camel-colored pants, his white shirt open at the collar.

He sent a smile to Vianne, and she pressed her lips together and looked away. Clearly, Miss Ellie had no toleration for bending the rules an inch when it came to young men. Not even a smile, not even a wink, not even as much as a second glance across a crowded street.

"Vianne." Once the elevator doors had closed, Miss Ellie's voice sliced like a rusted bread knife into Vianne's thoughts.

Vianne stared at the floor, her body moving upwards, her stomach going way down south with the elevator. "Yes, Miss Ellie?"

The elevator came to a standstill, and in the split second before the doors breezed open, Miss Ellie laid her hands on Vianne's shoulders and looked straight into her eyes.

"I am all too aware that man is gorgeous, and I'm all too aware of the way he looked at you from the moment he laid his eyes on you, but I have to make one thing perfectly clear. If you were to ever have a dalliance with a client's son, it would compromise the professionalism of my atelier. People gossip, and we would be seen as improper. I would lose business. All the other girls' jobs would be at risk, as well as your own." Miss Ellie lowered her voice. "I know that men don't have to live to such standards, but I'm afraid any unbecoming behavior in my girls will deem us as disreputable, and that, I cannot afford. I want to make that crystal clear, dear. I know you haven't done anything wrong, but I trust you understand me."

Vianne folded her hands in front of her borrowed dress.

The elevator doors opened, and Vianne felt the press of Miss Ellie's firm hand atop her shoulder.

"*Oui*, madame," Vianne said. "Of course."

Miss Ellie moved out of the black-and-white marble foyer in the Contis' fabulous building, swept through the glass doors that the doorman with his top hat and uniform held open for them, and clipped down Park Avenue, her arm linked with Vianne's, for all appearances as if they were a couple of fashionable ladies going on a shopping trip.

"Mrs. Conti admires your work." Miss Ellie smiled at a well-dressed woman who passed them by. "Anyone who is anyone in New York society will never allow their children to have anything other than a dalliance with a seamstress. That is the other thing to bear in mind."

They came to a stop right outside Miss Ellie's couture house, and in the window, the mannequin in the cape-sleeved dress stood there like a faceless wooden doll.

Modern women? Flappers? Who said the rules had changed? New York was supposed to mean freedom, and the very sight of Giorgio Conti had awoken something in Vianne that she'd buried along with her grief in the last months of the war. While she wasn't in love now, was she destined never to be allowed to experience the affection that Maman and Papa had enjoyed all their married lives? And as a working woman, was she so beneath other women that she was no longer worthy of loving and being loved? She'd blindly followed her dream, but now, she was blinded by what it might cost.

Vianne stared, huge-eyed, at her boss whose eyes pierced her own.

"Do you understand what I'm saying?" Miss Ellie asked.

Silently, Vianne nodded. She had to accept it; she had no choice.

CHAPTER NINE
AMELIE, SCOTLAND, FALL, 1924

Amelie opened her eyes, the gentle heathery light filtering into the bedroom. Tall windows framed the view of the glen from the grand old house on the hill, and the rich curtains were thrown wide to herald a glorious fall day. Amelie's arm lay stretched out over the deep-red counterpane, her head resting on a snowy white pillow, while at her feet, a tumult of red and gold embroidered velvet cushions were still all a tangle where she and Archie had thrown them after dinner last night.

Amelie rolled onto her side. She reached for the sparkling glass of water that a maid had refilled for her even while she slept. On the writing desk in the corner of the room, there was a vase of stargazer lilies filling the air with their rich perfume.

Maman had been allergic to stargazer lilies. She'd filled the apartment in Rue de Sévigné with roses, lavender, irises, daisies and daffodils. Maman had the knack of arranging flowers so that they were lovely. She had the ability to turn the prosaic into the extraordinary, a dull day into a ribbon of sunshine. Maman had brought all the joy in the world to her family, right until the day she died.

Amelie placed the clear, crystal glass of water down.

How could she ever go back to Paris and look Papa, Jacques and Vianne in the eye? How could she tell them that she, Anaïs, was alive after the abhorrent thing she'd done? After her actions had led to consequences so unspeakable, so unthinkable, that it was all she could do to hide her own shame?

And as well as running away, she'd had to obliterate the girl she'd once been. Anaïs was gone for good.

Now, she was Amelie.

Amelie closed her eyes. It was happening again. Her ears brimmed with the whistling that started low but would build and build. It could begin at any moment, no matter where she was. The terrors could strike at her any time of the day, or night. There was no discrimination. Yesterday, she'd been down by the burn that snaked its way through Archie's estate, the brown water rushing over the rocks and the air scented with fresh fallen leaves and rich Scottish earth, the Highland skies brooding and thunderous, threatening to drench the ground, until it was drookit, as Archie called it. The wilds of Scotland were as far away from genteel Paris as the moon was from the earth's hot core, but no matter how far she'd traveled, Paris would never leave her behind.

And neither would the war.

The low whistling ballooned, and Amelie was hit with a familiar, piercing, keening wail. Her skin bathed itself in a film of cool sweat, her heart curled in on itself, and now, she started to shake as there was that split second of silence before the thundering explosion, before the racket was drowned by a clatter of falling masonry, the air rupturing with people's hideous screams—her maman's screams.

Amelie eased herself up onto her pillows, her heart pounding, teeth chattering, hands clenched into tight balls, her damp fingers laced tighter than one of the corsets she'd always refused to wear before the war. She'd always been rebellious.

If she could turn back the clock, she'd change it all.

Her whole body shaking and her stomach searing, daggers

piercing her insides until she felt lacerated and raw, Amelie pushed her feet over the side of the bed and slipped her toes into the pair of white satin slippers that she had left at the precise spot on the Turkish rug. Every night, she did the same thing, placing everything just so, lining things up, each in their special spot to keep them safe. It was the only way to protect the future with Archie. There was nothing she could do about everything she'd lost in her past except cry herself to sleep every night, asking herself, why had poor, darling Maman been killed, only for she, Amelie to live in these eternal flames?

Amelie stumbled across the bedroom, checked, as she did every morning, her hair, inspecting it for any strands of blond. It was easy enough to purchase the dye. Dark hair was all the rage with flappers, and so Amelie had not had any trouble convincing her lady's maid that she was being a modern woman when she dyed her blond hair black. Removing all traces of her past was the only way she could live with the fact she'd survived.

And then, it was only just.

That afternoon, Amelie sat in her sitting room, her legs crossed at the ankles opposite Caitlin Calhoun. Amelie sipped tea as if she were any newly married woman entertaining another young woman in the neighborhood. The fire roared in the hearth, and a soft, misty rain fell against the windowpanes, while outside in the damp landscape, the River Clois threaded its way through the glen. Scotland had turned on all four seasons today.

Caitlin and her husband Malcolm were the very first neighbors whom Archie had invited to dinner when he'd brought Amelie back with him to Carrig as his bride. Amelie, still a whirl after meeting Archie at a cocktail party in Knightsbridge that she'd reluctantly gone to with a nursing friend, reveled in the wild, almost savage landscape in the Highlands. The cold, clear isolation had afforded her clarity, its sensational beauty a balm. At first.

Archie, she knew, had kept no secrets back from her. He'd told her openly how he was enchanted by her the first time they met, had courted her for a month before proposing, and in turn, she'd fallen deeply in love with him. All her dalliances with men so far had been fun, a grand joke. She and Maman had delighted in the way so many eligible Parisian bachelors had chased Amelie before the war. But if she were to tell him the truth, the hideous truth about her past, she'd lose him. For Archie, honesty and integrity were as important as the crisp clean air he breathed.

And sitting opposite her, vivacious, lively, and with a wicked sense of humor, Caitlin would have been exactly the sort of girl Amelie would have been drawn to before Maman was killed. But now, Caitlin must think her new neighbor a complete drip.

Caitlin, thrilled to have a beautiful neighbor around her own age after the dreaded days of the war, had inundated Amelie with invitations: shopping trips to London, because Archie and Caitlin's husband, Malcolm, owned mews houses in Knightsbridge right behind Harrods; tickets to the West End; invitations to sparkling cocktail parties with the bright young things in fabulous houses, followed by dancing at the Kit Kat Club or, better still, a pair of hard-won tickets to the utterly exclusive Embassy nightclub, where the cream of society danced the Shimmy and the Heebie Jeebie to the music of the new jazz bands, but Amelie had turned down all of these invitations.

"So," Caitlin said, her green eyes sparkling, her lips, painted deep red like the flapper she transformed into down in London, widening into a stunning smile. "I can't lure you away from the delectable Archie to London, but we're going to have a wee party here instead. Well," she chuckled, "not a wee one. A huge party, in the early spring."

Amelie placed her teacup down, her hands stilling in her lap. A party. No.

"My little sister, Annabel is engaged." She leaned forward, lowering her voice. "You know, she's been in Paris for two years, working with latchkeys and calling it a life?"

Paris? Not Paris. Amelie fought the urge to flee the room.

"Annabel's fiancé, Clyde, has a fabulous estate in Hampshire. You are most welcome to invite any friends of yours from Paris. You see, Annabel might just bring along someone you know!"

Amelie swallowed, her throat thick as treacle.

She stood up and went to stand by the window, turning the already wide-open curtains back a little more so she could stare down at the Clois River, with its famous stone bridge curving over the water. Archie had roared across that bridge when they'd arrived at Carrig, with Amelie in the passenger seat, clutching onto her cloche hat, her silk scarf whipping away behind her.

When she'd arrived in Scotland, being out of the city and back in the countryside, unhindered by war, she'd had to bite back memories of the country holidays she used to enjoy with her family, trips in the summer to a farm in the Loire Valley. Holidays that were in some golden past that would never happen again. They'd hired a house on a property out of Amboise each summer, and she and little Vianne had been allowed to walk into the ancient town center with its looming castle, where they'd bought fresh baguettes for breakfast, which Papa would spread with strawberry jam.

He'd taught Anaïs horseback riding, on the pony that belonged to the owners of the farm. Anaïs remembered the couple, along with some of their farmworkers, watching her ride, cackling at her earliest attempts to master the rising trot, which had only fueled her determination to perfect it. Soon, she'd tip her hat at them as they stood in awe of the way she galloped off with Leo into the forests, giving him his head, feeling the most exquisite sense of freedom and joy that she'd ever known in her life. She was the only one daring enough in the family to gallop. She'd *loved* to ride. She'd adored Leo, and when the golden summers came to an end, and it was time to return to Paris, she'd always felt a lump in her throat that she couldn't shift.

She'd been devastated when Papa had written to her where she was stationed in Belgium in 1914, telling her that Leo, like most horses in France, had been requisitioned for the war, and how the women on the farm were taking on all the traditional men's work. In the end, Anaïs had been saddened to learn that the farmer's wife whom they'd been so fond of had abandoned the struggle, faced with the loss of draft animals, fertilizer, and the constraints of price controls. She'd only been able to sow wheat on a small portion of her land, so the farm had been sold.

"Mummy and Daddy are talking about the cat's meow of a party, with a marquee for the young set, and Scottish Highland dancing in the ballroom, with the reception rooms of Kinloch decorated like a Parisian circus during the Belle Epoque. You'll be right at home. Simply give us a list of your friends in Paris." Caitlin's voice softened. "It was Archie's idea, Amelie. We want you to feel completely at home in Scotland and your friends are ours, you know."

Amelie stiffened.

Archie may have left no stone unturned to introduce her to his family and friends, but he could never know anyone from her past. Never.

In 1920, he'd told her, soon after his father's death, the estate lawyer had given Archie the keys to Carrig with his mother, Mary's blessing, but Archie had hotfooted it down to London, horrified at the idea of running the estate himself.

And then he'd met Amelie, fallen in love and wondered why he'd ever questioned his inheritance, or the life he was born to lead in Scotland. His mother had moved out of Carrig to a cottage on the estate, had it painted and freshened up, thrown herself into her garden and, in her own formidable way, had busied herself with the country life she'd always adored. She'd steadfastly not interfered with her son, and Amelie had been constantly grateful for the practical Highland woman's sensitivity when she made it clear that she did not need to talk about the war, or Amelie's past.

And it *must* remain that way.

Amelie took in steadying breaths.

Caitlin placed her piece of fruit cake down on her plate. "We have acres of room, but Mummy's starting to organize beds, and we're hoping you and Archie will accommodate any stray guests here at Carrig."

Amelie's hand shook on the curtain. Wobbling on her feet, she sat back down on the pale cream velvet sofa in the sitting room that Archie had insisted she redecorate for herself. Relieved to have something to throw herself into, she now realized she'd only channeled Papa's love of antiques. And here she sat surrounded by blue and white porcelain lamps and green silk walls with pretty portraits hanging on the walls.

But, confusing as this seemed when she stepped aside to look at what she'd done, this room felt like home to her.

Amelie turned her teacup around in its saucer three times. "I lost the young people of my acquaintance to the war. And..." she took in a deep breath. After all, what she was about to say was the truth... "My close friends were killed in the same bombing that killed my mother." She threaded her fingers through her pearls.

Caitlin leaned forward, drawing her soft cashmere cardigan close over her woolen skirt. "Of course, darling," she said, patting Amelie on the knee. "But there must be some of your old friends you'd like to invite. Do think about it and let us know."

Amelie remained silent, her heart beating like a wild bird bashing its wings against a glass window.

And then, her sense of preservation kicked in. Kicked in as it had so many times these past years. Without it, she would never have survived. "You're not going to have fancy dress?" she asked, tilting her head to one side. "After all, that was quite the thing during the Belle Epoque. Taking on other personas, people going to Paris and being who they really wanted to be."

Caitlin's eyes danced in triumph. "Why," she whispered, "you are quite brilliant. I'll speak to Annabel. Fancy dress."

Amelie watched her neighbor's mind whirl. "What about a masked ball?" she said, her nerves jangling and her heart pulsing like Vianne's beloved sewing machine.

"A masked ball?" Caitlin said. "Sounds like just the thing. Oh, I'm so glad you've joined our little community, Amelie."

Caitlin blew Amelie a kiss, and Amelie sent the girl one of her forced, false smiles.

CHAPTER TEN

VIANNE, NEW YORK, WINTER, 1924

Vianne sat alone in the workroom well after midnight, adding the finishing touches to Adriana Conti's diaphanous evening cape. Rain beat against the windows in the inky darkness, hail battered the roof, and Vianne, wrapped in one of Maman's favorite cashmere shawls, turned Adriana Conti's cape over and studied it under the bright lights.

She'd hand-sewed the layers of chenille trim, black, and cream onto the translucent black cape with the greatest care, and she'd worked into the early hours of the morning on countless nights, threading the black and cream ribbons into the flower and circle motifs, before hand-stitching them meticulously together until they formed her perfect vision of the dress.

Vianne drew the theatrical cape up onto her own shoulders, spreading her arms out like a ballerina and letting the exquisite fabric flow down her back. If she held her hands out wide, the chenille trim settled itself on her wrists, while the see-through fabric that would sit atop the dress hung in a perfect arc to the exact point she'd imagined just below her knees. She was a similar height to Mrs. Conti, so using herself as a measure for the cape made perfect sense.

Yawning hugely, satisfied that the dress was ready for Mrs.

Conti to try on one last time, Vianne hung the cape and covered it in one of Miss Ellie's bespoke garment bags.

As she trod, weary, up the stairs to the tiny seamstresses' apartment she shared with Lucia, Vianne turned off the lights, her mind in a turmoil of confusion because she'd see Mrs. Conti's handsome son, Giorgio, again tomorrow.

He'd insisted on coming to pick up the dress. Insisted on carrying it across the road to his mother's apartment building on the corner of Park Avenue in the morning because of the weather, and the forecast of more rain and sleet. He couldn't bear anything happening to all Vianne's hard work with the grand opening of his restaurant this weekend.

Giorgio had popped into the salon today to meet his mother for lunch after today's fitting of the dress. Gorgeously handsome in a dark suit, he'd stood chatting with Miss Ellie. Vianne had finished helping another client try on a day suit and was standing behind the desk in the salon. Lucia and Mollie had admitted that they too had their ears pressed to the closed seamstresses' door, relaying the suave Giorgio's words to Adeline and Goldie, both of whom had a crush on the good-looking Italian man.

And for her part, Vianne knew she was fighting an internal battle with herself because when Giorgio Conti sent her a smile, her whole being sparkled inside.

What was more, she'd become entranced with the entire world of the Conti family: the glamorous Adriana Conti had confided how Giorgio's late father came from a family who'd run two restaurants in Milano, but when he had died, Giorgio had been lost. He'd decided to start a new life in America, and Adriana, seeing only loneliness in Milan without her beloved husband and without her son nearby, had hotfooted it across the Atlantic too.

Being in Manhattan, with all its possibilities, had only affirmed Giorgio's passion for running his own restaurant. He'd decided to name his new venture after his beloved father, Valentino Conti. He was determined to turn Valentino's into an establishment worthy of his father's memory. And Adriana Conti couldn't be prouder of her only son. Vianne had seen Giorgio on the odd occasion when she'd gone to take measurements for his mother in her apartment, or to discuss slight variations to her gown, but any conversation with Giorgio had never gone beyond a smile or simply saying hello, so far.

Vianne slipped through the little apartment above the atelier, leaving her purse on the wooden table draped with a patterned cloth, two chairs sitting either side of it against the wall in the one room that did duty as living room, kitchen, and dining room. The sounds of Lucia's soft breathing filtered through the open door of her bedroom, and Vianne tiptoed past to her own room with its wooden dressing table and a pair of small prints of Degas' ballerinas hanging on the wall next to the single bed. She pulled off her work dress, laid it on the chair, washed quickly and slipped under her quilt, lying in the darkness with her eyes wide open, listening to the rain.

Giorgio would be listening to the same rain across the road, while his dream would be showcased for all of New York to see Saturday evening right on the corner of Park Avenue and East 63rd Street. And yet, thinking about him was the last thing she should be doing right now.

Vianne stared into the darkness; despite the impossibly late hour, her mind whirled. Giorgio Conti had insisted, she'd heard him, he'd insisted that both Vianne and Eloise should come to the opening of Valentino's. And she wanted to go. Every time she slipped past the blocked-off glass doors that led to the mysterious wonderland inside, she fought the urge to try to peek through a gap to see what Giorgio had designed on the inside.

He'd told Miss Ellie that he couldn't bear the thought of them not witnessing the wonderful reception of the marvelous gown Vianne had designed for his mother. Miss Ellie's atelier would be the toast of the party, featured in every newspaper on the East Coast. Vianne's dress, he said, should, in turn, launch her career.

Vianne turned on her side and hugged her knees to her chest.

Graciously, with a hint of reluctance that only Vianne had noticed, Miss Ellie had accepted Giorgio's invitation for them both.

So, Vianne was going to the party this Saturday evening at New York's newest and most dazzling restaurant.

Valentino's.

Giorgio arrived at Miss Ellie's door with his mother the following morning, a great black umbrella shielding them both from the drizzling rain. Vianne, her eyes bright despite her lack of sleep, and her hands folded neatly in front of her two-piece costume, opened the door to let the charismatic mother and son inside.

"*Santa Maria*," Adriana Conti exclaimed once Vianne had ushered her into one of the fitting rooms and she laid eyes on the dress.

"You are happy, Mrs. Conti?" Vianne whispered, barely able to cope with Mrs. Conti's reply. Hours, weeks, headaches, tears, countless pricked fingers, aching wrists from folding ribbons, had gone into the realization of this dress.

"Darling Vianne," Adriana said, "I have never seen anything so lovely in my life." She sat down on a chair, shaking her head and staring at the gown. "I simply cannot tell you how much I wish my beloved Valentino could see me tomorrow night." And the older woman reached into her little purse for a handkerchief, her beautiful almost-black eyes misting over with tears. "Oh, Vianne. This is beyond anything I had imagined." She reached out her hand. "You must come tomorrow evening, to Giorgio's opening. You and dear Eloise. Tell me you both will be there?"

"Madame Chappelle is going to permit me to attend, I believe," Vianne said.

Mrs. Conti sat up. "And why would she not permit you to come? Hmm?"

Vianne met Mrs. Conti's confident gaze. "I can't imagine..."

. . .

Once the final fitting was done, and Mrs. Conti had twirled in the oh-so modern black-and-white dress, fluttering the cape around her shoulders in delight, Vianne carefully put the outfit on a hanger and slipped it into a large garment bag, which she carried out into the front salon.

Giorgio Conti looked up from the *New York Times*, his eyes lighting up at the sight of his mother and Vianne.

"I can tell by the look on your face that you're enraptured," he said, addressing his mama.

"Oh, it's just marvelous." Mrs. Conti drew out the words so that her very utterance sounded luxurious.

Giorgio sent a wink Vianne's way, and she knew her cheeks turned pink. She had to stop reacting to him! Whether she got to see her final creation tomorrow night or not, Miss Ellie, rules aside, was right about one thing. Giorgio Conti would never show any serious interest in a seamstress. He was the last thing she needed right now.

Ten minutes later, Mrs. Conti had disappeared in a flurry of kisses for a morning coffee engagement, and Vianne, stroking the garment bag that contained everything she'd worked so hard for these past weeks, resisted the urge to bend down and place a kiss on it before she handed it across to Mrs. Conti's handsome son.

His dark eyes moved to the gown, and Vianne looked doubtfully outside at the steady rain that beat over Manhattan.

"Vianne," he said, tilting his head. "How about I carry the umbrella, and you bring Mama's dress. That way, you'll know that it's arrived safely."

She chewed on her lip. Accepting a gentleman's invitation to deliver a gown to his mother's apartment? Did that come under Miss Ellie's idea of appropriate behavior for her seamstresses? But Miss Ellie wasn't here, and surely she would want to see the dress safely delivered.

Vianne smiled. "Well," she said. "I don't see any harm in that." She couldn't help it, her French accent kicked in and her voice lowered a little to a salty growl.

"Perfect," he whispered, his eyes kindling with hers. He held the door open, and as she walked past him, her shoulder brushed on his arm.

She closed her eyes. *Stop it.* This was ridiculous. She had to get herself in check.

Vianne stood with Giorgio just inside his mother's apartment, having handed the gown to his mother's maid. She watched it go into the glamorous salon, feeling a little wistful, knowing that it was about to grace a fabulous party and hopefully make a grand splash. When the maid disappeared, Giorgio loosened his tie and ran a hand through his dark hair.

Vianne bit back her rueful smile. *Italian men.*

"Vianne."

"*Oui?*" He might be an Italian, but she was a Parisian and equally as sassy, she reminded herself.

His eyes crinkled. "You know, I'm feeling a little nervous. I want tomorrow evening to be the greatest success." He let out a sigh. "But, you see, there will be critics, and so many people to impress. We have over two hundred guests."

"Sure, I understand that," Vianne said, smiling at the way she'd picked up an American turn of phrase. "But I'm sure it will be wonderful. Everyone says it's going to be the cat's meow."

But Giorgio's handsome face clouded. He drew his brows together and shook his head. "Vianne, no matter how many times I check everything, I worry that Valentino's won't be good enough." He inclined his head to one side. "I don't suppose you'd be willing to look at my restaurant? Tell me what you think of Valentino's?" He lowered his voice. "You see, at the end of the day, I want it to be something of which my late father would have been proud." He looked at her with sadness in his eyes.

Vianne hesitated.

"I've kept busy ever since he died, too busy to think about

things. You know? But now, the restaurant is complete, and suddenly, I'm uncertain that I've done Papa justice."

Vianne swallowed, and a lump formed in her throat. "Yes, I do understand that, Giorgio."

"And now it's all ready, my tribute to my lost papa, I find myself worrying whether people will laugh at it. That it won't be a success, and then, I will have failed my father's memory."

Vianne frowned. "I'm sure he'd always be proud of you, Giorgio. No matter what. And the fact you've built a restaurant and named it after him, why, that is something wonderful indeed. No matter what other people think."

"Please. It won't take long." He sent her a sad smile and shrugged. "You know, if you hate it, I will cancel everything." He ticked off things with his fingers, as if they were a list. "The opening night party, the menus, the food, I'll sack all my waitstaff and my chefs..." he raised a brow her way.

Vianne swallowed her laugh. "Oh, phonus balonus to that!" She knew her eyes sparkled. Now she was using modern slang as if she were a girl born in New York.

Giorgio let out a burst of laughter. "You'd be the cat's pajamas if you'd come down and check everything's jake."

Vianne clamped her lips together to stop herself from giggling like a schoolgirl. "Well, five minutes, then, Giorgio!" Surely, five minutes wasn't going to do any harm?

Once he'd slipped the key into the locked double doors, stepping aside for Vianne to enter first, Giorgio flicked on the lights.

Vianne stopped suddenly still, right at the entrance, her eyes widening. "Oh, my," she breathed.

Three rows of yellow strip lights beamed into life around the edges of the ceiling, shining on the geometrical designs overhead. Rows of modern, hanging lights shone down the middle of the room, lending a honey-colored glow to the beautifully polished wooden floors. A long bar gleamed down one side of the restaurant, and behind this, glass shelving sparkled with tiny lights, and art deco mirrors reflected the room. On the wood-paneled walls, that gave out an air of an exclusive club, there were bold black-and-white photos of New York: tall buildings reached to powdery clouded skies, the Williamsburg Bridge, charming nineteenth-century brownstones in Greenwich Village, leaves cascading on the old New York streets, shots of bridges and ponds in Central Park and photographs of flappers in dazzling dresses dancing in the jazz clubs.

"I can't find the words," Vianne whispered.

Moving further into the restaurant, she forced herself not to fan her burning cheeks. Tables were set up throughout the middle of the room, and the edges were lined with cozy banquettes that overlooked Park Avenue. How New Yorkers, marching by out there in the cold, would ever resist coming right into this warm and stunning atmosphere, Vianne had no idea. She had to stop her own imagination from flying to thoughts of she and Giorgio sitting down right now in one of those intimate banquettes, sharing a cocktail while the rain beat down outside.

But there were to be no cocktails for them, and no getting-to-know-you chats. The 18th Amendment banning alcohol, not to mention society rules, made sure of that.

Even so, nothing was going to stop this beautiful restaurant turning heads.

Each table was set with a tiny glass candle, ready to be lit. Gleaming crystalware sparkled and reflected the warm glow of the art deco lights, and white napkins graced the tables, along with polished silverware in which Vianne knew she would see her reflection if she chose.

She stopped halfway down the bar, her eye alighting on a sketchbook that lay open. Vianne moved closer. The book was the same as the one she owned, in which she'd drawn up her own dreamy creations and let her imaginings run wild toward places that only she knew about. Slowly, she swung around to the man standing behind her.

His velvet eyes smiled softly at the open book.

"This is yours?" she whispered.

"Yes."

Vianne was still. Quietly, Giorgio pulled out a bar stool for her, its smooth feet barely tracing a sound on the floor. Outside, the rain streamed down in rivulets, but it was warm and beautifully cozy in here.

"Would you like to take a look?" Giorgio asked, standing next to her.

She glanced at him. He was standing so close by her that she could see his chest rising up and down with his breath. "I'd love to," she whispered.

She shouldn't. She should go straight back to work.

But, surely, one dreamer looking at another dreamer's imaginings was not against the rules?

He reached out, turning the pages, and her eyes roamed over sketch after sketch. Here it all was, the extraordinary geometric, golden lighting, the glamorous photographs, down to sketches of the tiny glass candles, the way the wick would glow when it was lit at night.

"All your ideas," she said, and he let her turn the pages, marveling at his work, the cross sections, thoughts, jotted notes in swift, rounded script. And then, she came upon his recipes. "Oh," she breathed, turning to him, her lips parting in a smile. "Well, I'd better not read these, Giorgio. I trust they are secret. If you Italians are anything like we French."

His lips formed a little grin. "*Bella*, I would like to cook them for your someday," he said.

Vianne started, her hand stilling on the page and her heart spun into tiny flutters. *Bella?* Perhaps it was just a turn of phrase. Frowning, she convinced herself it must be that.

"The recipes are adapted from my father's restaurant back in Milano," he went on, his voice silken against the soft, falling rain.

Vianne's fingers traced the page, the connection between Giorgio's papa and her lost parents feeling especially close. She closed her eyes, not wanting this moment to end, not wanting to lose the sense of their much-missed family members drifting between them. "Valentino must have been a very special man."

His lips parted in a smile. "*Sì*," he said, slipping into Italian. "Every time I cook, every time I make plans for the restaurant, I think of Papa." He pressed a hand against his heart. "He taught me to cook." He lowered his gaze. "It was something passed down from generation to generation. Cooking is something I will always hold close."

Maman taught me to sew. Vianne's gaze became a little unfocused, Giorgio's meticulous notes and drawings shifting on the page.

Giorgio pulled out the stool next to her and sat down. "Can I ask you a question?"

She nodded, her own heart far away in France.

"Why have you come to New York, Vianne?" he asked.

Vianne fought the stab that threatened to tear her insides apart. Anaïs, Maman, how much they would love this place! Papa would be suggesting a few tiny antiques to add to the overall charm.

Involuntarily, she reached up to wipe a stray tear that fell down her cheek. "Everyone knows New York is where it's at," she said. "It's the center of the world, so that is why I came here." She looked down. She was not ready to talk about her lost family with people in America. Not yet. "European cities were left in tatters after the war," she said quietly. "And New York is already filled with Italians, Jewish people. French. We Europeans are all migrants in one way or another here. I'm just another one, you know."

Giorgio was quiet next to her. "Would you let me make you coffee?"

She pushed her stool back, her eyes pricking with tears. "I should get back to work."

Slowly, she raised her eyes to meet his, but there was no hiding the solitary tear that slid down her cheek.

He searched her face, a small frown line forming between his eyes. "I know how bad the war was in France. I was too young to go, but... we had French friends who were living in the occupied zones."

She leaned against the counter, pressing down into the shining wood, forcing herself to take long slow breaths. She imagined herself walking into Papa's sanctuary, her hand lingering on the door outside Celine. Her memories of Paris made it seem like a charming village now that she was surrounded by the skyscrapers of New York, and yet, she wanted to cling onto the memories of her time there, never forget the elegant city that had been her home. She'd grown up there, she'd lived and loved, until there was no one left and they were all gone, killed in the most brutal way, dead of heartbreak, lost to her and, when it came to her brother, Jacques, consumed by anger.

She closed her eyes, imagining Papa, and no matter what he was doing, whom he was with, he'd pull his glasses off as if making certain it was her, and he'd open his arms, unrestrained, and pull her close into that embrace she could feel by memory. His soft woolen jackets, his crisply ironed shirts. And then, if it was after school, before the war, he'd take her hand, placing her little fingers in his warm palm, and they'd walk across the road from Celine to the patisserie, choosing something special. But she always chose a chocolate éclair. Her heart lifted a little as she remembered the texture of the delicate choux pastry, the sumptuous cream filling, and finally, the deep chocolate fondant icing. She'd lost her interest in beautiful food after the drabness of the war, and she'd thrown herself so hard into her designing to get through that she'd denied herself any treats, as if focusing on one thing would take all the pain of her losses away.

"*Bella.*"

Vianne looked up, startled. She'd gone away into her own thoughts, somehow, and now, Valentino's was filled with the most delicious scent. It was chocolate... How long had she been lost in the past that she'd never get back?

Giorgio was holding out a glass filled with frothy chocolate milk and topped with whipped cream.

Vianne looked at it. She'd not been able to touch chocolate since Papa's death.

"Have you ever tried *barbajada* before?" Giorgio asked.

Vianne shook her head. Outside, the rain pelted on the windowpanes. Even though they were blocked with drawn curtains, and the heating was on, she shivered.

"It's a Milanese specialty," he said. "A hot chocolate and coffee drink. It will give you strength to get through the rest of this cold day. Please, try it."

Vianne reached out, her hands warmed by the hot glass wrapped in a white serviette. She closed her eyes, sipping the delicious coffee and chocolate drink, the espresso waking her, bringing her back to the warm restaurant, the new restaurant that Giorgio had built as a tribute to *his* past, just as she would design dresses as a tribute to her past, to her parents, to Anaïs, and to the brother she used to have in Jacques. If she took her pain and turned it into things of great beauty, she'd be doing her family proud.

Gently, Giorgio reached out and pushed back a lock of her stray blond hair. "That is better?" he asked.

"*Oui, merci*," Vianne said. After a few moments, she smiled at him. "You know, I was supposed to be cheering *you* up."

"Well," he said. He leaned against the counter a little way up the bar. "You did that, Vianne. You did that just perfectly. Thank you."

And she gave him a smile, a smile that she knew was one of Maman's specialties. No one could take Maman's beautiful smile away from Vianne, and she knew all too well how special it was to meet someone who could draw it out.

But when she placed her empty cup back down, she caught sight of her flushed reflection in the mirror and stood deadly still. What was she doing? Giorgio Conti was a handsome Italian bachelor, who seemed to have more depth than she'd assumed by the descriptions she'd heard from the other seamstresses, but Miss Ellie was right. The last thing she needed was to damage her reputation, let alone the reputation of the seamstresses at the atelier. She must not risk losing everything she'd fought so hard for over a man.

"I've got to go," she whispered, sending him a fleeting glance. "Goodbye, Giorgio. And good luck."

His eyes stuck on hers for one moment. Too long. "I'm glad you like Valentino's," he said, his gaze burning into hers.

Flushing again, and her heart hammering something wild in her chest, Vianne turned around. She put one foot after the other, and she slipped out of the restaurant, and when she did so, the cold New York air bit at her cheeks. The wind picked up and whipped her short hair around. She pushed her hat onto her head, taming her wild hair into place, and, taking determined, steady steps, she went back to Miss Ellie's. Back to the atelier, where it was safe.

CHAPTER ELEVEN
VIANNE, WINTER, 1924

Vianne crossed East 63rd Street the following evening, her heart beating something wild in anticipation for Giorgio's grand opening, her footsteps clipping away on the sidewalk as she approached Valentino's. Well-dressed crowds milled about outside the building. Women in fur coats and cashmere scarves, their breath curling from their painted lips, chatted alongside men in formal black suits and polished Italian shoes. The very air on Park Avenue was scented with Chanel No. 5. Gentlemen of the press, notebooks in hand, vied with guests to get as close to the entrance as they could.

Vianne clutched her purse, one hand playing with the buttons on her coat. She jumped when she felt a tap on her shoulder. Her eyes were scouring for Miss Ellie, but she turned at the sound of a man's voice.

"Mademoiselle Mercier from Paris. How charming to see you."

"Good evening, Mr. Winter." Vianne fought a stab of disappointment that Giorgio Conti was not the one who'd tapped her shoulder, but then, she should be thankful for that. Yesterday's conversation with him had brought out too many treasured memories, and she'd stayed far too long talking with him, as if he was some sort of kindred spirit. It must not happen again. She'd been carried away, that was all, but she'd tossed and turned, not sleeping well last night after worrying that she might have put her career at risk. Miss Ellie trusted her. And she, Vianne, must prove she was worthy of that trust. She must show Miss Ellie she had what it took, and that meant steering clear of handsome young men.

She sent a genuine smile to Eddie Winter. The editor of *Bella* magazine had written a cracking piece about Eloise Chappelle's atelier. And he'd complimented the seamstresses most generously. The fact he'd bothered mentioning them at all had caused something of a riot amongst the girls. Mollie had pinned a copy of the article to the wall in the workroom, and Lucia had turned on the gramophone and danced the foxtrot around the room, only to have Miss Ellie tell her firmly to turn it down and to keep still. She was not one, she said, to blow her own trumpet and put herself on display. No, she had far more class than that.

"I hope you are planning to give Valentino's a favorable review," Vianne said to Eddie, rubbing her leather gloved hands against the cold.

"Giorgio Conti is a swell guy and his restaurant's going to be fabulous," Eddie replied, his gray eyes scanning the crowd, before turning back and alighting on her. "Tonight should be a gas, and I predict that Valentino's is going to be one of Manhattan's big deals." He pulled out a hip flask and took a swig. "That's how confident I am, Miss Mercier, before I've even set foot inside."

Vianne's eyes rounded. "Well, that sounds very good." Eddie Winter was not the only one pulling out a hip flask and taking a swig of something that did not look like fruit juice at all.

"Cheer up," Eddie said with a glimmer in his eye. "Medicinal whiskey is legal for influenza, darling. And you see, I've had a ferocious dose of the flu."

She turned away from him, shrugging.

"Come on," he said, turning her shoulder and holding the silver flask out. "Have some. You know it's being prescribed as the medicine of choice for all sorts of ailments. Anxiety, pre-opening night nerves…"

"Well," she said, sending him one of Maman's arch looks,

"lucky I don't suffer from *any* ailments, then, don't you think?" She might want to be modern, but taking a nip from Eddie's hip flask didn't seem so appealing right now.

He chuckled and turned to chat with a man in a bowler hat.

Right then, a cheer went up throughout the crowd, and those magical double doors opened. The guests surged forward and there was a fabulous swell of noise from a band playing the opening notes of "It Had to Be You."

Vianne's heart filled with pride for Giorgio, for all the hours he'd spent on those sketches that he'd shown her yesterday. And now, here was his chance to share those dreams with all of New York.

Vianne clasped her hands and followed the crowds. Finally, she had the chance to see the dress make its grand public debut, the dress that she'd held so close for the past weeks. Despite her assurances to Eddie Winter that she didn't suffer from nerves, every fiber in her being was on edge, and she couldn't wait to see what the reaction was to her design.

Inside, Valentino's was heaving, the jazz quartet was swinging, and the restaurant was a buzz with exclamations of how wonderful it was, the honey-colored lights on the ceiling and behind the bar lending the restaurant a theatrical air.

Waiters milled around carrying tray after tray of delectable Milanese food, Mondeghili—tiny meatballs made with ground beef and bread—little Michetta—stuffed puffy rolls fashioned into rose-like shapes—and tiny white plates filled with samples of creamy Risotto Alla Milanese, complete with saffron that gave the dish its precious hue. Trays filled with plates of creamy polenta topped with melt in your mouth Osso Bucco were being passed around, and tiny portions of breaded Veal Milanese, deliciously crisp with the light meat perfectly juicy underneath, were eaten with delicate forks, and folks were swooning over the food all around the room. Talk was, Valentino's was fully booked for two months already.

Vianne spotted Miss Ellie in the crowd and threaded her way across the room.

"This food is transporting me all the way to Milano," Miss Ellie declared. "It is divine and incomparable."

Just then, Adriana Conti swept to Vianne's side. There was a coterie of guests in her wake, and she clapped her hands together and held up Vianne's hand. "This is the designer of my metallic ribboned gown. I can tell you that this young woman has everything to do with how fabulous I feel right now."

"Bravo," an elderly gentlemen close by said, and Mrs. Conti's entourage all started a round of applause.

Vianne's cheeks flushed, and she allowed herself a grin. Adriana Conti was swept away again, and Vianne accepted, from a passing waiter, a Negroni in a pink and gold teacup, to hide the fact that the cocktail contained precious gin.

And later on, when the restaurant was filled with the scent of cream, coffee and chocolate, and waiters brought out glasses of chocolate and espresso *barbajada*, Vianne could only smile at the new memory Giorgio had created for her, of this warm drink from his beloved Milan.

"Vianne!" When Giorgio appeared by her side, Vianne almost choked on her hot chocolate and coffee, and she looked up at him, a line of froth covering her top lip.

His eyes danced, and, carefully, he took a white napkin and wiped her lip. "You are having a good evening?" he said, his eyes searching hers.

"Of course, I am, Giorgio. Congratulations." She took a step back because the chemistry between them was dangerous. Risky. She may be young, but she was not a fool. And Miss Ellie had picked up on the fireworks between her and Giorgio from the moment they first met. Vianne's boss was in this very same room, even if she was standing with another group of guests. There was no taking any risks.

To her relief, a shorter man with a good-looking face and an easy smile came to stand right next to Giorgio.

"Vianne," Giorgio said, "This is Jimmy Walker. And I can tell you with all confidence that he's going to be mayor of New York by the end of this year."

"This *wonderful* year," Jimmy Walker said. He took Vianne's hand and placed a kiss on her fingers. "Hello, gorgeous," he said. "Why haven't I seen you around town before?"

Vianne shrugged. "Nice to meet you, Mr. Walker, and as to your question, I haven't been in New York for very long."

"Vianne here has been hiding away designing Mama Adriana's wonderful dress," Giorgio said. "Vianne is a marvel. She's Eloise Chappelle's new second designer."

Jimmy Walker stepped back and blew Vianne a kiss.

She couldn't help it; she grinned right back at him. The man was as cheeky as a monkey, and he was holding a teacup filled with Negroni aloft. The man who was trying to be mayor. New York was outrageous. It was the kind of place Maman and Anaïs would have adored, and Papa would have adored them in it.

"A rising star in the New York fashion scene?" Jimmy Walker said. "Baby, if you want any support with your ventures, come see me and I'll lobby for you."

Vianne waved her own teacup around. "Oh, I'm not looking to start any ventures. But if I meet anyone who is, I'll send them your way."

He came closer and lowered his voice. "Your boss, Eloise? She's well positioned being close to Park Avenue," he said, suddenly sounding less like some theatrical swell and more like the politician he was clearly trying to be.

"Is that right, Mr. Walker?" Vianne said.

Giorgio was in a conversation with another guy to her right now. Vianne relaxed a little and focused on Mr. Walker because he was talking fast and sounding excited about his city.

"Fifth Avenue used to be where all the wealthy people lived, but now it's Park Avenue, baby doll. Fifth Avenue is where folks go to shop. Positioning a restaurant up here, right under New York society's noses and below their apartments, why, it's genius. And they'll all come to Miss Eloise's if they want something special, something bespoke, because Mrs. Adriana Conti is one of the city's most fashionable women, and you've just put a great advertisement for yourself right on her back. You," he said, lifting his cup her way, "are just the sort of girl New York needs. We're growing fast, Vianne. You know, we have a skyscraper being completed every fifty-one minutes each day. What do you say to that?"

"Every fifty-one minutes?" Vianne grinned. "I say it's uncommonly fine."

Jimmy Walker narrowed his eyes. "I mean it, honey. If ever you want to go into business, you come see me. You have a massive talent, and that dress you designed, well, I say your boss will be turning away clientele with a stick tomorrow morning." He grinned at her. "But New York's not all about hard work, Vianne. You know half the fun is enjoying the night scene. If I win the vote and become mayor at the next election, I plan to be known as Mr. Nighttime Swell, and I won't hold any meetings before lunch. It's the only way to do business. Now, you enjoy the giggle water, and hopefully I'll get to dance with you later on." Jimmy Walker held up his teacup and disappeared off into the crowd.

Giorgio was back by her side.

Vianne started, and she took a step away from him.

"I hope we New Yorkers are not tiring you out, Paris girl."

Vianne drew her hand out and looked at her little watch. She looked across the room, where Miss Ellie had sashayed up to an elegant couple and was engaged in animated conversation with them. She could talk to Giorgio for a few more minutes, before she'd risk her boss seeing her and taking down notes.

"You heard Jimmy's talk of speakeasies?" Giorgio asked.

"And he wants to be mayor? This is more ridiculous than France." Vianne searched the room for someone to talk to. She couldn't risk staying here with Giorgio.

Giorgio raised his glass, just like Jimmy had. "Welcome to New York. You ain't seen nothing yet."

She watched Miss Ellie walk right out of Valentino's into the night. In the background, she heard people talking about going dancing. To the clubs. Lucia and the other girls had tried their hardest to get her to come out with them in the past weeks, but Vianne had been dead set on getting Mrs. Conti's dress ready and she'd not taken a break until it was done.

Giorgio tilted his head to one side. "Are you keen to go out on the town after this?" he asked.

Vianne's brows drew close. At the rate she was going, she was never going to see anything of New York at night, other than the sight of her own pillow on her bed.

Giorgio's eyes danced. "Come on, Bella. Help us celebrate. We're going to have a ball. Surely you deserve a night out when your dress has been such a success."

She tapped her foot on the floor. "It's not that, Giorgio."

Giorgio pressed a fist against his lips. When he spoke, his voice was soft. "Eddie Winter and Jimmy Walker will be there, Vianne. In fact, there's a whole crowd of guests coming out. It will be..." Something unfathomable passed across his features, and Vianne's smile tightened and her stomach dived.

He stood there waiting, and suddenly she felt a little foolish. Perhaps she'd read it all wrong, and Giorgio Conti wasn't in any way singling her out. After all, why would he? The man must have girls falling at his feet. He'd be all over another girl before the night was done, so was she doing anything truly wrong by going out to a club with a group of his friends?

"Anyone who's anyone from Midtown will be heading to 42nd Street or, better still, to Harlem when midnight comes around. The Cotton Club stages a fabulous act at twelve, and another one at two a.m." Giorgio patted a man on the shoulder who was walking by.

Vianne tilted her head to one side. It had been so fun dancing the Charleston with Lucia in the atelier. Imagine how fabulous it would be to dance in a real jazz club, with proper musicians on the stage and not just some gramophone... and what would Maman say, not to mention Anaïs, if Vianne were to spend every night in New York sitting in her apartment while her friends went out? Maman had always said to live your life to the full.

Giorgio grinned at her. "You can't call yourself a New Yorker until you've stayed out until sunrise and sneaked back down to your apartment after dawn."

Vianne let out a sigh. What if she were to go out dancing in Anaïs's honor? "Very well, then," she finally said. "Excuse me while I go and freshen up."

His eyes lit up.

She nodded at him, turned away and walked straight toward the powder room. Once she'd pushed the door aside, she leaned heavily on the counter and closed her eyes. As long as she steered well clear of Giorgio, she'd not be breaking any rules. After all, Miss Ellie had not said anything about avoiding the clubs, and the other seamstresses went regularly.

Her fingers moving swiftly, before she could doubt herself again, Vianne applied lipstick, brushed her short, wavy blond hair, and powdered her nose. But her blue eyes were sparkling with something wonderful, and deep down, she knew it was not just the prospect of a dance in a crowded club.

Vianne stared at herself. Her dress was sitting as beautifully as it had done when she'd first put it on: its cream bodice coming down to a drop waist, with a vivid blue skirt below and one line of blue running over her shoulder, with silver filigree embroidered around the hem and the join of the skirt. She had on her T-bar dancing shoes too.

"Well," she whispered to her reflection. "My sister used to be one of the sassiest girls in Paris. Here's to you, darling Anaïs."

She blew herself a kiss and marched right back out the door into the gracious restaurant.

Giorgio was standing in the middle of the room, his black tie loosened and his head lifting at the sight of Vianne.

Vianne stopped for one long moment, her heart skipping a beat. But she came to a start when Adriana Conti came toward her and pulled her into a hug.

"Darling Vianne," Adriana Conti said, "I cannot thank you enough for making this night one of the most wonderful of my life. My son told me the night his beloved Papa Valentino died that he promised to one day open a restaurant that would make his father proud. And it took a move across an ocean, and a whole deal of confidence and hard work and outright ingenuity for him, to find the right time and the right place. And you, Vianne, have added something special and unforgettable to our family tonight. Valentino would have adored you and, sweetheart, he would have simply died for this dress. I only wish he'd seen it." Adriana pulled her into a hug.

Vianne smiled into the women's shoulder, careful to avoid getting powder, rouge or lipstick onto Mrs. Conti's precious, beautiful dress.

"I've told Eloise that I want you to design my entire spring and summer wardrobe," Mrs. Conti said, holding Vianne at arm's length. "You and only you. I think you've made me the happiest woman in Manhattan tonight."

"Thank you," Vianne said simply, though deep down, her heart was racing at the prospect of achieving this first step toward her dream.

Right then, Jimmy Walker came marching over with a group of bright young things, girls in stunning flapper dresses and several young men in tailored suits.

"Vianne's coming out with us all tonight, Mrs. Conti," he said. "I'm going to have to steal her away from you."

Adriana raised a brow. "Well, you take good care of her, won't you, Jimmy. She's very important to me."

"You have my word," the next mayor of New York said.

Vianne's eyes flicked over toward Giorgio, where he was standing with another crowd. She felt a frisson of nerves at the fact she was going to a destination she didn't know with a group of people she didn't know, but then, this was exactly the kind of risk Anaïs would take.

"The car's filled with champagne, and everyone's ready,"

Jimmy Walker said. He introduced her to some of the fellows and girls standing around him and tucked her arm into his own. "I hope you know how to do the Charleston."

She felt her shoulders relax. "We Parisian girls know how to dance."

Mrs. Conti patted her shoulder, and Vianne turned away, her feet floating off the floor as she followed the crowd out to the waiting cars.

If tonight was any indication of how wonderful New York could be, then Vianne knew in her heart that she'd come to the right place.

An hour later, Vianne stood outside the Cotton Club in Harlem on 142nd Street and Lenox Avenue next to Eddie Winter. The sidewalk was bursting with flappers waving cigarette holders and twirling long strands of pearls. Vianne stole glances at the oily-haired gangster types waiting to get into the famous club that was the talk of the town. Jazz belted out from the building, and everyone had an attitude.

"Ready to get in the mood?" Eddie Winter said.

"Of course," she replied, but she couldn't take her eyes off one of the flapper's light green silk crepe dresses with a diamond-shaped hem. It was decorated with diamantés that sparkled and shimmered under the pale streetlights.

Eddie scanned the crowds. "Owney is sure going to have a swell night tonight."

"Owney?" Vianne tore her eyes away from the dress. Giorgio was in a jovial conversation with some guy in a black suit and a cream scarf. The opening of Valentino's had been a triumphant success and Giorgio was the toast of the town.

Eddie's gray eyes narrowed, and he leaned a little closer and dropped his voice. "The Cotton Club is owned by a guy named Owney Madden. He bought it from a heavyweight boxing champion when it was known as Club Deluxe. Owney reopened it and changed its name."

"Is that so?" Vianne asked.

Eddie's lips curled into a rueful smile. "Listen, I don't know how precious you are, but I'll tell it to you straight. Owney bought the club when he was in Sing Sing prison serving a sentence for bumping someone off."

Vianne's stomach rolled. "Am I going to be murdered if I walk in those double glass doors?" She eyed the entrance nervously. A burly doorman was only ushering certain people in.

Eddie chuckled. "Not if you stick with me and Giorgio, honey. Owney's a mobster and a bootlegger who is buying up some of the finest clubs in town. You want to go out in New York, you'll be dealing with the mob. You want to drink champagne? It's all from the mob."

Vianne looked up at him. "The mob? So, who's policing them?"

"Turns out," Eddie said, "the folks that were so keen to introduce Prohibition aren't so keen to enforce it."

Right then, Vianne saw Giorgio pull out his wallet and produce a Cotton Club membership card. She'd heard how you needed to carry a card to get into some of the clubs in New York.

"The New York police don't want to have to deal with the 18th Amendment. They've got better things to do," Eddie explained.

Vianne took in what he was telling her. Well past midnight or not, the journalist in him seemed eager to give her the lowdown on how things in Manhattan were done.

They moved a couple steps forward in the queue.

"As for the Prohibition enforcement officers," Eddie continued, "owners of speakeasies learned fast that they have to pay those very officers off if they want to stay open, and if they don't pay them, well then, the Prohibition patrolmen will confiscate their liquor and sell it to their competitors."

Vianne raised a brow. "So, it's all a total racket?"

Eddie chuckled. "Sometimes, the officers confiscate the booze and make the owners buy their own stock back, or they go and open a speakeasy themselves!"

Vianne shook her head and grinned. "But where do the mob get their liquor in the first place?"

The line moved forward, and the doorman spotted Giorgio and waved him in the magical double glass doors. Eddie grabbed Vianne's elbow and whispered in her ear. "There are boats filled with booze sitting just outside New York, sweetheart, and a lot of illegal hooch is brought in from Canada as well," he said, waving his friends along. "It's all controlled by the mob, and by people like Owney Madden, who made a name for himself hijacking shipments belonging to other bootleggers. They bring the alcohol in under the cover of darkness, using delivery trucks. If they're caught, the drivers just protest and tell the police they thought they were delivering a haul of fish."

Vianne rolled her eyes, but in spite of Eddie's stories, she climbed up the stairs and followed him inside where the band swelled into life with 'California Here I Come' and her toes automatically started tapping along. She moved, along with the rest of the party, toward the round tables covered in white tablecloths. It looked like there were enough to seat seven hundred guests in here, and the club was full to capacity. No wonder the line outside was so long.

The music pulsing through her veins, she took in the guests, the stage. But one thing stood out. Everyone on the stage was black, from the jazz musicians, the pianist, the trombone players, and the men playing the double bass, to the women dancing in front of them on the stage wearing checked silk coats, little checkerboard hats and shiny ties and pants. And every guest in the club was white. There were no black guests at any of the tables. Not one.

Vianne had heard Papa talk of plantations and slavery in America's Deep South, but here, right now, in the modern world in this up-to-the-minute club that was owned by a gangster, it was as if that world of old had been recreated for twentieth-century eyes.

Unable to stop taking it all in, Vianne glanced around the

room, whose walls were lined with murals depicting plantations, and black folks working the cotton fields. The stage was set with a white-painted portico like the grand entrance to one of those Southern homes she'd seen photographs of, and across the vast club, a woman with pale black skin was being carried around on a man's shoulders through the crowds, her beaded costume barely covering her body, which the man was holding in the palm of his hand.

The waitstaff were dressed like plantation slaves, and the whole atmosphere was like a jungle inside. Vianne couldn't help but think how the black people were being depicted as savages, while the white clientele enjoyed the fruits of their labors. Did none of these guests have a conscience, or was the need to be in the mood more important than treating people the right way?

Her eyes burning, she slid down into a chair at the table Giorgio had got for them all, and a waiter placed a glass of beer right in front of her.

"Owney's famous number one beer," Eddie said.

Vianne turned right then, and swore she caught the eye of the burly doorman. Could he tell what she was thinking because she was staring so hard?

She picked up the beer.

"Vianne!"

Vianne jumped at the sound of the screech in her ear, only to have her shoulders sag with relief at the sight of a familiar face in these strange and unsettling surrounds.

"Lucia!" She reached forward to hug the girl with whom she shared her New York home.

Lucia's dark eyes lit up and she clicked her fingers at Vianne. "Oh, honey. You look like you're in a nightmare and you need to be woken up! You deserve a night off, so why don't you relax a little?"

"I am," Vianne said. She took a sip of the beer, and nearly spat it out. She was used to French wine, and the bitterness of this was something else. "See?" She burst into giggles.

Lucia sent her a delicious smile. "I can't think who, or what, persuaded you to finally get with the groove... *Oh.*" Lucia's eyes landed on Giorgio and stayed put. "Now, I see."

"Very well, Lucia," Vianne said, linking her arm through Lucia's and turning her friend resolutely away from Giorgio. "When are we going to dance?"

"How about right now!"

Vianne and Lucia's eyes met, right as the band on the stage struck up the Charleston. Lucia pulled Vianne up to the dance floor, and soon, Vianne was shaking her legs and waving her arms, her toes moving as fast as anyone's in her T-bar dancing shoes. Next to Lucia, a tall, sultry-looking girl with deep-red lips made the Charleston look graceful, if that was possible.

Vianne wiped her sweating forehead and nudged Lucia. "Are you going to introduce me to your friend?"

"Oh, honey, this is Gia Morelli. Gia, this is Vianne."

Vianne shook the tall woman's hand.

"A rare night out without my kids, or my husband," Gia said, her dark eyes warming to something special when she smiled.

"Gia's moved into the same house as my parents in MacDougall Street," Lucia said. "She's Sicilian, just like me, and like me, she loves jazz, which, you have to admit, these black folks play better than anyone else in the world. In fact, they own jazz. Everyone says the Cotton Club is home to some of the finest black musicians of this century."

So that was it. Vianne turned to the stage. The musicians were here for the music, they were here because they could play. They were doing what they loved but putting up with the humiliation that their own people could not be a part of the audience.

Vianne sighed.

"You should come down and visit us in the Village someday," the beautiful Gia Morelli said. "I'd wager you'd love Lucia's mom's cooking, and she'd adore you in return."

Vianne smiled at the woman, suddenly reaching out and grasping her hand. The idea of meeting some fellow Europeans seemed like a wonderful idea right now. "You know, I'd just love to do that. I miss..." she checked herself. "Some home cooking would be grand."

Vianne gathered her breath, her chest pounding, while the band struck up a slower tune. Recognizing George Gershwin's hit of the year, "Rhapsody in Blue," Vianne moved to go back to the table and sit down, but when she took a step forward, she walked right smack into Giorgio.

"Dance with me?" he said, his eyes darkening.

Vianne looked around for Lucia and Gia, but the two girls were hotfooting it off the dance floor, and it was only she, Giorgio and a whole lot of smooching couples under the dim lights. She looked up at him, and he smiled down at her.

"One dance?" he said, his velvet eyes melting, and his head tilted to one side in an endearing way.

Vianne shuffled about on her feet. "I really should go."

"I think you should stay."

"But..."

"The dance will be over and we'll both still be standing here."

Vianne swallowed. She took a step back, but before she knew it, Giorgio had gently encircled her waist in his arms, and without even thinking, perhaps deliberately without thinking at all, she placed her hand on his shoulder, promising herself that this was only going to be one dance. And his dark eyes softened further, and she couldn't help it, she leaned into his shoulder, and tried to get her beating heart to slow down.

"You're having a good time?" he asked.

"I am," she said. But her tone was not full of whoopee. She shook her head. "I'm struggling with the way the black people are treated, Giorgio."

Giorgio sighed. "The thing about the Cotton Club," he murmured into her ear, "is the fact that these musicians are the most talented in the world at what they do, and so, people come here to listen to them, because they cannot hear this sort of music anywhere else. I know the décor and the separation is upsetting. I hate it too, but I'm glad you care."

She sighed too, and leaned her head back on his shoulder, and allowed the music to glide them around the floor. A flutter of hope flickered to life in her belly as they cruised around smoothly to the gorgeous song. And for a few moments, Vianne closed her eyes and pretended everything was all right, that she did have security, and the warmth in her life that she'd missed for so long. For a few moments, while she rested her head on Giorgio's shoulder, she felt as if, for the first time in an age, she'd come home.

When the last notes of the famous tune petered out, she stood back, pulling out of Giorgio's arms.

"Vianne?" he said. "I—"

But she cut him off, her hand flying to her mouth. "I have to go." Because she'd not felt as safe as she did when she was in his arms since the day Maman and Anaïs had been killed. And that sense of security, of *family,* she knew, was what was missing in her life.

And it was the one thing she could not have.

Because she only had herself to rely on. There was no one on whom to fall back.

If she did lose her job, there was no Papa, no Maman, no Anaïs, no backup funds to save her. And Jacques would laugh in her face if she came home with her hat in her hand, a fallen woman who had been booted out of her job.

One more encounter with Giorgio, and she'd lose everything she'd worked for faster than Miss Ellie could dish out her Southern style.

No matter what her treacherous heart was feeling every time she saw him, no matter how she rationalized her position to herself and told her one conversation, one dance wouldn't matter, she had to stop whatever she was feeling in its tracks right now.

"I *have* to go," she said. "I can't stay here anymore." She chewed on her lip. "Congratulations on Valentino's. I wish you every success. Goodbye, Giorgio." She turned, but he caught her hand, and she swung around to face him, her heart racing, as she shook her head.

"Vianne?" He rubbed his hand over his chin, frowned at the floor, then raised his dark eyes to meet hers.

She stared at him for one long second, their eyes locking, and it was all she could do not to walk right back into the warmth of his arms. No matter how handsome he was, no matter how charming, how well they talked and shared the long-held dreams that they both, honestly, one day, might fulfill. It couldn't happen. Giorgio was closer to realizing everything he'd hoped for after his papa died than she was.

And there it was. He was a man. Giorgio had nothing to lose if they carried through this thing that was between them.

But she would lose everything.

What had she been thinking?

"Goodbye, Giorgio." She held her hand up and took a step back.

"*Bella?*" he whispered, shaking his head. "Talk to me."

But her ears pounding, she raised a hand. She'd be out on her ear when he tired of her, and she'd have no way of surviving in New York. It was a tough city. No one would protect her. There were wonderful things about this city, but New York had its share of darkness, that was certain. Tonight, goodness knew, had shown her that. Not one person in this room, not one person who was dancing under the cotton plantation murals and taking beer from black people dressed like slaves would give a hoot if she, a young seamstress with no family, was left to starve on the streets.

She looked at the man standing opposite her in disbelief. She did not even know him. She was a woman on her own. Since she'd lost her family, she was not of his world anymore.

"Goodbye, Giorgio," she said again, her heart hammering a treacherous warning as she whispered the words. If she wanted to get noticed, she had to make a splash and being Giorgio Conti's sweetheart was not the best way to dive into a pool that was infested by sharks.

She'd get back down to East 63rd Street, somehow.

But when she came right to the edge of the dance floor, she

jolted at the feel of a grip on her arm and, the small soft hands could only belong to a woman.

Lucia. Vianne almost collapsed with relief. Lucia was here, and they'd go home together. From now on, she would only dance with Lucia at Miss Ellie's. That was the only way to stay safe. And she'd design her dresses, and everything would be the bee's knees.

She pasted on a smile and turned to face her friend.

"Well, what do you think you're up to, Mademoiselle Mercier?"

Vianne lifted her chin and looked up at the girl standing opposite her. Not Lucia.

She looked down at the hand pressed into her arm. Pale skin with blood-red nails. Slowly, she lifted her head.

"Adeline?" she whispered to Miss Ellie's cherished embroiderer, her tailoress of beads.

Adeline's light blue eyes narrowed, and her lips moved into a thin smile. "So, Miss Ellie's bright star is happy to throw all our professional reputations out the window. Miss Ellie's bright star is happy to take us all down the nearest drain."

"*No,* Adeline..."

But Adeline cocked her eyebrow and looked straight at Vianne as if she were her hunted prey. Her red lips gleamed, and her brown curls bobbed under the dim lights. "My mother once told me that a woman's reputation is like a candle with a tiny flame." She clicked her fingers in front of Vianne's face. "You extinguish it, and it's out for good. And you, you've just burned yourself to the ground."

Vianne stood on the spot, transfixed. Horrified. "But Adeline, honestly—"

"You listen to me." Adeline leaned forward. "All Parisians think they are superior. You come here from Paris, determined to prove yourself, and you work on your own and do not care about the rest of us one jot."

"That's not true," Vianne whispered.

"Don't think we all don't see it. You're so determined to get noticed," Adeline went on, in her awful, nightmarish tone, and Vianne was transfixed. As transfixed and silenced as she'd been when Jacques had thrown her out the door on her own. "You go to client's events, to places that none of us, not one of us, have ever been invited in our lives. And we've worked for Miss Ellie for years before you came. And you sit up sewing, night after night, desperate to ingratiate yourself with Miss Ellie. And really? You're cavorting with Giorgio Conti. Making a fool of Miss Ellie and not caring one jot if all our reputations go down."

Vianne gazed down at the floor, her hands folded in front of her.

"I saw you dancing in his arms. I know Miss Ellie's warned you away from him." Adeline's eyes glittered with anger. "Pack your bags and get out of the atelier before I tell Miss Ellie what you really are."

And with that, Adeline swung around on her feet, and Vianne whipped her head back up, fury coursing through her, too late, because the girl was quite magically gone.

"Vianne?" Giorgio was back next to her, and she whirled around to face him, her cheeks burning.

"*Bella.*" He reached out, impossibly, to stroke her flushed cheek. "Is anything wrong? Have I done something?"

She jolted back from him.

"Oh, you haven't done anything wrong," she whispered, her words muffled, half formed. "It's I who have destroyed myself in just one moment."

Giorgio took her hands, covering her shaking fingers with his own. Confusion laced his features. "You are not well?"

But she pulled free of him, pressed her hand to his chest and pushed him away. "I'm perfectly well," she whispered. "Everything is perfectly fine." She lifted her chin. "But please. From now on, don't come anywhere near me. I can't see you anymore."

He jerked his head back. When he spoke, he stammered. "But I thought we had connected..."

Vianne shook her head. "No, there is no connection," she said, her voice as icy as a lake on a winter's day. "We must never see each other again."

If she had anything to do with it, her job would not be gone. Adeline would not destroy everything with Miss Ellie. She'd fight to the end to keep working at the atelier and she'd prove to the other girls that she was one of them, part of their team.

Vianne turned, wrapped in her treacherous lies to Giorgio, and walked out into the New York night.

CHAPTER TWELVE
ELOISE, WINTER, 1924

Eloise lowered her eyeglasses and held the fashion magazine at arm's length in disbelief, as if looking at the treachery from a distance would wipe out the heinous pictures on the page. For heinous they were. Lena Davis smiled out at the camera, those eyes, even in the photograph, chips of jade. The article shouted how "Miraculous Mrs. Davis" had come up with an original and striking dress, a design worthy of film premieres, nightclubs, weddings, or a formal afternoon tea where dignitaries or royalty were invited guests. And then the article went on to say once again how Lena had dreamed the dress up.

"Your dreams are my nightmares, honey," Eloise murmured, her neck cording tight as she read on about how Lena Davis was likely to take her place alongside such fashion luminaries as Gabrielle Chanel. "Come hell or high water, there is no stopping you, 'Miraculous Mrs. Davis.'"

Clearly, Eloise's stark warning last time they'd met hadn't put a dampener on Lena Davis's thieving ways. The dress was identical to the gown Vianne had toiled so hard over for the past weeks; the metallic thread ribbon work, the flower and circle motifs, the handkerchief hem trimmed with ribbon rosettes were all there, faithfully copied by Mrs. Davis to a T. And in a second, smaller photograph, the model on the page swept her arms out to demonstrate the diaphanous evening cape with contrasting chenille trim!

Mrs. Davis's copyists were quick. The fact that she had an entire team of them meant that she could produce imitations faster than Vianne could dream up her designs. There had been photos of Adriana's dress in the *Evening World*, and the *New York Times*, but clearly, this was not enough to stop Mrs. Davis from her devious ways. And the fact that Eloise's atelier was not even acknowledged made her boiling mad.

Eloise sat rigid at her breakfast table opposite Mama Pepper, in the small apartment on 84th Street that she had worked hard to buy so that she and her mama could have security. She'd never leave her mother out in the cold. The table was laden with the southern breakfast that Mama Pepper still insisted they share each morning.

"Ellie, dear, are you not hearing what I'm saying!" Mama Pepper's voice rasped into Eloise's thoughts and, as usual, would not let go. "I was telling' y'all how my friend Betty Radcliffe and I are fixing to carve out a couple of weeks to float around the continent once this weather improves."

Mama Pepper placed a pecan pie bar on her plate, pushing away her completed meal of fried potatoes and apple-infused ham. She reached for the small glass jar filled with homemade jelly, and a slice of bread, spooning the jelly onto her plate.

"A one-way trip to California only takes thirteen days, Ellie, and we'd stop in Havana, Cuba, on the way. What do you think about that? Oh, I love this decade, darlin'. It's so much better than that darned old war."

Eloise flinched when Mama Pepper reached her hand across the breakfast table, the diamond rings that Ellie's papa bought for her mother when she was still young sparkling on her fingers, and the scent of her rosewater and glycerin balm wafting through the air. Mama Pepper had decorated the apartment rooms with clean, crisp white paint, wicker furniture just like she'd had at home in the Texan ranch, overstuffed couches covered in cream silk to match the silk drapes, and a large dining table with plenty of seating for her friends. On the side tables she always had fresh flowers, and the ceramic lamps that dotted the room lent a warm and cozy air in New York's colder months.

In need of some outside air, Eloise stood up and went to the closed window, pulling up the sash and leaning out to 84th Street below.

"Oh, darling. You are welcome to come with us, you know," Mama Pepper continued. "Any daughter of mine is a friend of Betty's. And she's proud of you, as you know I am, Ellie. You needn't go over there and look so sore about it. Of course, you're welcome. In fact, I might invite several more of my old friends." Pepper clicked her tongue and busied herself with her bread and pie and jam.

Eloise leaned on the balustrade, her heart contracting at Mama Pepper's big-hearted kindness, as endless as the Texan skies. She would always admire and try to emulate her mother's manners, the way she treated others with respect. Those old Southern values would always be a part of Mama Pepper, and Eloise strove to keep them close. Her father's sudden plan to pull Pepper out of Texas and bring her to New York had not altered Eloise's mother in any way at all. She simply lived the life of a Southern woman here in New York as best she could, while marveling at all the changes going on around her and taking a keen interest in keeping up. It was why Eloise adored her mother, and it was why she always listened to her advice.

But how was she supposed to marry the intrinsic honesty and respectability on which she'd built the very foundations of her business when her ideas were being appropriated—no, stolen by the likes of Lena Davis, and the woman was showing no signs of slowing down?

She sighed. Down below, the street bustled as usual, cars honking, folks rushing here, there, and everywhere. Her plan to showcase Vianne Mercier's extraordinary talents had backfired and appeared to have advanced Mrs. Davis further ahead.

What was more, Adeline had made several snide comments about Vianne and Giorgio Conti. Eloise's stomach had curled with concern, but she had put paid to Adeline's insinuations on the spot. If she, Ellie, saw anything with her own two eyes, that would be different, but she operated on a basis of trust with all her seamstresses, and her instincts were that Vianne was a good person who would not do the business's reputation any harm. Eloise had already spoken to the girl, and Vianne had acknowledged the expectations placed upon her. Eloise would not have nastiness amongst her seamstresses, and she suspected Adeline was jealous of the wildly talented Parisian girl.

Eloise frowned. If only everyone lived by the generous values that Mama Pepper lived by, the world would be a much simpler place! But New York was moving at a hectic pace. The modern world had no time for yesterday's news, or yesterday's designers, and no one would care a jot if some seamstress from the Upper East Side cried foul and accused miraculous Mrs. Davis of ripping off Eloise's designs. You were top of the town one minute, bottom the next. Lena Davis was going to propel herself to the grandest heights and she didn't care who she trod over on her way.

And worse, New York was run by mobsters anyway. To survive in this decade, you had to swim with the sharks or be drowned.

But what if Eloise didn't want to swim in the same pool as the sharks? What if she didn't want to lower herself to Mrs. Davis's level?

"Sweetheart? You've hardly spoken a word since you woke up."

Eloise closed her eyes and turned to face her mama. "It's that woman again, Mama." There was no point hiding things. Eloise was a great believer that problems were better out than in. She held no truck with secrets, which is why she found Lena Davis's behavior so infuriating. "I just don't know." She turned back to face Mama Pepper. "Am I too old for this business? When I see my creations being shown all over town by someone else, I lose all my confidence." She lowered her voice. "I'm struggling to design."

Mama Pepper placed her knife back down before she spoke with great care, expressing the beautiful table manners she'd always upheld. "You're never too old until you tell yourself that it's so. I think you need to go one step higher than that copycat."

Eloise stifled a smile. "That copycat." If only she could see things in as black-and-white terms as her mama did. The last few days, she'd sat at her desk and drawn blanks. Every time she tried to design, all she'd see was Lena Davis's face, and her models blazing about in Eloise's and Vianne's gowns. There seemed little point in trying anything new because Lena Davis would steal it and emblazon it with her name. Eloise was almost at the point of letting Vianne do all the designing to keep the atelier afloat, and to ensure the girls would all have jobs. Eloise knew she owed them that.

But still, that would not stop Lena in her tracks. Eloise pressed her fingers to her temple. There seemed to be no answer to this.

She moved heavily across the pretty room and slumped down at the breakfast table, but her mother raised a tinted auburn brow. "Why, darling, you must make a splash of your own that will rival that woman and send her spinning right back down to the bottom of the pile where copycats belong."

Eloise shook her head. "I thought that Adriana Conti's dress might do that. But I was wrong." She reached for her cigarette holder, only to place it back down, aware of her mama's disapproving frown.

"Oh, you're never going to get where you want to get with *one* dress," Mama Pepper said, lowering her voice and folding her hands on the table in front of her in the way Eloise's papa used to when he was closing a cattle deal. "Darling, when I said you need to make a splash, I meant you've got to dive in head-first, no holds barred, and drown the woman once and for all."

Eloise waved her hands in the air and laughed, in spite of herself. "Oh, Mama. I do adore you, but sometimes you make no sense at all."

"My sweet, you need to outclass her." Mama Pepper nodded

her dyed auburn head, her red lips curling into a winning smile. "You need to host a grand fashion parade."

Eloise lifted her head.

Mama Pepper's voice was deadly low and deadly serious. "Schedule it for spring. Invite everyone who's anyone, collaborate with the charming Vianne Mercier to design a full collection, and show everything in one fell swoop. Have a signature look and that will make it much harder for this woman to copy you. At the moment," Mama Pepper said, "you are designing to please your clientele, rather than breaking out and coming up with the dresses you want to create in a style of your own, like Gabrielle Chanel, or the like. But this Vianne Mercier, she's capable of doing just that, and I think you are as well."

Eloise tapped her fingers on the table.

"Go see Robert Powers, hire professional models and find somewhere spectacular to host your show. Then, *everyone* will know these are your designs, Ellie. Not the work of Lena Rogers. Invite the press. She won't have a hope of passing your work off as her own if you are splashed all over New York as the woman who designed your garments first." Mama Pepper regarded Eloise. "What about Valentino's? I had the most wonderful luncheon there last week. And you know that the young man who owns it is a Rudolph Valentino dream."

Eloise chewed on her lip. *Somewhere spectacular to host it...*

Her heart stilled. The restaurant was the talk of the town.

"But the cost," Eloise murmured.

"Get Mrs. Conti to take a share in the profits. She and her son will love the publicity."

Eloise felt a sudden rush of energy. Could it work? Could Mama Pepper have just had the most ingenious idea?

Eloise stumbled over her words. "We could make it spectacular. Theme it. Magical Paris. Giorgio's Italian food is something marvelous, but I wonder if Vianne could talk to him about Parisian recipes." She bit back Adeline's prattle about Vianne. Vianne was a talented girl who could pull off a collection that would leave Lena Davis for dead.

Mama Pepper placed her coffee cup down in her saucer. "Now, if you'll excuse me, my darling, I have to go see Betty, and talk with her about this cruise we're both mad about. Not that anyone's interested, it seems, except me."

But Eloise already had her leather notebook out. She'd drawn a line down the middle of a page.

"Ellie?"

Eloise looked up at her mother, standing, resplendent in the doorway.

"I'm in a mind to meet this Vianne Mercier. Care to introduce me, soon?" Mama Pepper said.

Eloise sent her mother a winning smile. "She's charming. A real asset, and a hard-working sort of girl. I only hope the other girls can handle having her about the place. I'm aware there could be a touch of jealousy from Adeline, and I'm keepin' a close eye on it."

"Then don't let your girl go," Mama Pepper said. She turned out the door, and Eloise chuckled at the sound of her mother whistling all the way up the hallway to her bedroom.

Vianne stood by the window in the apartment above East 63rd Street. Snow had fallen during the night, and now it lay still and white as a cloud. Memories of vacations her family used to take to Val d'Isère floated in Vianne's mind, when she'd fallen about laughing with Anaïs and Jacques, pelting snowballs, their breath curling white into the cold air, before wrapping up warmly with Maman and taking sleigh rides, Vianne's small hand tucked safely into her mother's. She'd felt as safe holding Maman's hand as a girl in a castle protected by an unsurpassable moat.

Vianne tore herself from the unusually quiet New York vista outside. The lamplights still burned in the street. She grimaced at the thought of another day spent near Adeline. Vianne knew she should ignore the girl, but the embroiderer's knowing looks were unsettling. Adeline would brush past Vianne in the workroom, snide rumors slipping off her tongue, just loud enough for the other girls to hear and raise their heads. She'd whispered about Vianne's preference for Italians and her need to be the center of attention, both in the atelier and when it came to New York men. Adeline had even suggested it might be more apt to go down to the Village with Lucia to flirt with the boys of her own class than aim for Giorgio Conti, who was far too good for unimportant Vianne.

Vianne gathered her handbag. Wasn't there an argument for being entirely sick of knowing one's place in the world? After all, empires had toppled during the war, monarchies had collapsed. Women were voting, cutting their hair, they'd thrown out their corsets, years ago. And surely, by coming all the way to New York, finding work, and success, meant she'd cast off being viewed as insignificant Vianne.

She made her way downstairs to the atelier and stopped at the entrance to the workroom. Despite her circular thoughts, she smiled at the whirr of the sewing machines, and the dear, familiar sight of Lucia carefully measuring patterns, while Miss Ellie leaned over her and inspected her work, until her gaze landed on Adeline.

"Well, good morning, Vianne," Miss Ellie said. She looked up, taking off her eyeglasses and folding her arms over her green two-piece ensemble. "Now we are all here, I want to talk about our spring and summer collection, and I have some exciting news that I think will delight you all."

Vianne sat down at her worktable, forcing herself not to react to the way Adeline sniggered at the fact she'd arrived last to work this morning. She'd sat up late, legs crossed on her bed, sketching designs. It was her most creative time, and she guarded it carefully.

She held her head up, despite Adeline's stares, and waited for Miss Ellie to go on.

"I've decided to hold a fashion parade."

There was a silence amongst the girls.

"Our entire summer collection will be modeled and paraded for the press, for our clients and for a crowd of guests." Miss Ellie folded her arms, her eyes shining.

Lucia placed her pencil down. "In one of the department stores, Miss Ellie?" she breathed.

"Not quite," Miss Ellie said, "I'm fixing to hold it in Valentino's."

Vianne was still.

"The Contis have graciously agreed." Miss Ellie clasped her

hands together and the weak winter sun caught on her auburn hair. "And here's the exciting part, we are going to give the parade a Parisian summer theme."

Vianne smoothed down her skirt. A Parisian theme in Giorgio's Italian restaurant? She felt the need to fan her face with her hand.

But Miss Ellie was paying no heed to Vianne's confusion. "Eddie Winter has promised to give us a double spread in *Bella* magazine. I only hope we can build anticipation and attract journalists from the *New York Times* as well as from newspapers and fashion magazines well beyond Manhattan." She waved her arm in the general direction of the Upper East Side right outside the window. "I'm in a mind to have big dreams, girls. And I want you all right by my side."

Vianne curled her fingers in her lap. She kept her gaze stock-still on Miss Ellie, her stomach roiling. The Plaza? Macy's? Surely, they'd be the perfect venues for Miss Ellie's fashion parade... Vianne was working hard to bury the feelings she had for Giorgio, and she'd hoped that even though they worked across the road from each other, their paths may not cross directly again. In turn, Vianne was certain this would douse the insinuations surrounding Adeline's barely veiled remarks. But now, she was going to be thrown straight back into the lion's den.

Miss Ellie's eyes shone. "Vianne. We'll need sportswear, daywear, evening gowns, and..." she lowered her voice. "You can do a bridal gown for me as well."

"Suitably apt if Giorgio Conti will be watching," Adeline murmured. "Perhaps he'll use it as inspiration, for the bride he does marry, so that poor Vianne can see how her dreams were nothing but ill-founded fluff."

Vianne stiffened.

Miss Ellie's eyes shot to her embroiderer. "Adeline, Vianne will consult with you as to beading and embroidery for each garment."

Adeline nodded; her eyebrows raised to the roof. "Of course, Miss Ellie. You know I will never let you down, and as I have no other distractions, I'll give my all to your parade and the gowns."

Miss Ellie's brow knitted, but she turned to the other girls. "Mollie and Goldie, Vianne and I will ensure that you will be able to complete the garments to the timeframe. I have a date set for the spring, and Lucia, I want you to throw everything you have into the patterns we'll need for the designs prior to them being mocked up in calico. The volume of work will be challenging, but you know what to do."

Lucia clasped her hands together and Vianne sent the girl a warm smile. If Lucia ever heard any of Adeline's veiled remarks, she quite rightly ignored them, and Vianne loved her for it.

Miss Ellie leant a hand against the worktable. "A Parisian summer." Her eyes took on a wistful expression. "Imagine. You know, so many people around here adore France."

"So it seems. Some of the Italian locals are quite smitten apparently," Adeline muttered.

Vianne's breath caught.

"Vianne, you will consult with the Contis, particularly with Giorgio..." Miss Ellie appeared not to have heard Adeline's aside. "I want you to advise him on a suitable French luncheon menu for our guests. I'm sending you over there this afternoon, dear. You can tell them exactly what you'd have for lunch on a summer's day in Paris, and I want you to give the Contis some ideas for Parisian décor, for the decorations. Of course, I will oversee things. You can be sure of that." Miss Ellie sent Vianne a pointed stare. "I trust that will be acceptable to you, and that you will be happy to assist us in creating an authentic Parisian experience?"

Adeline snorted. "I'm not sure happy is the right word. Rhapsodic, perhaps?"

Miss Ellie shot the girl a glance. "Is there something I should be worried about, Adeline?"

"No, no," Adeline coughed, her blue eyes dancing. "Not a thing, Miss Ellie. You have nothing to worry about when it comes to *me*."

Vianne stood up and moved over to the edge of the room,

fighting the urge to press her flaming cheeks against the icy windows.

"Your thoughts on the French theme, girls?" Miss Ellie said.

"Well, I guess we'll all follow Vianne's lead," Adeline said. "And hope that she leads us well when it comes to marrying French and Italian arrangements."

Vianne shot the girl a look from underneath her eyelashes. To her horror, she saw Mollie and Goldie's heads swiveling from Vianne to Adeline and back.

"I think it's grand," Lucia said, oblivious to Adeline's undertones, and rubbing her hands together, her brown eyes lighting up. "A proper fashion parade inspired by Paris will be just the thing."

Vianne lifted her head. "I have an idea," she said.

There was silence. Out of the corner of her eye, Vianne felt Adeline's eyes watching her.

"Wonderful." Miss Ellie sent Adeline a reprimanding glance. "I'm always glad to hear constructive comments."

Vianne offered Miss Ellie a smile. "How about an opening with three dresses—one red, one white, one blue?"

The room was quiet.

"Three models," Vianne continued, "spinning on a moving base to the sound of traditional French accordion music, the sort of music that takes you right to the edge of the Seine on a summer night."

A flurry of wind fluted against the windows and Vianne was transported back to the banks of the Seine.

"Then, the music swells and we bring out the sportswear and then the daywear collection, but what if we start each new section with three models spinning on the spot? It would allow the viewers to see the featured garments in each collection from every angle at the outset, and the colors of the French flag... maybe we could decorate the room in the tricolors—red tulips, creamy white roses and blue hyacinths for spring. And I have ideas for food, because *le dejeuner*—lunchtime—in France is the most important meal of the day."

"Anything else?" Adeline cut in. "Would you like to host the parade, lecture us all about standards of behavior and take over Miss Ellie's role?"

There was silence.

Vianne could feel it, she was blushing visibly, but she held her chin up, her eyes locked with Miss Ellie's.

Miss Ellie laid her hand on Adeline's shoulder. "The only person who is on a soapbox today is you, Adeline. If you have something constructive and helpful to contribute to the conversation, then I'd like to hear it. We all would. But if you insist on undermining me at every turn when I am holding an important discussion, then I will have no choice but to assume you no longer wish to work here. Do I make myself clear?"

Adeline lifted her chin. Vianne was certain she saw the girl sneer at her.

But the other girls stared at Miss Ellie and Adeline in astonishment. Soon, Lucia sent Vianne a small shrug.

"Would you like to slip over to Valentino's now, please, Vianne," Miss Ellie said.

Vianne gathered her coat and moved toward the door, only to halt at the sound of Miss Ellie's voice.

"We are fortunate to have Vianne come to join us. Her expertise, her dedication and her designs are already lifting the profile of the atelier, and that will only help secure your futures here. I am pleased with the way that Lucia, Mollie and Goldie have all made Vianne feel welcome. We will all value your expertise when it comes to our Parisian-themed parade, Vianne."

Vianne turned around to face them all. "I'll do everything in my power to help make this an authentic French parade. You can rely on me, Miss Ellie."

Miss Ellie's eyes locked with Vianne's. "I know I can, Vianne."

Vianne's breath hitched, but she nodded at the older woman, and then turned and made her way out of the atelier.

. . .

A few moments later, Vianne came to a rushing standstill in the lobby of the Contis' building. Through the doors, Valentino's would be cool, modern, serene, but out here, Vianne was flustered, breathless, determined.

Miss Ellie trusted her, but Vianne was bound by traditional rules. She was tied to them. A seamstress must not socialize with wealthy clientele, and as for falling in love with an eminent New York businessman? Vianne may as well raise her glass and drown herself in a vat of bathtub gin. Adeline might have crossed a line when it came to pushing Miss Ellie too far today, but Vianne knew how she'd felt when she danced in Giorgio's arms. She had to make sure such a thing never happened again.

And now, she was about to see him and test her resolve.

She took a breath and raised her gloved hand to the restaurant's door, before knocking firmly three times. She would be professional, polite, discuss the Parisian luncheon menu and then walk right back across the road to where she belonged.

But when her eyes landed on Giorgio Conti, striding through Valentino's toward her, flicking on lights in a white shirt with his sleeves rolled up and his black hair slightly tousled, Vianne's hand dropped to her side, and she took a step back, drawing in a deep breath.

He came to a standstill opposite her behind the doors for a few moments, a frown line darting between his deep brown eyes, before he reached forward, unlocked the double glass doors, and held them open for her to step inside.

"Vianne." The lights of Valentino's shone on his dark hair, surrounded by the unusual hush that the paneled woodwork seemed to create in the magical restaurant, while outside, snow fluttered from the gray clouds through the freezing winter's air.

"Hello, Giorgio. Miss Ellie is very happy that you are hosting her fashion parade," Vianne said. "I won't keep you. She asked me to come and suggest some French dishes for the luncheon menu." Vianne took a breath. She was gabbling.

Giorgio's mouth twisted into a wry smile, and he looked down at the ground. "Well, I'd hate to hinder you or slow you down in any way, Vianne." He flicked his gaze back up to meet hers.

Vianne took in an involuntary breath. "You are not holding me up."

He flinched, his eyes, unfathomable, searching hers for a long moment. "I don't understand," he murmured. "I don't understand why you rushed off after we danced. I know that running away is not the answer to this, Vianne. If there is anything worrying you, I'd rather you told me so. And if I've offended you, I'm sorry."

Vianne swallowed. The truth was, she missed the way he called her *Bella*. Vianne didn't sound right when it rolled off his tongue, but she could hardly tell him that after she'd asked him to stop.

"You haven't done anything wrong," she said. "Oh, Giorgio, let's just discuss this menu, and then, I must get back to work."

Giorgio's gaze lingered on her for one long moment. "I'll bring our head chef, Lino, up to my office."

Vianne nodded, her hands knotting tight in front of her blue coat, the thought of sitting in Giorgio's office in close proximity seeming stifling somehow. "Why not show me your kitchens? I am happy to talk with Lino in the place where he works."

"The last place you want to go is down to the kitchens," he said, sending her a smile, by way of explanation, perhaps.

"I am a working woman, Giorgio," Vianne replied, her words coming out strong and clear. After all, was this not the cause of the problem? Did not the fact that she was a working woman mean she was not good enough for him? Had she come to New York with her parents and sat waiting for a beau in her father's apartment, then, she would be a suitable girl for Giorgio Conti, she supposed. She looked up at the straight, unrelenting lines that patterned the ceiling. "Just as your head chef is a working man, I am the same. I have no qualms in meeting him in his kitchen. It would be an honor for me, and more authentic if we met down there, don't you think?"

"Are you sure?" he said, his eyes locked with hers.

Vianne nodded. "Quite sure." Her eyes, she knew, held the

steel that her mother and Anaïs used to bring on at the pull of a thread. "I am happy to meet your head chef on his own terms, as an equal."

Giorgio's eyes were bright. "No woman has been down to Valentino's kitchens before. I am sorry, but—" He held his hands wide.

"Then why not let me be the first," she said, her voice softening.

He rubbed the back of his neck, but then led her out through the restaurant, into a side hallway, and down a flight of stairs.

The moment they hit the basement floor, Vianne's senses were assailed with the scent of delicious cooking. She followed Giorgio through a cool basement room, bottles of wine stored in the polished shelving that lined all four walls, a Persian rug spread over the flagstones, and a wide table with glass decanters was set atop this. There was something almost magical and reverent about this hushed, quiet space below the bustling city of New York, but the atmosphere in the quiet room shattered the moment Giorgio opened the door to the kitchens. The sounds of chefs chopping, someone barking orders, knives scraping, pots bubbling, and steam spreading out through the door into the wine room had Vianne stopping in her tracks. She pasted on a smile and hesitated, her fingers and toes tingling with nerves. But Giorgio, like a true gentleman, stood aside for her to go into the kitchens first.

Vianne took a step into the hot, sweaty room and stopped like a fox caught in a trap. Every head in the kitchen lifted, every working hand stilled, every one of the kitchen staff was male and the expression on all their faces matched. *Unadulterated shock.*

Vianne attempted a smile and removed her gloves.

"This is Vianne Mercier," Giorgio said. "Miss Mercier will be helping Head Chef Lino and I design the menu for the fashion parade we are hosting in April. Please, welcome Miss Mercier here."

Vianne sent the men a brave smile, men with lined faces and ashen skin in their sixties, to boys who looked barely out of school, their pink cheeks were so flushed. *"Bonjour,"* she said, slipping back to her French without thinking, and wiping a hand over the blond tendrils of hair that peeped out from her navy hat.

The men only gaped at her in silence, and she let out a little laugh, trying to think, for goodness' sake, how coolly and smoothly Anaïs would handle this situation. Anaïs, so used to having men fall at her feet. Maman, who would have made a grand joke or charmed them by asking if she could taste their soups and starters!

But before Vianne could come up with any witty asides, Giorgio was moving, his long legs striding through the steamy, filmy air.

Vianne had no choice but to follow him. She could hardly stand there on her own. She paced along beside Giorgio, fighting an overwhelming urge to pull off her cashmere coat and loosen the top button on her blouse against the heat down here. A line of sweat already beaded her upper lip by the time they came to a standstill at the end of the kitchen, and a tall young man with huge brown eyes came forward to greet Giorgio and raised his brows at the sight of Vianne.

"Vianne," Giorgio said. "Meet my head chef, Lino."

"Charmed," she said, finding her voice, and thrusting out her hand to the young man. He was taller than everyone in the room, and he had that unmistakable air of authority, despite the fact he didn't look much older than her.

Giorgio clapped his head chef on the back, barked to the kitchen to get back to work, told the sous chef to get everyone in line, and led Vianne into a small room off the kitchen, with an antique wooden desk, a pile of loose papers containing what were clearly recipes stacked upon its top, and a bookshelf filled with cook books in front of which stood a coat rack with a brown coat and hat. Vianne wondered how many hours Lino spent hidden away in this office, and she couldn't imagine what recipes he dreamed up here. For a moment, she felt a streak of kinship toward Lino and she was slightly humbled when he invited her to sit down in his creative space.

"You have my chair, Giorgio," Lino offered, his wide mouth moving into a smile.

"No, no, I wouldn't dream of it," Giorgio said, his vowels elongated and his tone as expansive as it was charming. "Please. Sit down at your own desk, and I'll perch on the edge."

Giorgio crossed his legs and leaned against Lino's desk, picking up a glass paperweight. "Now," he said, lowering his voice. "Vianne's boss, the inimitable Madame Chappelle, is planning on inviting all the big cheeses to her fashion parade. The menu's got to be entirely French, it's going to take some planning, and we want to get it right. Because I like the idea of collaborating with Miss Ellie for many parades in the future, don't you think so, Vianne?" He tilted his head to one side, his smile endearingly crooked.

Vianne raised a brow, determined to keep this professional. "Well, I'm glad you think it's a good idea, Giorgio, because I know Madame Chappelle has grand plans for her event."

Giorgio rolled up his sleeves a little further and sent Vianne a grin. "Wonderful," he said softly.

"I think so," Vianne replied, removing her gloves and placing them down on the table.

"Tell me," Giorgio murmured. "What does she have in mind when it comes to the luncheon menu?"

"I doubt she has anything special in mind, since she's not French," Vianne said, her Parisian accent kicking in and her blue eyes sparkling, she knew it, right at him. "This is why I am here."

Giorgio offered her a bemused smile.

She removed her hat and sat back, crossing her long legs. "Lino," she said, addressing the head chef, a sense of enjoyment rushing through her, as if she were born to be planning business functions. She unbuttoned her coat, her navy costume with its calf-length skirt practical and cool in the warm room. "Do you have any French recipes in your repertoire that you'd like to cook for the luncheon? Because, of course, I have many ideas."

The young head chef sent her a smile. "I'm Tuscan," he said, raising his hands in the air as if in mock self-defense. "Like Giorgio, who is from Milano, my father owned a restaurant in Florence. I love to cook my country's cuisine, introducing this to Americans, but, when it comes to French food, I have great respect for the traditions of the great chef, Auguste Escoffier."

Vianne sat forward, her eyes lighting up. "Well then. Escoffier believed that wonderful cuisine should be accessible to all people, so calling on his traditions will be especially relevant when it comes to the luncheon we are talking about. I'm sure he'd be delighted to know that you are cooking using his methods for Miss Chappelle's wonderful female clientele." There was a lull in the din outside in the kitchen, and for a moment, she felt as if she, Lino, and Giorgio were the only three people in the world.

Lino held her gaze. "Escoffier believed in simplifying high-class food, getting rid of the elaborate garnishes and rich sauces that could detract from the flavors and the look of a dish."

Vianne nodded. "Of course. My father was a great believer in these ideals himself. He loved every meal of the day and introduced me to some of the French classics. He taught me that simple food could be beautiful if the ingredients were beautiful too. That was before the war." She fought back a tear that wanted to streak down her cheek. How Papa had loved his food before everything had changed! Suddenly, she was overwhelmed with nostalgia for Paris. Perhaps it was this room, the antique desk, the way they were sitting here talking about French cuisine.

"Of course," Lino said, his eyes softening.

"Lino, Giorgio," she said, "I want to make sure that we honor France, so I would suggest we consider some of the most famous French recipes there are. Perhaps we could investigate some starters such as Coquilles Saint-Jacques, which are gratineed scallops, or a delicious bouillabaisse and perhaps a soupe à l'oignon, followed by some entrée choices including salade niçoise, cheese soufflés, coq au vin, confit de canard, or boeuf bourguignon. Moules marinières, which is a big bowl of mussels cooked in white wine served with shallots and parsley, is also enormously popular in France. All very simple, beautiful and classic dishes."

"My mouth is watering, Vianne," Giorgio said, his eyes intent on her.

Vianne nodded, turning her gaze away from him while she was feeling nostalgic for home. She would remain businesslike and professional at all costs. "Well, you must not forget the most important part: dessert. I would recommend tarte Tatin, or crème anglaise, chocolate soufflé, perhaps crêpes, and my favorite, crème brûlée."

Lino looked up from the notepad he'd filled with ideas while she'd talked.

"Yes," Giorgio said. "What a wonderful accompaniment this would be for your sensational designs."

"Miss Ellie's designs," Vianne corrected him, biting her lip.

"Miss Ellie tells me you will be designing several pieces," Giorgio said.

"To a collaboration, then," Lino's voice cut in.

"To a collaboration," she whispered.

Giorgio smiled at her, and a flush spread over her cheeks. She couldn't help feeling excited about the project, while she knew a small part of that excitement was at the thought of spending more time with Giorgio, however much she tried to deny it.

A half-hour later, Vianne walked back through Valentino's to the glass doors that would lead her back outside into the falling snow.

Giorgio came to a standstill by the doors, his head on one side.

Vianne opened her mouth to say goodbye, but he held up a hand.

"Vianne," he said. He cleared his throat. "Have you been out to Long Island yet?"

Vianne folded her arms. Long Island was one of the most glamorous places in New York. She'd heard the other girls chatter about the fabulous parties, the wildly beautiful mansions that overlooked Long Island Sound, not that any of her fellow seamstresses had ever been close to receiving an invitation to go to anything of the sort. But their clientele moved in those circles. Many of the wealthy Upper East Siders who came for fittings talked casually of their charmed lives, summers filled with ritzy house parties on Long Island, winters spent taking in the theaters, the restaurants, the crazy parties in New York.

"You haven't got to know New York until you've been to Long Island," he continued.

"I think that's what you said about the jazz clubs," she murmured. She was caught in the middle here, wanting to spend more time with Giorgio, but knowing she couldn't.

His eyes lit up, fine lines spreading out from them. "I may have. Because it worked, and you came out with us."

Vianne stood still. She interlinked her fingers and took in a deep breath. The best way to deal with this would be to tell the truth. "I can't break Miss Ellie's rules," she said. "And I'm afraid that Miss Ellie does not approve of my spending time with her clients... nor their sons. So, I'll have to go see Long Island some other time. I must go, Giorgio."

Giorgio came one step closer. "You are kidding me, *Bella?*"

She squeezed her eyes shut at the way he called her that, but she lifted her chin. "It's the truth, Giorgio. I won't risk my career."

Giorgio rubbed a hand over his chin. "But what if it was entirely innocent? What if you came out to Long Island on a Sunday, when Valentino's and the atelier are both closed? How could Miss Ellie possibly worry about that? I could take you to a party sometime. Introduce you to some new clientele for the atelier." He lowered his voice. "The moment they laid eyes on you, you'd have them all wanting you to design their new season's wardrobes."

Vianne folded her hands in front of her skirt. She looked away, her insides quivering at the thought of Adeline and her catty asides. "I've too much to lose, Giorgio," she said.

But he shook his head. "Vianne, forgive me, but in the nicest possible way, Miss Ellie does not own you, and she needs to keep *me* on side so she can have her parade in my restaurant."

Vianne's eyes rounded. "Giorgio!"

"Besides, there is the fact that my mother wants to adopt you," Giorgio whispered. "That black-and-white dress? She can't but help brag to all her friends how the sensational Parisian designer is one of the most talented people she's ever met. Imagine if you could have a hundred women like my mother all shouting about how wonderful you are all over New York? At a party at Long Island, they'd all be in one room. And," he added, "you wouldn't be alone with me. So, you see, there'd be no risk of upsetting your Miss Ellie."

Vianne fiddled with her necklace. Giorgio was so convincing she was almost believing him herself. What a businessman he was.

"Let me keep my ear to the ground," he whispered. "And next time there's going to be a fabulous party on Long Island Sound, why don't you come out for the day and see what the Jazz Age is really about."

Vianne shrugged. "Perhaps. We'll see," she whispered, knowing her French accent was coming to the fore. "But if I were to come see this Long Island Sound, it would only be for business purposes to benefit my boss."

"*Perfecto*," he whispered. "Until next time. *Ciao*, Vianne." He lifted her hand and grazed it with a gentle kiss.

Vianne rushed away before she could agree to anything else when it came to Giorgio Conti, and the way he had of making her change her mind.

CHAPTER FOURTEEN
AMELIE, APRIL, 1925

Amelie tucked the thick cream envelope deep into the pocket of her cardigan. She smiled at Duncan, the postman, and curled her fingers around the chubby hand of his little son, Hamish. Hamish had been a godsend to her this past winter, his company a delight during the rainy Highland days, with their foggy mornings, magnificent rainbows, and atmospheric clouds, days that had been made beautiful by the gray, snowy hills all lit up with beautiful Douglas fir.

But no matter how lovely the view, she'd realized she'd go mad sitting inside all day while Archie was busy managing the Carrig estate. And when Duncan had told her that his wife had begun working in the general store in the village, Amelie had stepped in and offered to look after Hamish while his father delivered the mail.

Amelie stood with Hamish near the bridge over the River Clois, watching Duncan wobble off on his bicycle, the mail packed in bags on a carrier that sat over the back wheel. She led Hamish up the fresh green lawn that ran up the slope to Carrig, dotted with cherry trees, whose pink-hued blossoms were vivid against the bright blue sky. Spring bulbs fluted in the sun at their feet, while across the glen, snow-capped mountains and hills full of flowers sat serene.

Amelie's fingers curled over the envelope in her pocket. Scotland, sleepy, cold, achingly beautiful in winter, was coming to life in the spring. As summer rolled closer, there would be a whole host of events—Highland Games, weekly farmers' markets, church stalls—and she, as Archie's new wife, would be expected to take part. She'd already staved off requests to help at the village church, and to contribute on committees for the spring fair, but she knew that some of her neighbors viewed her reluctance to throw herself into village life as reclusive, and this only added fuel to some people's gossiping about the fact she was French, aloof, and would never fit into Scottish country life. The last thing she wanted to be seen as was Archie's bad choice, but, if she did not move out of the safe circle of people she'd placed around herself—Archie, Caitlin, her mother-in-law Mary—she'd risk the locals viewing her in exactly that way. A mistake.

Archie had pounded off early this morning, leaving a light kiss on Amelie's forehead at breakfast, while gearing up for a day's fishing at the loch. He'd gone off with his ghillie and Caitlin's husband Malcolm, promising to bring home fresh trout or pike.

Amelie stopped, letting Hamish run around the lawn, his arms spread out like an airplane. She pulled out the thick envelope, tore it open, her eyes scanning the embossed card.

> *Mr. and Mrs. Angus Fife*
> *At Home*
> *For Annabel aynd Clyde*
> *Friends from Scotland and France*

Amelie frowned; her eyes stuck on the last line. *Friends from Scotland and France*. She took in a shaking breath and lifted her eyes from the card in her hand.

Hamish circled back to her.

"Sweet boy," she said, bending down, shoving the invitation

back in her pocket and pushing back some of his stray blond curls. He raised his extraordinary brown eyes toward her, and they lit up.

"What are we going to do today, Melie?"

She laughed out loud at the joyous way he spoke her name, even though her stomach curled at the firecracker that this party of the Fifes could turn out to be. "I thought we'd go and raid the kitchen, Hamish, do some more French cooking this morning. What do you think about that?"

The little boy's eyes nearly popped out of his head. "Aye, I'd love that. What are we making then?"

"You dear wee thing," Amelie said, the Scottish word slipping off her tongue as if she were already the long-standing Scottish landowner's wife that she hoped to always be. "Why, I thought we'd make crêpes, and we'll have them for morning tea. We'll serve them the way my mother used to, with lemon and sugar..." Her eyes misted over, and she bit on her lip. Maman would always bring out her pretty blue and white china for crêpes. They were her specialty, and she would don an apron and go into the kitchen to make them herself, pouring the batter into a thin stream in the pan, while Anaïs and Vianne would watch her, standing on wooden stools, their hands clasped together in anticipation of the crisp, thin, perfect crêpes that their mother turned out.

Amelie felt the warmth of Hamish's small hand in her palm. "Come on, Melie."

Amelie swallowed back her tears, locked her memories away, and followed her young companion up the slope to Carrig.

"Afterwards," she whispered, "we'll go out to the fields to see Gabriel," her voice softening at the thought of spending time with the gentle Palomino horse that Archie had bought her when the long winter came to an end. The sense of freedom she felt at riding him around the estate was going a long way to strengthening her connection with the sweeping Scottish landscape. The feeling of giving him his head and allowing him free rein to gallop, his hooves thudding on the rich, fertile earth, was something she never thought she'd experience again. "You can feed him an apple if you like, and I'll let you ride him on the lead rein, and then we'll sit in the sun, in Archie's old playroom and draw all afternoon."

Hamish squeezed her hand, and she squeezed it back as if her life depended upon it.

Perhaps it did.

She didn't tell him how she used to sit with her younger sister and show Vianne how to draw, and she didn't tell him how that small sister of hers had shown a prodigious talent for sketching, and how Anaïs had watched, astounded, while the little girl with her white-blond hair had sat in her pinafores and produced perfect reproductions of animals, flowers, anything she could put her mind to. Until she'd started conjuring up ideas of her own—dresses and exquisite costumes like the ones she'd seen at the ballet. Amelie could only imagine what her brave little sister was drawing up now.

Well then. Amelie lifted her chin and marched back up to the house.

Later that afternoon, when the shadows had lengthened across the garden and Hamish had gone home, Amelie sat in Archie's living room, the windows thrown open, filling the room with the scent of spring flowers and the evensong of the birds. Her mother-in-law, Mary Blair, appeared in the open French doors in a soft blue dress, her dancing eyes, eyes that she'd passed onto her son, Archie, now lighting up with warmth.

"I hope you don't mind me popping in, dear," she said, hovering on the threshold of the home she'd called her own for over fifty years.

"Not at all." Amelie stood up from the book she'd been trying to concentrate on and failing and came to kiss her mother-in-law on the cheek.

Mary accepted this, embracing Amelie in turn, but Amelie knew that this was all part of Mary's good nature, for she was certain her mother-in-law had found Amelie's French greetings a little overwhelming when her daughter-in-law first came to Carrig.

"Have you had a wonderful day?" Mary asked.

"Yes." Amelie smiled down at the faded rug on the floor. Because the truth was, she had enjoyed her day with Hamish. The little boy lived in the moment, and Mary, were Amelie to be honest, did the same thing. There was an art to it, and Amelie was more than aware it was eluding her.

She tucked her arm into her mother-in-law's.

"You will have received the invitation to the party at Kinloch," Mary said.

Amelie sighed. "I'll ring for tea."

She saw the way her mother-in-law's expression moved to being genuinely concerned. "Are you managing all right about it?" Mary asked.

"Yes..." Amelie sat down in a deep-red covered sofa, sinking into its plush depths. This room was the old family sitting room, and, apart from the morning room that Archie had insisted that Amelie decorate for herself, here was the room where she felt most at home in the grand old Scottish estate. She could wander the hallways for hours, stand about in empty bedrooms, the nursery, the old playroom, from which Mary had not thrown out any of Archie's old wooden toys, but here, the view out over the glen and then to the mountains was glorious in the afternoons, and the golden sun poured onto the furniture which was made to sink into.

Built for hiding.

Carrig had become her safe cocoon.

"Annabel is bringing friends from Paris." Mary settled down next to her.

Amelie appreciated the way Mary spoke with such directness. It was refreshing, and she'd worked out straight away that her mother-in-law came from a place of love and concern for her. While it was clear that any friend of Archie's was a friend of Mary's, and this, Amelie knew, showed a great faith on the part of a mother in her adult son's ability to make decisions. Also, Mary told her, she'd taken to Amelie after their first encounter.

Amelie had told Mary how she'd lost her family during the war, but she'd not elaborated, and Mary, bless her, had not probed. But Amelie knew that Mary noticed how her new daughter-in-law clammed up at the mention of France, and Amelie appreciated the respect the older woman showed to her treading carefully.

Amelie tapped her hands on the arm of her sofa. "I did suggest that Caitlin alter the party slightly, to turn it into a masked ball."

Mary nodded. "I see." A flurry of emotions passed across her face. "Well, then. How nice."

Amelie took in a shaky breath.

The tea arrived, along with a blue and white china plate filled with oatmeal and honey biscuits. Amelie poured and handed Mary a steaming cup. She sipped at her own tea, having taken to it since she'd moved to Scotland. Perhaps it was part of letting go of France.

"A masked ball will kick off the season very well," Mary said, eyeing Amelie over her porcelain cup "And you will manage, with people coming from..."

Amelie placed her teacup back down in its saucer, the warm handle suddenly feeling hot. "Behind a mask, I can hide the fact that I miss my family so much." This was true. Amelie swallowed the bile that rose to her throat.

She missed her family. But she did not miss Anaïs.

Anaïs had survived. Maman had not. If only it could have been the other way around.

"I hope you feel that you'll be able to make new memories here," Mary said.

The sun dipped behind the mountains, and the warm room was filled with shadows. "I already am," Amelie replied simply. "Scotland is my home now. Archie is everything to me."

Mary moved forward a little in her seat, her stockinged legs in their sensible brown shoes crossed at the ankle. "I am so looking forward to..." Mary cut herself off. "I know I'll never replace your mother, but I am very much hoping that one day, our family might gain—"

"You will make a wonderful grandmother," Amelie said, her instincts rising to the fore, knowing what Mary was referring to. She raised her tawny eyes to meet Mary's. "I could not ask for anyone dearer, or more wonderful."

Mary reached out, placing her wrinkled hand atop Amelie's. "You will manage this party, dear. I will be there, and Archie and I will do everything within our power to ensure you have only good memories from hereon, and, in time, I know that you will be able to only think of the wonderful memories you will always hold close from France."

Amelie felt the sting of tears behind her eyes.

It was all she could do to try to forget.

"So," Caitlin said, bringing a hand up to shade her face from the warm, golden sun, "the guests will be arriving on the Friday evening, and staying for the entire weekend. The first proper house party of the season. And what a weekend it will be!"

Amelie lay back on the tartan picnic rug, the ruins of Urquhart Castle framing the shimmering loch, blue hills sloping away to the east, while whitecaps scudded across the water, as if racing something ephemeral that she could not see.

"I know it's early, but the preparations are well in hand. Annabel says at least thirty friends are coming up from Paris. She lived in the Marais district, near the Place des Vosges. Such a gorgeous part of Paris. Do you know it?"

Amelie stiffened. Her hands gripped the edges of the rug.

Before she could quash the memory, she was back there, back in the apartment on Rue de Sévigné, Maman's laughter ringing through the hall, she and Vianne skipping home from school to the delicious smells of *goûter*, the French afternoon tea, always sweet, that Maman insisted on serving most afternoons at half past four on the dot, unless they were visiting Papa in Celine, and he was taking them to the patisserie for chocolate éclairs. If Anaïs and Amelie were not on time, Maman would become anxious, but her eyes always melted into smiles when they appeared, and she gathered her girls into her arms as if she had not laid eyes on them for months.

Jacques, walking from the boy's school closer to home, would already be there, sitting up in Papa's seat at the head of the table, which he thought a great joke, because Papa was still at Celine.

And Maman would clap her hands, and they would all begin on the sweet treats that were piled on the polished dining table, while the room rang with their voices and tales of the daily dramas at school. She and Jacques, Amelie remembered, her heart skipping a beat, would vie for the juiciest story, the story that would astound Maman the most, causing her to raise her blond eyebrows and exclaim. "*Non! C'est pas vrais!*" No! It is not true!

And, as the oldest, Anaïs would lean forward, waving her baguette filled with delightful squares of chocolate, or her tartine, an open sandwich with jam, or sometimes, a chocolate biscuit and she'd embellish her story until it shone. Always, she'd outdone Jacques. It had been her intention, her aim, and she'd always won. She'd make her stories more and more fantastical until he'd look at her with his adoring brown eyes, and sip on his milk.

Was the fact that she'd somehow won the right to live, in the face of Maman's tragic death, a cruel twist on Anaïs's ability to outshine everyone in her vicinity? Was her survival some awful lesson she needed to learn, while Maman had been slaughtered along with so many of Anaïs's oldest girlfriends and their mothers under the rubble in that beautiful old church?

Winning the lottery of life was a hollow victory when the loss outweighed the wretched gain. She came back to Caitlin's words.

Annabel... lived in the Marais.

Everyone in that part of Paris had known Papa and everyone had heard of Celine. The store was a neighborhood favorite. They'd been a golden family, and Maman was its heart and its light. Everyone would know of the tragedy that had hit the Mercier family at the end of the war, but those well-meaning people would turn into a pack of vipers if they knew that Anaïs was hiding up here in Scotland, and had not told her sister, Vianne, nor her brother, Jacques, let alone Papa, that she was alive.

A physical dart hit Amelie's stomach at the thought of Vianne. As for Jacques... her twin. She couldn't bear the pain of any of her family not knowing she was alive, and yet, were she to go home, they'd not begin to understand what she'd done. She'd break their hearts all over again if she told them the truth about herself and that was something she could not bear to do.

She could hardly look at herself in the mirror. How would she cope if she came face to face with those she loved?

Caitlin lay back, her green eyes staring at the blue sky, and her curls spread out on the rug. "After the winter we've endured, I cannot wait to bring some liveliness to Scotland."

"It's all about bringing people together again," said her husband, Malcolm, his blond hair ruffling in the breeze, and his expression thoughtful. "It's how things used to be. How I'd like things to be going forward. For Kinloch, for our family, for you, darling."

Caitlin reached out and laid her hand on her husband's arm.

Amelie stood up and walked down the steep slope to the very edge of the loch, her sturdy boots imprinting themselves in the soft green grass. She stared out at the water, constantly moving. Why did nothing in this world stand still? The plans she'd made, plans that seemed so secure when she'd met and fallen in love with Archie, were floating out of her grasp like dead leaves from a tree...

When she felt Archie's arms encircling her waist, she leaned her head against his soft argyll sweater.

"Sweetheart," he said. "We don't have to go to this party if it's too soon. I know that seeing people from Paris could be upsetting. Darling..."

Amelie disentangled herself, gently, from his arms. She picked up a stone, threw it, and watched it skim across the surface of the loch.

"Would you like to go away for the weekend, instead? We can give things more time. Caitlin will understand, and we can easily pop down to London, or Bath?"

Amelie turned to face him, her tawny eyes catching with his deep brown irises.

A weekend away? It would solve everything.

She took in a shaking breath and turned back to the loch.

"Sweetheart?" Archie said.

She turned and buried her face in his sweater. Dear, kind man whom she did not deserve. She could not hurt him. She could not act in the often wild, breezy way that Anaïs had done. Here was her chance to start afresh. If Anaïs had gambled with fate and lost everything, then Amelie would not make that same mistake. Amelie would do the opposite. She'd be the steady, sensible person Anaïs had never been.

The Scottish sky soared overhead. The crystal-clear water lapped at the rocks on the shore.

Amelie closed her eyes. "Of course, we'll go to the party, Archie. Caitlin and Malcolm would be hurt if we didn't go. I'll be there."

She'd conjure up the most elaborate disguise she could. No one would recognize her, and she'd manage, she'd not let her fears stop her. Most of all, she'd not risk her future in Scotland, even though she'd always have to protect herself from the girl she'd been in the past.

CHAPTER FIFTEEN
VIANNE, SPRING, 1925

Vianne surveyed the designs she'd conjured up for Miss Ellie's Parisian summer fashion parade, her eyes roaming over her collection of two-piece ensembles, complete with this season's double-breasted longer-line coats, her striped sports skirts with overblouses featuring the latest Peter Pan collars for tennis, and even a carefully curated set of riding habits, with breeches in checked linen, green, red or tan, with sleeveless coats over smart sports-shirts and Windsor ties. She looked at these wistfully for a moment. How Anaïs would have loved such gorgeous attire.

Vianne closed her eyes, pictures of Anaïs galloping across the fields in the Loire Valley on Leo filtering into her thoughts. Anaïs's blond hair would stream out behind her, and as a teenager, she'd struck a stunning figure and the farmhands had downed their tools to watch her fly freely past on her way off to the forest paths and the open countryside where she felt most alive and in her element. She'd never been a city girl. Anaïs had been born to ride and had done so without restraint. This ability of Anaïs's to let go, to truly be herself without any inhibition, was what Vianne had adored and admired. It was the one thing she'd always tried, and failed, to emulate.

Vianne tidied the myriad of other sketches that were spread

over her worktable: breakfast coats in silk and cotton with satin ribbon trims, lace-trimmed negligees of silk, and a selection of fashionable frocks. She'd negotiated with Miss Ellie and had convinced her employer to allow her to include bathing and beach costumes, one-piece swimming suits in wool jersey and a collection of beach capes.

Her drawings of her pièces de résistance—the evening dresses, and her bespoke collection of exquisite gowns—sat well away from everything else.

She'd worked long days, often late into the night and across weekends, to ensure that the guests at the parade would be certain to want to order copies of some of the daywear designs, which would be available on a made-to-order basis, while the evening gowns and some of the day dresses would be only bespoke so that Miss Ellie's clients could be assured they'd not bump into someone else wearing the same dress.

Vianne frowned, forcing herself to concentrate on the activities in the atelier, as Lucia, Goldie and Mollie joked over the night they'd enjoyed at the Savoy on the weekend. Adeline was in a fitting session with Miss Ellie and a fussy client who liked to check that not one bead on her gowns was missing, and that every button was sewed in a meticulous line.

"You're getting far too serious, Vianne," Lucia said. She paused from cutting out the patterns she produced with meticulous care and eyed Vianne over the worktable. "The Savoy was the cat's meow on Saturday night."

Vianne shrugged. "I'm so busy right now."

Lucia's eyes shone. "We never got off the dance floor for a second and there were enough ritzy guys there to melt even the hardest-boiled girl. Mollie's carrying a torch for some fella. She charmed him so, I think he'll be a pushover and we'll see him back with a big crush on her next weekend. You could have at least come to look at the dresses, Vianne, honey."

Vianne sighed. "I know, Lucia, but when I've completed the

designs for the parade, and they are all made up, I promise I'll come out dancing with you all night long."

Lucia heaved out a sigh. "Do you have to work so hard?" Lucia lowered her voice. "You are not trying to prove something?"

"Of course not." Vianne pressed her lips together and picked up her pencil again. The truth was she *was* taking a break this weekend, and she was pushing herself to her end point to justify doing that.

To justify going out to Long Island with Giorgio Conti this Sunday to a fabulous party in one of the most legendary homes in Sand Point.

Only because she wanted to see Long Island, and only because she wanted to lay eyes on the fashions the wealthiest women in New York were wearing at the party. There was no other reason. Vianne had made this clear to Giorgio as well.

Vianne frowned and added a pink silk godet—a lining that would peek through in a run from the waist to the hem when the wearer moved around—to a black dress with floral embroidery that was up to the minute yet inspired by the folk traditions of Europe.

Lucia heaved out a dramatic sigh that resounded through the room, and Mollie and Goldie fired up their sewing machines.

The truth was, Vianne had ended up designing nearly every garment for Miss Ellie's parade herself. What was more, Miss Ellie seemed distracted lately, diverted by something, and anxious over what Vianne was beginning to think was more than simply the pressure of planning the parade at Valentino's.

But it was not Vianne's place to ask if something was amiss.

More and more, Miss Ellie was relying on Vianne to pick up the threads that were falling from her grasp, and Vianne worried about the future of the atelier. Was Miss Ellie at risk of closing her doors?

When Adeline stepped back into the room, sending Vianne a smug smile, Vianne frowned. The girl still had said nothing explicit to Miss Ellie about Vianne's dance with Giorgio all those weeks ago, nevertheless her insinuations and asides stabbed Vianne like darts. Vianne held no doubt that the other seamstress was biding her time as to when to strike her most powerful match, but Vianne was never going to be anything more to Giorgio Conti than a friend and a business contact and she'd tell Miss Ellie as much with an open and honest heart.

Mollie's hands stilled on her sewing machine. "Let me tell you about this guy I danced with on Saturday night!"

"Vianne would never go for a man unless he was worth a million dollars. Save your stories, Mollie. Vianne isn't interested," Adeline muttered.

Lucia rolled her eyes and ignored Adeline's aside.

Mollie frowned and went back to her work.

Vianne gritted her teeth at the way Adeline skirted around her loaded gun like a murderer taunting his prey. She focused on the one piece that she knew she had to convince Miss Ellie to include in the parade, her ivory satin wedding gown, with seams that contoured the smooth fabric so that it clung to and draped the body.

She'd begun looking into the way seams emphasized the figure and gave meaning and definition to a dress. For the wedding gown she was planning for the parade, she'd started experimenting with more complex cuts. She bit her lip and looked at her sketch. She wanted the back seam in the fitted dress with its high collar to drop in a V-line to the waist to emphasize the shape of the wearer's back. Then, she planned to insert small darts to fit the main dress to the base of the yolk, shaping and highlighting the area around the hips.

"Well, then! Look at you all working away."

Vianne jumped at the sound of the slightly croaky voice. In the doorway, there stood a spectacularly well-dressed woman in her seventies, with dyed auburn hair and the same button mouth as Miss Ellie's.

"Mama Pepper!" Lucia, Mollie, and Goldie pushed their chairs back and ran across the room to crowd around the extraordinary woman who stood at the door.

Vianne's eyes flickered to Adeline, but the other girl simply raised her brow.

Miss Ellie's mother. The other girls had told Vianne tales of this extraordinary woman, who had been a Southern Belle in Texas, and had been at the center of the social scene as the wife of an important rancher, until Miss Ellie's daddy had lost everything and, tragically, had died trying to bring his family to New York. The rest was history, the rest was why they were all here working for Miss Ellie in her atelier.

Mollie and Goldie melted away from the elderly woman, and Mama Pepper's gaze landed on Vianne and stuck. Vianne cleared her throat and sent the woman a tentative smile. Being the focus of Mama Pepper's riveting stare was like being a deer exposed on a hilltop, antlers twitching in fear. Could Mama Pepper somehow know Vianne was going to Long Island tomorrow, no matter how innocent her plans?

Vianne stood up and held out her hand. When Mama Pepper's brown eyes crinkled with warmth, Vianne's shoulders sagged with relief. She had the feeling you had to stay on your toes when you were around Mama Pepper.

"Well, I'm delighted to meet you, Miss Vianne Mercier," Mama Pepper said, taking Vianne's hand. "My daughter insists that you've got more snap in your garters than any girl she's ever met. I'm Eloise's mother, and you can call me Mama Pepper, just like all the other girls do."

Vianne felt Adeline's eyes boring into her back, but she held up her chin. "*Enchantée*, Mama Pepper. It's an honor to meet you," she said, slipping back into her native tongue just as easily as the homegrown expressions seemed to roll from Mama Pepper's lips.

"Bless your heart," Mama Pepper said. "I can't express how my daughter appreciates that you have no slack in your rope. She says you're crowing before dawn every morning and are a real asset to the business. It's an honor to meet *you*, my dear."

Despite the doubts about her assignation with Giorgio bubbling to a boil in her head, Vianne felt drawn to the woman standing opposite her. She recognized something in Mama Pepper, and it was gumption. Gumption like Vianne's maman and her sister had once had.

Mama Pepper straightened the black-and-white woven coat that she wore—one of Miss Ellie's most successful garments of the spring season and designed by Vianne, with its woven Aztec pattern, in honor of the craze for geometric patterns, stripes, spots and zigzags that were so popular as surface decoration in daywear. The coat's wide collar framed Mama Pepper's striking features, and the simple design only added to the woman's cachet.

"I'm popping into say hello before taking my daughter out for lunch at Valentino's," Mama Pepper said. "Such a charming restaurant, and the owner, why he's a dream."

Vianne felt her cheeks blush as pink as the blossom petals that were falling in Central Park.

"Oh, we're all aware of that," Adeline murmured. "Vianne especially so."

Mama Pepper didn't miss a beat. "I'll be at the parade they're hosting for us with bells on." She sent Vianne a conspiratorial smile, her button lips curving just like Miss Ellie's used to do, more than they did these days. "And afterwards, why, we'll paint the town *and* the front porch. I want you girls to show me how to have a dinger of an evening in New York!"

Vianne gave the woman a warm smile. But as Mama Pepper waved at them, and flitted back out from where she'd come, the seed of doubt about her trip to Long Island this weekend grew into a strangling plant. What if someone from high society mentioned her presence to Miss Ellie? Why, Vianne might as well kiss everything she loved about New York goodbye.

Vianne sat at her tiny dressing table on Sunday morning and surveyed her Max Factor makeup. She had everything she needed to look the part, loose face powder in a shade lighter than her skin tone, liquid rouge in red, a black pencil for her eyes and brows, a matte red lipstick with matching pencil, and a dark matte eyeshadow in blue to enhance her deep blue eyes. She picked up the silver-backed hairbrush that she'd brought all the way from Paris to New York, unable to part with the soft brush that her mother had bought her for her eighteenth birthday.

Despite the treachery of disobeying Miss Ellie boiling around inside, she'd slept well after she'd taken a long walk in Central Park with Lucia yesterday afternoon, before returning to the studio and finalizing details for the ivory wedding gown she'd been designing all week.

She'd farewelled Lucia for the day a little while ago, waving her friend off to her usual Sunday luncheon at home in the Village with her family. Lucia had tried to lure Vianne down to join her so many times, but so far, Vianne had resisted, using work as an excuse, and then taking a cup of coffee up to the atelier and burying herself in her sketches to distract herself from her memories of all the Sunday lunches she'd once enjoyed with her parents, Anaïs, and Jacques before the war. One day, hopefully, her sadness at the loss of her own family might not tear at her heart quite so bitterly and she could manage a normal Sunday luncheon without breaking her own heart.

Vianne reached for the golden powder compact that she'd treated herself to, decorated with green leaf patterns, applying it with a fluffy powder puff in small sections, brushing downwards and following the contours of her wide cheekbones. She blended the merest hint of her rosy-red liquid rouge into a thin crescent moon on each cheek, letting the cusps fall away as they traced the curve of her cheeks.

She overdrew her top lip points with her lip pencil, making the fashionable Cupid's bow, and then, reaching for her lipstick, filled in the color, her lips looking most temptingly soft. She overdrew her bottom lip just a tiny bit, making her naturally full lip look even plumper than it already was.

Next, her hands shaking, she shaped her brows with a brow brush, brushing the hairs up from the bottom, then down from the top to create an arched line. Finally, she dabbed a little petroleum jelly on her brows to keep them in place, before drawing a line along her upper eyelid with a black pencil, and smudging that into her lashes, startling at the way this brought out the brightness of her blue eyes, before dabbing a little blue eyeshadow on the upper lash line to enhance her eyes even more.

During the day, she only wore face powder, her naturally dark lashes and blue eyes not needing enhancement, and now she'd painted her face with the makeup she'd gradually collected when she could afford such a treat, she looked like a glamorous girl she hardly recognized! But a glance at the clock on the wall meant she had to move. She was sitting here in her dressing gown and Giorgio would be downstairs outside the atelier in twenty minutes flat!

Her heart racing, she opened her wooden armoire. Outside, beyond her drawn drapes, she knew the sun was beaming from a vivid blue sky, as blue as her first glimpse would be of the famous Long Island Sound.

Every mention she'd heard of Long Island sounded seductive, glamorous, and alluring. She'd heard Miss Ellie's customers talk longingly of owning a house out there, with its rolling hills, deep harbors, mansions overlooking the tranquil waters, private beaches, yachts, summer houses, swimming pools...

Vianne carefully reached for the dress she'd created especially for the most exclusive invitation she'd ever had. Her brows drew together as she ran her fingers over the honey-colored sequins that covered the softly flowing drop-waisted garment. Miss Ellie had let her have the sequins, and she'd scrimped and saved to purchase the fabric, before sewing it up and decorating the dress's simple silhouette, lavishly enhancing it with a soft golden skirt, decorated with bugle beading and silk floss, embroidering the dress with trailing soft pink flowers and intertwining green leaves. She'd repeated this pattern on the front panel of the bodice, with a pair of interfacing modern, art deco tulips embroidered in deep red and pink silk, encased in a geometrical frame made of bugle beads, while the neckline was enhanced with a thin layer of gossamer silk just above the sequin line, sitting in a perfect V along her own honey-colored décolletage, before dropping a little lower down at the back. Vianne, knowing that sun-kissed skin was in, had deliberately worn a loose-fitting, low-cut blouse to Central Park yesterday, and her skin, which always turned a little brown in the sun, glowed.

The sequins shimmered all over her body, reflecting the pinks and greens in the flowers, and the lights that shone in the room, just as Vianne had planned, while she turned this way and that in front of her mirror.

At the sound of the clock in the hallway striking eleven, Vianne slipped on her cloche hat and a pair of T-bar shoes, grabbed the matching sequined purse she'd made to go with the dress, popped in her lipstick, her powder compact, a comb, and her keys, and slipped out toward the front door, her stomach pierced with nerves.

As she made her way down the wooden staircase, her shoes clattering mightily, she sent up a prayer of thanks that she was the only one here.

Swallowing this, she came to a stop outside the front door of the atelier on East 63rd Street. She drew a hand to her mouth. Opposite her, there stood Giorgio Conti, leaning against the most spectacular car. It was long and low, and the gleaming navy-blue paintwork was polished to a sheen. The tires had white inserts that were as pristine as a freshly washed cotton sheet, and the spectacular headlights shouted, "we have arrived."

Giorgio's face moved into a slow smile, and he came toward her in his three-piece camel-colored suit with its wide lapel, his long legs in their high-rise cuffed pants strolling as casually as if he took a girl out to a Long Island mansion every day of the week.

Vianne gulped. Perhaps he did.

Vianne was used to Anaïs's cavalier attitude when it came to men, but would even her older sister get stuck on Giorgio?

Lifting her chin, Vianne held his gaze, the sound of his feet encased in a pair of cap-toe Oxford shoes treading firmly on the sidewalk. His expression softened.

"*Bella*."

She sent him a little smile. "Hello," she said. She'd not reprimand him for calling her by that name when he was about to drive her out to one of the most famous places in the world right now.

"You are beautiful."

She held her hand out toward him.

He took it, his eyes raising for one split second to meet hers, before dropping a kiss on her hand. "Stunning," he murmured. "You'll be the belle of the party, Vianne."

"Well, thank you, Giorgio," she said, quashing the image of Adeline pouncing out of some wardrobe at the party and threatening Vianne with her superior smile. She closed her eyes a moment and channeled her sister, adopting a little of Anaïs's type of *je ne sais quoi,* and strolling down the front steps, she let herself enjoy the way Giorgio's eyes roamed over every inch of her fabulous dress, even though her heart was thumping something wild every time she took a step. As she landed on the sidewalk, a few people stopped to stare.

"My," a woman breathed. "Did you get that at Madame Chappelle's, honey, because I want one of those, please!"

Vianne lifted her eyes. "Why, of course, I did," she said. "And I know that Madame Chapelle would just love to design something just like it for you."

"You, my dear, are sensational," an older woman said. "If you don't mind me saying. I mean, look at the way that dress shimmers in the sun. Why, it matches your golden hair."

Vianne sent them a Parisian smile, and Giorgio held out a hand for her, intertwining his fingers with hers and giving them a little squeeze. Vianne jolted at the frisson that accompanied Giorgio's touch. No matter how spiffy a couple they made, no matter what a swell Giorgio was, today was all about trying to *help* Miss Ellie and maybe even get her a couple of new high-society customers who owned houses on Long Island Sound.

Well, that was the way Vianne was justifying it to herself.

Giorgio held out the door of the ritzy car and she stepped into the leather interior, her hands wanting to stroke the walnut paneling on the doors, the dashboard. She hardly knew where to put her feet.

But in a second, Giorgio was in next to her. "Well," he said, his words honey-soft. "Are you ready for a party you'll never forget?"

"Ready and racing," Vianne said, offering a fabulous smile.

His eyes crinkled with warmth. "You know, it's going to be a day I'll treasure. Thank you for accompanying me. It's an honor."

"I'm glad we can be friends, Giorgio."

Giorgio's expression was unfathomable a moment. "Let's blouse," he whispered.

Vianne chuckled at the modern term.

He pulled the car out from the curb, and a small group of New Yorkers were gathered to admire them. Vianne held onto her hat and didn't bother suppressing her grin.

Giorgio wove his beautiful Duesenberg along Long Island's exclusive Middle Neck Road, his elbow resting on the open window, as a gentle breeze wove up from the Sound. The car purred like a dream, the deep green fields spread down toward the serene still water, while the elaborate gates they passed only hinted at the chateaus and mansions beyond the verdant trees. Vianne felt all the tension slipping away from her shoulders. She'd worked so very hard for years, and were she honest, she knew she hadn't felt anything like the sense of relaxation she felt now in an age.

"Thank you," she said, turning to Giorgio's handsome profile, "for bringing me out here. You know, just driving here is doing me good." She sighed. "I have to admit, this all reminds me of France."

A tracery of lines fanned out from the sides of Giorgio's eyes. "Tell me about France, Vianne," he said. "Did you love living in Paris?"

Vianne swallowed. "I did." She'd not spoken openly about her life in France to anyone in America, not really. "I was very lucky," she said. "My parents were both, in their own ways, an inspiration to me."

Giorgio stayed quiet, only the tap of his fingers on his steering wheel giving away any movement as he drove.

"And my sister, Anaïs, well. If I could have been half as brave as she was…" Vianne gazed out, unfocused, as they passed a couple more entrances to old-money mansions. She caught a glimpse of an elegant white house with dormer windows through a bank of trees.

"No one could be braver than you," Giorgio said. "You came all the way to New York alone."

Vianne shook her head. "Oh, no. Anaïs served as a nurse on the battlefields in northern France and in a hospital in Belgium."

She sensed Giorgio's eyes flickering toward her, but he stayed quiet.

"And my…" her voice hitched, and she struggled to continue. "My brother, Jacques, was at the Somme. I knitted socks." She turned to him, as if willing him to challenge her statement.

He stayed focused on the gentle curves of the road. "But you were the youngest." His voice softened. "I was too young to contribute to the war in a meaningful way as well. I understand what it is to feel a sense of frustration that you couldn't have done more to help, but that is all it should be. Not guilt."

Vianne turned away from him. It was hard to explain the leeching ache inside her, that her courageous sister had been killed, while she still lived on, she, the one who had contributed the least when it counted most.

"You create pieces of such beauty." Giorgio's voice was soft. "It is the very best thing to do in life."

Vianne rested her head against the leather seat, Giorgio's words, so like Maman's, tender to her ears. How Maman would have adored him!

She pressed her lips together because she must not think like that. "Maman, Papa, and Anaïs are all gone now. They all died in 1918."

She heard Giorgio's sharp intake of breath.

"There are not words." He shook his head and turned to her. "I'm sorry. It always sounds so inadequate." His voice was soft. "You are doubly brave, then."

Their eyes locked for one second before he turned back to the winding road, and Vianne squeezed her eyes shut to halt the tears that threatened to explode down her cheeks. "Because of that loss, I want to make the most of my life, be someone, not just exist, you see. I want to be my own person, in my own right, not someone's adjunct."

There was a silence.

"I hope you understand," she said.

What was she doing? Giorgio would think she was crazy, but somehow, she wanted to explain to him that the reason she was keeping him at a distance was nothing personal.

Even though, deep down, she knew it was. Because if she gave into one iota of the attraction she felt for him, then she'd have to make an impossible choice. She was living in a dream world if she thought a woman could simultaneously have the two things men enjoyed—love and a career.

"I take it you mean that you don't just want to be someone's wife." His words whispered like a rustle of leaves into the extraordinary still air.

Vianne fidgeted with her handbag, her body freezing in place. What an awkward conversation. She sent up a prayer to Maman and Anaïs for guidance. She needed to be helped here. They would never land themselves in such an embarrassing state.

"Anaïs..." She swallowed, her throat closing over, but she took a breath and forced herself to go on. "Anaïs only had to walk into a room and she was somebody. I need to work a little harder to prove I have what it takes." She gabbled out the last words.

"No, no," Giorgio murmured. "If only you knew."

"Oh, but, my sister was something else. And as for Jacques..."

"He is still in Paris?" Giorgio said.

Vianne folded her hands tight in her lap. "My older brother is still alive," she managed. "He adored Anaïs. He never forgave me for living when she was killed, and after he learned Anaïs was gone, he... well, the truth is, he turned me out."

Giorgio frowned. Vianne flinched at the way his knuckles gripped the steering wheel and turned white.

She'd told him too much. Said too much.

She bit on her lip; her fists clenched tight in her lap. Giorgio Conti would never take her to a party again!

Right then, he ducked his head slightly, as if checking something, and they came to a set of magnificent gates.

Why had she mentioned Jacques? Now she had broadcast her shame! The fact she was an outcast, a woman with no family. She brought her hand to reach up to her forehead.

But just as she did so, Giorgio reached out and caught her hand as he turned into the driveway beyond the gates. "You could tell me a thousand things and it would never be too much."

She closed her eyes at the feel of his touch.

"Open your eyes, take a look at what's right in front of you right now, *Bella*."

Vianne lifted her gaze. And she gasped. The car had come to the end of a driveway, overhung with deep green trees, and the vista opened up, and there, in front of them, in the middle of a pristine lawn, a tall chateau covered in ivy stood, with a round turret at one end. Arched French doors along the rest of the building opened up to a long veranda set with tables and easy chairs, upon which beautifully dressed women and men lounged and smoked and the sound of laughter tinkled into the hazy sea air. Beyond this, the lawn only tapered away when it reached the glasslike water that lapped gently at a narrow strip of golden sand.

Vianne drank in the scene. The house was a reproduction of a beautiful home in France. Dear dormer windows, thrown open to the fresh air, winked in the sunlight, and the sky above was azure, threaded with only the finest gossamer clouds. Flowers spilled from the chateau's balconies, just as they did in France.

Vianne closed her eyes, allowing herself to imagine for one moment that Papa might appear, strolling down the lawn in a white summer hat and a pale suit, swinging his cane, with one of his customers trailing behind him, and there'd be a table set with lemonade for afternoon tea, and his dear eyes would crinkle in delight at the sight of Vianne, and she'd run into his arms...

The sound of jazz tinkled out to the lawn. Someone was playing a piano inside the magnificent home.

Giorgio turned to her. "Welcome, Vianne, to Katherine Carter's house."

She stilled. "Katherine Carter?"

"You have heard of her?" He reached out and tucked a stray tendril of hair behind her ear.

She shivered at his touch. Her lost, haunted brother suddenly filled her mind, the way his hands had shaken when he came home from the war. The way he had been so cruel. Giorgio's touch, so gentle, his kindness, was almost impossible to bear.

"I met a Katherine Carter on the ship from France. I wonder if it's the same woman. She was rather wonderful."

"How perfect—" Giorgio began. But he'd parked on a sweep of gravel not far from the house, and a uniformed valet was making his way toward the car.

"Welcome, Mr. Conti. Mrs. Carter is in the Great Room and is expecting you. I will park your car."

"Thank you," Giorgio said, smiling up at the middle-aged valet.

Giorgio climbed out of the car, and Vianne reached for her purse, her heart pounding at the thought of an encounter with the stunning Katherine Carter again. Chances were, Katherine would have forgotten the girl who mended her dress as easily as she'd let a sea breeze slip by.

Giorgio came around to her side to accompany her out and she placed her gloved hand in his own.

Five minutes later, they were through the French doors, past a group of men who'd slapped Giorgio on the back, past the women on the veranda whose eyes roamed up and down Vianne's dress and whispered to each other behind the backs of their hands. Gauzy curtains swirled from the French doors, and when they stepped inside the Great Room, Vianne caught her breath.

"Giorgio." The very Katherine Carter whom Vianne had helped on SS *Paris*, her blond hair tucked behind her ears, and her wide eyes dancing with delight, rose from a pair of enormous crescent-shaped velvet sofas, where a group of guests sat and laughed and clinked their cocktail glasses and waved their cigarettes.

Vianne did not know whether to gape at the view of the blue sea, to look upward at the wonderful white ceiling, decorated with inlaid patterns of white circles and corresponding squares, or to stare at her hostess, whom she was certain would not recognize her.

A pianist played Gershwin on the grand piano by the sets of doors that looked out to the Sound, and now, Mrs. Carter was placing her hand in Vianne's.

"*Bonjour*, Parisian girl," she murmured. "I'm glad to see you again. But how beautifully you are dressed today. I take it you made your own gown?"

Vianne flushed, aware of Giorgio's eyes on her. She nodded at her hostess. "Hello again, Mrs. Carter," she managed, turning to meet the woman's extraordinary green gaze. It was as green as the grass and as knowing as a cat, and her hostess held Vianne's hand for a second longer than she'd expected.

"*Ça va*, Mademoiselle Mercier?" Katherine Carter murmured. "You found Madame Eloise Chappelle?"

"*Ça va bien, merci*," Vianne said. "And yes, I am working for Madame Chapelle," Vianne said, captivated again by Katherine Carter's style. Her embroidered satin dress was the palest pink and was decorated with light blue and pink needlepoint in Chinese-style motifs.

Giorgio cleared his throat beside Vianne. "Well, I'm not keeping up, but I'm glad you two know each other. You'll have to fill me in sometime."

Katherine opened her mouth as if to say something more, and Vianne would have died on the spot to have a little more conversation with her beguiling hostess, but a dark-haired woman with a pair of bright brown eyes and a knowing look sidled up to them.

"Well, then. I see Giorgio's brought another exquisite companion today." A straight line appeared between the woman's black brows.

Katherine Carter's eyes did not leave Vianne's face. Katherine smiled again, and Vianne could not help but smile right back. "Vianne Mercier, this is Victoria Rose."

Katherine Carter paused, and Vianne winced. If Katherine revealed that Vianne was an unknown Parisian seamstress who'd come up from second class to fix a rent in her dress on the way to America, Vianne would be vilified before she talked to anyone at all.

Victoria linked her arm through Katherine's. "Who are your family then, Mademoiselle Mercier?" she asked.

Vianne stood speechless for a moment. What to say to that? "I'm afraid they are all gone," she almost whispered. "I have no family. There is only me."

"A young woman of no family?" Victoria Rose tilted her head to one side. "Well, I wouldn't be too proud about that. You must be honored that Giorgio found you," she said. "You should thank him sometime," she went on, looking Vianne up and down as if she were something that had been rejected by the cat.

Vianne flushed. She opened her mouth, only to close it again.

"Oh, come now, Victoria," Katherine said. "Don't be such a bore. You have to admit that Mademoiselle Mercier's dress is the most perfect thing you've seen all weekend."

Victoria raised a brow. "Where did you get it, Miss Mercier?"

Vianne raised herself up to her full height. "Why, I made it myself," she said, suddenly not caring what the woman standing opposite her thought.

Giorgio had been swept up into a group of chattering folks by the piano.

"I beg your pardon, dear?" Victoria Rose said. "What, did you sit at home with a sewing machine? Bent over it in the dark? Whatever next?" she tittered. "I can hardly imagine."

But Katherine Carter sent Vianne a sympathetic smile. "My poor friend here doesn't share our sense of humor, I'm afraid, Miss Mercier. And neither, it seems, does she share our manners."

Victoria Rose turned puce.

Vianne was aware of glances in her direction, the stir of voices. And as for Katherine's friend, why, as Maman would say, the woman had no class.

"Forgive me," Vianne said, standing to her full height. "I wasn't clear. The fact is, I am a fashion designer, and I designed and made this dress. In fact, I'm designing a range for Eloise Chappelle at this very time, and we are showing them at Valentino's in an exclusive parade for the atelier. If you'd like to come along, I'm sure we'd be honored to see you there."

Victoria Rose had the grace to look confused.

Katherine Carter laid a hand on Vianne's arm. "Let me introduce you to people, Vianne. And," she lowered her voice, "I'm going to ask you something, and I hope you will agree."

"Of course," Vianne said.

"Could I come in to see you sometime? Could you design something special for me? Because I wouldn't want to waste your considerable talents on daywear. No. You should be designing haute couture. I've never seen anything so beautiful as you in that dress right now. Could you begin to share some of that French flair with a boring old New Yorker like me? I'd pay you a million dollars if you could." And Katherine Carter linked her arm through Vianne's.

"I'd be honored," Vianne murmured, her pulse quickening in her throat as she followed her hostess through the room. "I'm so glad to have seen you again, Mrs. Carter."

Katherine smiled, her pearly teeth sparkling. "Now I'm going to show you off and make sure you dress all the fashionable people. I know I won't be able to keep you to myself," she added. "So, I'll see to it that I know your clientele." Katherine Carter let out a laugh and pulled a glass of champagne from a passing waiter's tray and handed it to Vianne.

And with that, Vianne felt a squeeze on her arm and a lift in her heart, and she moved with confidence right into the heart of the group where Giorgio stood.

"Darlings," Katherine said. "I want to introduce you all to Vianne Mercier, a fabulous new young designer who is nothing but the real McCoy, I can vouch for that. She's from Paris and she designed and sewed the dress she's wearing, and from now on, she's who I'm going to exclusively whenever I need a special gown. It will save me ordering from Paris." Katherine Carter raised her glass. "I am certain that Vianne Mercier is going to be the toast of New York."

Vianne's cheeks bloomed, and she broke into one of her most infectious smiles. A crowd of women gathered around her, while, from across the circle of gorgeous young things, Giorgio's eyes crinkled into a genuine smile.

CHAPTER SIXTEEN
ELOISE, SPRING, 1925

Eloise studied the breathtaking sketches that Vianne had left on her desk. Vianne was a marvel. She was not only working tirelessly to come up with designs for the parade at Valentino's, Vianne had also left a cache of decorating ideas for the restaurant during the event. Eloise turned through Vianne's arresting sketches, delighted at the tiny, perfect paintings of blousy red and white rosebuds lining the walls of the restaurant all around the catwalk. She'd suggested blue hyacinths could be set out in crystal vases on the tables. What a perfect idea! Vianne's ingenuity was going to bring Paris to New York.

Eloise cupped her chin in her hands, the familiar sinking feeling suddenly surging through her insides. The fact was, Eloise was waking up every night in the early hours bathed in sweat, haunted by nightmares that Lena Davis was right behind her, ready to pounce and copy her every move. Despite Mama Pepper's assurances that a parade would fix things, Eloise was not coping, and she had no idea what to do.

Thank goodness Vianne had not noticed the copy of Adriana Conti's sensational dress in the window of Macy's. Eloise suspected it had sold faster than it took a garter to snap, while in the meantime, Lena Davis remained as crooked as a dog's hind leg.

Eloise placed her glasses down on her desk and sat back in her chair. Every day, she sat at her desk between fittings and every day she'd come up with nothing, no ideas, no sketches, not a thing. If she did not have Vianne on board, she'd be the captain of a sinking ship.

Her little design book had been bereft of ideas for months. But no one must know that Eloise's inspiration had run dry.

"Eloise."

Eddie Winter stood at her office door.

Eloise stood up hastily, bustling around her desk.

"Good morning, Eddie." She closed the door behind the editor of *Bella* magazine. "Tell me you've brought me coffee, because I'm so busy I could be twins."

Eddie peered over Eloise's desk, but Eloise whipped back to her chair and turned Vianne's sketches face down.

"Oh, no, you don't," she said. "You go skin your own buffalo, Eddie. There are no stories on my desk."

"Shame," he murmured. "Because I've got something for you."

Eloise's hand stilled over Vianne's ideas.

Eddie took off his round glasses and ruffled his chestnut hair. He cleared his throat. "Look, there's no easy way to tell you this." His eyes bored into Eloise's, and she gulped.

Lena. The woman had become a go-to topic between her and Eddie and, despite her annoyance at this, Eloise couldn't let it go.

"Lena Davis is opening an atelier in Paris. I didn't want you to read it in the news."

Eloise slid back into her chair, picked up a pencil and twirled it in her fingers.

Eddie settled himself into one of Eloise's chairs, his hands between his knees. "I don't want a story," he said softly. "I wanted to let you know."

Eloise felt her lips curve into a sardonic smile. She looked off to the side.

"Apparently, she's going for the big cheese. Her old man's footing the cost." Eddie's voice filtered through the office.

Eloise focused on the potted palm in the corner of the room. It had seemed like such a grand idea to decorate with palms, lending the atelier a feeling of being in some swanky hotel. The only person staying in grand hotels was going to be Lena, hot as a two-dollar pistol with Vianne's stolen designs!

Eloise took in a shaking breath. Envy was a sin. Her strong values forbade her to give in to such heinous feelings, but something was turning her hot under the collar, and it wasn't her cashmere scarf.

"Apparently, they're kitting out a shopfront in the Place Vendôme."

Eloise looked up, sharp, her gaze hitting Eddie's. Place Vendôme was the most exclusive square in Paris. The idea of Vianne's designs, stolen and hanging in a window in Place Vendôme, was unthinkable. Eloise rose out of her chair and went to stand by the window overlooking the street, carving her hands through her short hair.

"Eloise," Eddie murmured. "You should act."

Eloise leaned her head against her window. The room was spinning and she closed her eyes tight.

"New York loves a scandal," he said, his tone laced with a dash of humor now.

Eloise swallowed down the bile that threatened to rise in her throat, turned around, and sent Eddie a hardened smile. "I can't afford any scandal, Eddie. I don't have the wealthy husband to provide me with financial support. And Lena Davis knows that. Which is why she's targeted my designs. Unable to come up with anything of her own, she needed someone to copy, someone who can't stand up for herself, and she thinks she chose well."

Eddie folded his arms.

Eloise heaved out a sigh. "Goodness knows, Eddie, I'm as hot as a billy goat in a pepper patch."

"I can imagine." He pulled out his cigarette case and offered it. She shook her head.

"Ellie?" he said, using the version of her name he'd only used so very rarely before. "Are you managing with it? It's not... affecting you. I mean, you've had your work stolen. There's no shame in dropping the ball."

Eloise pressed her lips together. Affected her? She couldn't design! "I'm fine."

He was silent.

"I'm fine," she said, again. She gathered herself. "Eddie, if you'll excuse me, I need to..." She knew what she needed to do. "There's someplace I must go."

She grabbed her coat, hat, gloves, and her bag, and held the door open for him. And as she sailed ahead of him, out of the atelier, she felt his eyes boring into her back.

Once she'd dodged her way through the crowds on Park Avenue, Eloise arrived at the entrance to St Ignatius Loyola church and almost collapsed with relief. The stone façade with its symmetrical windows and porticos looked as secure and confident as a bank. Her church was her safe place. It had always been that way.

She leaned on the handrails and climbed the front steps, her forehead lined with perspiration and her hands clammy in her white gloves.

Once she stepped inside the beautiful building, she crossed herself and sat down in a pew, lowering her head, and praying for some help, because she knew not what to do. For it was not only her business that was at stake. There was Mama Pepper to support, and her loyal seamstresses to consider, not to mention the burgeoning, brilliant talent that was Vianne Mercier.

All Eloise had been doing was working hard in good faith on her original work, and this impostor had...

Eloise checked herself. She swallowed. Her way of thinking was getting close to a sin and she was sitting in a church.

Taking deep breaths, she forced herself to stop thinking the awful, bad thoughts that had plagued her ever since Lena Davis had started copying her work, and instead, let the beauty and peace of the church wash over her.

All she could do was hope and pray that somehow things would be restored to their rightful place. Eloise and Vianne's designs, recognized as such.

Eloise closed her eyes, lowered her head, and bent to her knees. She did what she always did when things seemed impossible.

She prayed.

CHAPTER SEVENTEEN
AMELIE, SPRING, 1925

Amelie stood in the old nursery at Carrig, the sun beaming through the tall windows into the pretty room. Her eyes misted at the sight of the old Victorian dolls' house in one corner, just like the ones Papa used to sometimes sell at Celine. A set of wooden blocks sat atop it spelling out the names "Archie" and then "Flora," his younger sister who had been traveling for the past three years independently on the continent. There was a washstand, a round table covered in a soft white cloth, and a wooden chair with a teddy bear sitting jauntily at an angle and eyeing Amelie as if he, not Archie, was the true laird of Carrig. Old black-and-white photographs of Carrig's gardens lined the cream-painted walls, and atop the mantelpiece, a tiny white china tea set was arranged as if a petite gathering was about to unfold.

Mary had openly admitted that she always instructed the maids to keep the nursery cleaned and aired. She'd doted on Archie and Flora, and Mary had thrived in the years when they were small. Now, Amelie pressed her hand to her own belly. The news she'd had confirmed yesterday had kept her awake all the previous night. Every experience Amelie had of motherhood was intertwined with her maman, and the unfathomable hole that her death had left behind tore Amelie into little pieces. She had no idea whether she'd ever be able to stitch them together again.

The first thing she'd done when the physician had told her she was expecting was to mist over into tears because Maman would never meet her baby, never see her grandchild grow up, and the thought of raising a child without her family to share in the joys, the heartbreak, the ups and downs, was more than Amelie could bear. But she couldn't contact them. How would she explain she was alive and had not been in touch for several years, and how could she tell them something that would destroy them, even if she did feel like she was living a half-life without them around? Archie had his mother, cousins, neighbors, extended family, and she, Amelie, was like a lone bird on a perch filled with chatter that had nothing to do with her at all.

She closed her eyes at the memories of Papa taking her to the markets each week in Paris. How he'd introduced her to the bird market on Sunday, and they'd wander around, Anaïs's small hand in Papa's, staring at all the exotic and wonderful species—canaries, parakeets, and zebra finches. He'd told her captivating stories about the birds and the lands they'd come from, and Anaïs would always want to rescue them. On other days, she and Maman would go to the flower markets together, with blooms in a conglomeration of metal cubbies, all painted green, where Maman would pore over potted plants, hydrangeas, all different colors, and they'd choose houseplants, and proper garden roses for the pots in their courtyard.

But now, a dark fear circled inside her. She had more reason than ever before to keep her identity and her terrible past a secret from Archie now she was with child. He must never know who she really was because, if he did so, he would hate her, he would hate what she'd done, and if he were to turn her out, she could well lose her child. Already, she felt protective of the small life that would blossom inside her. More than ever, she felt like she must be completely a MacCullum of Carrig and not that Parisian girl she used to be.

No one in Scotland must know she was a murderer.

Amelie tore herself away from the nursery and made her way through the long gallery that lined the family's bedroom wing. The sky outside the vast windows was vivid blue, spreading to infinity as only the sky in Scotland could. She had to focus on the weekend ahead. She was wound up as tight as a coil over the engagement party at Kinloch. And she just wanted to get through it, for Archie and Caitlin's sake, and then retreat, back to her safe world at Carrig.

Now she had to drive up to Inverness to pick up her dress for the masked ball. Amelie walked to her bedroom, collected her coat, hat, gloves and car keys, and made her way down through the kitchens, patting Archie's Labradors on their obliging heads, and out to the garage, where her smart red Galloway 10/20 sat waiting for her.

For certain, she had everything.

And that meant she had everything to lose.

She climbed up into the raised seat, lowered the handbrake, and set off in a great roar for Inverness. The wide, green fields spread out on either side of her, the distant woodlands thick and impenetrable, the landscape dotted with remote farmhouses and villages with comforting Scottish names.

In the small city of Inverness, she parked her car in the high street and walked up the cobbled road toward the castle, its pink crenelated towers overlooking the old town. Amelie gathered her light coat around her as she made her way between the dark stone buildings, until she came to the dressmaker that Mary always used, a practical woman who'd turned out to be more than accommodating of Amelie's wish to be unrecognizable at the Kinloch ball. The reason, she'd said, was that she was a newcomer to Scotland, and wanted to be a little incognito, lending a sense of mystery around herself.

"Mrs. MacCullum." The dressmaker appeared through a red velvet curtain into the small front room of her establishment when Amelie pushed open the door and set off a small brass bell.

"Good afternoon," Amelie said, removing her gloves. "How did you get on?"

"Oh, perfectly well," the woman replied, her ruddy face softening into a genuine smile. "Your wee dress is all ready, my dear, and I think you will be very satisfied."

The woman turned and led Amelie into the room that did for a working room and a fitting room, where baskets were filled with offcuts of fabric, and canisters of buttons sat upon a row of shelves against one wall. The dressmaker's solid sewing machine was set against the window that looked out onto the back, narrow lane, and a rack of clothes hung in various stages of completion.

Amelie swallowed back the lump that formed in her throat at the thought of Vianne. How the darling girl would love this place. How she'd simply sit in here and swoon.

Amelie returned the woman's smile, her stomach hardening against her own duplicity. And when her eyes came to rest on the stunning garment that hung ready for her, even she brought a hand to her mouth. No one could have done better, except, perhaps dear Vianne.

"I appreciate this," she whispered. "Thank you, Mrs. Bay."

The dressmaker's eyes kindled with pleasure, and she went to remove the gown for Amelie to try on.

It was perfect.

Not a soul would guess a thing, and Anaïs could remain buried away, never to be heard of ever again.

"Amelie."

Amelie started at the sound of the still strange name. Having just left the dressmakers, she'd been lost in a reverie of memories: Vianne with her dear collection of antique pincushions, carefully set out on the windowsill of her bedroom at home in Paris. How she and Jacques had made fun of their sister. Collecting pincushions of all things, as a small girl! Maman had scolded her and Jacques and sent them to their rooms. But they'd giggled over it for days afterward, until Vianne had hidden her special collection away in the depths of her armoire.

Amelie gathered herself, and turned to face Caitlin, reaching forward to accept her neighbor's outstretched hand.

"You look well, Caitlin," Amelie said, taking in Caitlin's sparkling green eyes, her fashionable hat, trimmed with flowers and gold ribbon around the crown, sitting jauntily on her head. Her honey-blond hair peeped out from under her hat and curled just below her jawline.

Caitlin linked her arm through Amelie's, and started wandering down the high street, the sounds of car horns honking, and people greeting friends ringing through the air. Off to the side, cobbled alleyways wound their way through Inverness' old town.

"I can guess exactly what you've got hidden away in that bag you're carrying, but I wager you won't show me yet."

Amelie's fingers curled around the handle on her precious bag. She felt a sense of loyalty to the dressmaker of Inverness. The woman had single-handedly provided her with a way to survive Caitlin's party and remain entirely incognito, and she would be always thankful for that.

"But don't tell me you had Mrs. Bay make your costume for the party? Surely not you, a Parisian, darling?" Caitlin stopped outside a milliner's, peering closer to the window display to study the selection of hats—soft rolled brim hats of felt, cut off in the back as was fashionable, silk hats, rolled all around, one with a tailored bow on the side.

Amelie pretended to focus on a navy turban, trimmed with striped ribbon, and decorated with a huge side bow in contrasting red. "Mrs. Bay's done an excellent job." She clutched onto her carry bag.

"Oh, well, I suppose she can sew. But that's beside the point. Inverness hardly compares to London or Paris. I'm still waiting for you to accept my standing invitation for a weekend away, because you and I would have a ball in the jazz clubs together." Caitlin sailed on down the street, clearly unaware of her gaffe when it came to Paris. "You know," she said, suddenly. "It's too exciting. Your sister-in-law, and my oldest friend, Flora, is coming home for the party. I suspect Archie's told you. Which means it's going to be dreadfully fun. Flora's a gas. You'll love her. I saw her in London last month. She's most intrigued to meet her new sister-in-law."

Amelie chewed on her lip. Archie had told her his sister had quite the personality. She'd not come to their wedding because she'd been sailing around the Mediterranean with friends.

They came to Amelie's car, and she turned to Caitlin. "Can I offer you a lift?" she asked, although suddenly, desperately, wanting to be alone, needing the wide-open roads, the distant blue hills, the gorse, curlews wheeling overhead while she drove, and only the sound of the rushing burns to distract her.

But Caitlin sent her a smile and shook her head. "Mummy is up here with me. It's one of our shopping days, you see. She'd bumped into a friend and is having a cup of tea with her, so I said I'd leave them to it for an hour." She rolled her eyes. "I'd best run off, but so lovely to see you for a wee chat."

Amelie felt a sudden warmth for her neighbor. "Goodbye, Caitlin," she said. *Oh, to have a clear conscience, to have a normal life... a mother waiting for you, cups of tea together, shopping trips.*

Caitlin pressed Amelie on the arm. "Darling, there is one favor I do have to ask you. I can't believe I almost forgot."

"Of course," Amelie said. "What is it, Caitlin?"

Caitlin lowered her voice. "I know that Flora will be staying with you, of course, but we have one stray guest whom I can't fit in at Kinloch." Caitlin made something of a face. "Annabel's young friends all want to stay with us. And I'm afraid the house is going to be dreadfully full. But this one person, I don't even remember their name, needs a room. Can you help?"

Amelie's fingers slipped on the handle of her bag. The costume would disguise her at the party, but a guest? For the whole weekend? She'd be entirely exposed. "Do you... know if the person is French?" she asked casually. She pressed her lips into a small smile.

Caitlin tilted her head to one side. "Can't remember the particulars," she said. "But I'm sure she or he won't be any trouble. Do you think you can fit them in?"

Amelie stared at the clock tower further up the road and waited for the second hand to point to the top. "Yes," she managed. She could hardly turn her down without any reason. "Of course, Caitlin. I'll have one of the spare rooms ready, and you'll let me know when they'll be arriving, so Archie or I can be home?"

Caitlin's eyes widened at such particularities.

Amelie fought the urge to stamp her foot. She shouldn't have sounded so old-fashioned.

"Oh, I expect so," she said. "I'll drive them around." She nudged Amelie. "With Flora in situ, you won't even notice anyone else." Caitlin leaned forward, planted a kiss on Amelie's cheek and, with a wave of her gloved hand, was off into the distance.

Amelie reached for the handle of her car and sank into the blessed privacy of her seat.

All the way home, worries snarled in her head. How would she get on with Flora? Archie's mother, Mary, was charming, but his sister, from everything she'd heard, was something else.

Amelie could only hope Flora was not a woman who was able to see through a façade.

CHAPTER EIGHTEEN
VIANNE, SPRING, 1925

Vianne reached for a slice of Mama Pepper's Velvety Chocolate Butter Pecan Pie and placed it on one of the pretty pink and green plates that Miss Ellie's mom had brought into the atelier under a checked tea towel in one of her charming wicker baskets. Over the last tumultuous weeks, they'd all come to jump with joy when Mama Pepper arrived with one of her specialties: Divinity—a meringue-type confection—or her Green Mustang Grape Cobbler in a deep pie dish, while busying herself in the kitchen preparing hot chocolate, or iced tea, depending on the mood the Manhattan weather was in.

Vianne allowed the smooth chocolate in the pecan pie to linger on her tongue, while the pecan nuts added a deep richness that was as comforting as a warm pudding on a cold winter's day.

Outside, the springtime sun shone over New York, and in the atelier, Vianne looked around with pleasure at the industry that was going on in the room. Lucia was completing the final patterns for the parade, her dark head bent studiously over her tracings, while Mollie and Goldie were equally focused on sewing a fine light yellow silken dress and jacket that Adeline and Vianne would decorate with a geometric graphic motif, along with circlets of tiny fine beads that would give the ensemble a wonderful sheen under the lights.

Mama Pepper turned from where she'd been admiring one of the already completed pieces for the parade: a sequined dress with a peacock feather motif, and a graduated asymmetric hem. The sequins were sparkling black for the feathers, while their edges were vivid gold, and the peacock pattern was repeated all over the dress, with a golden layer at the top of the bodice. The effect was sophisticated, and shimmering.

"You know, I'm glad I can provide a good pecan pie, but these dresses are something marvelous," Mama Pepper said. "I only wish you weren't selling these charming garments, because if I were forty years younger, I'd be honored to deck myself out in one and go hit the jazz clubs." She twirled her hands in the air. "I'd make a humdinger of a flapper. What do you think?"

Miss Ellie looked up at her mother and rolled her eyes, her hands stilling over a stunning deep golden and black beaded dress, the base a soft pale yellow, scattered with tiny deep yellow beads running in darts toward the center of the bodice, while a magnificent floral centerpiece decorated the front of the dress in black.

"Imagine what the society ladies back home would think of that! You, a flapper? You'd never be invited anywhere again." Miss Ellie sent her mama a mock grin, and Vianne felt some of the tension she'd known these past weeks melt away.

It had been a long time since she'd seen Miss Ellie crack a smile.

"Oh, honey, you make the old ranchers' wives sound as exciting as waiting for paint to dry. Those girls? They'd be Charlestoning and foxtrotting with the best of them if they were young in this decade, I can tell you."

Vianne took the last bite of the delectable pie. "Mama Pepper?"

The elderly woman turned toward Vianne, as bright as a new penny.

"Why don't you come out to a jazz club with us?"

Vianne ignored the way Adeline suddenly raised her head.

"Why not?" she went on, her French accent lending a *je ne sais quoi* to her words. "We've all been working seven days a week. We deserve to enjoy ourselves."

Lucia's eyes danced. "Wait a minute. I've been issuing invitations for weeks, but you've insisted that you won't step your toes inside your T-bar shoes until this parade is done. So, what's Mama Pepper got that I haven't?" She folded her arms in mock-censure.

Vianne wagged a finger at Lucia. "Well, I will put it this way. Mama Pepper says she'd make a good flapper and I don't think there's any call to wait and see her dance. I'm certain, Mama Pepper, you'd outdo us all."

Mama Pepper clicked her fingers, wobbled her knees, and did a fine imitation of the Charleston, her auburn curls bouncing up and down and her brown eyes gleaming like a girl's. "Well, then. What do you say, Ellie? I think I'd be as fine as boomtown silk out at one of those jazz places. Who's in?"

"We'd struggle to keep up with you," Mollie declared.

Goldie giggled behind her hand.

Vianne shot a glance over toward Miss Ellie, but the expression on her boss's face was hard to read.

Finally, Miss Ellie stood up. "Well, since I'm the only person who sees the need for a little decorum in here…"

Mama Pepper threw a hand across her temple behind Miss Ellie's back.

Miss Ellie swiveled around and grinned at her mama. "There is one thing I know for sure. When my mama puts her mind to something, I always say it's as useless as two buggies in a one-horse town to stop her. So, I say, we're going out dancing! The only question is when?"

Vianne sat back down at her worktable with a sigh of relief. Truth was, she'd love to see Mama Pepper dressed up as a flapper, but she was increasingly worried about her boss. Miss Ellie had only turned quieter and quieter these past weeks. A night out dancing could be just the thing she needed to lift her spirits.

It wasn't as if the business wasn't thriving. But Vianne knew that it was she who was bringing in most of the new clientele, not Miss Ellie, and she hoped, fervently, that in doing so, she had not gotten on the wrong side of her boss or upset her ability to design.

Adeline cleared her throat. "I think it's a marvelous idea."

Lucia placed her pen down and cupped her hand in her chin. "You would fit in fine at the Casino Club, Mama Pepper."

"The one in Central Park?" Mollie said, sitting up. "Why, that's supposed to be awful glitzy. I don't know if we could afford to go there."

Miss Ellie raised a hand in protest. "Well then, I'll shout us all a table and Mama and I will bring the champagne. It will be a gas."

Mama Pepper nodded. "There, then. I'll wear a great big coat and hide two bottles inside. No one will think to inspect an old woman like me! Girls, I expect you all to get gussied up! In fact, let's not burn anymore daylight making decisions," Mama Pepper said. "I say we all put on our glad rags and go tonight!"

Mollie and Goldie clutched each other.

"Anyone got a hole in their fence about that?" Mama Pepper said. Her look was triumphant and would have stopped an elephant in its tracks.

Miss Ellie sighed. "I'll go and make a reservation for eleven o'clock. I don't see how they could refuse with you on board, Mama."

"Very well, then." Vianne's eyes lit up. "Shall we meet there, dressed up to the nines?"

The other girls let out an excited squeal.

Lucia hopped out of her seat and went to the gramophone, and when Miss Ellie was out the door, the room swelled with jazz.

That night, Vianne stood outside the glamorous club on Central Park's East Drive at 72nd Street with the other seamstresses, and Mama Pepper, resplendent in a navy silk and cut velvet cape, its large collar framing her strong features perfectly, and the baskets of cherries and flowers that were printed on it gleaming under the bright lights that blazed out from the windows of the grand house that had been jazzed up and turned into a high-society venue.

"I'll tell you what," Mama Pepper said, wagging her finger at everyone in the crowds who could hear. "I used to come here for regular dinners before the war. I was brought here by a couple of swell men who had a mind to become my beau. Before that, it was a ladies' luncheon place, one of the few places in town where women could come unchaperoned, because they weren't expected to take walks in the park alone. My, how things have changed!"

Miss Ellie chuckled. "But you got rid of those prospective beaus, fast and good, Mama."

"I most certainly did," Mama Pepper said, arching one of her painted brows. "I only ever loved one man, and that was your late papa, Eloise. I have no interest in anyone else."

"How romantic," Adeline said, her words suddenly cutting into the group.

Vianne turned to the girl in surprise. "You believe in true love?"

But Adeline shrugged and turned away.

Vianne folded her arms around her sleeveless black dress, a shiver pulsing up her spine, despite the warm evening. The silver beaded details glimmered under the beaming lights. She'd got out of that car as quick as a whippet when Giorgio had dropped her home from Long Island. She'd rushed away. No matter that she'd had a fabulous time at Katherine Carter's party, she knew she must not let any idea of romance with Giorgio take hold.

She was so very attracted to him, and as far as she was concerned, if anything were to develop with him, it would not be just some fling, like the fashionable flappers enjoyed these days. No, with Giorgio, Vianne knew she'd be in too deep.

He'd sent her flowers to her address above the atelier since Long Island, but she'd passed them off to an interested Lucia as thank you gifts from Adriana Conti, and she'd hidden Giorgio's card deep in her armoire. She'd been managing to avoid him since.

"We used to get a steak here for seventy-five cents," Mama Pepper continued.

Vianne forced herself to focus on Mama Pepper. Goldie and Mollie were distracted and looking out at all the handsome society men. Men in swell suits and white hats.

Suddenly there was a stir in the queues. "Well, I'll be," Miss Ellie breathed. "It's none other than Jimmy Walker, otherwise known as the swell Beau James."

Vianne swiveled around along with the rest of the crowd, keen to catch a glimpse of Jimmy Walker, the famous politician whom she'd met at Giorgio's opening, and who everyone swore would be mayor. He'd been at the Cotton Club, and now he was here. Vianne was of a mind to think that Jimmy Walker was going to be everywhere there was a party going on.

The crowds parted for the handsome man, and as he made his way up to the front of the crowd, he stopped, saw Vianne, came toward her, and lifted her hand to touch his lips. "Well, hello again," he said. "It isn't every day I see such beauty gracing the streets of my favorite city."

Vianne looked at him from under her eyelashes. He was awfully good-looking, with his chiseled cheekbones and warm brown eyes. Why couldn't she enjoy a flirtation like any modern girl with a guy like him?

Because her career was worth everything, and because she wanted something deeper and more lasting if she were ever to be able to afford to take the risk. Something like Papa and Maman had. And Maman had met her darling father when she was twenty-one.

"That's very kind of you, Mr. Walker," she said, addressing the politician by his real name. "Although, I think you tell a falsehood. You must see hundreds of pretty girls every time you step out into the street."

He took a step back, and chuckled. "Quite the diplomat," he said. "You should run for public service. You could have done if you weren't so darned good-looking."

Vianne folded her arms and raised a brow. "Well, I'm not sure politics and looks should go together hand in hand!"

He adjusted his cufflinks, and his handsome features broke into a wide grin. "Why are you waiting outside the door, my beautiful one?" He held out his arm, only to have Mama Pepper tuck her hand right in his other elbow and shuffle alongside him too.

"Throw your hat over the windmill, young man, and walk me in too!" Mama Pepper boomed.

The politician sent Mama Pepper the smoothest smile in the world and tightened his grip on Vianne's arm. "Well, my darling, if you put it like that, how could I refuse!"

When they were seated at their table by a liveried footman, the jazz band struck up "We'll have Manhattan," a velvet-voiced singer crooning in front of the band. Vianne allowed Jimmy Walker to lift her hand and place a kiss on it once he'd settled her in her seat before he filtered off into the crowds.

Mollie and Goldie buried themselves in the à la carte menus, pointing at the extravagant dishes and whispering with delight, and a waiter came and placed champagne glasses down for them all, with only a quiet nod when Mama Pepper produced two bottles from under her cape.

"My, this is special," Lucia said. "When I said jazz club, we sure picked the right one."

Vianne cupped her chin in her hands, letting the lyrics of the popular song drift over her. The jazz singer crooned about a couple too poor to afford a honeymoon but who were happy to save their fares and go for a walk down the Lower East Side's Delancey Street instead. Vianne let the last, exhausting few weeks slip away.

In the dark of night, she'd taken to wondering how a love affair with a man like Giorgio Conti could work in a world where Miss Ellie's and society's strictures did not exist. What if they both had their own careers, she an atelier of her own someday, and Giorgio, his beloved Valentino's? But then, she was pipe dreaming. Wouldn't Giorgio expect her to give up working to become a housewife if they were to marry?

Vianne sighed. Even flappers were only expected to have fun while they were single young things in jazz clubs like this one, but when they were married, in most cases, they were expected to follow traditions, be good wives and stay home.

"Vianne!"

Vianne started at Lucia's tap on her shoulder.

"You're sittin' there like a girl with a crush, and we're all off to the dance floor. Come on!" Lucia rolled her dark eyes, kicked up her legs, and threw a glance toward the crowded floor, where Mama Pepper was doing the Texas Tommy with some swell half her age, taking the acrobatic moves in her stride, and whirling around the room with this guy, before linking arms with Mollie, Goldie, Adeline, and Miss Ellie and twirling around in a circle, her jacket flying out in a balloon behind her.

"Oh, my," Vianne murmured, her eyes dancing at the sight in front of her, and linking her arm with Lucia's. "Will you take a look at that!"

"I *know*." Lucia's eyes lit up and she walked Vianne to the floor. "Well, honey, let's dance the night away like Mama Pepper and forget all about sewing for a while!"

At two o'clock in the morning, Mama Pepper was still up on the dance floor, and no one could get her to stop.

"Lucky corsets went out with the war," Goldie said, fanning her face and sitting down with Vianne after a rousing version of the Brazilian samba. "I don't know how Mama Pepper does it, but she's moving like a girl in her twenties, as if she grew up in this era, not in Victorian times."

Lucia leaned close to Vianne. "So glad you're having a break," she said.

Vianne squeezed Lucia's hand, her cheeks flushed from the good old exertion of dancing. She felt as if ten million spiderwebs had been cleared out of her system tonight. When she was shimmying and foxtrotting, her worries about the still mammoth amount of work that had to be done for the parade all but disappeared.

On her other side, Adeline was quiet, her chest heaving up and down from her efforts.

Vianne turned to the girl. "You are having a good time, Adeline?" she asked.

They both shared a commitment to hard work and perfection when it came to the intricate beading and embroidery that the current fashions demanded, and Vianne hated the bad blood that was between them over Adeline's misconceptions about Giorgio. After all, they may be working together for a long time and there seemed little point in not getting along.

Vianne attempted to smile at Adeline.

"I'm enjoying myself," Adeline said, her tone filled with that sense of mystery that Vianne had come to notice. "I suppose you wish someone was here."

"Adeline?" Vianne glanced at Lucia, Goldie, and Mollie, who were up to their sequined décolletages in gossip about one of the chaps on the dance floor. Across the crowded room, Miss Ellie was trying and failing to persuade Mama Pepper to come sit down.

Adeline turned to Vianne slowly, and then gave her full attention.

This was a little disconcerting, but Vianne took in a deep breath and plowed on. "I hope there was no misunderstanding between us that night at the Cotton Club," she ventured. "You see..." she chose her words carefully. As Maman always said, there was sometimes a fine thread between the truth and a lie. "I would never jeopardize my career with Miss Ellie over any man." Vianne placed her own champagne glass back down. "My work is the most important thing in the world to me. I hope you've seen my commitment to the atelier these past few weeks." Also, the truth.

Adeline was quiet. A myriad of expressions passed across her face. She spread her fingers out and looked at them.

Vianne waited, and finally, Adeline tapped her fingers on the table. "You walked in from Paris and were immediately given far more privileges than we've ever had. And still, you exploited that by dancing cheek to cheek with one of the customers' sons. Can you see how that looks to the rest of us?" Adeline turned to Vianne, her blue eyes intense.

Vianne folded her hands in her lap. "I'm sorry," she said simply. "I didn't look at it like that."

Adeline stood up, collected her coat, and looked down at Vianne. "You're lucky I haven't given your game away, completely, Vianne. But don't imagine I'm not aware." She clutched her coat in her arms. "I know that you went out to a party with Giorgio Conti again to Long Island. The only reason I haven't told Miss Ellie about that is because it would genuinely break her heart. The atelier is not just business to her, Vianne. It's her life."

Vianne flinched away from the other seamstress, and Adeline picked up her cloche hat, placed it atop her head, and marched out the door of the club and into the New York night.

The following morning, Vianne woke after a sleepless night, tossing and turning after Adeline's seeming threats to her. Was the girl right? Had Vianne simply been given more privileges than the others because she was from Paris? Did Miss Ellie know, too, that she'd been out to Long Island with Giorgio, and most importantly, was Vianne stepping way above her pay grade by associating with the likes of Katherine Carter and Giorgio? But then, she'd brought new business into the atelier by going to Long Island. Katherine Carter had made an appointment for a consultation about her summer wardrobe with Vianne, and surely that was helpful for Miss Ellie. What was more, Mrs. Carter had expressed sincerely that several of her friends also wanted a ticket to Vianne's designs.

But where did the line end between being a good business-woman and a lowly seamstress with no family? Papa used to discuss business and gather prospective clients all the time at social functions. People were drawn to him like bears to honey.

Vianne washed, dressed, marched out of the atelier and down

to her favorite patisserie in New York. For now, she wanted to be the girl from Paris, and nothing more. The modern world was strange and complex, and it seemed the rules for women in business were not set in stone. Katherine Carter had shown no discomfort at Vianne coming to her party. Might the rules be bent a little?

Vianne pushed the door open to the French bakery, and she was in Paris once more. Baskets sat atop a marble bench behind the counter filled with warm, freshly baked pastries, almond croissants, pain au chocolat filled with the highest-quality dark chocolate, delicious baked raisin breads filled with sweet sultanas and pastry cream, and handmade French brioches, so soft and buttery that Vianne could swear she was back in France.

"*Bonjour*, Madeline," she said to the owner, a fellow French expatriot who had worked for years to find her customers in New York.

"*Bonjour*, Vianne," Madeline said, her eyes lighting up at the sight of Vianne. "*Ça va?*" she asked.

"*Oui, ça va bien, merci*," Vianne replied. "Six of the best croissants in Manhattan, and one of your large quiches, please," Vianne said to Madeline.

Madeline bustled around behind the counter, carefully choosing her wares for Vianne, and packing everything in boxes and pale pink bags, which she tied with pink bows.

Vianne sent Madeline one of her most ravishing smiles and strolled back out into the New York sunshine, beating a familiar path down Park Avenue to the atelier.

Even though it was Saturday, the seamstresses had agreed that they'd all show up at work this morning to continue preparing for the parade.

Now, they had a perfect selection of fashionable pleated sports skirts and overblouses for their modern active clientele, as well as some charming two-pieces suits, or tailleurs, and daywear ensembles in a range of the latest season's colors—powder blue, biscuit, and white—along with riding habits, bathing and beach costumes, and even silk undergarments, which would be discreetly modeled for ladies' eyes only in a private room at Valentino's, for those who wished to view them. And then, there would be the pièces de résistance, the wonderful evening dresses, and Vianne's wedding gown.

Vianne hugged her Parisian specialties, pushing aside her worries about Giorgio and Adeline, and sashayed through the Saturday morning crowds to East 63rd Street. Sometimes, it helped to get out amongst people when it came to clearing her head.

"She's here!"

Vianne stilled outside the door to the seamstresses' workroom, tilting her head at the sounds of the girls inside bustling about. There was a shuffle, and Vianne pushed the door open.

"Good morning, girls," she said, almost singing the words.

Mollie and Goldie were standing so close to each other it was difficult to tell where one of them ended and the other began. Adeline did not even look up.

Lucia swung around on her work stool and sent Vianne a mock swoon when she saw the paper bags she held from Madeline's. "Oh, dearest, you know how partial I am to those French specialties. I swear, I love my Italian food, but those pastries, especially that hit of chocolate inside, I have never enjoyed my breakfast so much in my life!"

"I have pain au chocolat for you," Vianne called, briskly opening her parcels in the tiny kitchen off the workroom. "You know I would never forget."

"Well, you've made my day, Vianne," Lucia said.

Vianne fixed a pot of coffee, and one hot chocolate for her sweet-toothed friend. She brought everything out on a wide tray, setting it on the table that sat in their lunch room.

The girls crowded around her, and when everyone was holding a delicious plate with a treat, Mollie cleared her throat.

"Are we ready?" Mollie said, eyeing Goldie, Lucia, and Adeline in turn.

"Fire away," Lucia said.

Adeline shrugged.

"You have a secret?" Vianne said, sending the girls a look of mock concern.

Mollie's eyes lit up. "Well, no, but we happen to have a surprise!"

Goldie, her cheeks turned quite pink, placed down her plate of food, went out to the workroom, and hovered in the lunch-room doorway holding one of Miss Ellie's garment bags.

Vianne put her coffee cup down, her eyes narrowing with interest as the tall girl stood there, seeming awkward. "Goldie," she said, "you have made something special for the parade?"

"In a way." Goldie nodded, her very ears burning red underneath her fine blond hair. The room turned quiet. Until, with a flourish, Goldie removed the white cotton cover and revealed a full-length cream chiffon and lace dress.

Vianne gasped. She glided across the room, hardly aware of her feet, the gown was so gorgeous. "Well," she murmured. "May I?" She reached out to touch the gossamer-soft chiffon. "How ingenious," Vianne said, walking around to inspect the garment as Goldie held it up. The skirt flared asymmetrically from the waist, giving the most modern, wonderful feel, and gold embroidery wrapped around the back of the bodice. Vianne examined the fine gold stitching, large Oriental flowers that were spectacular on the front and the back, and even more rich gold embroidery flared at the base of the skirt. "It would flicker and shine as you walk," Vianne breathed. "You know how I love to play with light, and this is sensational."

Goldie was pink with excitement. "I'm glad you like it," she said, almost shy.

"Why? Like it? I absolutely adore it." Vianne turned to face the seamstresses. "Did you all come up with this or..."

But Lucia held her plate up, her dark eyes sparkling with pride. "It was Goldie's design," she said, "and her idea."

"Goldie," Vianne said. "We should tell Miss Ellie about this."

But Goldie shook her head. "Oh, Vianne, it took ever so much out of me. I'm going to stick to sewing from now on."

"We'll see about that." Vianne folded her hands on her hips.

"Are you going to tell Vianne, Goldie?" Lucia prompted.

"There's more?" Vianne said.

Goldie sent her a nervous smile. "You see, the thing is, we wanted to make this for you to wear at the parade. To show our appreciation for all you've done since you arrived at Miss Ellie's."

Vianne brought a hand to her mouth, suddenly overwhelmed with the thoughtfulness of this. Vianne knew she'd driven the seamstresses far harder than they deserved, and she knew this was because poor Miss Ellie seemed so distracted, she was hardly here in spirit some days, but somehow, Vianne had gotten them all this far, and they were all still working happily together.

"Goldie. I'm speechless. All of you," she said, her throat catching. "Adeline, the embroidery. It must have taken you hours."

Adeline raised a brow.

Vianne took a deep breath and plowed on. "Mollie and Goldie, the way the darts run on the diagonal just below the waist, and the way the fabric is cut in alternating panels flowing down and then across is perfection. And, Lucia, the whole pattern has translated to beauty. I don't know how to thank you." Vianne shook her head. "I value you all. Enormously," she whispered.

"And we you," Lucia said. "I can tell you that since you've come here, a new light has gone on in this room. I never thought I'd be making patterns for a parade at Valentino's, with all the press looking on. Me, just a girl from the Village who grew up in a crowded tenement. Honestly, I thought I'd spend my life behind the scenes slaving away for fussy clientele. But look at what you've done. Now, I can proudly say that I sewed garments for a proper parade, with illustrious guests."

Vianne caught Adeline's gaze and tried smiling at her. The other girl looked down, her expression hard to read.

"I'm glad you're all able to finally see the results of your hard work away from the atelier," Vianne said softly, directing her gaze at Adeline. "Goodness knows, you all deserve to do so. I hope... I hope that one day that will become a common occurrence, and no matter whether you are a seamstress or the head of a couture house, you can mix freely with the clientele, and all be respected for the part you play."

"Well, that sounds like utopia," Lucia said, holding up her hot chocolate. "But I'll drink to that."

"Thanks for the part you're playing in making it come true," Mollie said.

Adeline lifted her head sharply, and Vianne smiled warmly at her.

Mollie placed an arm around Goldie's shoulder. "You know, Vianne, when Goldie and I came here to work after sitting sewing twelve hours at a stretch in the factory in the Garment District, we thought we'd died and landed in a royal palace. We thought we were a pair of real princesses. But now, with you here, well... You've opened up our worlds just like you have for Lucia."

Vianne chose her words carefully. "It's a new century. Women can do anything. And why shouldn't we?"

Goldie smiled shyly. "So, you'll wear our dress at the parade?" she said.

"Oh, I'll tell everyone who asks and everyone who doesn't who designed it, too," Vianne said. "It's beautiful. Extraordinary. Thank you," she said.

There was a silence, and Vianne felt compelled to share something of herself, what with all these confessions from the others.

"And I never thought," she said, her voice low in the sun-filled room, "that I would ever get the opportunity to be a midinette in Paris, let alone a young woman designing for a parade in New York alongside some of the most talented seamstresses in the business. But, no matter how I came to be here, look how things have turned out."

"Well, cheers to us all," Lucia said, holding aloft her hot chocolate. "And may the parade next week be an almighty, rip-roaring, success!"

"To the parade!" the seamstresses said, holding their coffee cups high.

"There's one more thing," Vianne said, when the girls had quietened. "I have to say, that for the first time since the war, I feel like I've come home."

There was a stillness in the room, and Vianne took in a deep, satisfied breath.

Later that afternoon, when the girls were starting to yawn, and Vianne had insisted everyone go home and rest, she collected her pale blue coat, put on her hat and white gloves.

She was of a mind to go for a walk in Central Park. But just as she stepped out into East 63rd Street, she came to a sudden stop. A young woman was crouched in the doorway of one of the smart apartment buildings on the other side of the street.

If Vianne were not mistaken, the girl was Adeline.

Vianne didn't hesitate. She dodged the cars beetling past, walked straight over to the girl who last night had been so imperious as to suggest Vianne was risking the ruin of Miss Ellie's business and crouched down next to her.

"Adeline?" she said. "Are you okay, honey?"

The girl looked up at her, and shook her head, her blue eyes misted, her usually flushed cheeks pale and streaked with tears. Vianne glanced up and down the street. Thankfully, Mollie and Goldie had disappeared off into Manhattan, and the folks who passed she and Adeline by did not as much as take a moment to register the young seamstress sitting crying right in the center of New York's wealthiest neighborhood.

"Come on." Vianne tucked her hand beneath Adeline's elbow and gently lifted the girl to her feet. Vianne took a moment to check her fellow seamstress for bruises or scrapes, but there was no sign of any injuries.

Adeline stiffened under the touch of Vianne's hand. "Leave me be," she said. "Go away, Vianne."

Vianne frowned. "I'm not leaving you alone," she whispered. "Let's get you somewhere safe."

Just then, Adeline started shaking something terrible, her entire body shuddering, and Vianne led her like a rag doll back across the street. Pulling out her keys and opening the solid front door, she eased Adeline up to the apartment she shared with Lucia. Silently, she sent up a prayer of thanks that Lucia had gone to visit her family for the afternoon. Vianne's brows knitted together as she led Adeline into the small living room and offered that her to sit herself down.

Vianne asked no questions and busied herself making two cups of coffee in the kitchen. When she came back into the living room, Adeline was staring with that same glassy-eyed gaze out of the window to the building opposite.

Vianne sat down. Silently, she placed the steaming cup of coffee in front of the other girl. Traffic sounds and whistles and people shouting outside bled into the tiny apartment, while Adeline sat in a silence that Vianne didn't know how to break.

Vianne tried to extend a hand across the table. "You don't have to talk, but if you want to, I'll listen, and you can trust me. Please, let me know what I can do to help."

Adeline simply sat with tears streaming down her pretty face, and when she reached out to pick up the cup of coffee, Vianne frowned at the way the girl's delicate hand still shook.

"Have something warm to drink," Vianne soothed. "Have you had a shock, is that it? Did someone try to attack you, Adeline, because if they did, then—"

Adeline held up a hand. "What would you know," she said, her voice dark and treacherous, and coming from a place that even for Adeline was somber.

Vianne let these words linger between them a moment. Adeline took a few sips of her coffee, and a little color returned to her cheeks, only to suddenly leech out of them again, until the girl was again a ghostly version of herself.

"I might know quite a bit," Vianne whispered. "I understand what it is to suffer, Adeline. Remember, I traveled halfway around the world alone and left my home in France. Not that I had one," she added ruefully. "I really had nothing at all."

Adeline stared at nothing. "Well, nothing's better than a whole lot of baloney."

Vianne sat back in her seat. She cradled her coffee cup. "Adeline..."

"He said," Adeline went on, in that odd, monotonous voice, "that he loved me. That we'd have a wonderful future together when his legal guardian gave him his rightful inheritance. He told me we'd travel the world when he'd come into his money, that he'd support me through thick and thin, that we'd buy an apartment right up near the atelier, and that he'd buy me all the clothes I wanted, so I didn't have to work anymore, and I could parade past Miss Ellie's and just let her look at me in my finery."

"Ah." Vianne folded her arms and heaved out a breath.

"I met Arthur at a jazz club. I was out dancing with Lucia and there was something special between us from that very first dance. He had twinkling eyes and a gentlemanly way about him." Adeline was pale. "I thought I'd died and landed in the most heavenly lap. He told me how his guardian had raised him after his parents died in an accident when he was a baby, and how when he was twenty-five, he'd come into his rightful inheritance—a fortune that was worthy of a prince, he said." Adeline turned her bright blue eyes toward Vianne. "I thought it was all right. But now I know, I wanted to believe it was all right. Do you understand the difference?"

Vianne nodded. She laid a hand on Adeline's arm. "Oh, of course, Adeline. Of course, I do. At times, we all want to believe sweet words are more than treacle spilling off a spoon."

Adeline let out a bitter laugh. "I... thought it was real. I thought..." she bit out the words, punching them out one hard syllable at a time. "I thought he meant that he loved me, that he meant that he'd marry me, that he meant it when he said he'd take care of me no matter what." She took in a shaking breath. "I was thrilled when I was with child."

Vianne closed her eyes.

"I thought Arthur was the love of my life, and, at first, when he told me to wait, while he spoke to his guardian, to make arrangements so we could marry soon, I was as excited as a nightclub full of illegal pink gin. I almost told Lucia and the girls, but he asked me to wait, because, he said, he had a great big surprise for me."

"Ah ha," Vianne said. She crossed her legs and folded her arms.

Adeline smiled now, through the tears that fell freely down her cheeks. "I wanted to be able to tell my mom, up in heaven, that I'd made it, that I had met a man who'd do me no wrong. She had to make a living sewing sequins on costumes out the back of the Broadway theaters, only to die in her forties of exhaustion. She told me to find a man who could take care of me, a man like the fabled ancestors we had back in France before my family had to escape from the revolution to America, before everything changed. And I thought I'd done that. I thought I'd found one of the good men, Vianne. I thought, finally, I could get back for my family's memory, what we had lost so long ago."

"I'm sorry."

"Still, I trusted Arthur. Still, I believed him when he said everything would turn out fine. That we'd be married," Adeline continued. "I was riding high on confidence. But one by one, all his promises came to nothing. First, he told me we'd have to wait longer than he thought, then I saw him out dancing one night with another girl, they looked real close, you see. And then, he told me that he didn't know whether he could marry me after all."

"And the baby?" Vianne whispered.

"He paid for it to be terminated," Adeline said. She stared at the tabletop. "He made me promise not to tell anyone, lest his guardian found out and cut him off for good. And then, after that, I never heard from him or saw him again until... well, until a few moments ago." Her voice shook as she took in a deep breath.

Vianne reached her hand out across the table, but Adeline simply stared at it.

"I should have known. He hadn't done anything with his life, except follow his rich guardian around like some adoring puppy dog. He worked in a department store; he had no ambitions to do anything like I do. And today, he walked right by me, and on his arm was a well-dressed lady wearing a sparkling diamond engagement ring."

"I'm so sorry."

"Well," Adeline said simply, her words watery again. "I loved him. Maybe I was a fool for that, but my feelings and my actions were true, and they were based on the promises he made to me, that all came to nothing. And you know what?"

Vianne shook her head.

"The woman he is marrying? You can bet your bottom dollar she's not a seamstress. You understand what I'm saying, Vianne?"

"Of course. But—"

"No. You listen to me," Adeline said. She leaned forward and gripped Vianne's hand. "Miss Ellie won't let you down. I would fight to the end for her. But be careful around Giorgio Conti."

"Yes, but Giorgio is not making any promises, or in any way misleading me with false—"

"He's hard-working," Adeline continued. "I give him that. But he's a fella who also knows how to play hard in the jazz clubs, and you don't want to get yourself burned."

Vianne sat back in her seat. She folded her arms and let out a long sigh.

"Miss Ellie's the best thing you've got," Adeline said. "And she's all you need. Your job. It's everything. Don't do what I did."

"I'm sure Giorgio is a gentleman," Vianne whispered.

Adeline let out a sultry laugh. "So, I was right," she said. "You're falling for him, aren't you?"

"No," Vianne lied.

Adeline gazed at Vianne, her bright blue eyes two chips of ice. "You don't know a gentleman until he proves himself to be so," Adeline whispered. "Do you understand I'm looking out for you? Do you know why I don't want you to risk anything, Vianne?"

Silently, Vianne reached out and covered her strange companion's hand with her own.

After Adeline's departure, when the girl had insisted she was well enough to go home, Vianne wandered out of the atelier, desperate for some fresh air in Central Park. Everything was a whirl. The parade was coming up, her career seemed to be flourishing. But was Adeline right? Was she destined never to have the sort of love that Maman and Papa had all their lives? And would Miss Ellie really stop her from being happy with someone, even if she proved herself to be a worthy and valued designer on her own terms? Was Giorgio a cad or the hard-working man whom Vianne thought him to be?

Vianne came to Valentino's on the corner, her eye catching with Giorgio's through the window of the restaurant. He was chatting with a waiter. Vianne hesitated, and he raised his arm in a wave, indicating that she come on inside and talk to him.

Vianne's fingers tingled in her gloves.

He threw his arms in the air and grinned at her, and before she knew it, he was striding toward his glass double doors, his head poking around the main door to the grand building on Park Avenue.

"Vianne."

Vianne stepped aside to allow for a noisy group of shoppers to pass by. She closed her eyes, Adeline's stark warning ringing in her ears. How was she supposed to know whether Giorgio was an Arthur, or a good man like her papa?

"I was going to the park for a walk, Giorgio," she said.

His eyes locked with hers, and she bit her lip and looked away.

"Do you... mind if I join you?" he asked, after what seemed like an age.

She looked up at him. That was the last thing she needed. Or should she give him a chance to prove that he was the kind of man he professed to be?

Vianne sighed. Miss Ellie aside, if she didn't follow things through with Giorgio, she'd always wonder. And not knowing might be worse than learning everything. She wasn't a coward. And she'd heed Adeline's story. What was more, she'd not do anything wrong by Miss Ellie.

"I could do with a break, *Bella*," he said softly, taking her elbow to stop her from being bowled over by a man in a camel-colored suit. "And I'd love to talk," he added, his voice softening.

"It could be a business meeting," she said, deadpan.

"Let's go," he said, tucking her arm into the crook of his elbow. "Before you change your mind and drag me back inside to discuss menu plans."

Vianne was quiet as they wandered across to the park, and she was acutely aware of Giorgio's hand atop hers, resting gently on her glove as they navigated the crowds.

"I hope Eloise has not scared you with any more strictures about me," he said.

Vianne sighed. "I shouldn't be out with you. But I..." What? How to tell him she had to follow this through, no matter what Miss Ellie said, despite Adeline's warnings. Because if Anaïs or Maman were alive, they'd tell her to follow her heart and find out where things might lead.

"Let's go to Bow Bridge," he said. "It's a beautiful part of the park. We can talk."

Share their news...

Vianne crinkled her brow, forcing herself to focus on the incredible beauty that surrounded them in Central Park. Her eyes were drawn from the straight path they were walking on toward the deep green American elm trees that lined the walk, their overarching branches soaring like the ceiling of a cathedral overhead.

They came to the end of the pathway, where the lake spread out serene in front of them, the trees reflecting in the still water, the sound of birdsong breaking a rare moment of quiet.

"What a beautiful bridge," Vianne said, gasping at the almost perfect view in front of them. Bow Bridge spanned the lake, curving elegantly up to a gentle crescendo, before easing down over to the other side. The deeply polished wooden boards underfoot reminded Vianne of those on the decks of SS *Paris*. Perhaps this bridge would lead her somewhere new, just as the ship had done.

She turned to Giorgio.

"Would you like to walk along the bridge with me?" he asked, his lips curling into a smile. "You know, it's called Bow Bridge, because of the way it curves like an archer's bow."

Vianne nodded, and walked onto the bridge with him. She leaned on the balustrade, her eyes resting on the mirror-like water. For a moment, she thought about how she used to stare at the Seine, and she fought to turn away the image of Maman's face reflected in the water that awful day, near the Seine. Here, there was only opaque stillness and, in the distance, the busy sounds of New York. No one here knew of that dreadful day in Paris, no one cared or felt a whit about Vianne's family. Everyone here had their own lives to lead, their own stories to tell.

Suddenly chilled, she wrapped her arms around her body.

Vianne's brow furrowed, and she pushed her shoulders back and turned to face Giorgio. "I once told you that I wanted to make something of my life. To make the most of it," she said.

He leaned against the balustrade, his eyes searching hers.

Vianne stared at him. She'd lived too much to give up anything for a man. She'd also come to depend on herself, and this was not something she wanted to let go. Things were going to be different for the women of her generation than they were for Maman's, they had to be. But how would it work?

Giorgio's dark brows crinkled. "I admire women who have a career. I admire, you, Vianne."

A lone bird sang in a nearby tree.

Vianne sighed.

"I would never do anything to risk your job, nor harm your career. Surely you know that. Darling Vianne," he said. "You have a wonderful future. You must make it happen. This is New York and it's a new century. Anything goes. I think that's why we both came here. You from France, me from Italy."

"I know," she murmured.

He took her gloved hand in his and held it close to his heart.

"One day," he said, "I would love for there to be more between us. And I do think," he murmured, his voice barely audible, but his words as clear as a bell even though he spoke so softly, "it's time you made your own rules. And I know that, one day, you'll have your own atelier, and darling Vianne, I would be honored to be the man who was by your side while you soar to your greatest heights. You must not let anything stand in your way. And I would never stop you from realizing all your dreams."

She closed her eyes, and when she did so, she felt the lightest touch of Giorgio's lips grazing hers.

CHAPTER NINETEEN
ELOISE, SPRING, 1925

Eloise watched as the models from Robert Powers practiced, sashaying up and down on the catwalk in Valentino's above the tables that were all set up for the grand parade. Vianne was right up front, directing the girls, working alongside the choreographer. Every now and then, Eloise's most indispensable staff member would hop up onto the catwalk, carefully checking the flow of a garment, instructing the model to turn this way or that to capture a dress to its fullest advantage under the lights. Of course, Vianne could be a model herself, and the girls respected this and listened to Vianne's advice. Vianne was looking sensational in a frock of faille crepe in black, featuring the latest vogue for scallops on the skirt, with collar and cuffs in cream georgette.

"Vianne is doing marvelously," Eddie Winter said.

"I know." Eloise sighed. She had to open up to someone, and Eddie had proved himself to be a good friend. Despite her reservations about the fact he was a journalist, he'd not told anyone a thing she'd confided in him so far, and he'd promised to give her summer collection a double-page spread in *Bella* magazine. She pressed a hand to her temple. "Vianne is marvelous, but I, however, feel like I'm riding solo on the lower story of a double-decker bus and going nowhere, Eddie."

Eddie took off his glasses, his eyes lighting up in amusement. "Darling, that's the most original description I've heard in an age. Of what, I have no idea."

Eloise leaned against one of Giorgio Conti's round tables. They'd all been placed around the catwalk, and tomorrow, they'd sparkle with crystal glasses and silverware. And now, Giorgio was buried down in the kitchens with his patisserie staff. He'd kindly closed the restaurant this evening to allow for the dress rehearsal and had refused to take a cent of compensation for any loss of revenue on his part despite Valentino's now being the place to go in central Manhattan.

Eloise knew she was fortunate, and she also knew that without Vianne and Giorgio, this parade would have been well beyond her grasp.

She folded her arms and looked across the room at her mother. Mama Pepper was seated at one of the front tables, leaning on a walking stick she'd decided to use for effect lately, tapping it on the floor and clapping her hands whenever she spotted a dress she particularly liked.

"Brava!" she called out when the girls appeared in tennis dresses.

Eloise smiled at Mama Pepper's continual joie de vivre.

But that was the problem.

"It's like this," she said, looking up at Eddie, who still regarded her with a look of complete bemusement. "My mother, as you see, is riding high on the top deck of the bus, thrilled with everything she sees, and marveling at the joys each day brings in her advancing age. Young Vianne and Giorgio Conti are the new generation, the engines, carrying out all the work with the energy of ten people, and thriving on it. They have a direction, and they are both working hard. And me? I am standing by while a younger woman copies my designs and carries them off. I'm invisible, Eddie, and I don't know which way is up or down."

Eddie removed his glasses and tilted his head to one side.

Eloise saw this as encouragement to continue.

"I have lost both my sense of enjoyment and my direction." She shook her head. "I am in no man's land. I have no idea how to get to the place where my mother is, and I lack the energy to keep up with the likes of Vianne and Giorgio. As for Lena Davis, she is not my problem. I am."

Eddie frowned. "Not that you have anything against Vianne, darling?"

Eloise shook her head. "Of course not. She's a wonderful inspiration for the other girls." Eloise glanced across the room, where Lucia and Adeline were right beside Vianne, whispering with her, their expressions earnest. Eloise knew they were all in their element tonight. And she was glad that Vianne had convinced her to break one of her rules and allow the seamstresses to see their dresses out, away from the atelier. The idea that these young, hardworking women should be unseen was ridiculous. Antiquated. But where did a middle-aged woman fit in, in this new modern world? "I don't know where I'm going anymore Eddie, and this scares me."

Eddie was quiet, but he regarded her seriously.

It seemed a good idea to finish what she'd started to say. "I am certain, Eddie, that tomorrow's parade will give my atelier an enormous boost, and if Lena wants to imitate my designs, and has not the talent to come up with her own ideas, well then, perhaps that is only flattering toward me."

Eddie folded his arms. "Eloise?"

"I think that, as much as I've resisted change, department stores are going to copy designers more and more. But some women will always want dressmakers who can design a garment to fit them perfectly. And there will always be a market for people like Vianne who can design beautiful haute couture. She is an artist in herself, Eddie."

Eddie frowned. "I still think you could have a fantastic battle with Lena. I do wish you'd bite."

She rested her hand on his shoulder. "And I think, Eddie, we should stop talking about her. I don't think she merits our attention, to be honest. Anyone with a wealthy husband and money behind them can copy others and promote herself. I don't want to give her any more of my time."

Eddie sent her a slow grin. "Well done. But what's the answer for you, darling? I had no idea you were feeling so... lost."

She looked up at Eddie. "To that, I have absolutely no idea."

He patted her on the arm. "Let's go out tonight. Get your mind off things."

Eloise shrugged. She fixed her gaze on Vianne, watching as the young designer adjusted the hem of a black-and-white silk embroidered coat decorated with Egyptian art.

Right now, Eloise had no idea whether she was supposed to be young, or old. She had no idea how to be in-between.

"Sure," she said. "Let's go out, Eddie. Let's see if New York has any answers for me."

"Hello, suckers!"

Eloise rolled her eyes at the famous greeting from Mary Louise Cecelia "Texas" Guinan, hostess at the El Fey club. She clutched onto Eddie's arm as they walked through the club on West 45th Street, her senses assailed with the smell of alcohol. The parade was all prepared, Vianne and Giorgio had assured her they'd close Valentino's tonight and see that all the garments were correctly stored. She'd thanked them both, along with her seamstresses, and Lucia had said she'd see Mama Pepper home. Eloise, in a state because she shouldn't be going out the night before her huge parade, had left on Eddie's arm, hardly knowing what she was doing next.

The opulent interior of the El Fey club, famously grand, was utterly overshadowed by Texas, presiding from a stage-side table, her eyes rounded, and her hair curled in the latest style. Draped in ermine, she was wisecracking with the performers about to go on stage.

Everyone in New York knew the stories, how nothing honest came out of Texas' mouth. She'd convinced countless reporters that she'd ridden broncos, single-handedly rounded up cattle on some huge Texas ranch, attended an elite Southern finishing school, and run off to join the circus.

"I admit I'm a little terrified," Eloise said. "I'm not planning on emulating Texas, if that's what you had in mind."

"Everything she says is complete bunkum, darling," Eddie replied.

Eloise chuckled. She couldn't take her eyes off the woman, perched on a stool in the center of the club, armed with a whistle and her own booming voice.

The woman had confidence. If she was full of bunkum, she sure knew how to pull it off.

Eddie slapped a short, dark-haired, horse-faced guy on the back and introduced him as Larry Fay.

"Well, you're dressed to kill," Eloise said, eyeing the owner of the club's sharp dark suit, his black hat, his purple shirt and his tie. The tales about him were as legendary as those about Texas Guinan. Larry was a mobster who'd made his bucketload by driving a cab to the Canadian border, and loading up with whiskey, which he'd bring back to New York, selling it on for good money, and then establishing a fleet of cabs when he realized he'd hit pay dirt.

Larry lifted his hat and pulled his cigar out of his mouth. "Well then, that's a compliment coming from a lady of fashion." He raised a brow and waved his cigar about. "And I hear you've got a doll working for you. Word is, you're going to hit the big lights." He sent her a grin, and Eloise barked out a laugh.

Vianne, again, bless her heart.

"Well, I thank you," she said hopelessly. "Eddie, I don't know if this is helping me at all," she said truthfully when Larry had slipped away into the salon. If she was having a crisis of belonging, she sure didn't fit in with Larry's crowd. New York had answers for everyone's problems, but Eloise felt like she was lost in a great misty swamp.

Eddie led her to a table overlooking the stage, and a glass of champagne appeared right in front of her the moment she sat down. Eddie sipped the whiskey he was handed, and then slipped the waiter a ten-dollar bill.

Eloise raised a brow in protest. "Ten dollars?"

But Eddie waved this away. "The whiskey's outrageously overpriced, but plentiful," he said. "Drink up, Eloise, and forget your problems. It's the only way to manage in this town."

Eloise raised a brow and grabbed her cigarette holder out of her bag. She waved it in the air, hoping to at least look like a flapper, even though she felt as exciting as a mashed potato sandwich right now.

"So, now we can talk," Eddie said, just as the band struck up a riotous rendition of "Sweet Georgia Brown."

Eloise rolled her eyes and raised her glass in a toast. "Well, I don't know what my problem is. I only hope the answer I have in mind works."

Eddie lit up a cigarette and regarded her through plumes of smoke. "Talk to me."

She let out a dramatic sigh. "I don't know if you understand this, Eddie, but I've worked hard all my adult life."

He narrowed his eyes. "Of course," he said.

"And I've sacrificed many things, to take care of Mama Pepper, and to grow the atelier."

"It's a whirl," he said.

Eloise let the champagne bubbles rest on her tongue a moment. "Yes, but in the process, I've become as much fun as chopping wood."

"That's not true," Eddie shook his head and made a face. "I think you're fun."

She tapped him on the arm with her cigarette holder. "I think there's only one answer. There's only one thing to do."

Eddie leaned closer.

Eloise took in a breath, and she lowered her voice, determined to tell him exactly what she planned.

CHAPTER TWENTY
AMELIE, SPRING, 1925

Amelie stood outside Carrig's front door, her gloved hand tucked into Archie's. A lone curlew threw arcs high above the grand house, the bird's mottled brown and gray wings beating steadily, her haunting, sad call cleaving through the still, Highland air. The garden was serene as a pond in May. But Amelie's heart was reverberating as persistently as the beat of a Scottish drummer before the bagpipes swelled into action and the music began.

The sound of the car's engine burned into the air, and Amelie let go of Archie's hand, her fingers flying up to fidget with the pearls around her neck. Mary's pearls. They'd been a wedding gift.

Mary had telephoned this morning, informing Amelie that Archie's younger sister, Flora, was now at Mary's house and would be arriving at Carrig after lunch. Amelie had gone into a spin, checking Flora's old bedroom was properly prepared, picking fresh roses from the garden borders, telling the maid she did not want luncheon. She was in a state.

Archie clearly adored his younger sister. He'd disappear into his library, smiling to himself when her letters arrived, having missed her while she traveled Europe, working sporadically and leading the life of a modern girl.

Amelie needed Flora to adore her.

When a sporty little Crossley Bugatti roared over the bridge that arched over the burn, the busy brown water rushing over the rocks below, Amelie took in a calming breath, her eyes seeking out Archie's sister behind the wheel, fascinated to see if she was as beautiful as legend had it. Through the windscreen, as the car came to a halt before them, Amelie watched while Flora loosened the silk scarf that was around her neck and shook out her mane of lustrous chestnut hair.

"Archie!" In a flurry, Flora was out of the car, the driver's door left wide open, leaping coltlike across the neatly raked gravel driveway and throwing herself into her brother's arms, her green coat flapping behind her.

Amelie stood by.

"Flora, stand back," Archie said, chuckling and finally disentangling himself from his sister's embrace. "Let me introduce you to Amelie."

The pretty girl pulled away from her brother and turned her enormous brown eyes—the same deep color as Archie's, and fringed with long, dark lashes—toward Amelie.

"Hello, Amelie," she said. "I'm thrilled to meet you. So utterly thrilled."

Amelie cleared her throat. Unable to manage a word, she leaned forward to kiss Archie's stunningly beautiful sister on the cheek. "*Bonjour*," she said, closing her eyes against the girl's vanilla and bergamot Shalimar.

Flora held Amelie at arm's length. "You are just as beautiful as Archie described. The girl from Paris," she murmured, her sensational eyes lingering on Amelie's face, running up to take in her dark hair.

Oh, do not let her suspect my hair is dyed. "*Merci*," she said. She seemed to have forgotten her English, she was so enchanted by Archie's lovely sister.

But Flora seemed perfectly at ease, if utterly animated. She patted Amelie on the shoulder. "I cannot wait to get to know you. I insisted that I stay here at Carrig, so that we could spend as much time together as we need to really get to know one another."

Amelie gnawed on her lip.

Flora gazed up at Archie, threading her arm through her brother's. "When Mother told me we had another guest for the weekend, I was completely put out. I wanted you and ravishing Amelie to myself, at least until Annabel's party. Do we have to put up with another guest? What a complete bore!"

Archie chuckled. "Come inside and we'll have tea."

"Oh, nonsense," Flora said. "I want to go straight up to the loch." She lowered her voice and cast a look toward Amelie. "And I want to get to know my new sister. Amelie, you must let me drive you up there right away, and then we will walk around it. It's my most favorite part of Carrig." She waved a hand at the house. "I've never been one for the indoors."

Amelie laughed. "Well then. That runs in the family." Archie was barely awake in the mornings before he'd pulled on his boots and disappeared outside.

"Don't you overexert Amelie," Archie warned.

Flora's extraordinary brown eyes widened. "Darlings," she said. "Mother told me. Such wonderful news. A baby at Carrig. And you, a pair of parents so soon. Imagine how delighted Daddy would have been. And Mother will be in her element. I warn you!"

"How dare you be so serious." Archie chuckled.

Amelie reached out and took Archie's arm, sending Flora a warm smile.

"Oh, this is too much." Flora hugged them both. "Amelie," she whispered, "you have no idea how much joy you have brought into our lives."

Amelie frowned. She had brought joy to Carrig? She'd thought it was the other way around.

Barely an hour after her arrival, Flora brought the Bugatti to a stop at the end of the road that led from Carrig to the loch. Archie's

Labradors, thrilled at the prospect of a run along the water's edge, leapt out of the back seat. Amelie watched the Scottish-born girl as she stood a moment, her head held back, boots crunching in the leaves underfoot and breathing in the pure Highland air as only a Scotswoman could do.

Archie's sister turned to Amelie, her cheeks flushed, her extraordinary brown eyes bright. "I'm glad you've got your good Scottish boots," she said to Amelie.

Amelie stood with her hands on her hips, stretching her back after the bumpy ride along the rough road from Carrig. She smiled at Flora. "I'm Scottish now," she murmured. "I live in sturdy boots."

Flora sent her a grin of approval. "This way." She led the way along the track that was the continuation of the road, lined on either side by birch woods that wound along the hillside. Soon, these gave way to Scots' pine, and the track trailed along closer to the lower section of the loch.

Amelie glanced across at the magnificent trees that sat on the other bank across the water, here at the narrowest point in the loch.

Flora gazed at a tiny cottage that sat near the water and next to a curved wooden bridge in the shape of a bow. "Has Archie taken you down?" she asked, pointing at the little building.

Amelie shook her head. "He says there's nothing to see," she replied.

A shadow passed across Flora's face, and Amelie opened her mouth to say something, but Archie's sister pressed on, whistling to the dogs, who had leapt down to the water, hurled themselves about in the shallows and now came bounding back up the bank, only to shake their sparkling coats, before rushing off again, noses to the ground.

Amelie's eyes averted to the small cottage as they came closer. Its windows were closed tight, curtains drawn. This was Carrig land, but Archie had been definite when Amelie had asked about the tiny house. He did not want to show it to her.

She guessed there was a history there.

Flora came to a standstill by the bridge, her eyes narrowed. "Let's keep to the upper track," she said, switching away from the water and following the path upwards.

The trees were sparse here, and as they rounded a bend, Amelie's pulse quickened.

In front of them, the tall peak of a mountain came to view, its top painted with a mantle of snow, a ring of clouds hovering overhead.

"Marvelous," Amelie said, meaning it. Every time she came up here, the majesty of the Scottish landscape left her breathless and in awe of the small space she occupied in the scheme of things.

Flora had picked up a long stick and was using this to push herself up the hill. She paused a moment at a gate that broke a long fence running through the forest down to the water's edge. This, Amelie knew, was a deer fence, put up to keep deer out of sections of the forest to allow new plantings to seed and grow. This was Archie's initiative and was somewhat modern and controversial. He'd argued that overgrazing was preventing the forest from regenerating, and he wanted to see the natural pinewoods being able to expand.

"I didn't know what to think when I heard Archie was marrying a girl from Paris and bringing her back to Scotland," Flora said.

Amelie started at the girl's sudden words. The dogs barked, breaking the sound of the water rushing along at the bottom of the hill. "I love Scotland." She gazed out over the water. "It's my home, Flora."

They pressed on, following the track as it led them closer to the loch, still as a pond now, the clouds and trees reflected magnificently in the water, while on their right, old pines reached tall above the forest floor.

"It's not too dull for you?" Flora asked, turning to cross the next, more substantial bridge, leaving behind the pines, and then the loch. "I mean, it's a stark contrast to what you're used to. I hope you're not bored, Amelie."

The landscape became barer and stark. "How could one be bored out here?" Amelie murmured, her boots clattering on the bridge. "Scotland is a playground with as much beauty as Paris. But it is boundless. Scotland moves well beyond the realms of what people can do."

Flora gazed across at Amelie, her expression thoughtful. She stopped and leaned against the bridge. "I did hear about your mother," she said. "I'm so sorry." She sighed. "Even now, after several years gone by, the war touches us in so many awful ways."

Amelie clasped her hands together. Her breath curled from her lips in the wonderful, fresh air.

"What did you do during the war?" Amelie said, suddenly, wanting to know. Somehow, she did not think this girl would have been content to sit at home at Carrig. And Archie was often quiet about his sister. He said she was a free spirit, who'd roamed around Europe for the last few years.

"I drove ambulances in France," Flora said, her brown eyes narrowing. She turned to Amelie. "I collected wounded soldiers from the battlefields and drove them to hospital." She shook this off. "You nursed in Belgium and then France, I believe?" she said. "Belgium must have been tough."

Amelie nodded. Her gut twisted and Flora began walking again. Amelie wrenched herself away from the mountain scenery, following Flora along the path that would take them to the smaller bridge, and back to Flora's car. The dogs walked quietly next to them now, and to their right a small hillock led up to a summit that Amelie had only climbed once with Archie. From there, there was a magnificent view over the entire glen.

Amelie picked up a small stone, turning to the water and sending it skimming several times across the surface before it disappeared.

"I so want Archie to be happy," Flora said, her chest rising and down with the exertion of the walk. "This time."

"*This* time?" Amelie whispered, her words seeming lost in the bare landscape as they moved on again, the track winding as if leading nowhere ahead. Only one copse of trees broke up the still, bare landscape here on the other side of the loch, and the mountains rose to meet the blue sky in the distance.

"Archie's a romantic," Flora continued, her brows knitting. "Far more so than I."

Amelie frowned. "Is that so?"

Flora chuckled. "I'm afraid it is. Archie's heart was broken terribly during the war," Flora said, turning somber.

Amelie stopped, looking out over the loch, now impossibly blue, the sun throwing golden light onto the Scots pines on the opposite banks. "He mentioned a girl named Morag," Amelie said. "He didn't tell me she broke his heart."

"She led him to believe they'd be married," Flora murmured, her words getting lost in the clear, whispering landscape. "Only to dash back to the man she really loved when it turned out that he had survived the war after all. Because, by all accounts, he'd been killed. It was a complicated, awful situation, and unfortunately poor Archie was the one to get burned."

Amelie was silent.

"So," Flora came to stand beside her, nudging her with her elbow. "We are all absolutely delighted that you have joined our family, Amelie. And I'm thrilled that you love Scotland. Our girl from Paris," she said, her warm eyes softening. "I know for certain, that darling Archie would never have fallen for another Scottish girl. And, it is wonderful you have dark hair. Morag was blond."

Amelie flinched.

Her heartbeat racing, she turned to follow Flora back along the path that led to home.

"Of course, I adore her. Because you do, Archie. She's just a little secretive, darling." Flora's voice rang through the library.

Amelie stopped in the hallway, reaching for her pearls and twirling them in circles. One, two, three and back again. She took in three deep breaths. From inside the wood-paneled room came the clink of whiskey glasses, the pouring of the rich amber liquid, the chink of ice cubes falling into a tumbler. And then, Archie taking a match to the kindling in the fireplace, the crackle of paper and kindling taking to fire.

"How so?" Archie sounded bemused. "My wife was probably startled by your fondness for chatter. Muted into silence, Flora. You can be a little overwhelming, you know."

Amelie hovered in the hallway; her shoes pressed into the Turkish rug. They must not hear any clatter on the polished floorboards.

"I did all the talking." Flora yawned hugely.

There was the sound of Archie padding back across the room, settling in one of the sofas, turning on a lamp to both illuminate and throw shadow patterns across the myriad of old books that graced the glorious wooden shelves. Papa would have loved the room. Papa would have loved Carrig in its entirety. If he'd come for a weekend, he'd bury himself exploring all the family treasures, and they might never find him again.

"Amelie's a darling, but I couldn't get anything out of her. I do worry about you, dearest."

"Flora, no one talks about the war anymore," Archie pointed out. "And Amelie is nothing like..." his voice trailed off.

Morag, the last girl who had deceived Archie.

Amelie leaned on a polished table. Her wedding photo twinkled up at her underneath the lights. The village church. She'd worn lace and a family heirloom veil. She'd hidden behind this, her eyes watchful, the sense of relief that Archie and Mary had agreed to a small wedding doing little to assuage her nerves.

Nerves at the way she'd so boldly hoodwinked Archie into marrying her.

Nerves because she'd fallen in love with him, and she couldn't bear to risk breaking his heart.

She was jolted out of her reverie by the sound of Archie's voice.

"Amelie was in the thick of it in France, not able to hide away here and sit out the war, Flora. You must remember this and understand."

Amelie closed her eyes. In the thick of it... She bit back the memories that tried to force themselves into her mind.

"I wish she could have been safely installed at Carrig, darn it," Archie said. "If I had anything to do with it, I would have protected her from it all. From all she endured."

Flora was silent.

"It's done. Gone." Archie seemed to bite out the words. Amelie imagined Archie's brows knitting, contemplating this over his tumbler of whiskey. "All of it." There was a power to his voice, and Amelie drew her hand to the collar of her blouse.

"I hope so, Archie. I hope we never see anything like it again."

Amelie tried to still her shaking hands, her own treachery seeming to lurk in the very shadows in the hallway, in the crackle of the fire, and most of all, in her own, ominously beating heart, her heart that thumped in her mouth.

The strike of a match. Quiet, while Flora presumably blew smoke rings all around the beautiful old books. "Your girl from Paris. Let's hope she doesn't form a passion for one of the ghillies and run off."

"Flora."

"Well, it's true. You can be so insular, darling. Make sure you don't lose her to some fool, won't you, while you're off fishing on the loch?"

"Let's talk about you," Archie said, suddenly gruff.

Amelie brought her hand to cover her lips, the urge to walk in there, present herself, battling with her desire to slip to her room and sink into a bath, delicious, scented oblivion. But now, should she move, they would hear her footsteps, know she'd been lurking.

She stood silent as the grave, until Flora let out a burst of laughter, then Amelie seized her chance. Her dark head down, moving with catlike stealth, she slipped away into the shadows of the old Scottish house that was her home, but in which she suddenly felt uneasy.

. . .

The following evening, Amelie sat at her dressing table, the drapes drawn and the bedroom with its vast, deep red velvet-covered bed in disarray. Drawers lay open, several pairs of shoes, tried on and discarded, were strewn about the floor, and her dress hung, still draped in its cotton covering, on a padded hanger in the open wardrobe.

Archie, who'd refused to wear a costume, had proclaimed his Highland dress would be perfect. He'd reluctantly agreed to wear a simple black mask that Flora had bought in Inverness, put on his kilt and plaid, having asked the maid to polish his silver buttons until they gleamed, examined his handsome face in the mirror for a second or two, kissed Amelie on the top of her head, and retreated to the sitting room, where he'd set out drinks on the grand piano to wait with their guest, who'd turned out to be a woman in her fifties from Chelsea.

An obligatory inclusion at the engagement party, the guest was a distant aunt of Clyde's, and quite content to spend the day at Kinloch arranging flowers with Annabel and Caitlin's mother, Mrs. Fife, before coming back to Carrig in the passenger seat of Amelie's car, and then going off to dress in what she termed her "best velvet" for the ball.

Amelie stared at herself in the mirror for one long moment, her tawny eyes emphasized with black liner, her long eyelashes enhanced and falling deep onto her cheeks when she looked down.

She was the spitting image of Maman, and the very thought of that was too much.

Amelie stood up in her silk and lace negligee and knocked her velvet-covered stool to the floor. She went, determined, to her wardrobe and lifted the cotton cover from her dress, her fingers gliding over the midnight-blue silken gown she'd had made up in Inverness—a replica of one of the three dresses that had shocked Parisian racegoers at Longchamp in Paris, back in 1908.

She intended to shock in it tonight.

It was a risk, and one she was prepared to take. She would astound as Amelie. She would appear as Archie's exotic, Parisian wife, and that would be enough. With her dark hair, and her mask, no one would, for a moment, consider Anaïs Mercier.

Amelie slipped the gown off its hanger, quickly becoming buried in its folds. The dressmaker had first suggested she opt for a corset with minimum boning, but, after measuring Amelie, had announced that no corset was necessary. The dress draped itself over Amelie's natural curves, showing off her feminine hips and highlighting her creamy décolletage. Yet, there was no hint in her glorious figure that she was carrying Archie's child, who could be, if he was a boy, the heir to the entire Carrig estate.

Amelie remembered how Maman's eyes sparkled having returned from Longchamp, as she talked of these dresses, telling Papa how the racegoers had called the three models who wore them "*a monstrosity*". The women back then had been accused of being semi-naked and showing disgusting décolletage. Maman had laughed out loud at how Parisian society women had marched their husbands and sons out of the racing enclosure.

Papa had clamped his hands over little Vianne's ears, while Maman remained in hoots of laughter. But later that week, Vianne, fascinated, even as a child, by the idea of a fairy-tale dress, had insisted that Anaïs show her the pictures of these risqué garments in *La Nouvelle Mode*.

Amelie remembered every detail of those dresses because Vianne had examined them most seriously, tracing her small fingers over the pictures of the beautiful garments that outlined the hips and thighs.

The designer who'd shocked Longchamp went by the name of Jeanne Margaine-Lacroix. She'd chosen the Parisian racetracks as her catwalk. But everyone could see that the women were not wearing bulky undergarments, no full corset, no petticoat, and no chemise.

Amelie turned this way and that before her oval mirror, tears pricking the backs of her eyes, because darling Vianne would have understood immediately how the dress, even after all these years, showed off a woman's natural body, rather than the old-fashioned artificial silhouettes. The skirt, just the same as Lacroix's, hugged Amelie's curves and was split to the knee. The sassy, slimline dress was modeled after the Ancient Greeks.

Amelie reached for her pièce de résistance, her complete disguise, her mask in gold and black filigree in the shape of a swan. She secured it over her eyes with a black ribbon and walked out of her bedroom, to head down the grand staircase to where Archie, Flora and the Fifes' aunt were waiting for her.

She paused at the top of the staircase.

Let the party begin.

Kinloch was ablaze with golden lights. Lights from the glorious old home's mullioned windows spilled out onto the great lawns, high-lighting the billowing white marquee. Amelie, her hand tucked into Archie's arm, waited while the prospective bridegroom, Clyde, kissed her hand in the receiving line, and something kindled within her at the way guests turned to stare at her from across the crowded marquee. Amelie only stood up taller when she saw them whispering behind the backs of their hands, women ruffling their pretty fans, leaning closer to look. She felt the old power that she used to revel in when she walked out in Paris or went to the theater with her striking Maman. Tonight, she could leave nervous, silent Amelie behind. Behind this mask, for one night, she could be Anaïs.

She stood, enigmatic and sure in the face of the fired-up gazes of every man whose eyes alighted on her in the luxurious tent, a small smile playing on her lips while she was alongside her hand-some, popular husband dressed so magnificently in his Highland tartans.

In turn, Archie seemed to have come to a new lease of life. People laughed at his witty jokes.

She and Archie were not left standing alone for one second,

the marquee aswirl with men lining up to kiss Amelie's hand, strangers keen to introduce themselves to the most sensational couple at the ball.

Amelie stood with her lace-gloved hand entwined always with Archie's, her eyes dancing with fire behind the mask that made her appear like an exotic, mysterious bird.

Flora drifted around the party, enchanting in a pale pink dress and long black lace gloves, exclaiming and chatting with old friends and admirers lined up to speak with her. The party from Carrig were lending a real cachet to the ball, and that was something of which to be proud.

When Archie led Amelie to the dance floor, his fingers caressing hers with only a featherlight touch, she allowed herself one quick glance around the couples, in case, heaven forbid, her eyes should alight on anyone she knew from Paris, but there was not a soul she recognized.

Perhaps, everything was going to be all right after all.

She moved into Archie's arms as the band struck up "Les Roses Blanches," and if she closed her eyes, she could imagine she was in Paris. Swept along to the lyrical music, and the songstress singing in the language of her country, she flowed, and the dress caressed her just as Archie's hands caressed her back. She leaned her head onto Archie's shoulder, stunningly aware of his lips, so close to her ear.

"I have neglected you, darling," he murmured. "I tend to get lost in my own world up here. You must be terribly bored. We need to fix that."

Dear Archie. "Why?" she said.

She felt his soft sigh against her cheek. "Because here, tonight, you are shining. You are being you and I want you to always feel as alive as you do now. I can sense the difference. And so can every person in the marquee. Everyone is admiring you, in love with you. I am a little jealous, but, darling, you need to shine."

Amelie closed her eyes, letting the music flow over her. "I think I understand why you really ran to London, Archie," she said.

His hand stilled on her back.

"Flora told me about Morag," she continued. "And that locked-up cottage by the loch? Was that something to do with her?"

Archie took in an audible breath.

"Sweetheart," he said. "Love is sometimes weakening, but it is sometimes a source of strength. Morag weakened me. You, my darling, are my strength."

Amelie felt butterflies' gossamer wings fluttering in her stomach.

When the song was finished, Amelie, in need, desperately, of fresh air, laid a fleeting hand on Archie's cheek, excused herself, and worked her way through the crowds, her chest heaving, to the still lawns outside.

Out here, a group of gentlemen stood smoking, catching Amelie with their nonchalant gazes. They'd removed their masks, and she, suddenly unable to breathe for loving Archie so very much, for the lies she'd told him, for the fact she was carrying their child and her baby would not know its mother's real name, pulled her hand up to her swan mask, and still fighting for air, she slipped it over her head.

Just for one second. She needed to breathe.

The mask slithered out of her hand and fell to the grass. Facing upward, she grimaced at the empty face of the black swan, so gilded and decorated, and yet, with nothing of substance behind its empty eyes.

And then, it happened.

"Anaïs."

Amelie turned instinctively, and her mouth fell open. She staggered backward, tried to gasp for air, but it stuck in her throat.

But the woman who had spoken stepped out of the shadows, standing in the golden light that that beamed from the blazing windows of the house and now shone around her like a halo.

"Anaïs."

One word, one name.

One revelation that would rip everything she knew into shreds.

Amelie's hand flew to her blackened hair, as unfathomable as her own ghastly lies.

Her gaze bore into the woman standing opposite her.

It could not be.

But it was, and she knew it, and Amelie's eyes bulged, her very breaths hitched at her throat. And she raised a hand to ward the woman off, before gripping the sides of her ears, which were buzzing. She was hot, so very hot, and there was a whirring, as if the propellors of some faraway plane had come to life, and yet it was getting closer, and louder, and she felt most awfully sick.

She fell, and all the golden light around the woman's face turned black.

CHAPTER TWENTY-ONE
VIANNE, SPRING, 1925

"It's an oasis of calm out there in Valentino's." Miss Ellie appeared through the door in the wood paneling. The door led to the room out back where the models were sitting at mirrors, makeup artists painting their lips into fashionable Cupid's bows, hairdressers curling tresses into waves and placing hats to sit just so atop curls. Lucia, Goldie, Mollie, and Adeline were helping slip dresses onto the first round of models, and despite the frenetic activity, the mood was quiet, concentrated. They were all perfectly prepared for the parade.

Vianne looked up from where she was straightening a model's dress, checking the hemline and the chiffon skirt for tiny, stray pieces of cotton or, heinously, loose threads. She ran her eyes over the entire garment like a hawk, inspecting every inch of it, even though each piece in the show had been checked seven million times.

The model was one of the first three girls to go out, and she took a twirl in the stunning deep-red afternoon frock trimmed with contrasting black ribbon around the drop-waisted skirt.

The second of the first three models dressed in the colors of the French flag came sashaying toward Vianne next, beautiful in her white georgette frock with its pintucked front, the front of the skirt circular and swinging marvelously around her legs.

Vianne moved down to the last girl of the trio, dressed in blue, who'd appear on the spinning panel with the other girls to open the show. Despite everything being prepared to perfection, Vianne's insides pierced with nerves, every fiber of her being was on fire, and she'd hardly slept last night after the rehearsal for going over the choreography, the order of garments that were slated to be shown off.

The hum of chatter came from outside the room, exclamations at the tiny, wrapped gifts of chocolates that Giorgio had placed on each table, sighs of appreciation for the springtime hyacinths, the magnificent red and white roses lining the walls around the catwalk, and the large photographs of Paris that graced Valentino's for the parade.

"Go out there with confidence and certainty," Vianne told the three girls in their French colors, a slight twinge piercing her insides at how much Maman would love to see all of this. How proud she would have been. Her youngest daughter, finally having made something of herself, having proven that, like Vianne's idolized sister, Anaïs, she could contribute to the world. She may not be nursing, but she hoped that in her own way, she was helping to enhance people's lives.

The music swelled as the jazz trio struck up their opening notes, and Vianne squeezed the girls' hands and sent them out to the catwalk.

The parade had begun.

After this, things moved quickly. Vianne hardly shepherded one girl in from the catwalk before it was time for a new model to walk out. She cast her expert eyes over every garment, every hairdo, every glove, stocking, and shoe. Soon, she was as lost in her work as Papa used to be when he was immersed at Celine, and the girls from Robert Powers were as professional as ever, changing out of their garments in a few minutes flat, while the other seamstresses assisted them.

Mama Pepper, resplendent in a vivid red coat, sat in a chair in the corner, leaning on her walking stick, her eyes roaming over every outfit. Miss Ellie stood with a master list of garments, checking them off and ensuring each girl was wearing exactly the right thing.

"I owe so much of this to you, Vianne," Miss Ellie said when Vianne came to stand beside her, turning a model in an evening dress of midnight-blue satin this way and that.

The sound of guests' applause rang through the restaurant and Vianne sent Miss Ellie a tired, but satisfied smile. "But every opportunity I've had in New York is down to you, Miss Ellie." Vianne squeezed Miss Ellie's arm as the guests' polite clapping moved to thunderous applause. Sequins sparkled and skirts swished around long, coltlike legs.

Vianne moved over to stand near the velvet curtains that led to the catwalk. Through the gap in the curtains, Vianne could see the guests. There was Katherine Carter at a front table, looking fabulous in a black, sleeveless tubular dress decorated with climbing white irises in glossy beads, their leaves curling in soft green, and the hem gleaming under the lights with a running beaded pattern that flickered dreamily. It was a dress Vianne had designed specifically for the wealthy, influential client. She'd visited Katherine Carter in her magnificent Fifth Avenue mansion and had tried to stop herself from gaping at the opulent interiors, the vast garden in the middle of the city tended by an army of staff.

There was a gasp now, back in the dressing area, when the model who'd been selected to wear Vianne's bridal gown came over to have her garment inspected by Lucia. Even Vianne wanted to clap her hands with joy when Lucia motioned the model out to the catwalk.

She clutched Adeline's hand, feeling closer to her since her confession. She was so thrilled at the way the model carried herself, her head high with pride, the rich, lustrous cream satin that Vianne had labored over for nights with Lucia by her side. Vianne had known that the simplicity she sought must rely on clever pattern cutting and, in Lucia, she had the best pattern cutter she could ever hope to find. The single bow placed at the back was elegant, flirtatious, and sophisticated all at once, and the way the neckline dipped into a V-shape at the back, with the elaborate use of darts in the cut, worked like a dream.

Vianne shook her head with a smile, now, at the deliberations she'd gone through while designing that dress, the fabric of the skirt pulled toward the center back, where it fell in a drape either side to a pointed hemline, giving the effect of a relaxed bustle.

But it had worked.

Vianne hugged herself, her eyes locking for one long second with Giorgio's where he stood by the catwalk behind Katherine Carter's table. Their gaze met over the wedding dress, and his lips curved into a small smile. Checking no one was watching him, he raised his fingers to his lips and blew Vianne a kiss.

She blushed, looking down at the floor a moment, before the girl in the cream satin dress turned back up the catwalk, and came to an elegant, final pose right near the curtains where Vianne and Eloise stood.

Her heart pounding, Vianne allowed Miss Ellie to hold her hand as she waved all the models and seamstresses out onto the stage for a final bow.

The guests stood up, the applause filled the restaurant, and Miss Ellie held Vianne's hand above all their heads.

"*Brava!*" people shouted.

When Giorgio sent two waiters to present Miss Ellie and Vianne with flowers, the room erupted, and it was all Vianne could do to stop herself from collapsing with relief.

The fashionable ladies' eyes shone, and all their faces turned to Vianne and Eloise.

Vianne knew her eyes were dancing and her face glowed. The dress she wore, designed so meticulously by Goldie, flowed beautifully in cream folds, the gold embroidery delicate and perfect. She felt as if she were floating on the stage, floating through this wonderful new world in which she'd landed.

New York was a place where anything could happen, a place where she'd been able to realize her own dreams.

Vianne knew right then, standing on that stage with the seamstresses and Miss Ellie beside her, with Giorgio sending her a ravishing smile, she was the happiest she'd ever been since that one dreadful day seven years ago. Perhaps there was some hope that she could rekindle the joy she'd once taken so for granted before the war.

When the crowds spilled from their tables, Vianne held her hands out as Giorgio came toward her, and she leaned forward as he placed a kiss on her cheek.

"Well done," he murmured. "That was wonderful. *You* were wonderful, *Bella*."

Vianne, lost in the swirl of the crowds, was only aware of his hand holding hers, as Katherine Carter came and enfolded her in her arms. "Vianne. You will be the talk of New York. The only problem is I *still* don't want to share you, but I fear I'm going to have even less choice after today!"

"Oh, don't you worry about that," Vianne assured her beautiful client. "I'll always make sure that my bespoke clientele only receives designs that are entirely made for them. I would never do anything less."

Katherine squeezed her hand. "You know, I remain certain you're going to be famous, dear," she said. "I can feel it."

And then Eddie Winter was there, leaning in to shake Giorgio's hand, and kissing Vianne on the cheek.

"Well, Miss Mercier," he said. "That was sensational. I want a double spread on you this week."

"But what about Miss Ellie? It was her parade, Eddie."

He laid a hand on her arm. "I promised Eloise a major feature, and I'll do that for her. Of course, I will. But after that, I want an exclusive interview with you. I want a feature on the girl from Paris so that all of New York know who you are."

The room seemed to still, all the whirl and noise and congratulations and models slipping through the crowds showing details of their perfect garments lost, as Vianne stood opposite the fashionable editor about town.

"The girl from Paris," he repeated, his hand resting on her arm. "What do you think of that?"

And Vianne couldn't help it. She leaned forward and pulled Eddie into a hug.

Later that evening, after darkness had fallen over Manhattan, and the stars studded the night sky overhead, Vianne placed a calico cover over the last of the dresses that hung out back of the atelier. The atelier had been inundated with bookings for appointments after the parade, and now, she sank down on her chair in the workroom.

Miss Ellie stood by the window, her cigarette holder tapering in her hand. She gazed out over the narrow street below. Slowly, she turned around to face Vianne.

"That was a sensation," she said. "I am incredibly grateful, Vianne. To you, to the seamstresses. To everyone who made it possible. You know, it was an incredibly special day for me."

Vianne watched Miss Ellie. Her boss came to sit down opposite her, placed her unlit cigarette holder down on the table between them, and folded her bejeweled fingers in front of herself.

"I destroyed another demon today, Vianne. One I have not told you about."

Vianne tilted her head to one side.

Miss Ellie's fine brows creased into a frown. "I hadn't told you this, but another designer, associated with a big department store, has been copying my designs, replicating them. And claiming them as her own."

Vianne sat up in her chair. "But this happens in Paris. You must do something—"

Miss Ellie held up a hand. "I have been struggling, Vianne, with who I am, how I was to respond to this, and, most of all, the fact that I am getting tired. I've worked for years, you know. Hard work. I think I've never wanted to let go of that, to admit that, perhaps, it is time for me to move to another phase."

Vianne's brow crinkled.

"The woman's name, so you know, is Mrs. Lena Davis. If you come across people like her in this business of ours, please, simply rise above her tricks and play the game properly, Vianne. It will stand you in good stead."

Vianne held her breath. "Of course, but—"

Miss Ellie eyed her. "The best way to deal with such difficulties is to create beautiful things."

Vianne's eyes softened. She swallowed, a lump forming in her throat. "My maman used to say something similar," she whispered.

"Well then," Miss Ellie said, "I'd say your mother and I were on the same page."

A breeze fluttered through the open window into the atelier, and if Vianne closed her eyes, she could see herself, that girl, sitting all those years ago, fixing the rents in her maman's white lace gown in the restaurant on the Champs-Élysées during the long, cold years of the war. Years that seemed so distant now. Surely, they could never return to the world again. Surely, the world had learned its lesson, and Europe would not ever again endure such darkness.

Miss Ellie went on, her words coming slowly, as if she were choosing them with great care, "I'm not ready to retire, Vianne. It's not that. I'm not going to be kicked out of what I love doing most because of some designer trying to copy my ideas. But..." She took in a breath. "I have worked out a solution to my... distress. To the sense of being stuck that I have felt lately. And, to that end, I do want to ensure that I have someone by my side from now on. Someone with whom I can create ideas."

Vianne sat up.

Miss Ellie's lips curved into a thoughtful smile. "I would like you to be a partner in my business, Vianne. And when I do retire, I cannot think of anyone more worthy of taking over the atelier and building it into something even more magnificent, than you."

Vianne's whole body tensed. For one split second, she forgot to breathe.

"I've considered it carefully," Miss Ellie went on, her voice filtering into the workroom while Vianne sat, unable to move. "I've been thinking about it for several weeks. Your talent and your drive are inspiring to the other girls. I'd like to change the name of the couturier to Chappelle and Mercier, and..." she paused. "When I retire, you can call it by your own name."

Vianne's eyes teared up. Not knowing what to do with her hands, she pulled them away from the sides of the chair and sat on them.

Miss Ellie held her gaze. "You will be an equal partner from this day onwards. Fifty percent of the profits. And together, I believe we can take on the risks of being in business, the likes of Lena Davis. I've always been alone. Operated by myself, after Papa lost everything. Refused, point blank, to take on a partner, in life or in business. Now, for the first time, I see the value of sharing things with someone. You have been a big part of that. She reached a hand over the table. I hope you will consider my offer, Vianne?"

"Consider it?" Vianne whispered, slight-headed. "I am honored and thrilled."

Her voice shook.

Miss Ellie's lips turned into a smile. "Now. Something else."

Vianne waited.

"I have eyes, Vianne, and notwithstanding what people may say, I also have a heart. Not all women in business are hard and unfeeling, despite what people think of us. We are human too, you know."

Vianne simply nodded. Right now, she did not trust herself to speak.

"I can see how you've put the couturier first. But for now, I would suggest that it's time for love and career to merge."

Vianne stared at her. "But—"

"You and Giorgio have my blessing, should you wish to find out where your feelings for each other might lead," Miss Ellie said. She sighed. "I think the emptiness I've experienced lately could be partly due to the fact that I've devoted my entire life to my career and only that. I've come around to thinking that if a woman wants to do so, there is no reason why she cannot have love and work, just as men do. So, I retract my strict rules, and you have my whole-hearted support to love and thrive in your career to your heart's content." She chuckled. "Who knows, one might inspire the other!"

Vianne's eyes glittered. She took Miss Ellie's hand and held it for a long time. Her feelings for Giorgio? Who knew, but perhaps there was a chance they'd lead to something wonderful, to places and feelings in her heart she thought she'd never experience.

Vianne sat alone in the quiet workroom of the atelier after Miss Ellie had returned home. The other girls had gone out for the evening, but, exhausted, filled with irrepressible excitement and in a reflective mood, Vianne had turned down invitations to go to the jazz clubs, and now she sat, a cup of coffee warming between her hands, while moonlight pooled through the windows into the room that had seen such bursts of energy these past few weeks. It was peaceful to realize that this space of frenetic activity could also be still, and it was more than exciting to think about what the future might bring for the atelier. For Chappelle... and Mercier. It was still too hard to believe.

When there was a knock on the front door, Vianne raised her head. It was late for a visitor.

She unlocked the front door, frowning at the boy who stood there, his bicycle leaning against the stairs that led to the atelier.

Her eyes dropped to the envelope he held in his hand.

A telegram delivery boy. At this hour?

Her hand dropped to her side, her thoughts flying. *Something urgent for Miss Ellie? Lucia?*

"Telegram for Miss Vianne Mercier," he said.

Vianne's heart started beating wildly, and without knowing what she was doing, her hand floated out to accept the envelope from the boy, her arm moving in short jerks.

"That is I," she murmured, even as she turned the paper over in her hands.

The boy nodded, trotted down the stairs, and disappeared on his bike.

A cool breeze scuttled along the street, sending flotsam fluttering above the pavement, leaves swirling in the wind, and a couple walked by, drawing their coats around them.

The marvelous day was going to end with the winds of change. She knew too much of telegrams during the war to ever suppose they brought anything but bad news.

Vianne turned, the envelope tingling in her fingers. She pressed the front door shut behind her, and slipped up the stairs to her apartment, turning on lights as she entered, closing curtains, reaching for the letter knife she and Lucia kept in a kitchen drawer. She sliced the paper with a clean cut.

And sank down at the table, blinking, her eyes scanning over and over the words that swam in front of her eyes.

NEW YORK POST AND TELEGRAPH

MISS VIANNE MERCIER
2 E 63rd ST, NY,
NY, 10065
UNITED STATES OF AMERICA
MESSAGE: ANAÏS ALIVE STOP COME HOME TO PARIS
IMMEDIATELY STOP
SENDER'S NAME
MADAME MARGUERITE CLEMENT
CARRIG, SCOTLAND

Vianne, nausea rising through her insides, clamped a hand to her mouth, and the telegram fell to the floor like a dead autumn leaf, the words that had at first blurred in front of Vianne's eyes imprinting themselves in her mind, etching themselves in a way she was never going to forget until the day she died.

CHAPTER TWENTY-TWO
ANAÏS, BRUSSELS, BELGIUM, SPRING, 1915

Anaïs climbed out of bed, the soft breathing of the other young women the only sound to break the silence in the Red Cross hospital where she was working under the administration of one of the most famous matrons in the country, Edith Cavell. Anaïs, still honored to have been accepted back in 1914 for her post by the English woman who had turned nursing into a respectable profession and raised standards no end in Belgium at her teaching hospital, had arrived just before the war broke out. Refusing to go home to Paris, she'd stayed by Matron Cavell's side as the Germans invaded Belgium, entering the city of Brussels after burning homes across the country, razing villages to the ground, murdering women and children, raping, looting, mutilating, before finally reaching Brussels, and cutting it off from the rest of the world.

Anaïs reached for the simple skirt and blouse that were set out on the wooden chair by her bed. She dressed, quickly, expertly, her fingers nimble in the pitch darkness that was heaviest right before dawn. The darkness that enveloped the occupied city of Brussels was something Anaïs had come to know well during her time working for Matron Cavell. In the evenings, Matron Cavell went out into the streets and cared for the sick and injured, and in the pearly mists of dawn, she smuggled Allied soldiers to her homeland, England, recruiting her nurses to accompany them through the streets in the dark.

Her feet sure on the immaculate wooden floorboards, swept clean at Matron Cavell's command several times a day, Anaïs slipped out of the nurses' sleeping quarters and down the stairs into a locked, small room, lined with shelves filled with men's clothing. Clothing that those nurses who could sew fashioned behind closed doors.

Anaïs checked the thick black curtains were closed tight, and working with the door open to the corridor, her eyes adjusted to the irrevocable deep black, she reached, instinctively, for the pair of trousers that she'd prepared for the mission she was about to carry out. She had exactly ten minutes because her schedule was clear-cut, and time was paramount. If she were one minute late, two minutes late, Matron Cavell would be aware. The whole operation had to be precise. If it was not, it would fail and the penalty for those caught harboring, protecting, or aiding Allied soldiers was execution.

Anaïs was working against the odds of her own death.

She pulled the scrap of fabric that she'd covered in tiny print last night in Matron's office from the pocket of her skirt. Matron Cavell had dictated to her, whispering in Anaïs's natural French as Anaïs wrote, her head bent under the light of Matron's desk.

Anaïs turned the trousers inside out, unpicked the seams of the lining, and slipped the piece of incriminating fabric inside, before sewing it up again until no one would guess she had touched a thing. When she was done, she tied off her stitches, clipped shut the sewing box and carried the trousers, a clean shirt, jacket, socks, a pair of shoes and a belt up the corridor of the patients' wing. On her way, she unlocked the door of another room, and collected the kitbag that Matron Cavell had prepared for this particular English patient's flight out of occupied Belgium.

Her heart beating, Anaïs carried her quarry down the silent corridors of the hospital, past the nurses' station, where one nurse sat reading a novel, to the English patients' section of the hospital.

There had been great complaints from the nurses when they were informed that they would be treating German wounded soldiers, but Matron Cavell had admonished her girls, telling them that they must do their duty for everybody who needed their help. Anaïs had treated men from both sides of the battle lines with trench foot, severe shell shock, missing limbs, bubonic plague, shrapnel wounds, and the devastating effects of chlorine and mustard gas.

In the face of the devastation that they witnessed every day, Matron Cavell had confided in her nurses that she had never before done anything subversive, but that she felt that, in the circumstances of war, obeying God's law was more important than German rules.

Anaïs moved past the wards, taking care not to let her shoes clatter. The young Englishman she was smuggling out today would have no idea he was carrying any information back to England until he was intercepted in London. No one would find a thing. If he were captured and questioned, even tortured on the way home, he would not have any information to pass on to the German secret police.

Anaïs had become inured to the information she'd written in ink onto fabric concealed in the garments in the past weeks. Matron Cavell's network was actively engaged in espionage, using handkerchiefs and slips of paper tucked into the soles of shoes, as well as the scraps of soft, undiscoverable fabric that were sewn into the lining of thick tweed suit jackets and trousers that they made for the men returning home. The information was random, anything that could be of use—she'd written out notes about the position of German munitions factories, the gatherings of army reserves, talk that was overheard in coffee shops, and the locations of new trenches in the deadly, stinking, lice-infested German lines.

Last night, an informant had reported that the Germans were focusing more on shipping targets. Anything was valuable to the Allies. Matron's network met information gatherers in coffee shops, sliding dockets covered in invisible ink across the tables in the restaurants of Brussels. The underground network was active and alive, and Anaïs was more than happy to play her part toward helping the hungry, terrified occupants of the country that neighbored her beloved France.

Outside Brussels, there continued horrific stories of Belgian villages being destroyed as the German army advanced. The people of Brussels, while hungry, controlled, scared, were defiant in their minds and hearts.

Anaïs tiptoed past the ward that housed the German patients and made her way to Matron's wing for wounded English and French. Matron Cavell was at the door, her arms folded, and her hair already dressed neatly for the coming day. At 6.15 a.m. precisely, she would preside over the nurses' breakfast in the refectory. If anyone was a minute late, their daily shift would be extended by two hours.

Anaïs lowered her eyes and Matron clicked her tongue in disapproval at the fact Anaïs's long blonde hair still flowed down her back.

In the ward, she followed Matron to the farthest bed, waking the patient who had been deemed ready and able to take on the pre-dawn walk through the otherwise sleeping city armed with a kitbag containing food, money from Matron Cavell herself, and extra rations to bribe any officials on his flight to the neutral country of the Netherlands.

But he needed to pass through the Belgium border, and this was surrounded by an electric fence.

"You have checked the kitbag?" Matron whispered to Anaïs. She led the soldier, impossibly young, out of the ward, into the refectory, where she sat him down in his nightshirt and handed him a warm bowl of broth.

The young man, eyes still sleepy like a boy's, raked a hand through his tousled hair, did not open his mouth to say a word lest he woke anyone, as instructed. Instead, he bent his head forward, scooping up the broth, wiping the bowl with bread, and taking the bundle of clothes from Anaïs before slipping into the corner of the darkened room, and getting dressed.

Anaïs and Matron turned their backs to him.

Anaïs clutched the kitbag to her stomach. "Food, money, water, Dutch identity card," she whispered. "And Jane Austen."

Matron's expression did not falter, but Anaïs allowed herself a small smile.

The soldier, dressed in the clothes that fitted him to a T thanks to Anaïs's precise measurements, came to stand near them, tucking his shirt into the high-waisted pants.

Matron shook the young man's hand, and Anaïs led him down the next flight of stairs, and straight out of the door of the hospital onto the silent, misty street, the street that, in three hours' time, would be teeming with German secret police, military personnel and hungry Belgian citizens. Locals would be seeking food and supplies in the city that saw no hope of freedom from occupation if this brutal war still held Europe's great nations in a stranglehold.

Anaïs, her eyes alert for anything untoward, let her training kick in as she led the young man down the alleyways and through the narrowest streets of Brussels, avoiding the magnificent thoroughfares and the grand buildings that made the city famous. Their steps were soft and eerie in the darkness, and the shrouds of early-morning mist hung in the silent air.

When they came to their destination, Anaïs halted at the entrance to a lane. On the wall opposite, she glared at one of the many signs pasted all over the city, proclaiming that anyone who hid the enemy would be severely punished. She would spit at it if she were alone.

A girl around her age stepped out from the steps of a house a little way further down. The soldier, standing still next to her, placed a hand on Anaïs's arm.

"*Yorc*," the other girl said, her voice low and yet carrying through the mist, and Anaïs nodded, accepting the password that was used by the Belgian resistance.

"Godspeed," she whispered, daring to use her tongue for the

first time since she'd left the hospital. The young man would require all his courage to face the German secret police at the border with the Netherlands as they checked identity papers, controlled travel permits, and all matters under security in the occupied zones.

"Thank you," he murmured. He stopped a moment in the still, silent lane. "I'll send word when I arrive in London."

Anaïs's lips curved into a derisive smile. "No, you will not," she whispered. Matron had been tight-lipped and furious when a former patient had sent her a postcard from England, thanking her for saving his life and affording him safe passage home.

Recently, Matron had reluctantly allowed a group of English patients one night out at a local hotel, but they'd come home, rowdy, the strains of "It's a Long Way to Tipperary" belting through the streets. Now, Matron was insistent with her Allied patients. They must be entirely discreet.

The boy disappeared into the mist, and Anaïs turned to go back to what was, now, her home.

Screams ruptured the hospital corridors, flinging through the still, dark air. Anaïs's fingers froze on the handle of the front door that led directly from the sidewalk, and a sudden coldness bit at her core. She reached up to remove her hat, her gloves and the light coat she wore over her civilian dress, and then grabbed for the chipped banister in the old building. Abandoning any attempts to prepare herself, she ran up the stairs in the darkness, her hair streaming down her back.

She knew exactly who was howling like a trapped animal, and she was the only one who could calm him down. Anaïs rushed along the corridors, her feet clipping a profound beat upon the floorboards. She held no truck with keeping herself quiet now. All she had to do was alleviate her patient's suffering, and fast.

It was hard to say when Johannes Meyer had become her patient, hard to say when her attitude toward the men in the

German ward had changed. Hard to say when she'd stopped scoffing at Matron Cavell's insistence that all men were equal in the eyes of God, no matter what side of the battle they were on.

Over the past few weeks, Anaïs had served as Johannes' confidante. She'd come around to see a real man behind the soldier, a man who'd been educated in Heidelberg, at the oldest university in Germany. Johannes, trying to distract himself from the searing, constant pain of his wounds, had told Anaïs how much he missed working as an engineer. He'd sometimes ask Anaïs for pieces of paper on which he'd sketch his funny little designs, complete with specifications and minute drawings. Anaïs, not an engineer, had no idea what they were, but she'd tried her best to copy some of them and show them to Matron Cavell, because they were always wary that the Germans might send a spy into the hospital in the guise of a wounded soldier.

Anaïs came to a wild, sudden stop outside the German ward. The other patients, in varying states of injury, were inured to Johannes' night terrors because there was always one soldier suffering nightmares, whether in the trenches, in a hospital, or in a military camp. Bravery, Anaïs was coming to learn, was only a front.

Johannes' narrow survival after a shelling attack had left him anguished, tormented, and distressed when he was trying to sleep.

But he'd confided in one person. He'd confided in his nurse, Anaïs, who'd been moved, terribly, by his stories of life in the trenches. She'd recognized that he needed to talk of his experiences, and she'd sat and listened, even though her blood curdled, and her insides recoiled with fear. Fear for all the young men in the trenches, and especially, an internal, confounding fear for what her own brother, Jacques, might be going through, because she felt bound as closely to him as she was to her own heart, for he was her twin, her other half.

Johannes was sitting up in bed, face wild, eyes blazing, hands flailing and beads of sweat dripping from his forehead. Anaïs clipped across the room, shoving aside the stern warnings in her mind that if Matron Cavell caught her out of her nurses' uniform, she'd be severely reprimanded.

She could not leave her patient like this, even if he was German.

Her blond hair swinging around her face, and her blue coat flapping open, she flung off her gloves, rubbed her hands together to warm them up, and placed her hands squarely on Johannes' shoulders.

And when she did so, a single piece of white paper fluttered to the floor.

But Johannes was screaming, crying for his *"mutti"*, his mother, while the tears streamed down his narrow, pale cheeks. His brown eyes were wide with terror, but when Anaïs tried to soothe him, he stared beyond her at something she could not see, at something no one but Johannes could understand or endure, something that was playing over and over in his mind like a broken record on some warped old gramophone.

Would men like Johannes ever find peace after war?

Anaïs lifted her skirts and leapt up onto the bed next to him, pulling him down to sit from where he knelt, howling like a wolf. She whispered soft words to him, grateful for her rudimentary understanding of German, grateful that Papa had insisted she and Vianne be taught English properly, and German well enough that they could get by.

She reached for one of the white towels she'd placed on Johannes' bedside table for his episodes and wiped it across the poor young man's soaking face. When he buried his head in the crook of her arm, his body racked with uncontrollable sobs, she comforted him, stroking his hair like she would that of a little boy.

"Johannes," she whispered, crooning his name as Maman use to croon to Jacques when he was in one of his anxious moods. "It is all right. You are safe. It is over. Nothing bad is going to happen anymore."

How she wished her words held some truth.

Johannes whimpered. Gradually his heartbeat, wild and

erratic and as hot and rattling as the engine of an airplane, steadied, and his body stilled in her embrace.

She sat there, her long hair curtaining his body, her head bent over him.

"Nurse Mercier," he whispered.

"I have told you to call me Anaïs." Her understanding extended across the lines of a battlefield that neither of them had drawn. They were both too young to be caught up in lines drawn by older men.

His shoulders began shaking again. "The only solace I find is in my drawings. Please, you must understand this."

Anaïs frowned. She glanced down at the piece of white paper on the floor, her practiced eyes taking in the drawings. At the top of the page, there looked to be a railway track. This was nothing surprising; Johannes had told Anaïs how he used to design railways. Underneath this were several incomprehensible words in German, measurements, and a dotted line traveling in a wide arc. In the bottom left-hand corner of the page, a tiny drawing of a cogged wheel peeped into the page.

Anaïs tore her gaze away. She would report this to Matron later on. Now, she wrapped a hand around his shoulders, swaddling them like a baby's. "Johannes," she said, "Take life one day at a time."

But Anaïs frowned at her own, useless words. One day back at the battlefields and he could be dead. If only she could do more than tend, assist, soothe. If only she could help her patients in a more substantial way. She'd drawn on all Maman's joyous philosophies and tried so hard to share them with these battered, bloodied men, but this war was stronger than Maman's words.

Johannes had been here two months, recovering from an unspeakable head wound, which Anaïs had tended, bathing him, caring for him like she would her own kin.

She climbed off the bed, lay him flat again, but remained next to him, her hand clasped in his own. His pulse still jumped erratically.

"I had just completed my engineering degree and had started working at an engineering firm in Essen," he said, his breaths shuddering. "But I was conscripted and pulled away from my work."

"Of course, Johannes," she murmured. He'd told her the same story a thousand times.

The thing about this war was that the soldiers were only boys. Untrained boys who were sent to become murderers. Governments were throwing their young to the slaughterhouses, to fight or be killed, and then what?

"See," he said, his thin, pale fingers fumbling for the piece of paper that had floated to the floor.

Anaïs swallowed. She handed him his sketch.

"You are a creator," she whispered. "I understand."

His eyes, dead, dull, beforehand, lit up with a new glow. "Yes, that is it. But it is more than just creation. I have long been fascinated with the way science and technology have the power to completely transform our lives. To modernize our world in ways we could never have imagined."

Anaïs waited. He was settling down, forgetting his pain. She would listen a while longer and then return to the nurses' quarters to get dressed for the day's work.

"I believe that this century we can break through technical challenges to bring an end to wars such as these once and for all. I know you are against my country, but we have some of the greatest scientific minds in the world in Germany who relish challenges and that is what we must focus on as we move forward. We must lift ourselves out of the muddy battlefields and dream up better ways of living and of conquering our problems, Anaïs."

Anaïs's brows drew tighter. She looked away, her eyes roaming across the other forlorn men in their hospital beds, torn, half-mauled remains of once healthy boys.

Johannes squeezed her hand, and she startled at the warmth of his gesture. Papa always used to squeeze her hand.

Johannes' grip tightened. "I cannot go back to the trenches." Her bony fingers were cold. "Please, will you ask Matron to speak to my doctor. Please? Will you ask if I may return to my work as an engineer in Essen?"

Anaïs closed her eyes. She had no business in doing anything other than nursing these German soldiers. Outside the hospital, their fellow countrymen's boots would stamp on the old cobblestones all too soon, and the very sound of this was a tattoo of domination and misplaced power over the citizens of Brussels.

And yet, when the young German engineer's eyes locked with hers as the sun rose in the Belgian sky, and tiny chinks of golden light broke through the almost imperceptible gaps in the deep, formidable black curtains, Anaïs heard Maman's voice whisper in her ear.

What if Jacques' fate was down to a nurse on the other side? What would any of the Mercier family desperately pray for that nurse to do?

Anaïs stood, straightening herself. A couple of nurses swung by down the corridor, tending, first, to the Allied patients, marching straight past the untold sufferings that were playing out in the German ward.

She closed her eyes, and silently sent up a prayer for help. Help in making a decision for her German patient. Should she send him to a certain death because he was on the other side of the war?

She stood there, in silence, and when his chest rose, unsteadily, and she saw a single tear fall down his cheek, she let out a deep, weighted sigh.

That evening, after a day spent assisting the doctors in an operating room, then monitoring her patients, tending to treatments for German, English, Belgian and French men alike, Anaïs made her way back to the nurses' quarters. Only to come face to face with a man standing in the hospital corridor.

"*What do you want?*" she asked in her rudimentary German, barking out her words. She took a step back, blinking rapidly.

The man lifted the lapel of his suit, revealing his badge. German Secret Field Police, known as the GFP or *Geheime Feldpolizei*, the police system that functioned side by side with the uniformed Belgian police, who served under veiled German tutelage.

Anaïs shuddered, clearing her throat. The German Field Police acted solely as a detective branch and were famous for their utterly unscrupulous modes of work, Matron had warned the nurses who were part of her network. These were the men who worked in plain clothes, and who infused the entire occupied population with a terror of German rule. Everyone knew they depended on the effects of fear and the dread of the unknown on the human mind when they sought their captives.

"We have reason to search this hospital for any suspicious reactions to our government and for any activities that are intended to shake our hold on this city."

Anaïs took in a quick breath. She understood what he was saying very well. "There is no reason to suspect anything here. We are tending to German patients just as carefully as our own. Let us get on with our work in peace."

The man's lips curled at her last word, and she closed her eyes, placing her shaking hands behind her back, and clasping them hard. Her breaths shuddered. *Had the worst happened? Had someone walked into an estaminet, and started whispering rumors, or worse, was the hospital housing a German patient who was a spy?*

Anaïs swallowed. She'd slipped out this morning. She'd slipped back in, and the German patients had witnessed her coming in fully dressed, not in her nurses' uniform, to attend to Johannes.

"We have reason to search this hospital on suspicion of espionage."

Anaïs held the man's gaze now, lifting her chin. Her eyes widening, she picked at her fingernails behind her back. "No," she said simply. "There is no reason for any such suspicion here."

Matron had warned her that there were also instances of unscrupulous Belgians and French living in Brussels, who were not above turning informers, and currying favor with the occupying authorities by betraying a real channel of espionage. It may not have been a German who had reported them.

Anaïs's heartbeat began to race. Her legs wanted to buckle underneath her, and she fought the urge to slide down the corridor wall. Nevertheless, she squared her shoulders and took in a shuddering breath.

The man stood to attention. "We will be carrying out a systematic study of this entire building, with the intention of discovering any channels of espionage, nurse." He sneered and looked her up and down.

Anaïs brought her sweating hands forward and folded them firmly over her chest.

"We will not tolerate any sabotage. If any of our subjected population in this institution are breaking the rules, we will take appropriate measures. Do I make myself clear? Now. Go. Leave me to my operations."

Anaïs wasted no time. She turned around, a metallic, bitter taste rising from her thumping chest to her mouth. She wanted to scream, to sound the alarm to warn the other sleeping nurses.

If only Matron Cavell was not out on her nightly rounds tending to the sick in the streets of Brussels. If only, for one evening, she had absconded from her duties, and had stayed here in the hospital, she would handle this. But that was not Matron Cavell.

And it was not Anaïs. She would not succumb to fear.

Her feet managing to beat their way down the hallway, she winced at the sounds of the German entering the English patients' ward. Her legs moving automatically, steadily, she walked up the hall staring straight ahead but not seeing anything in front of her eyes.

She entered Matron's personal office.

Inside, she shut the door, locked it behind her, and pressed her palms into it. Anaïs slipped off her shoes, and rushed, frantic, to Matron's desk, where her hands fumbled like a pair of fools and she grabbed the false identity papers that Edith Cavell had already appropriated to help English wounded soldiers get home to safety. She stuffed these into a plastic sleeve and, then taking some tape, she placed all of this underneath her uniform, pressing them tight against her belly before taking in a shuddering breath, and stepping out into the corridor, where, her head held high, she marched, feet steady, to the women's WC.

Anaïs stepped into the furthest cubicle, closed the door, climbed up onto the toilet seat, and slipped the papers into the cistern, where she taped them to the inside of the lid, and then prepared to step back down.

But the door into the room swung open. Anaïs closed her eyes at the sound of footsteps. The steady thump of heavy soles on the wooden floor. Her eyes slammed to the closed cubicle door. Had she locked it? Had her fingers, slick with sweat, her palms glistening, managed to slide the bolt across?

He was opening toilet doors, grunting, slamming them shut again, muttering in German. She'd heard how the occupying government employed their agents ad hoc, paying them miserably. This man would think nothing of murdering her, of taking her to one of the infamous torture cells, a bare lightbulb, a single table, decaying, rotting walls.

He was coming closer.

"What are you doing?"

She slammed her fist in her mouth, forcing herself not to cry out at the sound of the greeting in German. *Johannes.*

"That cubicle door is broken," Johannes said. "There is nothing to find in here."

Anaïs stilled, her knees wanting to buckle, to collapse underneath herself.

"The hospital is simply a hospital. There are no spies here, sir. I can assure you. I have been treated here for many months."

Anaïs flexed her fingers, curling and uncurling them. Was Johannes saving her? She a nurse on the other side?

There was an unnatural stillness, and she stared at the back of the implacable wooden WC door.

The German policeman muttered something indistinguishable. "We will be carrying out random inspections," he went on. "In the coming months, we will be maintaining a rolling barrel of arrests. If you or anyone here is lying to me, we will find out. We will be inspecting this hospital regularly. The staff here are not free, and they never will be again."

"Please," Johannes said, "I understand, but focus your investigations elsewhere. There is nothing to find in this hospital. The nurses are exceptionally kind. Exceptionally." Johannes lowered his voice. "They have treated me with as much concern for my health as they have those patients on the other side."

There was a silence, and Anaïs could almost hear the ruminations in the secret police officer's head.

"I warn you, we are watching them. I will be back."

Anaïs slipped down on the toilet seat, and the room resumed its terrible silence.

The only sounds outside were the beating boots of the secret police officer on the hallway floors and the shuffle of Johannes' slippers as he accompanied his fellow countryman.

CHAPTER TWENTY-THREE
VIANNE, PARIS, SUMMER, 1925

"Vianne."

Vianne dropped her suitcases on the platform in Paris, throwing herself into Marguerite Clément's arms. A porter approached and Marguerite spoke to him, instructing him to load Vianne's luggage onto a trolley, and he busied himself with this. Vianne rested her head in the crook of Marguerite's shoulder. Throughout the entire journey from New York, she'd focused on the moment she'd be in Marguerite's arms, and now, here she was, and it felt like home.

Vianne's eyes filled with tears. "Darling Marguerite," she said, linking her arm through that of her mother's best friend. Unanswered questions had bothered her ever since she'd received Marguerite's telegram. Arrangements were made for Vianne's immediate voyage to Paris, a passage booked, luggage packed, so swiftly, and then she was on the liner sailing to Plymouth, the ferry to France, another train to Paris.

Throughout the entire journey, she'd fretted, impossibly confused as to what was going on. Was the woman whom Marguerite claimed to be Vianne's sister really Anaïs? How had the authorities got it so wrong, proclaiming Anaïs dead, announcing there were no more survivors after the attack on Saint-

Gervais church? Vianne had been shaky all the way to Paris. *Why had her sister taken so long to find them?*

The train let out a belch of steam. People rushed by, women in light sundresses and matching hats, their eyes alight, children in prams pushed by nannies. Vianne held back the memories of train stations in Paris during the war, the subdued atmosphere, women burying their heads in their mother's shoulders, handkerchiefs. All those black armbands. And the young men, packing the carriages, hands flailing out of the windows, eyes burning with excitement to go to war.

Anaïs had gone off with such bravado. And so had Jacques.

Marguerite squeezed Vianne's arm, and she forced herself out of her reverie.

"You must be exhausted. A warm bath and a rest?" Marguerite said, the hint of a crease line forming around the sides of her brown eyes.

But Vianne shook her head. "Dearest Marguerite, I have to see Anaïs."

Marguerite's expression was full of sympathy. "Prepare yourself."

She followed the porter along the platform to a street taxi, and he began loading Vianne's luggage into the back. Vianne could have wept with relief. The driver lifted his peaked cap toward Marguerite, who thanked him, and they climbed into the jaunty automobile, its white-painted tires barreling along the streets of Paris.

Vianne held onto her hat. "You must tell me everything. Please, Marguerite. I don't understand what's going on. I mean, I am thrilled, overwhelmed, to hear my sister is alive, but I don't understand what happened. I am perfectly fine, after my journey," Vianne went on, suddenly remembering her manners. "I slept well, traveled well, wanted for nothing."

"Oh, dearest Vianne," Marguerite said. "You have no idea how relieved I am to have you back." A shadow passed across

Marguerite's face. "You have no idea how much your family needs you."

Vianne wiped a stray tear from her eye and stared out the window as the taxi bumped over the narrow, cobblestone streets. Her stomach churned with nerves.

"Thank goodness for you," Marguerite murmured.

"The *Mauretania* was extraordinary. I meant to thank you for reserving me a passage on such a wonderful liner. There was no need to choose such an elegant ship, you know..." Vianne said.

Marguerite frowned, but Vianne continued.

"It was, just like the SS *Paris*, more like traveling in a fashionable hotel than a ship," she said truthfully. "Salons like Italian palazzos, dining rooms inspired by sixteenth-century French chateaus. There was a dome dotted with the signs of the zodiac above and for the upper-deck passengers, a constant round of games out in the fresh air. Honestly, I would have traveled third class to come, under the circumstances, but I will repay you for the cost of the trip. You know, now I have my partnership with Eloise lined up, I..." her voice trailed off.

Marguerite shook her head. "I assumed you knew," the older woman said.

Vianne turned to her mother's friend.

"Dearest, a Mr. Conti insisted on paying for the *Mauretania*. And he refused any offer of reimbursement. I assumed he was... that is... you and he were close."

Vianne brought her gloved hand to her mouth. She shook her head, her eyes widening. "But I had no idea." She had told Giorgio about Marguerite's telegram and he'd held her hand for one long moment, before rushing off with the piece of paper in a whirl. He'd driven her to the shipping terminal, seen her onto the *Mauretania*, but he'd only told her that her fare was paid and sorted and that he'd been in touch with Marguerite.

Marguerite smiled.

Vianne folded her hands in her lap. She would write to Giorgio immediately and thank him. Or, better still, she would send a telegram tomorrow, and insist on paying him back.

She took in a deep breath. "Where is Anaïs now?" Vianne whispered, her eyes darting to the driver. "And what on this earth is going on?"

There was a pause before Marguerite responded.

Vianne waited.

"Anaïs has amnesia. She does not appear to remember anything about her time in Paris before the... dreadful day in March, 1918. Not me, not—"

"No." Vianne pulled away instinctively. Instinctively, she shook her head. "No," she said. "That cannot be. She does not remember us? She has forgotten her childhood?" Vianne raised her voice. "She could *never* forget Jacques. She could never forget her twin."

They had been inseparable. Until the war had forced them apart.

"Sweetheart, all we can think is that she must have suffered a blow to the head. Falling masonry, perhaps. Apparently, she was not actually in the church, but left before the service, because she had dropped her necklace outside. As she searched for it in the surrounding square, she was knocked over in the street by the blast. She cannot recall anything before that."

Vianne shook her head. "*What?*"

"She was not taken to the same hospital as the other wounded, but picked up by a doctor and his wife, where she rested for several days and then apparently left of her own accord, confused."

"I'm sorry..." Vianne covered her mouth with her gloved hand.

"The doctors are confounded, but they are dealing with so many cases of... mental weakness from the war, I'm afraid it's just another case. They say that all we can do is wait. I'm hoping that seeing you will help her. I'm *praying* that it will."

A lump formed in Vianne's throat. It was the only explanation, of course it was, otherwise how could Anaïs possibly have been living and not contacted them? Not even Jacques. Vianne stared out of the window. They were driving alongside the Seine. Barges made their slow way down the river, and the sunlight twinkled on the tiny ripples atop the water. In the distance sat the Eiffel Tower, majestic, solitary, looking down over all of Paris.

Vianne turned back to Marguerite. "If she had remembered, if she had come home, everything would be different," she said, the words bursting out before she could rein them in. "I would have a family. None of this would have occurred. Anaïs would have stood up to Jacques. She would never have let him turn me out."

They turned up Rue Brosse, and the church of Saint-Gervais loomed into sight. Vianne turned away, sickened.

"Oh, bother this," Marguerite said. "I'm sorry, dearest. I should have told the driver not to come this way. How silly of me." She tapped on the driver's seat. "No need to take the scenic route! Straight to the Places des Vosges."

"But where is Anaïs now? When can I see her?" Vianne asked, her eyes rounding, tears threatening to pool and slide down her cheeks. She leaned away from Marguerite, unable to tear her gaze away from the familiar, dreadful, beautiful old church. She sat, rigid, her arms crossed over her chest, her ears beating with the sound of crashing bricks, the yells of people, the thud of her own heart in her chest, which she thought might explode, as she had stood there, helpless, her feet like lead.

Marguerite was quiet as they moved through their beloved Marais district, driving by the boulangerie where Vianne and Papa used to buy their after-school treats, the boutiques where, as a young girl, she would stop and stare at the windows, trying to figure out how they had fashioned such beautiful garments, and then they came to Celine.

Vianne gasped. "But what has happened to the store?" she said, fighting the urge to stop the taxi, climb out and rap her hands on the front door of Papa's treasured antique store. As they passed, she could see it was dusty, the front doorstep needed a good sweep with a broom. Paint peeled from the black and gold painted sign that used to shine so brightly on Papa's windows, the letters half faded away. "What on earth is going on?"

"Jacques happened," Marguerite murmured. "He has not proved to be the manager we hoped."

Vianne loosened the collar of her blouse, cords in her neck tightening, as the small car pushed ahead. She tried to crane her head around, search her papa's beloved store for signs of life, but they had passed. The streets widened, and they were in the Place des Vosges.

Vianne climbed out of the taxi and her stomach dropped like a heavy stone to the bottom of a pool. Stupefied at the sight of Papa's store in such a state, she offered to pay the driver, but Marguerite brushed this aside.

Like a wooden doll, her stare fixed on Marguerite's back, she picked up her suitcases, and followed her mother's friend through the arched stone gallery that flowed gently under the redbrick and limestone building, the address fit for kings, where Marguerite lived.

She followed Marguerite in silence. The beautiful stone arch, unlike Papa's dear store, was all intact, and the ancient wooden door into which Marguerite inserted her key was polished, tended to with care.

Had Jacques ruined Papa's business after sending Vianne away?

Vianne climbed the steps up to the familiar fifth floor, to the apartment where Marguerite had afforded her refuge after Jacques' confounding behavior following the war.

Marguerite unlocked the solid polished front door, and Vianne curled her fingers around her suitcases, anger threatening to take off inside her like a flock of swallows in flight, before her cheeks began to burn red.

"I cannot believe what I saw," she muttered. She was overwhelmed. Tears glistened in her eyes. What was wrong with her brother? What madness had overtaken the boy she grew up with?

And what of Anaïs?

A maid bustled to the front door to take Vianne's luggage when they stepped inside Marguerite's calm, beautiful home.

Marguerite took Vianne's hand, her older eyes serious now. She held Vianne's gaze. "She is in the morning room. Would you like a refreshment before you see her? Do you need to gather yourself?"

Vianne's mouth opened and closed, but her words stuck in her throat and her feet felt as if they were glued to the spot. "Of course not." She pushed away the images that fought to take prominence in her mind. The store, tattered, beautiful Celine.

Somewhere behind all this destruction lay the siblings she'd lost. But how to find them?

"What do the doctors say?"

Marguerite's brown eyes were full of sympathy. "I have had several physicians examine her. They all think she had a bump to the head and has not recovered her memory. And the opinion is that she needs to see you. Seeing Jacques has not triggered her memory, but because you were one of the last people, she saw..." Marguerite's eyes cast downwards, "we are hoping that you being here will help."

"But where has she been?"

Marguerite raised a brow. "The Highlands of Scotland."

"*Scotland?*"

Marguerite's face fell into shadow. "I was in Scotland for an engagement party. One of my dear friend's daughters, you see. Annabel had been living in the Marais and I'd shown her around Paris, so I was delighted to travel up to the Highlands for her party. It was a chance to see old friends. But I was astounded when one of the most beautiful women at the party turned out to be none other than Anaïs." Marguerite twisted her hands into knots. "I would know her anywhere. You know that."

Vianne drew her hand to cover her mouth. "But—"

"I cannot tell you how confused I was at first, and I cannot tell you how strangely Anaïs reacted when she laid eyes on me. She appeared to not recognize me at all and was utterly mortified when I introduced myself to her husband."

Vianne frowned. *"What* did you just say?" Anaïs was married? Vianne reached out for the wall to stop herself from falling backwards to the floor.

Marguerite lay a hand on Vianne's arm. "One thing at a time, darling. All her husband, Archie, knew was that his wife had lost her family in the attack. Other than that, she had told him very little of herself. He'd fallen in love with her in London and they'd had a whirlwind romance."

"Archie?" Vianne murmured. It couldn't be true. Had Marguerite made a terrible error? Had she brought back the wrong girl to Paris with her? Anaïs was the very last person to marry a Highlander and to go to the wilds of Scotland. The very idea was mad.

"Archie told me he had not pushed her for more as Anaïs, or Amelie, as she called herself, was so distressed, but he is honestly a charming man, Vianne. Your Maman would have adored him."

Vianne simply shook her head. It was as if the carefully constructed world she'd built since the war was based on nothing but lies. And yet, it couldn't be true. Anaïs alive and living in Scotland all this time?

"Archie encouraged her with all his heart to come back to Paris with me. To rediscover her past. I knew I needed to take care of her, just like I took care of you after the war."

Vianne felt a lump form in her throat at the sincere kindness of her maman's dearest friend.

"But Anaïs refused to accompany me for days," Marguerite said. "Eventually, she agreed most reluctantly to part with Scotland, but then she prohibited her adoring husband to join us!" Marguerite threw her hands in the air, her beautiful lips turning downward in a grimace. "He remains in Scotland." Marguerite shook her head. "Vianne... this is why I need you here."

Vianne's expression grim, she followed Marguerite into the room where her sister was in wait.

. . .

An hour later, Vianne sat on a bench in the Places des Vosges. The most beautiful square in Paris. Once, to Vianne, Anaïs had been the most beautiful girl in the world. Now, her sister sat next to her, her eyes staring straight ahead, her hair dyed black underneath the hat Marguerite had placed upon her head to walk out of the apartment and a few blond tendrils starting to appear around the crown of her head. Vianne had no idea why Anaïs had done this, and she didn't dare to ask. Around them, children ran in the sunshine, and Parisians walked along the raked gravel paths, stopping to admire the lawns that were sheltered from their footfalls, lest they taint the beauty of the park.

"Dearest," Vianne said, taking a deep breath.

Anaïs's chest rose and fell in the loose cotton frock that she'd apparently brought down from Scotland, where Marguerite had said she'd started a new life under the name Amelie.

Amelie MacCullum. She'd married, and no one in Paris knew.

Vianne's hand rested atop her sister's, and bravely, she reached up and stroked a dark tendril from Anaïs's delicate cheek. "Remember playing here, when we were children?" she murmured, fighting to keep the desperation from her voice, fighting to stop herself from throwing her arms in the air with frustration, fighting to stop herself from collapsing in despair at the fact her sister seemed to be gone for good.

Anaïs's hand stilled underneath Vianne's.

There was a silence for a long moment. Vianne took in a shaking breath. She'd said too much. Upset her sister. Then Anaïs turned to her and, for a split second, there was something in the flash of her eyes that spoke of the old Anaïs, and Vianne's lips opened, she shook her head.

"*Anaïs?*" she murmured. She clutched with her free hand onto the hard wooden bench.

Marguerite had warned her not to take Anaïs away from the apartment. But Vianne had insisted. Something inside her knew that she must be allowed to speak to her sister on her own, out of the still, quiet room where she was sitting, her every move observed by a pristine nurse. Vianne had been certain she'd seen a flicker of recognition when she'd walked into Marguerite's salon and Anaïs had laid eyes on her.

Anaïs's grip tightened. "I remember everything, Vianne. All of it. If only I could forget."

"I beg your pardon?" Vianne's voice rose to an incredulous pitch. She loosened her hold on her sister's hand, remembering, remembering, instinctively how it felt to hold Anaïs. How her older sister had always pulled back slightly, whenever Vianne tried to embrace her as a child.

"I can never go back to being Anaïs," she continued in her quiet voice. "Not ever again and you must never tell a soul. Promise me. Or I shall do something even more drastic."

Vianne's lips opened, but she could not form any words.

Anaïs stared out at the square. "Maman's death was my fault."

Vianne stiffened. Her breathing seemed to catch and hitch, and she leaned forward in her seat, her hands falling between her knees. Next to her, her sister sat, implacable, and Vianne was silently, violently, sick.

That afternoon, Vianne stumbled out of Marguerite's apartment. Her head spinning, she left Anaïs with her nurse. After her breathtaking statement, Anaïs had stood up, faced Vianne, who was sitting blanched white as snow on the park bench, and insisted they go back to Marguerite's apartment. Despite Vianne's entreaties, Anaïs had closed like a book.

Vianne's brow furrowed as she marched along the familiar streets, head down, toward Celine. Did Jacques know anything more? Had Anaïs opened up to him despite the fact that Marguerite had insisted that he had not triggered her memory? Despite her misgivings about her brother, her infuriation with him,

Vianne had to find out if he, Anaïs's twin, was the confidant to whatever secrets she was hiding now.

Vianne turned down Rue de Sévigné, her heart lurching as she passed the apartment building where she'd grown up. Her memories of her last encounter with Jacques and the inobtrusive Sandrine tore at her, and she had to stop herself from walking straight up to the front door of her the old building and ringing the brass doorbell outside. If Jacques had landed Celine in terrible financial trouble, what had become of Papa and Maman's beautiful home? The home they'd treasured along with every special antique inside it, as well as their children?

Vianne focused and walked straight ahead. It had all seemed so formidable: her family, her life. What she had thought of as a fortress had fallen over like a pack of cards.

She'd have to stay a while, so she had organized a telegram to be sent to Giorgio to thank him for his generosity and had asked Marguerite's maid to send one to Miss Ellie to inform her Vianne had safely arrived in Paris.

Vianne curled her fingers into tight balls in her white gloves. Her tiredness from the journey had been thrown out into the wind. The blue summer frock she wore was neatly pressed, and her cheeks were flushed with a determination and, more than that, an irritation that she'd not known since she last spoke with Jacques.

When she came to Celine, Vianne couldn't hold in the sob that escaped from her mouth. She'd been perfectly correct as she passed by in the taxi earlier today. Cobwebs dangled above the window, and grime smeared the once gleaming glass.

Her heart ripped in two when she pushed the front door open and it gave out a piercing squeak. Her eyes alighted on the dusty counters, grubby floorboards, the pathetic meager offerings in the store. She stood with her hands on her hips, and bellowed.

"*Jacques!*"

There was a commotion out back in Papa's old office, the place where he used to chat with his clients, sort out deliveries from vast chateaus or apartments filled with a cache of riches in the suburbs of Paris. He used to call the people who were kind enough to trust him with their treasures to sell, and the people who would buy from him, his friends.

What on earth had Jacques done with everything Papa had worked so hard to build? After all, her brother had been so pompous about inheriting the apartment and Celine, making grand claims about the fact that he was the only son, not Vianne, that she was some vessel who he had to be rid of, so that his wife and he could take their rightful place as the head of the family home.

Vianne stood face to face with her sister-in-law.

"Sandrine."

"Vianne?" Sandrine, blinking rapidly, her gray eyes were dull and traced around their edges with fine lines that had not been there on the one occasion that Vianne had met her. Sandrine brought a hand up to pat her fading blond hair. She had not cut it in the modern style, instead, it was pulled back into a gaunt bun at the nape of her neck, and she had the appearance of a woman twenty years older than herself. "You had a safe journey home?" she asked, uselessly. "Marguerite said you were coming."

Sandrine twisted her hands, reddened, in front of the dowdy skirt and blouse she wore.

"As you see," Vianne said. She pulled off her gloves and held them in one hand. "Sandrine, where is my brother? And what on earth has he done with Celine?"

Sandrine flushed from her creased forehead to the base of her throat. "I... well, I can't say," she said, looking away.

Vianne sighed. "Very well," she replied. "I shall find him, and he shall tell me. Is he out back in Papa's office, Sandrine? I heard a great crash when I walked into the store. It sounded like a bottle..."

Sandrine came forward to stand right near Vianne, her reddened hands gripping Vianne's own.

"I am glad you are back," Sandrine whispered, shooting a glance behind her toward the open door of Papa's office. "Vianne, I need your help with Jacques. I need you to stay and help us.

Please..." Sandrine loosened her grip on Vianne's hands and covered her mouth with her palm. She let out a sob.

Vianne opened her mouth, but Sandrine tightened her grip.

"We need you here, Vianne. Jacques has made an awful mess of the store."

Vianne tried to move toward the office, but Sandrine went on, intent.

"He can't run a business," Sandrine hissed. "He is not capable, Vianne."

Vianne looked straight into the girl's worried gray eyes. "And why not?"

But right then, there was a bang in the office. A chair, clearly, being knocked to the ground.

And in the whip of an instant, Vianne's eyes shot to the doorway. For there stood her brother Jacques, a bottle of wine in his hand.

Vianne closed her eyes. Oh, dear goodness. She had not thought it as bad as this.

"Hello, Sister!" he said, grinning at her like a fool. And he tipped the bottle up, and took a great swig out of it, only to glare at it when not a drop of liquid came out.

"Jacques." Vianne's voice dropped. Her hands fluttered away from Sandrine, and she clutched her stomach. "Jacques," she said helplessly.

She closed her eyes, beating back the images of Giorgio, and New York, the fact she'd worked so very hard and had a wonderful opportunity that was slipping through her fingers and was seeming more and more like a dream in another world. The girls: Lucia, Adeline, Mollie, Goldie, and Miss Ellie. She'd have to give it all up because her family was in such a state.

"So," he said, "you didn't find a husband in New York?" He waved his bottle in the air. "Ever'one will be thrilled." He slurred his words. "We can marry you off to a Frenchman."

Vianne's mouth fell open and she swallowed, hard. "What is going on?" she said. She'd hoped for, but not expected, an apology.

Now, it was all she could do to deal with the problem at hand. The man standing in front of her. Vianne grimaced. When she thought of her brother, the boy she'd grown up with, and his dark lashes, his very blue, clear eyes, the way he'd said he wanted to be a sheep farmer or a vet, the young Jacques, he'd been sensitive, and kind. What a mess he'd become. What complex creatures they all were.

She folded her arms.

He was her brother.

No matter what.

"Sandrine," she said. "Get me the broom. And a duster." And she glared at her brother. "And when you've sobered up, Jacques, we shall sit down, and talk."

CHAPTER TWENTY-FOUR
ANAÏS, BRUSSELS, BELGIUM, SPRING, 1915

Anaïs stood outside Matron Cavell's office in the Red Cross Hospital, her hands wound tightly around the clean white apron she wore over her skirt. From inside, she heard paper rattling, drawers being opened and closed with a snap. Matron Edith Cavell was never idle. Anaïs ran over the favor she had to ask of her boss in her head for the millionth time.

"Come." Matron Cavell's voice rang out clear and strong into the hallway, and Anaïs, biting on her lip, entered Matron's neat room. The request she was about to make of her senior was something she would not have dreamed of doing, but Johannes' very real distress had changed that.

She'd dug deep within herself, and only come up with one answer, every time. No matter that he was German, as his nurse she could not stand by and see him go back to the trenches. If she did so, Anaïs knew her inaction would haunt her until her dying day.

Anaïs halted in front of Matron Cavell's plain, wooden desk. Shafts of sunlight flickered onto the middle-aged woman's fair hair and the pale skin on her cheeks. It was strange to think the sun still shone outside, while the German occupiers patrolled the streets of

Brussels, their ominous presence terrifying all the citizens of this good city into submission. Or some of them...

Matron removed her reading glasses and smiled kindly at Anaïs. "Nurse Mercier?"

Anaïs pressed her lips together. There was no point beating around the bush. Matron was simply not that kind of person.

But, before Anaïs could open her mouth, Matron Cavell had started to speak. "You are proving to be excellent at all aspects of your job. The patient that you guided through Brussels last week made it safely over the border. I have had word. He is now on his way to London. But..." a reflective look passed over Matron's face. "I have another proposition to put to you." She indicated that Anaïs sit down in the stark wooden chair opposite her own.

Anaïs slid onto the hard benchlike seat.

"You are due to go back to France for leave very soon, Miss Mercier."

"Yes, but I don't have to, Matron. I can stay here."

"Oh, no. I think you must." Matron Cavell turned away; her light eyes filled with a sadness. "I have a favor to ask of you when you are on your way." She leaned forward, her work-hardened hands folded on the plain table. "But it will be dangerous, and it will put you at further risk."

Anaïs folded her hands in her lap.

"Intelligence documents from Herman Kappio, a very important member of our network, need to be transported to Paris. The information is critical, Anaïs. It will contain precise information about the German's munitions stores around Valenciennes. It is exactly what the French government need to know. Because it is such vital information, I want to send you as soon as possible. Tomorrow, Miss Mercier." She held Anaïs's gaze. "It will mean supplying you with false papers to use until you make it over the border so that you are not questioned. You speak some German. You are content to comply with this?"

Anaïs sat tall in her seat. "I will conceal the documents in my clothing myself. My German is passable, and I will only speak if necessary until I'm over the border. It is not myself that I worry about, Matron. I—"

"Wear your hair down. It will distract the German officers."

Anaïs's stomach curled. "Yes, Matron."

"Very well, thank you, Nurse," Matron said.

Anaïs held her ground. "Matron Cavell?"

Matron looked up, her hand stilling on the papers on her desk.

Anaïs wove her hands into a knot. "It is the young German patient, Johannes Meyer. He is not... he is not fit to go back to the trenches in my opinion. You see, he has a terrible case of shell shock, worse than I have seen since I've been here. Tremors, confusion, nightmares. I have observed all the symptoms on multiple occasions. When he wakes, his vision is often impaired, and he takes a long time to recognize... even me."

Matron eyed her.

Anaïs sat forward in her seat. "Johannes Meyer is an engineer. He spends his time sketching, doing mathematical calculations. Bridges, railways, the drawings that I have shown to you. The trenches are not for him. Might he not be sent back to work as an engineer? He mentioned that he'd worked for a large firm in Essen. He talks of how much design means to him." She looked down. "I understand he is the enemy. I understand that my request is irregular in the extreme."

"Nurse Mercier, no one is the enemy in God's eyes. We must have compassion for those who are suffering on both sides of the battle lines. You know that I hold hatred for no one."

Anaïs nodded. "This is why I have come to you."

Matron folded her arms. "You know, there is a prevailing view that this condition is simply caused by cowardice, Nurse Mercier."

No. Anaïs leaned forward in her chair. "But—"

"Some think these terrors are best addressed by military discipline."

Anaïs closed her eyes. "That would kill him."

There was a silence. "There are also increasing cases where soldiers are being discharged from hospitals as invalids, incapable of employment. I imagine you don't think that would be the best outcome for the patient, Nurse?"

"Not at all." Anaïs sat taller in her seat. The relief of being able to care for someone, for another human being, just as she used to care for Jacques, was almost palpable. She could almost see it surrounding her like a soft, protective haze. All her life, she'd been thought of as brave, invincible, fearless Anaïs, but deep down, she'd always felt a deep yearning to help others, to take care of them, to make a difference somehow. Nursing fascinated her, science and medicine too. And now, these things had come together, and if she could help Johannes, she could make a difference that was tangible, that meant something, that she'd always remember and for which she could be proud.

She chose her words with care. "I believe, with treatment, and if he is allowed to return to his regular work in an engineering firm, that Johannes might have a chance of healing, but it will take time. His wounds are deep, and internal."

Matron sat back in her seat. "And, based on what you have observed, if the patient were to return to the trenches?"

Anaïs lifted her gaze. She eyed Matron and spoke with great clarity. "I believe he would not survive another bout in the trenches. I don't think he'd stand a chance." She swallowed, the sound of German military personnel barking orders outside in the street perforating the stillness in the room, and her eyes met Matron's for a glimmer of a second. The reality was right outside this building. Governments might protect the weak while they were physically injured, but as soon as soldiers were sent out again, they would be thrust into a cold, cruel world where they had no choices, no control and were expected to slaughter their fellow men, look them in the eye and kill them-or be killed.

Matron stood up. She moved to the window, flicking the soft gauzy curtain aside for a moment and gazing out into the street.

"I will speak to the doctor on duty today. I will recommend, based on your observations, that they send him back to his engineering firm, Nurse Mercier."

Anaïs's shoulders sagged with relief.

"I suppose he was working at Krupp, if he were in Essen. One of the most famous German steelmakers, an important manufacturer of industrial machinery," Matron said. "He will be safely employed." Matron turned back to face Anaïs. "Perhaps he will design the perfect bridge." Her features softened into a smile. "Well done, Nurse Mercier. I am proud of you for your humility, in the face of..." she glanced out the window again.

Anaïs let out a shaky breath. She would never forget the sound, the sight, the anguish she'd felt at seeing that young man, terrified, damaged, deranged by this war. If she had to go away and leave Johannes Meyer tomorrow, at least she would do so in the knowledge she, as his nurse, had helped to save his life.

"You."

That night, Anaïs stilled in the hallway. She'd just finished her rounds and was about to go to bed, to get a good night's sleep, if possible, before her trip to Paris the following morning. Slowly, she wheeled around to face the man whose voice she would recognize anywhere. The German secret police officer who had pushed the doors open in the Nurse's WC while Anaïs had balanced in the cubicle, having hidden Matron's incriminating papers into the cistern, stood face to face with her.

"I want to talk to you. Now."

Anaïs flushed. She tore her shaking hands behind her back, clasping them until her fingernails pressed into her palms.

"Come with me," he said.

Anaïs lifted her chin. The officer of the secret police seized her, pressing his firm hands into the soft flesh of her upper arm.

"God keep me brave," she whispered.

The officer yanked her down the hallway and into the night.

CHAPTER TWENTY-FIVE
VIANNE, SUMMER, 1925

Vianne stopped on the Quai de l'Hôtel de Ville, right at the spot where she'd looked into the Seine on that cold, March, day back in 1918 when Maman had been killed. Back then, her fantasies had only been about the peach silk dress she was preparing for Anaïs and Jacques' birthday. A tear streaked down Vianne's cheek for the loss of her innocence and for the price her brother and sister had paid during circumstances that were unendurable for everyone in their generation. The loss was insupportable. In the last few years, Vianne had thought she'd be able to put the pieces of her life back together. Coming back to Paris, she'd only seen them fall apart all over again.

But, looking down at the opaque water, standing in the exact same place as she'd stood, a young girl of just eighteen as the wheels of war drew to an awful, final close, there was no reflection of Maman's face looking back at her, no shimmering, blond hair waving amongst the ripples that tumbled across the water's surface, only to disappear back down into the mysterious depths of the Seine.

Vianne felt a leaden deadness spreading over her. She could go back to New York, and pretend none of this existed, that none of the ache and pain of the old world was real. She could return to the fabulous New World with all its wondrous opportunities and leave her brother and sister to rot.

But to do so would be unforgivable. She could never live with herself.

Fashion designing had only been a fairy tale. Fantasies and whimsies were just that. They had no place in real life. Vianne's smile was rueful. She'd always been distracted by dreamy imaginations, sewing Maman's lace dress when she should have been knitting balaclavas, then sailing off to New York to follow a fantasy.

Her time, fleeting as it had been, in America was over. The life she'd built for herself amongst the golden, dreamy towers of Manhattan was gone. The new world with all its promises, opening its arms to so many displaced people from Europe, was not for her.

And if there was any doubt in her mind about staying in Paris to help Jacques, Vianne knew she had to ignore it and show him compassion. She recognized his bravado and now saw that when he had sent her off, it was not a show of strength but of weakness. The quick marriage to his nurse, Sandrine: the posing, the posturing. Vianne would not succumb to such a thing. She would not treat him the way he'd treated her.

Of course, her brother should have taken care of her after the war. After their father's death, the least Jacques could have done was to ensure his little sister was safe and had access to a home, food, safety. He had been, to all intents and purposes, the eldest surviving member of the family and he'd inherited the entirety of Papa's estate.

Vianne shook this aside. All she could do was deal with what was right in front of her, and, leaning against the railings, the hot summer sun beating down on her hat, she knew that she could not return to New York.

And that meant turning down the opportunity to be a partner with Miss Ellie. It meant kissing goodbye all she'd worked toward.

It meant leaving any chance of happiness with Giorgio behind for good.

Vianne fixed her gaze on the river. The Seine had always been her compass. She'd come here whenever she was at a turning point, no matter how small. The river had flown through and around her life in Paris, and here she was, back again, come full circle, unable to see anything but shadows in its depths.

Vianne clasped her hands together over the railings that divided herself from the water.

Her family could not continue as they were. She would have to stay in Paris and build up Papa's beloved Celine, to protect his legacy. She would have to help Jacques get well, or her brother and her sister-in-law would be destitute, and goodness knew Anaïs needed Vianne if she were to climb out of the dark place she'd inhabited these past few years. Taking care of Anaïs would have been exactly what Maman would have done, and having her sister back was miraculous. After all, looking after family was still living her life, and following her heart, just not in the way Vianne had planned. In some small way, she knew she had to be happy about that.

Sighing, Vianne turned away from the river and made her way through the cobbled streets to the Place des Vosges.

In the three weeks she'd been in Paris, she'd swept the floors of Celine every day, and mopped them until they gleamed, carefully dusted the stock they did have, scrubbed the windows and polished them until they shone, thrown Jacques' empty bottles into the bin, gone to speak with his doctor, and made him an appointment with an eminent psychologist. Vianne had written to Papa's loyal clientele and let them know she was back and was running Celine. That she would love to sell on any beautiful heirlooms they might not want anymore.

She'd had enthusiastic responses from Papa's old clientele. Of course she had. Vianne had run Celine for much of the last year of the war while Papa was gravely ill, and she'd always been in there, whenever she could manage to be as a girl. She'd met all of Papa's clientele.

She'd closed the little book of fashion designs she'd brought with her from New York, hiding it right at the back of the armoire in her bedroom at Marguerite's house.

Vianne exhaled. She would push on.

But now, exhaustion was biting at her after sitting up for count-less nights attending to the accounting for Celine, after meeting with the bank manager, impressing upon him that the business would be solvent by the year's end and that they had to keep it afloat in the meantime.

So, tomorrow, she'd have to send two telegrams to America that would break her heart.

Hardly aware of the Parisians enjoying the summer warmth, parasols up, cloche hats jaunty, laughter and plans for summer vacations to the South of France ringing through the air, Vianne came to the edge of the Place des Vosges.

Before she did anything more, she had to take care of the matter that was pressing upon her more heavily than anything else at present.

She had to talk to Anaïs.

That night, after she had dined with Marguerite, and the kindly, smiling woman who only served to remind Vianne, every day of her darling Maman, had gone out to the Opera Garnier with friends, Vianne trudged up the stairs in the beautiful apartment. Outside Anaïs's room, she knocked softly on her sister's closed door.

"Come," Anaïs said.

Vianne entered her sister's bedroom. The last vestiges of long summer daylight filtered through the window, thrown open to the Parisian square with its charming gardens below. Anaïs was propped up in her bed, her beautiful face pearly and almost translucent in the soft light. Her body, still slim despite the fact she was with child, was encased in a soft negligee of pale blue chiffon.

"How are you?" Vianne said, going to stand by the window, gazing out at the green lawns where Parisians sat in the long shadows and the odd burst of laughter rang through the quiet air. Birds sang the last of their songs for the day, their sweet voices loudest before they tucked their heads under their wings and turned silent in the Parisian trees.

She turned to her sister, whose eyes, as always, diverted away toward the white-painted wall. Vianne worried desperately that the fact Anaïs was confining herself so tediously would only hinder her situation, lengthen her illness, make things much, much worse.

"Anaïs?"

She came to sit on the edge of her sister's bed, reaching out and grasping the hands that had once seemed so confident, so strong, and capable. Now, Anaïs's palm was as soft as a child's.

A trickle of a tear passed down Anaïs's cheek, and Vianne, her heart melting, squeezed her sister's hand. She leaned closer, drew Anaïs into her embrace.

Anaïs's husband Archie was worried sick. He'd offered to come to Paris, his telegrams arrived daily, and Marguerite was sending dispatches back to him, as if from the battle lines of this family's private, unfinished war. Marguerite felt that him being here might overcomplicate things. She wanted Anaïs to have a chance to be alone with Vianne, and Archie, dear-sounding man that he was, had agreed to this. Vianne had written to him too, and he her, their letters crossing these past weeks and both wanted the same thing.

They wanted Anaïs to get well.

Vianne knew Marguerite had tried to get her sister to talk to doctors, knew Anaïs had simply closed up.

Vianne held her sister at arm's length, before settling her back on her pillows, and climbing up.

"Talk to me," Vianne whispered. "Please, darling."

And waited until, finally, she heard a great sigh come through the entirety of her sister's frame.

"You know that I worked in a hospital in Brussels at the outset of the war," Anaïs said, her voice lingering in the growing shadows that cast around the room.

Vianne pulled the bedcover up a little higher, tucking their legs inside. "Of course," she whispered. "And after that, you were stationed in Northern France, in the military hospitals from the middle of 1915. You were far braver than me, Anaïs."

Anaïs let out a low moan. "Don't."

"You faced danger head on," Vianne whispered.

"In Brussels," Anaïs said, her voice cracking, "the head matron of our hospital was engaged in a network of espionage."

Vianne stiffened. She remained silent.

"Edith was extraordinary," Anaïs went on, her voice soft in a way that Vianne had never heard in her sister. "She helped over nine hundred men back to England, patients who'd been at the hospital, prisoners of war. She was the instrumental part of a network of guides who gave them safe passage through to neutral Holland." Anaïs lowered her voice. "But she did more than that, she also gave them information, vital intelligence to carry home to the War Offices in London, or Paris, and for this, she took great risks, often accompanying them through Brussels in pre-dawn escapes, meeting with informers, organizing false identity cards for them, money, and food and bribes for the German secret police, who were all-seeing and everywhere."

Vianne was silent. Her hands shaking, she placed them atop Anaïs's own.

"I helped several soldiers get home to England. I carried information, I... But Vianne..." her voice broke. "I also helped a German patient. A young man for whom I came to care."

Vianne hugged her knees to her chest. "And that makes you doubly brave and strong."

Anaïs held out a hand and cut her off. "No. It does not. Johannes was... he was young. Vulnerable. He reminded me," she said, "of Jacques."

Vianne's brow clouded. "But you always took care of Jacques," she whispered.

Anaïs let out a wry laugh. "Yes, but in my arrogant, confident state, no one thought of me as maternal, Vianne. It was not the way I was viewed, not the persona I was in our family."

Vianne frowned. Had they had a choice? She, the baby; Anaïs, the warrior; Jacques, the indulged, sometimes anxious only boy? Or had they adopted these attributes? It was certain that they had become defined by them.

"I always wanted to be a nurse, Vianne. It was just not my role in the family. Not the way I was seen."

Vianne was quiet. "No, I understand that. Go on, Anaïs."

"So, I made nursing adventurous. Edith Cavell was a role model for me. She was revolutionary in so many ways, in her training of nurses, in the way she lifted the reputation of the profession from the ridiculous, and the scorned, to become well regarded. She had the finest reputation of any matron in Europe, which is why I chose to train with her."

"Of course, it was an honor for you to work with her, but it was also a privilege for her to have you working there," Vianne said. She squeezed Anaïs's hand. "Tell me what is so wrong, Anaïs."

Anaïs shuddered violently. "My German patient couldn't bear to go back to the battlefield. So, I advocated for him to be excused."

Vianne shook her head. "Well, that is a good thing."

"No." Anaïs only spoke in a whisper, but the strength of her exclamation was profound. "If I had not spoken out, Johannes Meyer would never have returned to his former work at the famous engineering firm in Essen, called Krupp."

"Krupp?" Vianne asked, frowning.

Anaïs barked out a strange, deep, throaty laugh. She buried her head, speaking into her knees. Her words came out in a hushed and haunting tone, and Vianne simply stared at the black and blond strands of hair atop Anaïs's once proud head. "If you had seen what I had seen, if you had done what I had done, you would wish yourself dead."

"Anaïs!" Vianne's hand flew to her mouth. As much as she wanted to comfort her sister, she knew that if she were to do so, Anaïs would accept none of it.

"A few days after Maman's death, the name Krupp, the master gunmakers in Europe and the world that had designed the Paris

Gun, the very same firm who had shocked the world with Big Bertha, was all over every newspaper in France."

Vianne reached for her necklace. Her shoulders quaked. "He was working at the firm that designed the gun that killed Maman? But still, this does not mean..."

Anaïs's shoulders heaved, and her knuckles were white around her knees. "It gets worse. I *knew* that Johannes' notebooks were filled with designs, but on the last day I saw him, he was drawing something else." She lifted her face, and her cheeks, white as snow, almost blended into nothing with the graying light. "A train track, and below this, a multitude of descriptions in tiny German words, and then, underneath that, a dotted semicircle in a great arc rising up from a flat line." Anaïs shuddered. "I saw that exact picture replicated in the newspapers in the days after Maman was killed. The arc showed the angle that the cannonball had taken over Paris, and the train tracks were for the gun emplacement, not railway carriages as I had thought. And I never reported these drawings to Matron Cavell. Instead, like a fool, I let him go free, and those designs of his? They murdered Maman. You have no idea how the images burn in my mind."

Vianne stood up.

"Johannes even *told* me how he was passionate about designing something to end the war, about making some grand statement that would turn trench warfare into a thing of the past. The engineers at Krupp designed the Paris Gun in just fourteen months, and I sent Johannes back there in 1915. By 1918, his work was done. We now know that Professor Rausenberger and his team at Krupps got approval by the German High Command to design this ultra-long-range gun firing heavy shells over distances of over fifty miles."

Vianne moved across to stare out the window, rubbing her arms. The air had become so very chill inside.

"Vianne, I lived. Maman died."

Vianne turned around. Her eyes locked with her sister's, and in the silence, Vianne's chin trembled.

Anaïs clutched at the single strand of pearls she wore around her neck. "I had to kill Anaïs. I don't want to be called by that name. Ever. Do you understand, Vianne?" She tried to kneel up in the bed, only to slump down again. "You must not tell a soul."

Vianne opened her mouth.

But Anaïs held up her hand. "Especially not Archie. Just let me go back to Scotland. Let me bear this child whom I do not deserve. Let me live quietly in my own fuming pool of guilt until the day I die." Anaïs buried her face in her hands.

"Anaïs!" Vianne threw herself back across the room, cradled her sobbing sister in her arms.

And still, Anaïs went on. "I dropped my pendant while we were walking into Saint-Gervais on Good Friday for the service," she said, "just as the service was about to start, I ran back out to look for it. I was knocked out by the explosion, by the impact of the blast. I was taken in by a doctor, and not sent to the same hospital as the other patients, but when I... came to, it was all over the news. Krupp's latest invention, the Paris Gun, and there were the measurements, the engineering behind it. Our countrymen had worked it out and had provided the basic sketches in the newspapers, just the same as the designs Johannes had drawn. In the days after the attacks, when I saw the list of names of the victims in the paper, saw Maman's photograph, mine... it was better to *lose* Anaïs than to be her. I had to leave her behind. After all, to you, I was dead and gone."

Vianne closed her eyes.

Anaïs went on in her strange, soft, shaking voice. "It wasn't just 1918, either. I was questioned by the German secret police before I left Brussels in 1915. They warned me if I returned to Brussels I would be watched. I would be on a list of suspects. So that is why I did not go back to Brussels and Matron Cavell after 1915."

Vianne was sickened. "Did they hurt you? The secret police?"

Anaïs's eyes clouded, and Vianne had all the answers she needed. Vianne wrapped her arms tight around her waist, while Anaïs, her voice quiet, continued.

"The summer of 1915, during a raid at the hospital in Brussels after I was safely home in Paris, one of my fellow nurses in Belgium was caught with compromising documents, and two thousand copies of the underground newspaper, *La Libre Belgique*."

Vianne moved back to sit with her sister.

"The German secret police came for Matron Cavell. I, whom she had trusted, was not there to help her when she needed me. They took our brave Matron Cavell to their headquarters and imprisoned her." Anaïs lifted her head, and her eyes were agonized. "While I was safely back in Paris, thirty-five members of my network were arrested, Vianne. Matron Cavell," she whispered, "was sentenced to death. I escaped freely, time after time, outside the church in Paris, from the espionage ring in Brussels. And all those good people gone." She placed her head in her hands. "Now, Vianne, you understand why Anaïs does not deserve to live."

Vianne swallowed. "Darling..."

But Anaïs ground out the words. "The brave Matron Edith Cavell, who helped so many Allied soldiers to get home, was shot on a cold October morning in 1915 by the German secret police in Brussels. The last thing she would have seen was an arc of soldiers. How terrifying it must have been," Anaïs whispered. "Her kindness, the way she spoke to people, the way she fought so hard to get others to respect nurses, and the nursing profession. All gone in the gloomy mists of an autumn morning."

"I'm sorry..." Vianne whispered helplessly.

But Anaïs's voice was wretched, bitter, laced with something she'd thrown over her memories and burned until only the chars remained. "Maman, gone in the flicker of a cold Paris afternoon. The matron who taught me everything I knew shot in cold blood. And I fought to free the young man who went to work for the very engineering firm that famously designed the gun that butchered Maman. So, no, Vianne. I'm not your hero. You should walk right out of this room and get away from me for good."

Vianne held her sister's hand. Darkness fell, and the room was bathed in shadows.

"Anaïs," she whispered. "Please. Listen to me."

But her sister only stared at nothing, her fingers still grasping her strand of pearls.

Vianne swallowed. She reached out and stroked a stray dark hair away from Anaïs's cheek. Her sister was still beautiful, and she knew that beauty shone through. If it hadn't, she would not have felt any guilt. But her guilt was too much, and she must not bear it alone.

"I think you should tell Archie the truth. I think he should be here with you, until you feel well enough to go back to Scotland. And in the meantime, I also think we should go to the doctor and help you find the care you need to deal with all you've been through. You and Jacques, both so affected by the war. I'm only sorry you've had to suffer alone, Anaïs. I promise, you won't live another day bearing this torment by yourself."

Vianne stroked her sister's head, and then, she heard her mother's voice, talking to her, to them both, in her calm way.

"Darling Anaïs," Vianne whispered. "Look at it this way. You helped a man despite the fact he was on the other side of some war. And the fact is, that was exactly what Maman and what Matron Edith Cavell would have done too."

Anaïs raised her head, tears streaking her cheeks.

Vianne took in a deep breath and went on with conviction. "You had no say in what happened to Maman. But one thing we all can do now is accept that the war is over. The war is done for good. And we have life. We have the life that Maman and Papa gave to us. And there is a new life burgeoning inside you, and your child deserves to know that their mother was filled with compassion for the suffering of a human being. Please, Anaïs, accept that all you tried to do was to help. You never killed a soul, but you helped hundreds by the sound of it. For the sake of our pasts, for the sake of our brother, and for the sake of your child, you must not take responsibility for something that was beyond your control. Let it go, Anaïs."

And there was a silence. Then Anaïs, her heart beating so

wildly that Vianne could almost sense it drumming in her own breast, lay her head down on her younger sister's shoulder, and they sat in the gathering darkness, together, at last.

"Send for him," Anaïs said, her voice shuddering, but despite this, her words were perfectly clear. "Send for Archie, Vianne."

Vianne cradled her sister's head and closed her eyes in relief.

CHAPTER TWENTY-SIX
VIANNE, PARIS, FALL, 1925

2 E 63rd St,
New York,
NY 10065

Dearest Vianne,

I was so very moved to read your letter. And, while I am, of course saddened to hear the news that you will not be returning to New York since your brother and sister-in-law need your help far more than we do, I also write in the hope that you might still change your mind.

The girls miss you dreadfully. While we are battling on to meet all the new orders that came in after the wonderful parade, the atelier lacks something. A spark. Your genius. You know, if, and I still say when, you want to come back to Manhattan, the lights will always be on for you.

Lucia is complaining of life being extremely dull in the apartment. She says she is finding it far harder to become motivated and realizes how much you inspired her. She and the other girls send their love, and tell you that when you come back, they will take you out and you shall dance all night to celebrate! I have no truck for such energy anymore, but, you know, I wonder if my mother, Pepper, does! In any case, Mama Pepper also sends love, and says to tell you that you are in her thoughts and prayers.

We are starting to design more dresses with flaring tunic tops. These are charming for the afternoons, and I have several orders in for frocks in flowered chiffon. We are trimming them with contrasting ribbon, and underneath, they have a slip of satin that is built in. Lace is also popular for trimmings, and most interestingly, we are seeing more of the color tan, in combinations with other colors—blue-and-tan, tan-and-green. Scallops are terribly in vogue. Every customer wants them. A little design I came up with in faille crepe has been popular too. I'm making it in navy or black, with collar and cuffs of flesh georgette.

We are churning out daywear, but without you here, I'm afraid we are not achieving those couture pieces that were making us stand out so very beautifully! However, the effects of the parade, and all your hard work, are still resulting in much interest in the atelier, and I've had to lie to several of my clients and say you will be coming home to New York soon.

I do hope you view the atelier as a home, a home that will be yours to own one day. But more than anything else, what I wish, Vianne, is that you are designing, because you must not let that spark of yours be put out.

Finally, my dear, I am certain you have not given away, in your letters, the real atrocities of what your brother and sister have endured, but please know that from New York, I send my deepest sympathy to you all, and I hope that you understand you have family here. We all miss you,

Yours truly,

Eloise Chappelle

. . .

Vianne looked up from the desk in Celine. In the sparkling, polished store, Sandrine was attending to customers, a well-dressed couple from the country who had walked in while strolling around the Marais district for the afternoon. Vianne cupped her hand in her chin. Sandrine looked professional. Her blond hair now cut short, she was dressed in a silk crepe frock that Vianne had whipped up for her in smart blue and red.

Vianne smiled encouragingly when Sandrine turned toward her as if seeking her approval while she showed the couple around the store.

Vianne slit her letter opener through the other envelope that had arrived in today's post.

Valentino's
Park Avenue,
New York
NY, 10065

Bella,

I read your sister's story with my heart on my sleeve. What horrors are these that our fellow men inflict upon each other? I am so saddened to hear she has endured so very much. But I am also incredibly pleased to hear that Anaïs's husband has come down to Paris from Scotland, and that he, whom you describe so beautifully as a "dear man," is staying to take care of her. It is wonderful that she is receiving treatment, and I hope that she will make a full recovery.

Your brother sounds like he, too, is making steady progress in the sanatorium. And as for you, you are a marvel, I can tell it, bringing Celine up to scratch again.

I'm glad you had a grand reopening with all your papa's old friends, and I'm glad my suggestion to do this, in some small way, helped. I also think I would have loved to have known your Papa. He sounds like an incredible man. I, too, see my patrons at Valentino's as my friends just, like he did at Celine.

Darling, Vianne, I know you have work to do there, and I know you are worried about the future for your brother and sister, but please, I beg you to ensure you are following your dreams, your heart.

And you know that heart is so very dear to me, so very dear that I cannot put it into words.

I am thinking of you, always, and I am always yours.

All my love,

Giorgio

Vianne stared down at the letters from New York, and then taking a deep breath, she hid them away in the drawer of Papa's desk.

Sandrine finished with her customers and moved over quietly to stand by Vianne. "The lady and gentleman are interested in the eighteenth-century table," she said, her voice tentative. "And they are coming back tomorrow to make arrangements to have it sent to their home in Aix-en-Provence."

Vianne smiled, and absently, with an aching chest for all she'd left behind in New York, she laid a hand on Sandrine's. "Well done, dear. We'll continue to try to increase our acquisitions and sales together. I've several promising pieces lined up in the coming months, and I'll make a list of people whom I think might be interested in them..."

But then, Vianne frowned. For outside the window of Celine, a showstopper of a motorcar had just pulled into the curb. While most automobiles still looked like boxes on four wheels, this gleaming, stately vehicle was all about the curves. Vianne was unable to peel her eyes away from the car and a small crowd had gathered on the sidewalk to stare.

Vianne stood up and wandered over to the window to take a closer look at the beauty that had parked right in front of her eyes. The automobile was like haute couture in the form of a luxury motorcar.

"Why, look at that statue on the front of the car. She looks as if she has wings," Vianne breathed, staring at the beautiful figure of a woman, leaned forward with her arms stretched out behind her on the hood of the vehicle. "She looks as if she could take off and fly."

"Oh, my," Sandrine whispered next to her. "Have you ever seen something so sublime?"

Vianne smiled, wistful. She hadn't seen a motorcar so classy since she'd driven out to Long Island with Giorgio in his Duesenberg, and another pang of regret needled her insides. For one split second, she indulged herself by imagining how it might be if Giorgio stepped out of the vehicle onto the sidewalk right now and came into Celine.

But then she frowned. A gray-haired uniformed driver climbed out of the driver's seat and came around to open the passenger door for a dazzlingly dressed woman, who stepped out and turned to stare right at Celine.

"Well then, it's a lady's car," Sandrine breathed. "Oh my, she must have a very wealthy husband."

"Perhaps." Vianne leaned closer to the window, her heart beating wildly as she glimpsed the gleaming red leather interior of the car before the driver snapped the door shut again.

The woman stopped for a moment, clearly taking the time to thank her driver, and as she did so, Vianne gasped.

"Emilie Grigsby," Vianne breathed, taking in the sight. "What on earth brings her to the Marais?" Vianne could only stare and admire the vision who stood on the sidewalk. Miss Grigsby's hair shone reddish gold under her hat and her face had that sad sort of expression that was often the company of true beauty. Her complexion was like alabaster.

Miss Grigsby turned gracefully. She moved beautifully, her form was exquisite, and yet she was not more than five feet five inches in height. Vianne staved off the ideas for stunning haute couture gowns that whirled through her mind.

Sandrine leaned closer to have a look. "How do you know who she is?"

"I met her on a boat. She's a New York heiress who has been acknowledged as the most beautiful woman in the world."

Sandrine turned to Vianne. "Vianne. She looks like an empress!"

Vianne almost fell backward into her gaping sister-in-law when the front door to Celine opened, and Emilie Grigsby stepped inside. Vianne stood transfixed, while, clearly, Sandrine waited for her to take the lead. But Vianne's professional eyes, eyes that had been starved of inspiration for weeks, were drinking in the low-waisted number Emilie Grigsby wore, with its rectangular neckline, echoed in a modern black-and-white rectangular pattern that was repeated over and over right to the hemline. She looked like she'd stepped out of *Vogue* magazine and landed on the front doorstep of Celine.

Vianne sighed, memories of the gowns she'd designed in New York for Miss Ellie threatening to overwhelm her, along with the busy sound of sewing machines and the perky chatter of Lucia, Mollie, Goldie, and Adeline.

Emilie Grigsby paused for effect in the doorway, before turning her extraordinary violet eyes toward Vianne. Her red-gold hair was styled in soft waves. To Vianne's relief, the woman's expression softened into the sweetest of smiles. "Why, there you are, Miss Mercier," she said. "I'd know you anywhere." Her voice was gentle, and Vianne felt a pierce in her heart, because Emilie's Southern accent reminded her so much of Miss Ellie.

"And how could I ever forget you, Miss Grigsby," Vianne said. "Surely you have not come to Paris to see me?"

"But why not?" The Kentucky-raised belle, who had caused New York millionaire Charles Yerkes to fall in love with her, raised a perfectly shaped brow.

When Vianne had mentioned how she'd met Emilie Grigsby on board SS *Paris*, Miss Ellie had told Vianne how Charles Yerkes had built a palace on Fifth Avenue for his wife, Mary, but two blocks away, he'd built another home, a mansion of white granite, for his "ward," Emilie Grigsby, that stretched one hundred feet along Park Avenue, halfway to 68th Street. She was a legend in New York.

Miss Ellie had told Vianne how Charles Yerkes had lavished Miss Emilie Grigsby with the funds to furnish her New York palace, and she'd done so with exquisite taste, filling her library with a collection of rare and valuable books, her salons with price-less art, Flemish paintings, and tapestries, and how she'd had a Napoleonic bedroom, and a music room that engulfed the fourth floor, with a piano covered entirely in gold leaf. She had a box at the Métropolitan Opera House and was infamous for her grandiose traveling style.

Vianne came to realize it had been something special and very rare to meet such a famous woman as Emilie Grigsby aboard SS *Paris*, even if Vianne had only been fixing a loose thread in one of Katherine Carter's dresses at the time.

She squeezed Sandrine's hand. Here in front of them stood the woman who'd famously sailed away from New York, sold her home and all her treasures, including her golden piano, the silver, furniture, Oriental lamps, and carpets, and moved to London after the death of her Mr. Yerkes.

"Katherine Carter sent me," Miss Grigsby announced. She leaned her pretty hand onto the very eighteenth-century table that the visiting couple wanted to buy. "You have some charming things in here," Miss Grigsby went on.

Vianne blushed. She could hardly imagine what such a collector with rarefied taste and an unlimited budget would think of the small pieces they had on display at Celine. Vianne fought with the conflicting desire for Miss Grigsby to state her business and leave, and a yearning for her to stay longer and fill Vianne in on all the wonderful things that must be happening in the fantastical world of haute couture, parties, the world of modern women who didn't appear to have a care in the world.

Vianne frowned. It was a fantasy, and not for the likes of her. She had her sister-in-law and brother to take care of. Look what happened when she entertained thoughts of anything else. She'd been away far too long from Paris as it was. No, she must stop herself from indulging in any ideas that Miss Grigsby's affluent world was in any way a place for her.

"I came to Paris from London to tell you that my dear friend, Katherine Carter, is in a state," Miss Grigsby explained. "Katherine telegrammed me and informed me that she wants her personal designer back."

Vianne stilled. All of this, just for her? "I am honored, but—"

Miss Grigsby held up a hand, quite imperiously for one so small in stature. "Miss Mercier, I won't waste my words. The thing is, apart from Katherine's anguish, there is another reason I am here. I have come about something I think might interest you, a woman named Josephine Baker. You *have* heard of Miss Baker, I take it?"

Vianne heard Sandrine's quick intake of breath. She reached out and laid a gentle hand atop her sister-in-law's arm.

"The most famous showgirl in the world?" Sandrine breathed, clearly unable to wait for Vianne's response. "Oh, I'd love to see her dance. But my husband, Jacques, won't hear of it."

Emilie turned her sparkling gaze toward Sandrine. "That, my darling, is one of the reasons I've never had a husband. I prefer to make my own decisions as to where I shall go, and when."

Sandrine nodded, two spots of pink blooming on her cheeks.

"Josephine Baker came from America to Paris recently and is starting to make a sensation of herself here," Emilie went on, still addressing Sandrine. "Much like Miss Mercier moved from Paris to New York. A reversal, it seems."

Sandrine's head swiveled from Emilie to Vianne and back again.

"It's hardly comparable," Vianne murmured.

"Why couldn't it be?" Emilie said. "The city of Paris will continue to transform Josephine Baker, a girl who famously arrived here in a checkered dress with pockets held up by two checkered suspenders over her checkered blouse. She enraptures people with her dancing. Katherine wants you to come home and enrapture New York again. Your talents are wasted here, Miss Mercier."

Vianne folded her arms. "I appreciate your kindness. Honestly, I'm honored, but my brother and sister are not well. I need to be nearby them, and there is my sister-in-law's livelihood to consider."

"Did you realize," Miss Grigsby interrupted, in a stern voice, "that off stage, Miss Baker adores high fashion just as much as I know you do, Miss Mercier? Do you realize that every designer in Paris is fighting to dress her, as we speak? Poiret, Ada Smith, Jean Patou?"

Vianne frowned. She'd deliberately avoided reading fashion magazines since she arrived in Paris, and she'd not picked up her pencil to sketch one dress. To do so would be her undoing, she knew that. "Well, no, I didn't know that Parisian designers were clamoring to dress Miss Baker," she said, honestly. "Forgive me, Miss Grigsby, but I'm not certain how that has anything to do with me."

"Well then. I have come to tell you that Katherine Carter has gotten you an interview with Miss Baker this very afternoon. Now." Miss Grigsby drew herself up to her full five-foot-five height. "I have come with the express intent that you will climb into my Phantom Rolls-Royce immediately and drive with me to Miss Baker's apartment so that she can see for her own eyes the young breath of fresh air that her friend Katherine Carter has recommended she have to design the dress she will be wearing on the cover of *Vogue* magazine."

Vianne placed a hand on her chest to still her beating heart. The photos she had seen of Miss Baker were exquisite. She was perfection itself. Vianne couldn't begin to imagine being able to design a dress for her. One sighting, and Vianne knew she'd be gone. She would have to rush home and pull her sketchbook out of the drawer where she'd safely hidden it away. "I'm afraid I mustn't," she said, waving a hand around Celine. "You can see, I am needed," but she knew she sounded uncertain.

"Oh, for pity's sake, Vianne. Just go! Or you'll regret it all your life. How could you turn down the opportunity to design for Miss Baker, choosing to sit here with boring old me, instead? I'll be here tomorrow, and the day after that," Sandrine burst out.

Vianne turned to Sandrine. The quiet, unobtrusive creature's outburst was even more unexpected than even Emilie Grigsby turning up at Celine!

Emilie's lips curved into a small, but satisfied smile. "Quite," she said, turning to Sandrine. "You seem like a sensible girl. Would you like to come with Miss Mercier to meet Miss Baker? Shake up your husband a bit?"

"Oh, would I! More than anything," Sandrine said. She dived for her blue coat on the rack by the door and tugged it over her shoulders.

Vianne bit on her lip. If she did this, she'd break her vow to steer clear of designing and fashion. One single step down this road, and she'd be lost to that world again. But then, perhaps one drawing, one dress wouldn't hurt?

"Well," she murmured. "Seems like I'm about to have my first ride in a Rolls-Royce."

"Keep designing like Katherine says you were in New York," Miss Grigsby said, "and you'll be driving in many more Rolls-Royces, Miss Mercier."

Sandrine's eyes were round as saucers. "You never told me, Vianne," she whispered. "I thought you'd just worked as a dressmaker."

"I will fill you in on the way, dear," Emilie said, reaching out and tucking her hand into the stunned Sandrine's arm. "I think you can help me. You can be my accomplice in getting Vianne Mercier back at the drawing board, Mrs...?"

"Sandrine Mercier," Sandrine supplied, her eyes widening toward Vianne.

"Come on, then, Sandrine Mercier," Emilie Grigsby smiled. "Let's go and paint Paris with one of Vianne's stunning gowns. Let's see how it feels to adorn Josephine Baker, and let's see if we can convince your sister-in-law to return to the thing she was born to do."

Emilie made a show of waiting for Vianne to walk ahead of her, and when she stepped out onto the sidewalk, the chauffeur held the door open of the magnificent Phantom Rolls-Royce. Vianne slipped into the vehicle, and it was as if she was stepping back into her New York life. She let the rush of excitement at the glamor of it all course through her system, because she hadn't felt anything like it since returning to Paris.

Josephine Baker sat in her modern apartment with her long legs crossed over the armrest of a Louis XV Empire chair. When Emilie introduced Vianne and Sandrine, she waved her hand in the air. "Well, you took your time, Miss Mercier."

Emilie leaned forward and kissed the famous showgirl on the cheek.

Vianne stood next to Sandrine, who was barely hiding her exclamations of delight. Vianne folded her arms, half relishing and half admonishing herself for the feeling of confidence and ease that was spreading over her as she took in the elegant surrounds. The fact was, she felt at home here. The windows of the salon were thrown open to the sounds of Paris, and on the floor, there lay a pool of discarded haute couture clothes. Vianne eyed them.

"Oh, ignore them," Josephine said. "Tomorrow, all those designers will come and take those away and deliver more."

Vianne took in a sharp breath. If she were to design something for Josephine, it would have to be spectacular, and how could she compete with the likes of Paul Poiret?

"What *Vogue* needs," Emilie Grigsby said, sounding businesslike, "is a high-fashion image that will seal Miss Baker as far more than the girl who was only a chorus dancer in New York, where audiences were segregated."

Vianne nodded. She remembered the Cotton Club and the troubling Southern plantation decorations that graced the stage.

"*Vogue* want to show her off as the beautiful woman she really is. If things continue the way they are going, Josephine Baker will be the toast of the continent. Did you know, Miss Mercier, that Miss Baker used to have a mind to design fashion herself once?"

"Oh, I did some sketches sometimes at Paul Poiret's shows," Josephine shrugged. "I added some fringes to some of his dresses." She chuckled. "I would look at *Vogue* magazine when I was a dancer in America and correct the drawings!"

"That hardly reduces the pressure," Vianne said, but her eagle eyes were drinking in Miss Baker's form. Her long, long legs, the way she'd cut her hair like a French man and parted it on one side. Miss Baker was a trendsetter. She was not, in any way, a little lamb. "Have you a piece of paper?" Vianne whispered, ideas already racing through her head.

Miss Baker swung her long legs over her chair. She reached to the floor for a notepad and held it out for Vianne.

Vianne went over to the window, her hands moving in a flurry, not worrying whether she'd ever go back to New York, not worrying whether she'd ever get the chance to design again after this one day. Because if she could come up with something that Miss Baker would wear on the cover of *Vogue* magazine, then she'd die happy, that was for certain. Vianne, her fingers working feverishly, let her imaginings take the reins, and several minutes later, she turned back to Miss Baker and held out her sketch.

Josephine extended her hand, and as she did so, her deep brown eyes caught with Vianne's, and Vianne saw something kindling in them, something that she recognized in herself. And

Vianne knew what it was. It was determination, it was gumption, and it was persistence in the face of all the odds.

Josephine Baker had grown up in the slums of St. Louis. As a young girl, she'd cleaned houses and babysat for the wealthy, but in an unprecedented way, she'd then risen above everything, and now, she was catnip for designers, for the stage, and for the world.

"I want to present you as an incredibly important, strong icon for women, Miss Baker," Vianne said. "I want you to feel like a goddess. I want you to use fashion to project an aura of glamor and sophistication, something you can maintain throughout your life."

Josephine Baker looked down at Vianne's sketch of a stunning, shimmering dress made of glimmery silver fabric that hugged her curves, and wrapped around her body, and was held at the waist with a jewel clasp, just like the one Vianne had used on that very early dress she'd designed for Maman. But Miss Baker's dress had diamond shoulder straps, and a flattering, scooped neckline that would show off her caramel-colored skin.

A single tear fell down Josephine Baker's cheek. "Thank you," Miss Baker said simply. "Thank you, Miss Mercier." She pressed her lips together, and she reached out, and she clutched Vianne's hand. "I love this. I've never seen anything so gorgeous in my life. I shall wear it for you on the cover of *Vogue*, and, my darling, it will make you instantly famous too. Now, you listen to me," she whispered in that famous voice of hers. "You believe in yourself, and you make whatever you want of your life. Don't follow trends, just follow your inner voice. That's what I do."

Next to Vianne, Sandrine covered her mouth with her hands.

"And that goes for you too, my girl," Miss Baker said, addressing Vianne's sister-in-law. "You were telling me you'd like to run the family business on your own two feet while Miss Mercier was sketching away just now."

Vianne turned to Sandrine. "Is that true, Sandrine?" she whispered. "Would you like to take over Papa's business? Would you like to run Celine?"

"If you think I am worthy," Sandrine said. "If you'd trust me with it, then you could go back to New York. And I'd love to run Celine, now that I know Jacques is getting better," she went on, her voice sounding more confident. "I would like to do your papa proud and take his business and grow it until it shone again."

"Oh, girls, I think we'd all be doing our papas proud, and our mamas," Emilie Grigsby said, her own deep Southern accent kicking in. "I think they'll all be smiling down on us and sending us their blessings."

And right then, Vianne was reminded of Miss Ellie, and her Southern values, values that she held close to her heart, and the way she'd pushed through and stayed true to not only her dream but, importantly, to her strong beliefs and ways of treating people all her life, no matter what challenges came along.

Vianne couldn't think of any better company than she was in at this moment, nor could she think of anyone she'd rather be around than the inspirational women she'd be working with at Miss Ellie and *her* atelier, when she *did* return to New York.

CHAPTER TWENTY-SEVEN
VIANNE, NEW YORK, FALL, 1925

Vianne held onto her hat. Next to her, Giorgio drove his fancy car at top speed toward their beloved Manhattan, and Vianne gasped at her first glimpse of the city after so long as they drove over Queensboro Bridge. It was that magical time right before sunset. Below them, the river shimmered, still as a pond.

"Isn't it magical?" Giorgio murmured.

"It is," Vianne murmured, "But, you know, I've decided to give up hoping for fairy tales."

He turned to her, taking his eyes off the bridge for one second, but he was driving at top speed, so he moved his handsome profile back to face the wheel. "No," he said. "I can't believe that, *Bella.*"

"It's true," she said. "I used to think New York was my fairy tale, but now I realize…"

"Yes?" he whispered, reaching over and squeezing her hand. She felt the way it tensed when he touched her skin.

"Now," she said. "I don't want fairy tales. I want to embrace every part of real life. *All* of it, the whole lot. The good, with the bad. I don't want to escape anything anymore," she continued, turning to him, her voice softening. "I've come to understand that's how things are meant to be. Reality, losses, awful as they can be, only make us appreciate the beauty in life. All the things since that day in 1918 have brought me here. To New York. With you... And without those sad things, I may not appreciate all the good things, which I will never take for granted, Giorgio. The only way to cope with life is to accept it, and then to rise high, and create something beautiful that inspires people, and that's what I want to do with my life now."

He was quiet a moment. "*Bella?*" he murmured. "I would love it if you embraced it all, the whole of it, with me. Darling, marry me?"

She turned to him. What a modern proposal, flying over the bridge toward Manhattan! "A modern arrangement," she whispered, "where we both follow our dreams on equal terms?"

His eyes crinkled. "But of course!" he shouted into the breeze. "Anything's possible!"

"And to that," Vianne said. "I utterly agree."

Giorgio reached across the car and placed his free hand in Vianne's.

And right then, the lights came on. The lights of Manhattan beamed over the water, pouring a flood of shining, golden darts into the dark depths below. And above this, the skyscrapers were a deep, rose gold in the glorious sunset.

Vianne was certain she saw reflected in the brilliant, shining water, the smiling, lovely face of her maman.

A LETTER FROM ELLA CAREY

Dear reader,

I want to say a huge thank you for choosing to read *The Girl from Paris*. If you did enjoy it, and want to keep up to date with all my latest releases, just sign up at the following link. Your email address will never be shared and you can unsubscribe at any time.

www.bookouture.com/ella-carey

This book was an absolute joy to write. I fell in love with gorgeous Vianne when I was writing the first book in this series, *A New York Secret,* and Vianne appeared as an inspiration for my lead character, Chef Lily. In that book, set in the 1940s, Vianne was a highly successful fashion designer in New York. I knew then that I wanted to write Vianne's story, and it was wonderful to be able to set her tale partly in Paris, which many of my long-time readers will know is incredibly close to my heart.

I am so fortunate to have a career which I love. I wake up every day and cannot wait to get cracking, and I am only appreciative of the women of past generations. I am also enormously appreciative of each and every one of you, my readers. Thank you for the time you have spent reading the book.

I hope you loved *The Girl from Paris*, and if you did, I would be very grateful if you could write a review. I'd love to hear what you think, and it makes such a difference helping new readers to discover one of my books for the first time.

I love hearing from my readers—you can get in touch on my Facebook page, through Twitter, Goodreads or my website.

Thank you,

My best wishes,

Ella

www.ellacarey.com

facebook.com/ellacareyauthor

twitter.com/Ella_Carey

AUTHOR'S NOTE

Edith Cavell was executed in the gloomy mist on the cold morning of October 12, 1915, by a German firing squad in Brussels, Belgium. She was part of a secret underground network behind enemy lines in Belgium helping English soldiers to get safely back to England during the First World War. She was betrayed, interrogated, and subjected to a show trial, during which she admitted to her offenses. Edith Cavell had served for several years in Brussels, Belgium as the matron of a nurses' training school before the First World War broke out in 1914, choosing to remain at her post, looking after both German and Allied soldiers until her death in 1915. On the night before her execution, she vowed to have no bitterness or hatred toward anyone.

On March 29, 1918, a shell hit the roof of the Saint-Gervais church during one of its Good Friday services. The whole roof collapsed, killing eighty-eight worshippers and injuring sixty-eight. More than a third of the total deaths from the Paris Gun came from that one shell. The attack was part of Germany's spring offensive, a massive attack on the Western Front that brought German forces within seventy-five miles of Paris. The long-range cannons were specifically built to attack Paris from the unheard-of range of seventy-five miles. The psychological damage impact was massive. These attacks were the harbinger of a new and terrifying warfare, in which civilians were intentionally targeted in a way that would break their morale.

The Paris Gun was designed by Professor Fritz Rausenberger and his team at Krupp of Essen—the master gunmakers in Europe at the time. They had already designed the infamous Big Bertha earlier in the war, a type of howitzer that was among the largest mobile artillery pieces in use by any army.

Emilie Grigsby was the daughter of a Kentucky slave owner and brothel owner. She had an affair with fabulously wealthy industrialist Charles T. Yerkes, and in her day, she was acknowledged as one of the most beautiful women in the world. It is said that she remained sweet-tempered and generous all her life.

The famous American dancer Josephine Baker was born in the slums of St. Louis, Missouri. She cleaned houses growing up and babysat for the wealthy. At the age of fifteen, she was recruited for a local vaudeville show, and from there, she performed in musicals in Harlem. It was in Paris that she found widespread fame, when she clowned and subverted stereotypes, and advanced her career in ways unprecedented for a woman of her era. Paul Poiret and Madeleine Vionnet, two of the leading couturiers in the 1920s, dressed Josephine Baker offstage. In 1927, she was interviewed for *Vogue*. While fabulously famous, she also remained a woman of the people throughout her entire life.

I read many books on fashion during the research process for this book. I will post a blog on my website sharing some of the wonderful books on fashion that inspired Vianne's dresses and designs.

ACKNOWLEDGEMENTS

This book has been an absolute joy to write, and at times, heartbreaking too. I am indebted to many people for their support and expertise. My sincere thanks to my new, lovely editor, Sonny Marr, for your fabulous ideas to develop and enhance the story. It is going to be so fun and creative working with you! Huge thanks to Caroline Hogg for your expertise and insights during the structural editing process. It was an honor to have you read and edit my work and your insights were fantastic. Thanks to Laura Deacon for overseeing my career at Bookouture. I appreciate you enormously and am grateful for your incredible support. Hugest of thanks to the brilliant publicity team at Bookouture, Kim Nash, Sarah Harvey and Noelle Holton, for your phenomenal, tireless efforts and enthusiasm in promoting our books. I am always in awe. My thanks and appreciation to my wonderful copyeditor Jade Craddock for your detailed work and expertise. Thank you to the lovely Anne O'Brien for reading and reviewing the final proof. To Lauren Finger, my thanks for coordinating the final editing stages of my books. Thanks to cover designer Sarah Whittaker for the stunning covers for this series. They really are gorgeous covers and I know my readers have loved them as well.

My deepest thanks to my agent, Giles Milburn. You are the best, and I am incredibly fortunate to work with you. I am always so appreciative of your being by my side and I cannot thank you enough for managing my career. Thanks to Emma Dawson for managing things on a day-to-day basis. Huge thanks to Liane-Louise Smith, Valentina Paulmichl and the foreign rights team at the Madeleine Milburn Literary Agency for selling my Daughters of New York series, and my backlist books into so many new territories. It is most rewarding to see all the different editions as they are being published and to hear from new readers all over the world. Even more so in these times.

My special thanks to Maisie Lawrence, my former editor, who was the first person to fall in love with Vianne in *A New York Secret*, and who told me I had to write a book about her!

I would like to acknowledge the brilliant Bookouture authors. Your support and friendship is invaluable, and I am honored to be a part of the Bookouture family.

Deepest thanks to my children, Ben and Sophie, for your ongoing wonderful support of my writing, and to Geoff for his support and wonderful belief in my work.

Thanks to my readers, some of whom have been with me since *Paris Time Capsule* was first published back in 2014, and my thanks and hugest of welcomes to my new readers—it has been lovely to chat with some of you so far. My thanks and special appreciation to the bloggers and reviewers who read and review my books. I appreciate your time and effort enormously.

You all mean the world to me. Thank you.